MW01165461

GOLDEN STATE

ARNOLD
4 GOVERNOR

DAVID PRYBIL

iUniverse, Inc.
Bloomington

Golden State

iUniverse books may be ordered through booksellers or by contacting:

iUniverse
1663 Liberty Drive
Bloomington, IN 47403
www.iuniverse.com
1-800-Authors (1-800-288-4677)

ISBN: 978-1-4502-7302-2 (sc)
ISBN: 978-1-4502-7304-6 (ebook)
ISBN: 978-1-4502-7303-9 (dj)

Library of Congress Control Number: 2010916858

This book is set in Californian FB, a typeface originally designed by Frederic Goudy in 1938 for the University of California Press.
Printed in the United States of America

iUniverse rev. date: 11/23/2010

To my wife, Robin,
and my sons, Jackson and Ryan,
the best inspirations a guy could ever ask for.

I
MODEL CITIZENS

1

SPENCER

Late morning in early August, downtown Sacramento, and it was already a hundred degrees in the shade, if you could find any. Sun beating down directly overhead; no clouds, no breeze. The air was so bone-dry it was hard to draw a breath. The city streets shimmered like some kind of black magic. It was the type of weather that drove men mad.

Of course, insanity is not a condition exclusive to cases of extreme heat. From his desk in the air-conditioned offices of the Sacramento *Bee*, Spencer Brine could certainly attest to this. He was sitting there, directly beneath an air duct that was blowing so hard and cold he actually contemplated putting on a sweater.

Then again, a sweater would not have been nearly enough to solve Spencer's problems, because that duct was also dripping some kind of refrigerated fluid on him. Which made even more like Chinese water torture because it was taking place in a windowless basement, in a claustrophobic, gray-cloth-walled cubicle, with harsh fluorescent lighting and a mysterious, odd-smelling brown stain on the wall beside him, where he was toiling as a lowly paid junior staffer, writing obligatory back-page pieces that absolutely no one read, the crafting of which made him want to stab himself through the brain with his own pen and end it all right then and there, before it could get any worse—if, indeed, that was even possible.

And it was on this hellish day that things *did* get worse for Spencer. It was on this day that he lost his mind, just a little bit. For while Spencer had somehow managed over time, and with much effort, to resign himself to the woes of his workspace and the tedium of his daily labors, this feat had only been made possible—at least, up until now—by the fact that no one else around him seemed to be having much fun, either.

This collective state of relative misery was due to a number of factors. The first being, they were all in Sacramento. Capital of the great state of California, it's true, but bearing no resemblance whatsoever to the California most of the world knew and loved. No beaches. No celebrity sightings. No iconic signs or bridges or hills or theme parks. Though an attractive enough place by most standards, it quite simply paled in comparison to the Golden State's larger, starrier, and more picturesque coastal brethren. Nobody ever bought "I Love Sacramento" T-shirts. And despite the city's valiant efforts through the years to change that, the area and its people retained an inferiority complex that was hard to shake.

The same was true with the newspaper itself. After all, how can a paper called the "*Bee*" ever be taken seriously as a journalistic enterprise? Though the name had been in use since the paper's founding back in 1857, most people, especially Spencer, secretly hated it. Rife with overly folksy connotations, it sounded more like the title to some cow-town gossip column written by an old biddy in a Minnie Pearl bonnet. And this was so even without the added disgrace of their cheesy, animated-bee mascot, Scoopy. Together, the name and accompanying cartoon image somehow infused everything they did—and mind you, they did a lot of things extremely well—with the faint but undeniable stench of second-rate amateurism.

On this day, however, a dazzling ray of new hope had appeared on the horizon. It came in the form of a big, breaking story, one that seemed destined to put Sacramento right at the white-hot center of the news-world map; that was, the petition to get rid of the state's flailing governor, Gray Davis, had been officially certified. As a result, an unprecedented recall election had been announced for October 7 to replace him, mid-term, in just a little over two months' time. With such a brief run-up, minimal qualifying standards, and no cap on entrants, this had set the stage for an utter free-for-all, a political carnival of a kind only California could produce. Candidates of all stripes and competence levels were racing to sign on, with over a hundred already declared, and more on the way. Among them were a number of famous names, some with reasonable prospects and qualifications like telegenic gadfly Arianna Huffington and Olympic organizer Peter Ueberroth, others just unashamedly desperate for attention, like former child star Gary Coleman and hardcore porn actress Mary Carey. And while that was more than enough to generate the media's interest, rumors were swirling that an even bigger name player, indeed the very biggest of them all, was plotting to join in the fun, too: former bodybuilding champ turned movie star Arnold Schwarzenegger.

Add to that the state's dire financial straits and the energy-crisis corruption scandal that caused them, which led to the call for Davis's head in the first place, and if that wasn't a blockbuster scenario, what was? The *Bee*'s entire staff was salivating at its potential. Reporters and columnists manned their desks and marched the newsroom hallways with a newfound sense of urgency, hoping with every ring of the telephone to receive a tip that could lead to something big, as if sensing that a searing, front-page exposé with their name on the byline, perhaps even a Pulitzer-worthy one, might be lurking just around the corner.

But for poor Spencer Brine, toiling away down in his damp basement cubicle, that dream was not being shared. For, you see, Spencer chased no leads, employed no snitches, and fielded no scoops. He won no awards, and appeared on no local newscasts. No. Spencer wrote obituaries. Even worse, he wrote the local obituaries. And in Sacramento, that meant a lot of sewage commissioners and Rotary Club presidents. Ever try to write an interesting school paper on a member of your own family? Imagine that kind of futility, then multiply it over three obituaries a day, five days a week, fifty-two weeks a year, for four long years. That was Spencer's life, and he hated it. And with the added indignity of a big, juicy, career-making story being dangled right in front of him, just barely out of reach, that hatred became unbearable. Especially when he heard this:

"Got one for ya, Briney."

Spencer looked up to see his boss, the editor of the Metro section, Morris Sutphin, fast approaching, a print-smeared facsimile clutched in his bony, claw-like hand.

Morris, unlike Spencer, loved his job; thought working Metro at the Bee was as good as it gets—which, for him, it probably was. And if anybody dared besmirch such a notion, or even vaguely hint that its underlying logic might be faulty, Morris made sure to make that person's life as miserable as humanly possible. Spencer could almost hear him now: *Don't like the obits? Okay, Shakespeare, how's about you try some classifieds on for size?* Therein lies the rub; no matter how shitty a situation might be, there's always a way it can get worse.

Morris walked off and Spencer slowly dragged the fax into his direct eyeline. The newly deceased's name was Jarvis Kovacs. Spencer stared at his photo and tried to surmise what the rest of his life story might contain. As usual, he wasn't far off; the faces don't lie. Like his parents and their parents before them, Jarvis had been a farmer, growing pumpkins with and of no particular distinction, until the city's creeping growth reached his property and Jarvis was able to sell the family land to commercial developers. That land was now a nirvana of strip malls and gas stations, and Jarvis—until his recent passing—had resided in a big house on a small bluff at the end of a street he named after himself (Jarvis Lane), staring down upon all that his ancestry's purchase had wrought.

But, Spencer asked, does this truly merit a feature obituary? All the man really did was sell some undistinguished property that was fortuitously situated, and then sit back and reap the profits. Yes, there were the pumpkins, bought by locals every year to festoon their front porches on Halloween. And yes, Jarvis also owned the local go-kart and putt-putt emporium, which entertained the kiddies, while also serving as an impromptu lovers' lane for the teenage crowd. But was this really a life of great accomplishment? One of genuine newsworthiness to the community? This was a question that Spencer grappled with on a daily basis. And oftentimes, the answer hinged on a second query, one that was far more cut-and-dry in its resolution: namely, who else has died? So far, Jarvis was all Spencer had, and if things stayed that way, he would be memorialized as a benevolent land baron, a man who brought joy to the masses. But if Spencer received more faxes? Well, then, the passing of Jarvis Kovacs would likely be relegated to a few short lines at the bottom of that same page. Such are the vagaries of life, even in its twilight.

And it is precisely these vagaries that occupied Spencer's mind much of the time. In his case, while it was true that he'd chosen to leave his home state of New York after college and go west, to broaden his horizons and carve out his own slice of the California Dream, he nevertheless had to ask himself—and often did, especially now, especially today—how in God's name had he wound up *here*, in the sun-scorched armpit of the state, doing *this*? He'd had such high goals for himself. What had happened to all his drive and ambition? His talent? How will history remember him when he passes?

These were awfully weighty matters to be pondering, especially when you're barely thirty years old, but that's what writing death notices for a living did to a person. It forces you to constantly dwell on the end of things, even when they're still at their beginning. And that can't be healthy, can it?

Thirty years old. Shit. Might as well be sixty, Spencer thought to himself. Going from his small condo to his small Volvo subcompact to his small, gray-walled cubicle. And then right back again, day after day after day. It might as well be one space. One small, continuous space. A prison cell. Or a coffin.

A headline suddenly flashed before his eyes: JUNIOR STAFFER DIES AT DESK, NO ONE NOTICES.

Spencer blinked, wiping the image away. He got up from his chair as if it were on fire. He took the stairs, up a flight to the side exit. Out the door and down the sidewalk, with no sense of direction or purpose other than to *get out of there, right fucking now.*

And once that was done, there was nothing to do but keep going, away from the *Bee*, from Morris, from the faxes, from the boredom, from the death. Spencer walked for miles, aimlessly, through the scorching midday heat, in a fog, only vaguely aware of his surroundings—enough to avoid oncoming traffic, but with no real cognizance of where he was or what he was doing.

Until he heard the music. It was rock and roll, and it was loud and raunchy and alive. And it was just what Spencer Brine and his job and indeed his whole sorry excuse for an existence were sorely lacking. It was coming from inside a purple concrete bunker with a large neon sign out front bearing its name: ShowBar.

A bar. Hmm. Spencer suddenly realized his throat was parched and that his shirt was drenched with sweat. And though it was barely past noon, it also dawned on Spencer that a cold beer would really hit the spot. On impulse, he made a beeline for the door, only to be stopped in his tracks by a huge bearded man with mirrored sunglasses and a black, sleeveless Harley-Davidson T-shirt.

"Five dollar cover, ace. And I need some ID."

Spencer was taken aback. "Five? But ... I just want a beer."

"Save it for your wife."

Spencer protested, "My what? I'm not—"

But the bouncer didn't care. "Look, bro, you want a beer, there's a liquor store down the street. Otherwise, it's five bucks."

The mountainous man crossed his forearms threateningly. Spencer felt the hair on the back of his neck stand up, like a cornered animal, and he considered fleeing, but the music and the air conditioning and the promise of refreshments within were all calling out to him like the Pied Piper. He finally reached into his wallet and proffered the money and his license.

The bouncer smiled now, the blazing sun gleaming off his gold-capped incisors. "Okay, boss, you're good. Enjoy the show."

The show? Spencer thought nothing of this, his parched throat calling all the shots. He headed inside, the jarring transition from sunlight to darkness leaving him stumbling around like a latter-day Mister Magoo. However, aided by the blinking beer signs that lined the walls, Spencer was able to navigate his way up to the bar. There, he straddled a stool, and wasted no time placing an order.

As he waited for his drink, Spencer drummed his fingers along to "Welcome to the Jungle" by Guns N' Roses. Doing so, he felt better already. Though not exactly one of his favorites, it nevertheless conjured up fond memories from the carefree days of college. Keg parties. Co-eds. Cutting classes—which, come to think of it, was kind of what he was doing right now. Spencer smiled to himself as the bartender returned and set down his beer, a Corona longneck, icy cold, with a fresh wedge of lime perched in its mouth, just the way he'd imagined. He took a long pull off the bottle and sighed contentedly.

Then, as his vision adjusted to the dim lighting, he glanced into the large mirror behind the bar and finally caught sight of the "show" to which the bouncer had alluded. And only then did Spencer realize, despite what anyone now or at a later date may believe, that he was in a strip club.

Spencer spun around on his stool. Onstage, there were two women, both of them completely nude and dancing seductively around a pair of firemen's poles. But Spencer only saw one of them, a blond stunner with tan, supple skin and the body of a Greek goddess. She was exactly the kind of sun-dripped beauty that he had always hoped he'd meet out here. Spencer couldn't take his eyes off of her. And maybe he'd led a sheltered life up until now, or maybe he'd just been cooped up in that horrible basement too long, but sitting there, he swore that she was the most gorgeous creature he had ever laid his eyes on.

The golden-tressed goddess danced to two more songs. First, another hard-rocking number called, disturbingly enough, "Nookie," that allowed her to show off her slinky athleticism. Then, slowing it down for her apparent encore, she writhed and crawled and did the splits in a dazzling variety of increasingly provocative ways to another Guns N' Roses classic, "Patience."

And then, she was gone.

The jaded DJ mumbled out a rote exit line, "Give it up for Roxy and Veronique, fellas. Thank you, ladies. Next up, Candy and Carly. "

But Spencer didn't care. Bolted to his chair, thoroughly gobsmacked, he stared at the stage door, waiting desperately for Veronique—it had to be Veronique—to reappear. And, after twenty excruciating minutes, she finally did. Dressed now in a lacy camisole and a sheer ... what? A robe? A jacket? A scarf? Whatever it was, she looked fantastic in it. Working the room, she stopped by several tables, thanking her tippers and flirting a bit. But then, she looked up and caught Spencer's eye. Spencer was so overwhelmed at first that he shyly looked away, but when he turned back, she was smiling—and not only that, but she was heading right for him. And she kept right on coming until she was perching herself onto the faux-leopard stool right beside him.

"Hi, you must be new here. I'm Veronique."

Off this kismet-confirming introduction, Veronique flashed another brilliant smile and extended a soft, well-manicured hand. Taking her hand into his own, Spencer inhaled her intoxicating scent and stared deeply into her entrancing, azure-blue eyes. And with that, everything else fell away. His disappointing morning. His unfulfilling job. His whole, soul-crushing life.

Maybe, Spencer thought, he would never get the big break and the big career he had always assumed would be rightly his. Maybe his name would never be hailed, his talent never recognized. Maybe he would die as completely unknown as the day he was born. But this was something, at least. Something tangible. Something worth living for, and fighting for.

This was his California Dream, right here, right now.

2

MISSY

"**A**nd don't forget the signs! I want those signs up tonight, and I want them everywhere. North, south, east, west; I want that place impossible to miss. Like Disneyland, do you hear me?"

In her state-of-the-art home gym, astride her top-of-the-line elliptical trainer, real estate agent Missy Carver was pedaling away, while also barking orders via headset to her assistant, Jerome.

"Okay, good, now what about the flyers? Did they correct the color? Tell me they corrected the color."

Missy had left her office at Eureka Realty much earlier than normal today, a little after 5 p.m. (she usually stayed until at least 7, then went straight to dinner or coffee with a client), but that didn't mean she was being lax or irresponsible. Far from it. Missy never gave less than one hundred percent to anything she did. Otherwise, what was the point of even doing it?

"I don't care, Jerome. We need those flyers up by 9 a.m. tomorrow morning. *All* of them. Do you hear me? Get it fixed, ASAP. Or do I have to find someone else to do it?"

August was always the busiest month for Missy; houses showed best in summer, with pools open, trees green, and flowers in bloom, and families preferred to move when their kids' schools were out of session. As such, Missy had a jam-packed schedule of open houses to host, private preview showings to attend, stagings to oversee, and clients to attend to. She had to make every moment count.

Missy had a philosophy, you see, about real estate sales, one that had served her in excellent stead throughout the nine years she'd been in the business. To her way of thinking, success was all about optimal preparation and thorough follow-through—nothing more, nothing less. Other realtors may be full of pep and smiles and gift bags and good humor, but when it came down to it, it was about moving people and properties at the fastest possible rate and the best possible price. Being popular only gets you so far. Jolene Wyatt, her colleague and chief competitor, may be a godmother to three of her clients' children, but if you ever saw her desk or her car, you would know what a catastrophe in the making she was. That wasn't Missy. No. She made it a point to always be more organized and on the ball than anyone else.

Case in point was the recall of Governor Davis. The second it was announced, Missy had recognized how dramatically this would affect the local housing market, as well as who might have to move, and who might be looking. She had thus contacted all of the people in the current administration and, mincing no words, had told them she could maximize their transaction outcomes for them. And even if a few of the need-to-unloaders got a bit huffy at the implications, it had already resulted in three new clients, with more surely to come. It was that kind of hustle that had won her so many Top Realtor awards, and it was that hustle which would soon score her the biggest, most important account of her entire career.

"And what about Arnold? Did his office call yet? What about Maria's? Well, call them both again, send those new listings I got, and remind them that the clock's ticking, okay?"

Arnold and Maria—a.k.a., the Schwarzeneggers. Landing them as clients would be the ultimate coup. After all, they were far too famous, wealthy, and tasteful to live in that gaudy Governor's Mansion. When Ronald Reagan was elected back in the 70s, his family had only lasted a few days there before wife Nancy declared the place a "firetrap" and insisted they buy a home in an exclusive gated community up in the hills. The even-more-patrician Maria was sure to follow suit. And who could possibly be better suited to help the new Governor and his fabulous First Lady find their dream estate in this difficult market than her? Nobody, that's who! Even though Arnold hadn't won yet, and indeed hadn't even officially declared his candidacy, Missy knew it was only a matter of time, and that her tenacious wooing of them would pay off. And once it did, it would surely bring her the one thing, the one career validation, that she still lacked, and that she both wanted and deserved most of all: to be elevated to full partner at her firm.

"Okay, Jerome. Let me know if you hear anything. I'll be on my cell. And get those flyers done, and done the way I want them done, do you hear me? Okay? Okay."

Missy hung up, set the phone to vibrate, took a quick sip of her vitamin shake, picked up a book to read, and also picked up the pace on her elliptical for a final, end-of-workout sprint. She was a cool customer, all right, and a multi-tasker without peer, but even *she* was feeling the stress today. Some people turned to alcohol when they were anxious, some people ate, and some people prayed. Missy treated food as fuel, she rarely drank, and she didn't pray, either. Instead, she worshipped at the temple of her own body, religiously and without fail, for one full hour, from 6 a.m. to 7 a.m., every day of the week.

This day was a special one, though, which was why she was rewarding herself with a second, invigorating spin on her elliptical. Yes, there was all the work she had on her plate, which she was confident would soon bear fruit. But there was something else, too; a final item on her daily planner, which was unique in that it had nothing whatsoever to do with real estate. That was, she had a date. Missy had turned thirty recently, and she had—in her inimitable, no-nonsense, no-stone-unturned style—determined that the time was right for her to start thinking seriously about marriage. She had the big house, the luxury car, the thriving career. It was time now to focus on finding the proper mate.

"*Res ipsa loquitur*—the thing speaks for itself," Missy said, reading aloud from her book, before repeating the phrase under her breath to memorize it. Then, on to the next: "*Res judicata*—a matter already judged ..."

To succeed in this endeavor as she did in every other, Missy had realized, right from the outset, that she would have to step up her efforts considerably. Up until now, dating had never been much of a priority for her. Certainly, not in the way that it was for most women she knew. She didn't need a husband by her side to feel complete. She was at ease with herself, she was self-sufficient, and she always had been.

This kind of fierce independence had, she knew, scared off some eligible men in the past. Others—most, in fact—weren't even worth the trouble. And being a pragmatist, Missy was able to recognize a lot of the dating process as being total rubbish, anyway. As a result, romantic companionship for her had often come in synergy with other, more central components of her life—namely, her career. She had been courted by coworkers, for instance, which was easy and convenient and offered a common area of interest upon which to build. Over time, however, the inherently competitive nature of the relationship had always proved a hindrance (yes, she'd poached a few listings this way, but if the colleagues in question had been performing up to par, she wouldn't have been able to do so in the first place, now would she?). There had been clients who had pursued her, too;

unfortunately, the mix of work and play never seemed to work out particularly well there, either (despite what they may have said, she could compartmentalize better than anybody). Finally, she had allowed herself over the years to be set up on a handful of select blind dates—mostly by her pushy, ever-intrusive mother, Mamie, who wouldn't take no for an answer—all of which had been, no surprise, utter nightmares.

It was thus time for a new approach. A better, more calculated approach. One that would be both more efficient and higher yielding. And after much research, Missy had found what she was looking for in the form of "Matchmaker to the Sacramento Elite" Heidi Horowitz. Heidi, a zaftig, fast-talking yenta with whom Missy had felt immediately simpatico, had come highly recommended from several reliable, upscale sources. And indeed, when Missy stated her prerequisites— college educated, preferably with a graduate degree, at least six feet in height, with an athletic build and a salary of no less than $100,000 per annum—Heidi hadn't even blinked.

"Don't you worry, honey. I'll find you your soul mate. He's out there," Heidi had said with a wink. And for the first time, Missy had allowed herself to believe it.

Thus, while it was true that Heidi's first two referrals hadn't quite lived up to her expectations—one spoke with a slight lisp and wore way too much cologne, the other drove a Hummer and enjoyed karaoke—Missy's hopes remained high for tonight's match, Steve Manning. Steve, a partner at a local litigation law firm, had an MBA and a law degree from prestigious East Coast universities, competed in triathlons, and donated his time on weekends to Habitat for Humanity. On paper, at least, he certainly fit the bill; and indeed, their two phone conversations had only reinforced her faith in his credentials. Much like herself, Steve was a hard charger with lofty ambitions who now had his sights set on finding an equally high-aspiring partner. That was why Missy had devoted the extra time and effort to her preparation for their evening together, leaving work early to buy a new dress and squeeze in an extra workout, and even boning up on her legal jargon—ergo, the book—should it come in handy.

Ding.

As soon as the beep on her chronograph watch sounded, signaling that her workout was complete, Missy was up and off the elliptical like a rocket. Time was tight, and she still had to get herself looking date-ready before Steve arrived. Heading into the bathroom, she quickly disrobed, tossed her sweaty workout attire into the waiting hamper, and leapt into the shower. But even there, Missy couldn't help but multitask. While lathering and rinsing, she repeated to herself, over and over, her personal mantra: "You deserve only the best, and you'll get only the best. You deserve only the best, and you'll get only the best."

Five minutes later, she was back out, wrapped in a towel. She checked her watch again. Still on schedule. Racing into her meticulous master closet, she put on her silkiest French undergarments, which she'd laid out like a store display on her toile-covered dressing bench, then rushed back into the bathroom to style her hair and apply makeup. Another ten minutes—after nearly a decade on the job, she had this routine down to a science—and she was back in the closet putting on the new dress, a classic-cut navy-blue sheath with gold accent trim by Donna Karan, her favorite designer. Finally, back to the mirror for one last look, and one last swish of blush on her cheeks. Missy smiled at the results, confident that Steve would like what he saw.

Just in time, too. From the corner of her eye, Missy caught the sweep of a pair of headlights turning into her driveway. A quick peek out the window revealed the outlines of a gleaming silver Jaguar coupe, a top-of-the-line model by the looks of it, if not brand-new than at most a year old. Missy's face lit up anew. She approved.

As her date, Steve, stepped out of the car, she closed the blind and turned off the lights, headed for the front door to greet him with an eager, well-toned skip in her step, all the while repeating the words, "You deserve only the best, and you'll get only the best. You deserve only the best, and you'll get only the best..."

That was her mantra, and her plan. And when Missy Carver set her mind to something, it got done—or else, she'd certainly have to die trying.

3

ROWENA

As long as she could remember, Rowena Pickett's favorite day of the week had been Friday. It signaled the end to a long workweek, the arrival of a fresh paycheck, and a full forty-eight hours of good times to come.

But not this Friday. This time, Rowena's Friday had gone all sorts of wrong. As a result, she had not cashed her check, or gone out to the bars to party, or even had so much as a single drink. Instead, she had stayed in her trailer, staring out the dust-caked front window, waiting anxiously for the busted headlight of her boyfriend Randy's motorcycle to come into view. And with every tick of the clock, that wait had only gotten tougher, her worries made even worse.

It had all begun, this sorry state of affairs, a little over nine hours earlier at the Vittles Pet Food factory up in Rio Linda where Rowena worked. She had headed to her locker at the end of her shift, chatting over weekend plans with the other ladies as always, only to find a letter from her bosses, informing her that she was being laid off, effective immediately. It was a cold blanket dismissal, no doubt written by the Vittles corporate attorneys, citing the economy, market conditions, blah blah

blah ... like the economy was really going to rebound off the
$10.75 an hour she had been making. And this was done, mind
you, even though she had worked there two full years, longer
than she had ever held any job, and had gotten along well with
everybody, too, even her shift supervisors. It still wasn't enough,
apparently.

The whole thing had made Rowena sad. It made her angry.
Worst of all, it made her feel utterly disposable, like some greasy
fast-food wrapper or empty beer can. But the truth was, the
job itself was no great loss. Working on the line, seeing what
went into the various Vittle products, from the popular chuck
wagon-themed Cat and Dog Vittles to the offshoot ZooSelect™
label for more exotic creatures, had made her lose respect for
both the company and the animals themselves. Nothing was
off limits; it all went into the vats, churned into the company's
"secret home-style recipes," whether it was horns or hooves or
internal organs, or even if it was from the intended consumer's
own species.

And now, it had ground her up and spit her out as well.
But, again, it wasn't the loss of a job that had gotten Rowena
so upset. She could always find another job, a better job, at the
Target, or the Costco, or maybe that new Sam's Club they were
building out on Interstate 80. No, what troubled Rowena most
was what had happened in the hours after she left work.

Returning home that night, Rowena had been looking
forward to a shoulder to cry on and a warm body to cling to,
namely that of her boyfriend, Randy. To be loved and comforted
and supported; at the end of the day, that's all that really
matters, right?

But when Rowena arrived back at the trailer—the trailer
she and Randy had shared for nearly six months—he wasn't
there. And as the evening slipped away and the clock struck
two and the bars all closed, he still wasn't there. And at a little
after three, still with no word, Rowena was worried sick. Her

mother had stayed up late one time waiting for a call from her father that never came, and she had been a wreck ever since.

This fear had loomed large in Rowena's mind as she stared at the clock, pacing back and forth in front of the window. *Is Randy riding drunk again?* she had wondered. *Did he get in another accident? Another fight? Is he hurt? Does he need my help? Should I start calling the hospitals?*

It was just then that Randy's old Harley-Davidson had finally roared onto the trailer park's gravel drive. Rowena had raced out the door and down the stoop to greet him and make sure he was okay, only to find that he reeked of pot and booze and at least three different kinds of cheap perfume, none of which were hers.

With that, Rowena's concern had quickly turned to fury.

"Where the *hell* have you been?" she demanded to know.

"Out," Randy replied succinctly.

"It's three o'clock in the morning!"

"So?" Randy replied, keep his side of the argument to one-word answers only.

"So? So! I'll tell you what's so," Rowena countered, before turning back into the trailer and returning with an old gym bag, a Magic 8-Ball, and a motorcycle helmet, all of which she threw at him, one after the other, scoring at least one direct hit and possibly two.

"Do you have any idea how worried I was? Do you have any idea how shitty my day was even before you decided to be a total asshole? I lost my job, Randy! The factory laid me off. And now this!"

Randy, ducking behind his bike, remained remorseless. "Jesus, Rowena! Is it my damn fault you lost your job? Shit!"

Rowena raced over and kicked him, hard, right square in the ass.

"Is that all you have to say for yourself? Do you think I'm stupid? Do you think I don't know what you've been up to?

Screw you, Randy! Screw you and your sorry-ass motorcycle and everything else. I want you out of here! Now!"

In response, Randy had simply dusted himself off, offered up a sloppy shrug, and said, "That's what you want? Fine by me, babe." Grabbing the gym bag and walking past her as if she weren't even there, he had gone inside, gathered some clothes, and then hopped back on his Harley and tore out of there without even so much as a look back.

That was four days ago.

Ever since, Rowena had remained in her tiny trailer bedroom, on her twin-size futon, curled up like a fetus. And although she initially wondered if maybe she had been too harsh, now that she had nothing but the void of unscheduled hours and days on her hands, the truth flashed before her like a beacon, in gaudy neon lights. Randy had *wanted* to get kicked out. He had never been serious about their relationship. After six months, he had grown tired of her. Tired of sharing her bed and eating her cooking and seeing her naked, with that cellulite on the back of her thighs and the appendectomy scar and the faded "Poison" tattoo on her left breast that she got back when she was sixteen and got falling-down drunk for the first time on Long Island iced teas. That was why he got so wasted all the time. It was why he stayed out late, and went to strip clubs (he denied it, but she knew). And it was why he had smacked her that night, right there on the very bed she was lying on now, blackening her eye so bad she had blurred vision for a week.

So when Rowena called him on all his crap, Randy couldn't leave fast enough. He was packed and out the door in five minutes flat. And true to his word, she hadn't heard so much as a peep from him since. Which was, undoubtedly, the plan all along. Looking back now, Rowena realized he'd probably had someone else on the side those last couple months. Hell, he was probably bedded down with one of those skanky lap-dancers from the ShowBar at this very moment, while she was lying here, crying and all alone and needing him more than ever.

Rowena wiped away a tear, sniffled, and looked at the clock on the wall. It was mid-afternoon, a time she used to spend on the line in the Vittles rendering room. Uncoiling from her womblike state, she reached over and grabbed the remote, turning on her dusty wall-mount Panasonic with a no-look click over the shoulder.

A crackle of static and the sound kicked in, breaking the silence with a jolt, before the picture tube finally sprung to life as well. It was a local newscast, doing a report on the upcoming gubernatorial recall election. The anchorman seemed genuinely excited, calling it an unprecedented event in California state history.

Rowena couldn't have cared less.

Punch-punch-click. The newscast disappeared.

After a moment, the screen lit up anew with the sights and sounds of a different channel and the one thing, the one show, the one person, that she hoped might somehow make her feel better about things:

"...Oprah."

Rowena smiled for the first time in days. Call it crazy, but she loved Oprah Winfrey, she really did. Loved her like her own flesh and blood. Oprah might be rich now, and she might hang out with movie stars and wear fancy designer clothes and throw glamorous parties for herself, with her tall, handsome lover Stedman at her side. But deep down, Rowena knew, Oprah was still a plain, slightly overweight small-town girl with a rough-and-tumble past, not unlike herself, and that made her miraculous transformation into a millionaire superstar icon an inspiration to Rowena, who didn't begrudge her even one little bit of her fabulous lifestyle. You go, girlfriend!

As fate would have it, the theme of Oprah's show this day was "Good Women Who Love Bad Men." Rowena sat up with a start. This was a subject she knew about, in spades. Not just because of Randy. Rowena had dated guys like that, almost exclusively, right from the moment her loins had first started tingling back in junior high school.

The object of that initial attraction had been Rodney Stanzler, a leather-clad chain smoker who hung out by the auto shop and wanted to be a racecar driver. They dated all through eighth and ninth grade, and Rowena gave up her virginity to him one night, willingly, in the back of his souped-up, mint-green Chrysler Cordoba—at which point he immediately dropped her for Debra Hartwig, an overdeveloped eighth-grader with the body of a porn star and the mind of a ... well, with that body, who really cares, right? Rodney sure didn't.

After Rodney, it was Chet Rollins, who had a fake ID and bought them beer and Jack Daniels at the Korean grocery store on the edge of town. Then Lance, a star tackle on the varsity football team thanks to the steroids he took, which gave him horrible acne and a vicious, volcanic temper. After Lance, it was Hank, who played drums in a heavy metal band, and Carlos, who collected guns and knives, and Johnny, who grew pot in his garage, and a string of other moody losers just like them.

What was it about bad boys that made them so attractive? Rowena thought she knew, although she hated to admit it to herself. Part of it was the challenge. To tame them and make them your own, at least for a little while. To have something you knew all the other girls wanted, even if they bent over backwards trying to pretend like they didn't. Another part was the unpredictability they offered, which brought a little excitement to life, even if that excitement often came in the form of a long walk home after being kicked out of the car because somebody had flirted with her, or a black eye that stubbornly refused to heal—anything to distract from the day-to-day routine of life, whether that routine was work or school or sudden, thudding unemployment. And, finally, Rowena knew deep down that a big part of the appeal stemmed from the unresolved issues she had with her dearly departed father, Eddie Pickett.

Eddie had been a bad boy, too, in his day. Big and tan and strong, with a lantern jaw and a buzz cut and blue tattooed anchors on his biceps from his stretch in the Navy. When Rowena's mom Connie met him, he had just gotten discharged and started a new job as a long-haul trucker, driving loads of produce back and forth across the country.

The job suited Eddie. He'd never been much of a people person, really. He liked the solitude. Liked the freedom it gave him. Liked the chance to have a woman in every port (a term, and a practice, that he picked up in the Navy). And, last but not least, Eddie also liked the amphetamines he took to stay awake on those long, lonely hauls.

Liked them a bit too much, unfortunately. Her mom got the call one Saturday morning. Eddie had been coming back with a load of cigarettes from Winston-Salem, when he lost control of his rig on a Colorado mountain road going nearly 80 miles an hour. There was no indication that he ever applied the brakes, or even noticed that he was driving off a cliff. The truck was found at the bottom of a steep gorge, in four feet of fast-moving water. The police found over a hundred amphetamine tablets in the glove compartment, and it was impossible to know how many he'd already taken, or whether he had slept so much as a wink since leaving that Carolina warehouse with his load three days before. But the fact was, he was dead. All around the country, in trucker-friendly hubs like Omaha and Amarillo and the Picketts' hometown of Sacramento, women wept. As for Connie, after that call, which had come after a long night's vigil waiting in vain for Eddie to check in, a shell-shocked glaze came over her pretty hazel eyes and she had never been the same since. Eddie Pickett was the love of her life, even if he was a boozing, incorrigible, amphetamine-addicted womanizer.

On the TV, Oprah was now deep in conversation with a mall-banged divorcee named Sandi about her own lifelong "bad boy addiction." Sandi was telling Oprah about her latest relationship with a gentleman currently in prison down in Lubbock, Texas. She had seen the man's personal ad in the back pages of the *National Enquirer* and had answered it on a lark. The two became pen pals, and over time their letters had grown more and more intimate. She felt like Buck, the inmate, really understood her. As a result, when he proposed to her, Sandi said yes, sobbing with joy even though she knew that Buck was on death row for killing his previous wife with a hatchet, and that he would never be eligible for parole. The ceremony had taken place six months ago, on Valentine's Day, and was conducted through the bulletproof glass windows of the visitors' lounge, with the wedding bands exchanged via prison guard.

Oprah let this sink in for a moment, screwing up her face and casting a raised eyebrow in the direction of the shocked, disapproving, and overwhelmingly female audience, before turning back to Sandi and asking, in her trademark sassy-but-sympathetic way, "Girlfriend, what *were* you thinkin'? Why? Why?"

But Rowena already knew why. And she knew exactly what Sandi was thinking, too. She knew it so well, in fact, that—as if in some kind of trance—she found herself saying it out loud: "Because she'll always know where he is. Because she already knows the absolute worst thing about him and she still loves him." Then, to herself now, a revelation of the highest order: "Because he'll never leave her."

Rowena got up out of bed. Suddenly, there was a light at the end of her dark, four-day-long tunnel. She opened the curtains and checked her hair in the mirror. Maybe there was hope, after all.

4

TODD

For the last fifteen years and counting, Todd's Tuxedos had been *the* place to go for rented formalwear in Westside Sacramento. All the kids, the prom-goers, came to Todd's. So did the black-tie wedding crowd, and even the occasional fancy funeral. And why wouldn't they? Todd's had the best selection and the best prices.

But the sad truth of the matter was, even though it was the capital of the great state of California, Sacramento wasn't really much of a formalwear kind of town. Just as it was back in the gold rush days when it was founded, Sacramento was a working-class city, populated largely with working-class people, wearing working-class clothes. Even the politicians who toiled there tended to dress down, donning mostly white shirts with loosened ties and rolled-up sleeves (*"Working Hard for You!"*).

And for Todd—Todd Tisdale, sole owner and proprietor of Todd's Tuxedos—this was a major problem, bringing with it an endless roll call of days and weeks with slow-to-nonexistent business, as well as a load of debt that didn't go away no matter how hard he worked at it.

Which is why Todd was so totally fired up about this whole recall-election deal. Not only were they finally getting rid of that drab idiot Gray Davis, but even better, and more importantly, there was also a good chance that the person who would take his place might actually bring a little pizzazz back to the old capital city. A little glamour. And, not incidentally, a reinvigorated need for rented formalwear. That man was Arnold Schwarzenegger.

After weeks of rumors and denials, Arnold had finally booked an appearance on *The Tonight Show* with Jay Leno, and with no new movie to promote, it was widely believed that he would be formally announcing his candidacy right there, live, on national TV. Todd was giddy at the mere thought of it.

Sitting behind the counter of his empty shop on yet another sweltering August morning, he read the *Bee* front to back. The early polls showed Arnold already leading the pack by a mile over a bunch of wacko long shots and pasty-faced dullards who might as well be Gray Davis all over again. You could feel the excitement in the air. It was going to happen.

Todd smiled to himself and allowed his mind to drift, imagining all that a Schwarzenegger victory might mean to him. More business, for sure. Hell, *booming* business. Arnold was married to a Kennedy, for God's sake, and she was a gorgeous TV personality in her own right. A new version of Camelot right here in the heart of central California seemed like a real possibility.

Todd's mind drifted further. He could expand the store, like he'd always dreamed about. Take over the space of that struggling yogurt shop next door. Maybe add some casual wear, some sportswear. The new governor, accustomed to the best men's shops in LA, would swing by one day, like what he sees, and become a customer. A loyal regular. A friend. Todd and Arnold. Arnold and Todd...

Todd snapped back to reality. His store was still empty. The new shipment of cummerbunds needed folding. He got up from his chair and headed into the back to get cracking.

From the storeroom, the sound of a door chime up front, followed by a chirpy male voice calling out, "Hello, sir! Hello?"

Todd's head snapped up off the pile of bow ties he'd been sorting, their knots leaving a trail of sleep marks all across the left side of his face. "Yep," he responded groggily. "Be right there."

It was a Tuesday, always the slowest day of the week, and in this case, slow meant basically inert. Whoever was calling out to him was Todd's first customer of the afternoon, and only his second since he'd opened his doors seven hours before. Todd rubbed his eyes, tucked in his shirt, and raced out to greet the man.

"Hey there, partner. Welcome to Todd's Tuxedos. Todd Tisdale, owner and proprietor, at your service. What can I do for ya?"

The customer was a young Asian fellow named Fook. In need of a tuxedo for his upcoming nuptials, Fook had—before Todd could lend his expertise to the matter—already zeroed in on the ugliest tux in the shop, a shiny powder-blue number with wide lapels and maestro tails that Todd referred to as his "Sopranos Special" because it looked like something only a low-level mob guy would even think about trying on. But Fook loved it. It fit his cheery personality; it made a statement. And what are you supposed to say? It was his wedding. His choice.

Truth was, Todd envied Fook. The guy was so happy, he was practically walking on air. He clearly adored his fiancée, Lulu, and talked about her the whole time he was getting measured. He said they were using the wedding money from their parents back home in Bangkok to open a donut shop in a strip mall being built right next door to a police station out in suburban Bridgeway. He even showed Todd a picture he took at the shop, still under construction, with Lulu posing in a little tool belt, flashing a flirty little smile for her man behind the camera. Todd could tell already that both the couple and their shop were destined for success. The two lucky lovebirds would probably be making bear-claws and babies together in utter bliss for years to come.

If only Todd's own path was so certain. There was the whole Schwarzenegger situation, of course, which could be great, but who really knew? And outside of that? Well, to be honest, things weren't so hot. His own business was barely staying afloat. His social life, what there was of it, was mostly confined to his league bowling night and the occasional wingding at the Elks Lodge. And as for his love life, well, that was basically nonexistent, and had been for years now.

Not that Todd hadn't had his turns at the plate. In fact, he'd been quite the ladies' man back in the day. A star athlete at his local high school, he had sowed his wild oats like a champ before finally locking down the one girl every other guy his age lusted after, head cheerleader Katy Kapowski. He and Katy quickly ascended to the throne as the school's golden couple, named Homecoming King and Queen for two years running. And the good times rolled on at nearby CSU, Stockton, where they both went to college, Todd starting for the football team and Katy cheering from the sidelines, as always, which was where Todd proposed to her at halftime of his final home game, senior year.

And she said yes, of course. It was like a fairy tale.

Unfortunately, fairy tales don't last. After college and their wedding at the Golden Nugget in Las Vegas, the couple moved back to Sacramento. Still remembered as a local sports hero, Todd landed a good position as a sales rep for a pharmaceutical company, and Katy started throwing Tupperware parties from their apartment. And this is where things started going awry, because while Todd could barely tolerate his own job, Katy loved hers with an unbridled zeal. She was like a cult member, with all the mottos and pep talks—not to mention the parties themselves, which were pretty stupid once you stopped to consider that it was all about showing off a bunch of lame plastic bowls. Todd used to tease her about this, especially when she would get overly rhapsodic about her new Tupperware "family." Katy would get defensive, then pout, and then—worst of all—withhold sex.

And without that, the very thing that had brought them together in the first place, the whole relationship started to suffer. Todd's teasing became more barbed, and Katy's pouting got more pronounced. Soon, Todd found himself spending more nights out with the boys, so as to avoid the pointless sexual tension and any more fanatical diatribes regarding the benefits of airtight lids. As for Katy, she found herself being groomed for "bigger things" within the Tupperware empire, a grooming that led her to spend an increasing number of evenings huddled with district manager Kenny Chitwood, whom Todd would only later discover had become the surrogate beneficiary of Katy's estranged affections.

The final straw came when Katy was promoted on the same day that Todd quit. While Todd was certain that there was a greater destiny for him out there than hawking arthritis pills and eczema creams, Katy was not. Instead, rubbing her own career ascent in his face, she told Todd that he was turning into a big, fat loser—that was the exact term she used: "Big, Fat Loser"—and that she had no intention of sticking around any longer to watch his steep and sorry decline. That hurt, of course, and the subsequent discovery that she was already hatching exit strategies with the aforementioned Mr. Chitwood didn't help much, either.

But, again, Todd had always been adept with the ladies, so getting divorced at twenty-seven ultimately didn't turn out to be such a bad thing. He was still in pretty good shape, still with a full head of hair. And once he got back on his feet and started tending bar at a hot new dance club called Funkytown, he soon found himself with more female attention than he could handle. Oh, yeah, it was high times, indeed. Todd felt like a king again, ruling the roost with a smile on his face and a keg-tap in his hand. Katy Kapowski could suck it, for all he cared.

Then came Angela Marino. Sidling up to his bar one sultry summer night in white hot pants and a low-cut halter top, Angie had asked for a beer, and a shot, and a light, and a dance, and his phone number, all in one breath. And Todd knew, he *just knew*, that this little firecracker was gonna be more than just a one-night stand.

And he was right.

After they got hitched, it was Angie who came up with the idea of the tux shop. She knew how much Todd had detested his boss at the drug company, Carl Zitron, a pencil-pushing toady with problem skin. She also correctly surmised that the problem hadn't so much been Carl himself, but the fact that Carl got to tell him what to do, and when and how to do it. Todd was a guy who liked to call the shots. He needed to be the boss, the captain of his own team. Knowing, too, how fond Todd was of his high school glory days, when he was the big hometown sports hero, Angie posed the question: What better way to combine those two things than for Todd to open his own tuxedo shop, where he could vicariously be a part of every prom, every wedding, and indeed every festive occasion his beloved metropolis of Sacramento had to offer?

Todd was intrigued, and when he did the research, he found there was only one other tux shop on the entire west side of town, and that one was run by some sketchy Pakistani guy— needless to say, a far cry from a beloved local figure like himself. Sure enough, with the value of his good name, plus the papers to his Trans Am and most of Angie's life savings thrown in for good measure, Todd was able to secure a loan to open up a shop of his very own. Todd's Tuxedos was born.

"Is that all?"

"Hmm?" Todd snapped to. "Oh, right. Yes, yes. Got your card number right here, Fookster. We're good to go. See you next week."

"Next week. Yes sir!" Fook gave Todd a little salute and headed out the door.

Todd shook his head. Drifting again. He was a dreamer, always had been, but it had been getting worse lately. And now with a paying customer right there in front of him, too...

Part of it, Todd knew, was the loneliness. Angie had left him two years ago this October. Not another divorce, but cancer, from those damn Virginia Slims she always smoked. And when it got a hold of her, it spread like wildfire. Watching her wither away, trying to ease her pain and keep a smile on his face for her sake while doing it, sucked whatever youth was left in Todd right out of him. When he looked in the mirror after the funeral, what he saw staring back at him was a sad, lonely, middle-aged man. A two-time washout. A widower.

Todd tried to be okay with that. He'd had one great marriage. No kids, but the two of them had had a blast. How many people can say that? Still, working in the shop, seeing all those young couples in love, hands all over each other, made it tough. Call him greedy, but Todd still wanted some of that for himself.

Unfortunately, it wasn't as easy as heading on down to Funkytown anymore. For starters, Funkytown had been closed for over a decade; it was now a Chuck E. Cheese's. But more than that, Todd had changed, too. He was older, and slower, and less cocksure. Sure, he did a requisite check of the new, happening places in town, like Teasers and Rattlers and the Rhino Room, but he felt out of place there, an old man leering at girls who could easily be his daughters, bouncing around to music that only served to give him a headache. It was as if time, and life itself, had passed him by.

***

In a funk, Todd closed up early and headed straight to the bar that had become his watering hole of choice: Hair of the Dog. There were no coeds here. No strobe lights. No fruity umbrella drinks. This was a bar for serious drinkers, populated with booze-hounds and wastrels and pathetic fifty-something two-time losers like himself—*or*, like Vic, a grizzled Vietnam vet who was sitting next to Todd and yakking away even though the topic of his slurry monologue was the last thing Todd needed to hear.

Turns out, Vic was a frequent habitué of the infamous Asian red-light districts, where a guy like him could find all sorts of young and willing female companionship for a reasonable price. The last trip over, Vic—who, with his gnarly skin, distended belly and unruly Fu Manchu made Todd look like Sean Connery in comparison—had actually fallen in love with one of these women and married her, right there in Phuket.

"And, heh heh," Vic added lasciviously, "you wouldn't believe some of the things that little lady can do."

In no mood, Todd tried his best to shut out Vic's drunken boasts, and instead focus on his own brew and the song on the jukebox, "Bad Moon Rising" by Credence Clearwater Revival.

But it was no use. The fuse had been lit, and so his mind kept wandering, back to Fook and his fiancée, Lulu—and to that beguiling photo of her, with the taut body and the flirty glance. Even the tool belt seemed like a come-on now. Fook was one lucky guy, all right. And so, he hated to admit, was Vic. Certainly no prize, yet the guy was going home every night from his job on the docks to a hot young Thai babe who apparently treated him like a king. And for her part, hey, she was out of whatever landmine-ridden hellhole she came from, living in the Land of the Free with a little place in the suburbs, nice clothes, and food on the table every night. She was probably even able to send a few bucks back to her family. So, he got what he wanted, she got what she needed, and they were bonded together by that mutual betterment of circumstance. Just like every other marriage, if you really stop to think about it.

Todd pondered this some more, from several increasingly loin-stirring angles. Then, he shook his head, dismissing the whole sordid vision that was brewing in his beer-soaked brain. He wasn't prejudiced, not really, but he just couldn't see himself being with any lady for the long haul unless she was white. That's just the way it was.

Todd polished off his mug and glumly signaled for another, as the depressing tune about bad moons finally ended, and was replaced by the opening chords of a new, more up-tempo song, featuring an urgent drum-line, driving bass, and the screaming sounds of a supersonic jet coming in for a landing. It was "Back in the USSR" by The Beatles. Todd got his refill and started bopping along, tapping out the beat with his fingers, actively willing himself into a better mood.

And that was when he suddenly realized: Hey! Didn't some Russian women do the same thing as Vic's gal? Marry American guys so they could escape Chernobyl or Siberia or some other similarly frigid turd-patch and come live over here? By God, of course they did! All those Eastern European women did! And no red-light districts or any of that; it was all totally aboveboard and legal, too.

Todd didn't have the faintest clue how he knew this, and with such clear-headed conviction to boot. Or, how such arrangements were struck. Or, for that matter, who might orchestrate them. But he knew it, with all his heart and soul. And he also knew, like a sign from God above, that it would be just the thing for him to seal the deal with Arnold, too—an Eastern European émigré himself, after all.

It was almost too good to be true, as if all his hopes and dreams were converging in this one crystalline moment, and fate itself was guiding his hand. With thoughts of this dancing through his head, and John Lennon singing, "*You don't know how* lucky you are, boy" as if to him personally, Todd pounded the rest of his beer, grinning like a newly certified lottery winner.

Well, *Todd old boy,* Todd thought to himself, *looks like you just might have a few big plays left in you, after all.*

II
CAMPAIGN TRAILS

5

DARLING NIKKI

Spencer had become a regular at the Showbar. The bouncer who'd nearly sent him fleeing that first day, Ivan, was practically a buddy now. He and Spencer called out to each other by name, swapped fist-bumps and man-hugs. Then, Ivan would wave him through the line and past the velvet ropes, no charge, like he was some kind of VIP. It felt good. After hours spent toiling anonymously down in the catacombs of the *Bee*, where life and opportunity seemed to be passing him by with total disregard, it was nice to go someplace where people were actually happy to see him for a change.

This was especially true with Veronique, who Spencer now knew as Nikki, which was actually short for Nicole, her given name. There had been a connection between the two from the very first moment. Spencer knew it was crazy. He was a Jewish Phi Beta Kappa from Cornell by way of Long Island, while she was a high-school dropout from Yuba City whose mutt-like melting pot heritage and utter lack of intellectual curiosity left her with an indefinably exotic beauty and almost no cultural or ethnic point of view whatsoever.

And maybe that's why it worked. For Nikki, things were simple. She liked to dance. She liked to laugh (Spencer had been honing his largely-dormant sense of humor ever since). She liked Italian food. She liked margaritas. And she *loved* sex, although Spencer had to take her word on this, as they had yet to see one another outside the club's confines, much less engage in any actual hanky-panky. Still, Spencer's hopes ran high, and Nikki encouraged those hopes with her vast repertoire of intimate glances and coos as he slipped bill after dollar bill into the razor thin waistband of her silky G-string.

Yes, indeed. Spencer was no regular-Joe customer. He was special. Every guy in the club knew it, too. When she was done onstage, Nikki would always stop by his table first, then loop back to him after she had made her rounds. The two would sit and talk, nothing particularly deep or meaningful, but always with an ease that reflected their growing familiarity and comfort with one another.

Occasionally, during these little visits, Nikki would ask Spencer if he wanted to go back to the "VIP Lounge" for a private dance. Tempting as it was, Spencer always declined this offer. He didn't want to cheapen the bond they'd been forming, at least not at such a crucial, early juncture in their relationship. And at first, Nikki, who was of course trying to earn a living through such enticements, had appeared mildly annoyed by this. Then, as time went on, she actually seemed amused, and perhaps even charmed, by it. Though she never addressed the topic directly, Spencer had the sense that Nikki had grown accustomed to being in the company of men who were drunk and vulgar and sometimes even worse. Spencer's chivalrous manner set him apart, and he could see it was having the intended effect.

Nikki finished her last number of the night, helicoptering her way around a brass pole to the closing strains of "Cherry Pie" by Warrant as all the men in the club cheered lustily. Nikki was nothing if not a crowd pleaser. She was a gifted dancer, too, infusing her routines with real choreography and style, which Spencer viewed as a sign of character and artistic integrity on her part. Most of the other girls at the club didn't bother with such technicalities; instead, they would just strut out, whip off their clothes, and then stick their privates in the customers' faces until a tip was forthcoming. Crude, but—Spencer had to admit—startlingly effective.

Still, the fact remained that Nikki was the class of the field. In fact, to Spencer's way of thinking, Nikki was another kind of performer entirely. She could have been a real star back in the 50s, in the heydays of burlesque theater, when it wasn't just about big hair and boob jobs and piston-like pelvic thrusts; it was an art form. And that's precisely what he had been trying to tell her. That she was selling herself short; that she was capable of so much more if she just gave herself the chance.

But such ruminations were quickly set aside as soon as Nikki came into Spencer's line of sight, headed straight for his table, as always. She still took his breath away. And although Spencer had grown accustomed to it on some level, the sight of her coming toward him still made his hands sweat like a teenager on a first date. Especially tonight, when he'd decided it was finally time to take things to the next level.

"Hey there, big boy."

"Hey, Nikki. Boy, you were really great up there tonight."

"Oh, that's so sweet," Nikki cooed, sitting down beside him and coiling a spiky stiletto heel around his right ankle. "And look at you, with that cute little jacket and tie."

If it weren't for the amber glow emanating from the stage lights, Nikki might have noticed that Spencer was blushing bright red. Why did a simple compliment from her always get to him like that? Spencer could never quite put a finger on it, although one might guess that it had something to do with the fact that she was rubbing her chest against his while saying it, and wearing no clothing whatsoever while doing so.

But again, Spencer had more on his mind than simple compliments. There was an agenda, a higher purpose, for his visit this evening. After a month of almost daily visits, Spencer had a plan to ask Nikki out on an actual date, one that would be both off the clock and non-tip-related. All he had to do now was conjure up the words.

Alas, for a man for whom the use of language was a source of livelihood, Spencer found himself painfully at a loss. As he hesitated, Nikki's eyes slowly started to wander, to other men, other tippers, at other tables. And it was precisely this outside competition for her attention that finally forced Spencer to show some cajones and simply spit it out.

"Hey, Nikki?"

Nikki turned back, brow raised, sensing something different in the timbre of his voice. Spencer leaned close so that no one else could hear, and Nikki responded by doing the same, the waft of her perfume nearly making Spencer lose his concentration. But no, he was a man on a mission. He soldiered on: "Listen, you and I, we've gotten to know each other pretty well, right? I mean, I know this is your job and all, but—"

Nikki stopped him, stroking her long lacquered nails across his cheek. "Baby, of course you're special to me. You know that."

"Well, I feel the same way. I do. And that's why I wanted to ask if I could take you out sometime, just the two of us. Maybe we could grab a bite at that Italian place you said you liked, Luigi's? Whatever you want."

Nikki pulled back a bit. A line was being crossed here, and Spencer knew it. There was a pause, broken only by the Motley Crüe ballad emanating from the speakers and the hoots of horny strangers huddled around the stage. But to Spencer, it was utter and excruciating silence. He waited for his answer, trying to play it cool, although his eyes were clearly begging.

"For dinner?" Nikki finally asked.

"Or lunch. Whatever you want," Spencer said, before adding the magic words, "I just want to make you happy."

Nikki smiled, but the meaning of it was hard to decipher. So was the sigh and slight aversion of her eyes that followed. And when she looked over to the entrance, where Ivan and the other bouncers were busy comparing bicep flexes, as if ready to call them over for assistance, Spencer was certain that he was about to be rejected—that he had misread the signals, and was in reality just another pathetic strip-club chump with an unrequited crush.

He said nothing more, for fear of making things even worse and having the bouncers' collective fury unleashed upon him. But then, suddenly, she turned back, leaned in close again, and whispered, as if it were the juiciest of secrets, "Okay, big boy. I get off in five. How about right now?"

Surprising as this reply may have been, it was like music to Spencer's ears. And not just any music; it was a whole freakin' philharmonic orchestra, accompanied by a choir of angels. Because the fact was, no matter why or how it happened, his invitation had been accepted. He wasn't crazy. This vision of beauty, this goddess, this California Dream Girl, was actually agreeing to go out with him. To be seen on his arm. To make him the envy of every man in the club, and beyond. He took her hand and kissed it, over and over again. He was on cloud nine.

The next hour or so was a blur for Spencer. He had been so eager for this moment to arrive, and imagined it in so many different ways, that the sudden actuality of it felt almost surreal. He was conscious of waiting for Nikki to punch out and change clothes. Then, of stiffly walking her out to the parking lot, to the Volvo that his father had bought for him after college because of its safety record and good gas mileage.

From there, his memories came only in brief, strobe-lit flashes. Driving to the restaurant, trying his best to engage Nikki in casual small talk without ruining things by crashing en route. Pulling up to the entrance, as the wide-eyed parking valets fought over who got to open her door. Then, following the maître d' to their table, as all the other men in the room turned on a pivot to watch them pass. And finally, best of all, ordering manicotti and margaritas, Nikki's favorite meal, as her face lit up, her hands clapped, and her breasts did a mesmerizing shimmy right there on their tabletop.

But while Spencer was physically present for all of this, it was also as if he were observing it from afar, in some kind of altered state. And with it came a pair of voices, calling out to him from the deep chambers of his own roiling mind.

"What are you doing, Brine? The girl's a *stripper*, for God's sake!"

This was the voice of reason, informed by Spencer's strict, East Coast Jewish upbringing, and by years of largely inept encounters with members of the opposite sex, most of whom were jappy debutantes from the same elite schools and good Jewish families as himself, whose privileged upbringings were just as strict and repressed as his own, and whose companionship thus left him with little exposure to, much less experience with, the less inhibited and more sexually astute exemplifications of the species.

"Yeah, but holy crap, just look at her!"

This second voice was Spencer's desire talking—in this case, a rebel yell of pure unadulterated lust, bottled up like a genie over years of largely unsated sexual desires and curiosities, and coupled with far too many lonely nights spent perusing Playboy magazines and Girls Gone Wild videos, wondering what kind of lucky bastards actually ended up with those kind of girls. "She's an angel. And you saw her dance. She's damn good. Is it her fault she hasn't had the right opportunities in life?"

"Wake up, champ, she's gonna chew you up and spit you out like that pasta you just ordered!"

"Maybe she will, but what a way to go! And look at those—"

"—you know? Spencer? Hello? Anybody home?"

Spencer blinked, suddenly realizing that Nikki was talking to him; that, indeed, she had been asking him a question of some sort. Not wanting her to think he hadn't been listening, he fumbled for a recovery. "Oh ... right. Yes. Sorry."

"So?" Nikki pressed, quickly growing peevish.

"Ummm." Spencer was lost. Hopelessly lost. Adrift without a paddle.

"I mean, if you don't want to," Nikki huffed. "Whatever."

"No, no! Whatever you want, I want, too. Believe me. I'm sorry, I just ... I was just thinking, you know. How happy I am that we're here. That you're here. Just tell me what you want, I'll make it happen."

Nikki seemed assuaged by this. She bit her bottom lip, drawing out the moment, fully engaged again. "Oh. Well. Okay..."

Spencer hung on her every gesture now, eager to fulfill the request that would certainly open the door to an exciting new chapter, a new level of intimacy.

"But actually, I was just wondering if you liked calamari. You know, those little fried rings?"

Spencer blinked again. Was this the breakthrough he'd hoped for? Not exactly.

Did he like calamari? Absolutely not.

But he certainly wasn't going to let it show. The fact was, this minor blip had been a godsend, a wake-up call. Nikki clearly demanded a suitor's full attention. To win her, he would need to stay on his toes. And from this moment forward, that is precisely what he planned to do.

With a voice full of renewed vigor, he called out, "Waiter! We'll need an order of the calamari as well!"

The waiter nodded, in a way that indicated that he now saw Spencer as a customer not to be taken lightly. The calamari would indeed be theirs. And, by God, if not tonight then soon, Nikki Balodouris would be his.

6

LADIES' NIGHT

"**W**ant another drink, Ro?"

Rowena was huddled at a corner table in a crowded bar with Vicky and Estelle, two of her coworkers from her new job at the Golden Child tanning salon.

"Another Long Island iced tea, maybe?" suggested Estelle with a wink.

Estelle, Rowena's best friend since seventh grade, was the one who had gotten Rowena the job at the salon, where she was assistant manager. And now, seeing as it was Rowena's first night out since her little "setback," Estelle was equally determined to show her a good time. That is why they had come here, to Teasers, a slick suburban-mall nightclub where the gaudy decor, dim lighting, and loud music all served to make heavy drinking and late-night hookups seem almost obligatory. Adding to the mood was the fact that tonight was Ladies' Night, which not only meant they got in free, and that all their drinks were half price, but also that the place was packed with hot guys out on the prowl—all the elements of a great, forget-your-troubles kind of night, which is precisely what Estelle thought Rowena needed most.

As the over-exuberant DJ cued up yet another crowd-stirring, party-hearty dance anthem, the ladies pondered what to order next from the plethora of bars and drink stations that, along with the bikini-clad "shot girls" roaming the floor hawking their wares, were trying their hardest to create a rowdy Spring Break atmosphere in the club's far less paradisiacal surroundings.

"Maybe we should *all* get Long Island iced teas," Vicky chimed in, her eyes locked meaningfully on Rowena's. She and Estelle both knew Rowena's weakness for the sneakily potent concoction. They also knew that if anything would help her loosen up and have some real fun for a change, that would be just the thing to do it.

But Rowena knew something, too. She knew what they were doing. It was the same thing they had been doing ever since they stopped by her trailer earlier that evening with a large pepperoni pizza and a jug of cheap Chablis, hoping to boost her sagging spirits, only to find her already up and about, ironing her favorite jeans and humming along to the radio with a big Mona Lisa smile on her face.

Naturally, the girls had suspected a secret behind these mysteriously improved spirits. And they were right. Rowena did have a secret. But she also knew that there was nothing her friends could say or do that could get her to divulge it, even if they got her totally wasted, and even though they were her best friends in the whole world. So, with a casual shrug of her freshly-bronzed shoulders (the main perk of her new job—free tanning), she boldly accepted their challenge.

"Sure, why not? Long Island iced teas, it is."

The reason Rowena knew she wouldn't reveal her secret is that she knew that no one, not even Estelle, would understand it, much less approve of it. The fact was, she had followed up on her "Oprah moment" by looking into a prison pen pals program, and had started corresponding with a number of single men (they had to be single, Rowena made sure of this) from several different penitentiaries around the state. And although some of these men had proven to be a little too forward—and in some cases, downright freaky—there were a couple guys she thought she might really like. Guys who seemed like they had truly learned from their mistakes, and just wanted someone to write to. To confide in. To understand.

"So what's the big secret, Ro?" Now that Vicky was off to get the drinks, Estelle was scooting her barstool closer, moving in for the kill, dying for the details. "Come on. It's just you and me now. You been grinning like a jack-o'-lantern ever since we came and got you."

Rowena sat back and let her eyes go wide, as if utterly at a loss. "I don't know what you're talking about, Estelle. I'm just happy being out again, that's all."

Estelle leaned closer still, hovering over her friend like a police interrogator. "Come on now, girl! There's something goin' on. Spill it already."

"There's nothing, really. I swear."

Estelle backed off and looked away. She seemed angry now. Betrayed, even.

"What's wrong?"

"What's *wrong*? Girl, who do you think you're fooling? You think I can't tell when somebody's getting themselves good and laid? Shoot." Estelle whipped out her pink lighter with a pout and fired up another Capri Menthol. "I thought we was friends."

"We are, Estelle, jeez. It's like I said, okay? It's nothing like that. I just decided I was done worrying about Randy McCracken and all his bullcrap. He wasn't worth it, anyway."

Estelle turned and stared hard at Rowena for several seconds, deciding whether to believe her or not. "You sure? You aren't holding out on me, now?"

"That's all, I swear. It's over for good this time. I'm ready to move on."

With a final, squint-eyed drag off her cigarette, Estelle eased forward again on her stool and, having apparently decided that she had truly squeezed her friend out of every scrap of information worth getting, offered up a conspiratorial whisper. "Okay. Guess who I see over by the bar, then?"

Rowena froze, in a dead panic. "No! Is it Randy? Randy's here?"

"Not Randy. Screw him. It's Wade."

A regular at the same Westside bars they frequented, Wade Watson was a ruggedly handsome construction worker with a deep tan, bulging biceps, and silky, feathered hair, just like Erik Estrada's on *CHiPS*. When Rowena turned, he was looking right at her, smiling and waving. Embarrassed, she tried to look away before realizing that he had already seen her and that looking away only made it worse. She turned back and forced a self-conscious smile of her own.

Wade started over, with his distinctive bow-legged swagger, which made him look like he was wearing a tool belt even when he wasn't.

"Hey there, ladies. Thought I saw you over here."

"Hey, Wade," the girls replied in unison. "Come on and sit down," Estelle added, with a sly glance thrown Rowena's way to let her know it was all for her benefit.

"Don't mind if I do." Wade spun a chair around and sat down, legs spread wide, giving the ladies an unobstructed view of the faded crotch of his tight Wranglers. He turned his attention, and his dazzling smile, to Rowena. "Haven't seen you in a while, Ro. You're looking good."

Rowena flushed. "It's the tan. Never had one when I was working at the factory. Always inside, with those bad fluorescent lights—"

"Never smelled so good, either. Smell her neck, Wade," Estelle interjected.

Rowena tossed a glare her way; Estelle was pushing it now. But since the subject was already out there, Rowena felt the necessity to add, "It's Passion. You know, the one with Elizabeth Taylor in the purple bottle?"

Wade dove in and gave her neck a long sniff, lingering far longer than what might be considered proper. Not that Rowena minded. She hadn't felt a man's touch in nearly a month now. "I like it. Is that the only place you have it on?"

Estelle giggled, "Why don't you two just get a room already?"

Wade took the bait. "Not a bad idea. Ro, what are you doing Friday night?"

Rowena hesitated, blushing again. "I don't know. No plans, I guess." Then, opening a door that she knew she shouldn't: "What about you?"

Wade flashed that smile again. "Taking you out dancing. Say, eight o'clock?"

And there it was. An invitation to another bad boy, the absolute last thing in the world she needed right now. The voice in her head called out to her, urgently: *Don't do it, don't do it, don't do it!* But Rowena couldn't help herself. "Okay. But make it nine. I don't get off till eight-thirty."

"Eight-thirty, it's a date." Wade got up from his chair, leaning over to smell Rowena's neck again. "Mmm-mmm-mmm. And you better put on some of *that* again, too." And with that, he was off again, with that same cocky tool-belt strut.

"Guess who I just saw?" Vicky said, returning a moment later with the drinks.

"We know. He was just here."

Vicky looked confused. "Him? No. I was talking about Missy Carver."

Estelle's eyes went wide with wicked glee. "Oh no, you gotta be shittin' me! Miss Prissy-bitch is actually in a *bar*? Where?"

Vicky pointed, and the girls all craned their necks in unison to sneak a not-so-subtle peek at the attractive but rigid-looking woman sitting in a corner booth with a tall, handsome man in his early forties, who looked almost as uptight as she was.

Rowena knew Missy, too. The most stuck-up girl in her high school class, Missy was the same way even now, more than ten years later, with her upright posture and prim little walk, not a hair or a thread out of place, gazing about the dimly-lit room as if it was all beneath her. None of Rowena's friends could stand her, but Missy was one of those types who didn't even seem to notice—too sure of herself to worry about the impact she made, or the people she had to step on to make it. And that's probably why she was such a big success now, a fact that only made her that much more loathsome.

Estelle snorted. "Jesus! Who does she think she's kidding? Is she actually drinking a glass of *water* over there?"

Vicky nodded, adding sarcastically, "It is *sparkling* water, though."

Estelle cackled. "Watch out! Missy's cuttin' loose tonight!"

Rowena sat back and sighed, looking on silently as Estelle and Vicky continued lacerating Missy from afar with a barrage of insecurity-induced, mean-girl putdowns— relieved, more than anything, that she was no longer the center of attention.

Her secret was still safe.

7

ONLY THE BEST

6:02 a.m., the morning after Missy's big date with Steve Manning, and she was back on the elliptical for her daily one-hour workout, same as always. This morning, however, every step felt like a muddy slog. And although she tried her best to convince herself that it was because she had exercised twice the day before, Missy knew the truth. It was because of the date, which had proved to be yet another unmitigated disaster—and this, after everything had seemed so perfect. Where had it all gone wrong?

The truth was, part of her already knew. As a realtor, Missy could always tell with potential buyers whether they had a deal or not. It was all in the eyes. And last night, Steve's eyes were saying "No Sale." God, why couldn't she have just loosened up a bit and ordered a second chardonnay? The way he looked at her when she had asked for that glass of water...

Then again, Missy reminded herself, it wasn't as if it was *entirely* her fault. After all, what kind of man would ever take a date to that sleazy meat market Teasers in the first place? Then there was the way he had looked when he picked her up, with that criminally scraggly goatee, which was decidedly *not* there in his prospectus photo, and his clothes, which were badly wrinkled and ripe from work. Couldn't he have at least changed into a fresh shirt? Overall, it made her wonder: did he actually believe this was making a good first impression, coming to the door looking like some kind of stinky beatnik? In Missy's case, all it had done was make her lose interest and respect right from the very start.

Steve *had* tried to make up for lost ground, though. At dinner, in a downtown restaurant clearly chosen for its romantic riverside views, he had directed the conversation her way, politely asking questions, seeming interested, trying to learn more about her. The problem was the type of questions he asked. Missy didn't really care to drum up vignettes from her schoolgirl days, or her family tree, and she *definitely* didn't care whose alma mater was going to have the better football team. Religion was a no-no, too, even though Steve had clearly broached the topic to help establish himself as a solid marriage prospect with proper values. Missy was a firm non-believer, and she frowned upon those who refused to accept the cold, hard facts of the situation.

But then, hallelujah, Steve asked about her career. Missy was more than happy to tackle *that* subject. Unfortunately, by the time it was finally broached, dinner was almost over, so when Steve proposed that they go somewhere else for a nightcap, Missy had no choice other than to say yes. That is what led them to that garish, low-rent nightclub in the first place. And while Missy had tried to make the best of it, continuing to tell Steve about her work as best she could over the blare of the god-awful music, before she could even get to the best part, about her courting of Schwarzenegger, she noticed that his eyes had begun to wander away from her—his date!—and over to the pagan gyrations of the nearby dance floor. This was yet another strike against him to be sure, and a big one at that, but she was willing to keep an open mind, she really was, until he suddenly interrupted her to say that it had been a long day and that he was getting tired. Can you believe the nerve? Missy sure couldn't.

Back at her house, Missy had watched as Steve tore out of the driveway in his Jaguar, already chatting away on his cell phone. But to whom? And at 10:30 at night? *So much for being tired*, Missy thought, fighting a sudden wave of exhaustion herself. Turning away from the window, she had then headed right off to bed, already knowing that she was going to have to pay a little visit to Heidi-the-Matchmaker first thing in the morning and set things straight, once and for all.

And now, after a long night of tossing and turning and replaying all the evening's miscues in her mind, Missy's sense of outrage had only grown. After all, she had paid a handsome retainer and done everything that was asked of her, and what did she have to show for it? So far, just three lousy dates with three disappointing bachelors, all of whom were a far sight shy of what had been promised.

Her anger reaching a crescendo now, Missy churned the pedals furiously until the chime on her chronograph went off, signaling that she was done. With that, she got off and threw her towel hard against the wall, missing the hamper completely as a sign of her rage.

"You better get ready, Miss Matchmaker to the Elite," Missy growled, psyching herself up for the showdown to come. "It's time to reap the whirlwind."

"What is this?"

Missy stared at the check that Heidi had just handed her, fully taken aback. This wasn't how things were supposed to play out, not at all.

As planned, Missy had driven straight from her house to Heidi's office, arriving right when the doors opened with the intention of letting Heidi know all about her dreadful experience with Steve. Heidi was supposed to listen and cluck along sympathetically, then atone for it by offering up one of her "gold standard" bachelors—the crème de la crème doctors and entrepreneurs that Missy assumed she had held in reserve for her top clients on precisely these kind of occasions.

But no. Across the desk, Heidi's face was stone, bearing no resemblance whatsoever to the amiable yenta that Missy had met weeks before. She pushed the check to the edge of the gleaming glass surface, practically jabbing at Missy with it. "It's your deposit, returned in full. Take it."

Missy was flabbergasted. "But I just ... I was just making the point that—"

"And this is *my* point. I don't think I can help you anymore. I'm sorry. Let's just part ways now, as friends, and let me wish you all the best."

"I ... Heidi, I would think, as one businesswoman to another, that you'd at least want to hear what I have to say. As I was saying, Steve was—"

"Steve was fine, honey, okay? Steve's a doll, a total catch, a ten! So was Charlie. And Jeff. They aren't the problem."

"You already spoke to him? But ... you haven't heard my side of the story."

"Honey, please! I haven't heard? That's *all* I've heard, ever since I met you! That's all you know. And that's the problem."

"So, you're implying that the problem is *me* now, is that it?"

Heidi offered no reply, but her raised eyebrows and poorly concealed smirk spoke for her. Missy was aghast.

"Heidi, I'm sorry, but I simply will *not* just sit here and listen to you unjustly malign my character any longer. I will not!"

Heidi tilted her head, as if a battle were waging inside her as to how to proceed. She finally leaned forward. Her features softening now, back to yenta mode. Missy smiled, pleased with herself at having called the bluff.

"Honey, let me do you a favor here, okay?"

Missy nodded, waiting expectantly for the favor she expected to receive in the form of a handsome plastic surgeon or Internet mogul.

Heidi sighed. "I'll be blunt. Have you ever heard the phrase, 'Life's too short'?"

Missy chuckled, although she was unsure whether it was to signal her agreement or her disdain. "Yes, I have, as a matter of fact, and that's why I tried to—"

Heidi cut her off. "That's how I feel about working with you, okay? That's how the men I tried to set you up with feel about you. You told me you were picky? Fine. I know from picky. That's not what you are. You're just snobby. And rude. And bossy. And self-absorbed. And from what I can tell, the only person who seems to meet your ridiculously high standards is yourself."

Missy gasped, now in utter, highly offended disbelief. "*Excuse me?*"

Heidi remained unflinching, as if she had total conviction in the appalling accusations she had just made. *My God,* Missy thought to herself, *the woman is positively nefarious!*

Heidi continued, unrelenting. "It's just my opinion, but I know I'm right. You're too tough on people. You make them feel inadequate. And that makes them hate you."

"Hate? Who said anything about ... about hating anybody?"

Heidi refused to go into any specific details on this, which to Missy's mind was yet further evidence that the shameless yenta was just making poor excuses for her own shortcomings. Instead, she simply folded the check in two and silently slipped it into Missy's purse.

Missy started to protest. *This was wrong! She was the wronged party here! She was there, Heidi wasn't.* But curiously, for once, Missy could not manage to summon forth the words for her own defense. Instead, she simply grabbed her purse and scurried out the door.

Exiting the building in a huff, Missy got in her Lexus, slammed the door, and tore out of the parking lot with an alarming screech. The meeting with Heidi had flustered her, more so than she would ever care to admit, and that fluster had followed her like a bad smell. She needed to put it behind her, along with that bitchy matchmaker, as quickly as possible.

"You deserve only the best, and you'll get only the best. You deserve only the best, and you'll get only the best," Missy barked, a bit more shrilly than usual, before performing a series of deep, rhythmic yoga breaths. In and out, in and out, in and out.

This seemed to help. Missy repeated the cycle. Then, did it again. Slowly, the sense of weakness and uncertainty she had felt subsided. Indeed, by the time she made her turn off the commercial loop and onto the main road, headed now for her own office at Eureka Realty, Missy had already started feeling altogether better. Maybe it was for the best, she thought. Clearly, Heidi couldn't deliver the goods, and she must have known it. That was why she had returned Missy's retainer, in full. She had failed, just as the three men she had chosen for Missy had failed.

Or.

Was it possible?

That she had, somehow, failed *them*?

Driving along in a deepening daze, Missy found herself pondering this heretofore-unthinkable possibility. She recalled one date she had gone on a couple years back, with a young writer (Jewish; a problem) from the Sacramento *Bee* (where he wrote obituaries—ick), whom she'd placed in a nice downtown condominium, and who had a refreshing East Coast prep school polish about him.

The journalist, whose last name was Brine (another ick), told her something that she nevertheless remembered. Talking about himself and his own experiences (self-absorbed, slightly morose—more problems), he told her that life was never exactly how he had imagined it would be, but that by learning to embrace the unexpected, and view it as fate, he had become a much happier and healthier person. Maybe, Missy thought, that could have applied to her first date's lisp, or the second one's love of karaoke, or even something as vacuous as going to Teasers and talking about college football with Steve. Maybe she needed to learn to loosen up a bit, and roll with the punches, and be a better sport, and all that.

Maybe. But right now, it was all too much for Missy to even ponder. And with the offices of Eureka Realty now dead in her sights, she had to store away all those negative thoughts and focus on the workday to come. At Eureka, she was a Master of the Universe, and she had all the perks—like her own parking space, branded with her name and designation as Realtor of the Month, which she was pulling into now—to prove it. Nothing could stop her; not here, not now.

Sure enough, bursting through the front doors into the office lobby, her game-face now fully on, Missy felt it right from the start. An expectant buzz, an aura of excitement. This was going to be a great day. She could see it in people's faces, in the way they moved more crisply than usual. And when they saw her, the buzz only amplified. Spotting one of the senior partners, Richard Block, a chubby man with awful hair plugs, she grabbed him and asked what all the commotion was about.

"You mean, you haven't heard?"

"I just got here, no." Then, feeling the need for an excuse for her atypically late arrival, she added, "I ... had a meeting."

"Well, okay, then. Great news. Looks like we landed Schwarzenegger!"

Missy swooned. This was a dream come true, the coup she had been waiting for, the one that would finally seal her ascent to full partnership. Beaming, she grabbed Richard by the shoulders, fighting the urge to kiss him—only her innate sense of decorum (and his hair plugs) holding her back. "I knew it! I knew my persistence would pay off! I just knew! And I know just the place he's going to want, too!"

Richard coughed uncomfortably. "I ... glad you're so excited, Missy. We are a team, after all. And I'm sure Jolene will be happy to hear any ideas you may have."

Missy's face fell like a brick. "Jolene?"

"That's right. She bumped into Maria on a flight out of New York. Apparently, the two got along like peas in a pod. They traded numbers, and Jolene says they've already made some preliminary plans to get together again."

"I ... but I ..." Missy was reduced to sputtering now.

"Hey, look, I know you were trying to chase him down, too. Who knows? Maybe Jolene'll take you on as a second. She's always been a team player, and since she's getting bumped up to partner, that'll certainly take up a fair amount of her time. Besides, nobody works a deal like you. You two can play good cop, bad cop. You're the best bad cop around."

Incredibly, Richard seemed to intend this as a compliment. But for Missy, it was a cruel, backhanded blow. Bad cop? What's bad about negotiating a good deal? But Missy didn't say this. For the second time in less than an hour, she couldn't speak at all. It took all her strength to simply nod and offer up a rictus-like smile, her body rigid, frozen in place, as Richard patted her absently on the shoulder, then trundled off towards the snack room for another Krispy Kreme as if it were nothing.

Standing there, Missy slowly came to realize that a whole room of eyes was upon her. Summoning every possible ounce of intestinal fortitude at her disposal, she willed herself to put one foot in front of the other—one-two, one-two, again and again—until she finally disappeared into the stark confines of her beloved office. And there, in the privacy of that hard-earned space, decorated with the trophies and plaques and gold-plated pen-and-pencil sets celebrating her many years of success, Missy headed to her desk, sat down, hid her face in her hands, and began to cry, the tears flowing like they hadn't since her childhood.

8

DATE WITH DESTINY

Todd closed the shop early again. It was Friday, typically his busiest day of the week, so he hated to do it, but this was a special occasion. He had made plans to meet with the West Coast rep for Czech-Mates, a company he found online that facilitated introductions between single American men and eligible bachelorettes from all over Eastern Europe who were looking for serious relationships, and perhaps even marriage.

The meeting place was in a hotel in downtown San Francisco, which meant a three-hour drive for Todd, there and back. It was a haul, sure, but Todd had high hopes. The man he had spoken to over the phone, Andrei, had asked him a battery of questions, and seemed to like what Todd had to say. Furthermore, he had made Todd feel much more at ease about his interest in their program, saying that many guys in his position were doing the same thing. They were usually older and established, he said, often divorced or widowed, and tired of the game, of all the hoops that American women made men jump through before there was any kind of romantic payoff. He made it clear that Eastern European women were different.

Sexier, for one thing, and not afraid to show it. But also, happy and grateful to find men—successful, responsible men like himself—who would appreciate them, and take care of them, and help them build better lives for themselves than they could ever hope to in their own sexist, repressed cultures.

This was just what Todd had needed to hear. Despite his initial bravado, he had still harbored some doubts. Was he just some dirty, pathetic old man? Would people look down on him for it? Think he wasn't able to attract women the conventional way? Andrei's soothing words erased those fears. He wasn't a loser. He was a liberator! Hell, when he shows up with his new Slavic sweetheart on his arm, he'll be the envy of every man in the room. And with his tuxedo business, too, it'll be perfect. He'll be like some kind of international playboy—the James Bond of Sacramento!

Todd quickly embraced this image, and it had sustained him through the days that followed. At the wheel, he began to drift, imagining it yet again, in vivid detail, now with the inclusion of his soon-to-be-pal Arnold, both of them in tuxedos, smoking fat Cuban cigars, drinking stiff martinis (shaken, not stirred, of course), and staring appreciatively at Todd's new lady love in all her—

HOOONNNK!

Off the furious horn-blast from a neighboring semi, Todd snapped back to the present in a full-on panic, as he realized his speeding Ford Bronco had drifted across the dotted white lines and nearly into the side of the wailing truck's waste-spattered trailer, filled with cows heading off to slaughter.

Frantically re-gripping the wheel with both hands, Todd white-knuckled his way back into the dead square center of his own lane. Then, for good measure, he veered over an additional lane, steering his vehicle well clear of the truck and its still-irate, still-honking driver.

It was a close call, all right; far too close for comfort. Todd's heart was beating like a jackhammer. And had it not been for his lightning-fast reflexes and sure-handed maneuvering, it would have undoubtedly been one hell of a messy collision, too. But despite all that, Todd soon found himself easing back into a dreamy little smile. For the fact was, he saw his destiny lying clearly ahead of him now, and it didn't involve any crunching metal or hobbled livestock. Oh, no. He was on his way to an exciting new chapter in his life. A chapter that would bring to him all the happiness, companionship, and financial success that he had been so desperately yearning for.

It was his time to shine.

Todd met Andrei in the lobby bar of the Fairmont Hotel. Andrei, who looked to be about his age or maybe a couple years older, was a big, swarthy guy, built like a tank, obviously Russian, wearing a double-breasted pinstripe suit with a gangster-like fedora, and bathed in a heavy musk cologne as thick as his accent.

Off this intimidating first impression, Todd's worst fears began to run wild. What exactly had he gotten himself into here? Was this all really on the up-and-up? Was it possible that Andrei could actually be a front man for the Russian Mafia, overseeing some kind of seedy slave-trade operation?

Fortunately, Andrei sensed Todd's concerns and quickly dismissed them with a hearty laugh. "You have seen too many movies, my friend!" Andrei said, taking off the hat and unbuttoning his jacket, making himself look far less fearsome in the process. He then explained that Czech Mates had been operating successfully in their chosen field of "foreign relations" for well over twenty years, and that they currently had offices throughout Eastern Europe and the Russian Republics. Andrei was, in fact, heading to Moscow the very next morning for another scouting trip. If Todd put a good-faith payment down now, he'd be first in line for the new batch of lovelies.

Todd was naturally intrigued, but he remained cautious.

"So how does it all work? Do I write letters, look at pictures, what?"

"Excellent question, Todd," Andrei replied, in the silky-smooth patter of a born salesman. "And the answer is, that is entirely up to you. The process can take many forms, and that process can be very slow, or very swift. Allow me to offer an example. There was a client I had; he was from Boston. He needed to get married, and fast, to a Catholic woman, or else he would lose a huge inheritance. I was able to find him a sexy Polish girl—practically a model, this girl, and devout as the Pope to boot—and it was done, the whole thing, kit and caboodle, in less than two weeks."

"Wow."

Andrei shrugged humbly. "Like I say, just an example. On the other hand, there are men—they are more on the shy side, you understand; never much luck with the ladies here in the States—who have been writing to girls for years now, and they still haven't made any attempt to meet even one of them! Ha ha!"

Todd laughed along. He liked Andrei.

"But this is not the case with you, Todd. I can see it in your eyes. We are both men of the world, yes? Our tastes demand more. For us, only the very best is good enough."

Todd wasn't entirely sure that this was true, but he wanted it to be, so he found himself nodding along.

Andrei winked conspiratorially. "So let me tell you, then, Todd. What you *really* need to do? It is to book a trip for one of our Berlin Wall parties. They are legendary, my friend. It is like being inside an Arabian sheik's harem—except at our parties, the women, they are all there for *you*. And for you to choose."

Todd liked the sound of this. He liked it a lot. For one thing, it had been years since he had taken a real vacation, and even then it was just to Vegas. He was long overdue for a little getaway. This would also, he realized, allow him to concoct a suitable story for exactly *how* he met whichever lady he ultimately chose.

It wasn't some sleazy green-card thing—oh, no, no, no—this was a real honest-to-goodness, love-at-first-sight whirlwind romance, like something out of a fairy tale.

"Maybe you could tell me a little more, Andrei," Todd said, trying his best not to sound too eager.

"Gladly," Andrei answered, and he proceeded to provide all the enticing specifics, about how the parties worked, who attended, and where they were held. When he was through, Todd was convinced. It sounded exactly like something the James Bond of Sacramento would do. This, indeed, was the plan for him.

"So I suppose I should ask what all this costs."

"Ah, yes, the bottom line," Andrei nodded. "Okay, then. You shoot straight with me, I do the same for you."

With that, Andrei produced a single sheet of embossed paper from inside his briefcase, and set it face down on the table. "The figure at the top is for the Premium Courtship Package, which is the one I would recommend for you."

Todd turned the sheet over, looked down at the numbers, and nearly choked. "Holy Mother! Do you know how many tuxes I'd have to rent to cover that?"

Andrei lifted his palms in a show of sympathy. "It is not cheap, Todd, I know. I wish I could say otherwise. But I have found, in my many years of experience in the field, that one gets what one pays for."

And with that, his hand disappeared back into his case and emerged holding a thick, leather-bound volume, which he then slid in front of Todd.

"What's this?" Todd replied, wary now, still reeling from the numbers he'd seen.

"Just give it a look," Andrei suggested, as he opened the cover and slid the book even closer.

Todd looked. Staring up at him was the face of a gorgeous woman, with blazing eyes the color of the bluest ocean, hair like platinum silk, and cheekbones you could cut diamonds with. She was possibly the most beautiful woman he'd ever laid eyes on.

"Our placement portfolio. All satisfied customers," Andrei added helpfully.

Todd nodded dumbly and kept turning pages, all featuring alluring photos of exotic-looking women, all of them leggy, smooth-skinned, nubile. Mouth agape, he just stared, completely and utterly entranced.

Oh, yes. This was the clincher every time, the deal-closer, and it was clear from the look on Andrei's face that he knew this.

And Todd knew it, too. How could he pass this up? It was a chance to make all his dreams come true.

After several moments, he finally wrenched his eyes away from the book. "So, Andrei," he said, pausing to clear his throat before pulling out his wallet with a badly-trembling hand, "would you be willing to accept a check?"

9

ENDLESS SUMMER

Rowena's new workplace, the Golden Child Tanning Salon, was located in a strip mall just a short drive up I-80 from her trailer park. Situated between a dry cleaners and a vitamin-supplement shop, it featured eight tanning beds and two spray-on booths, as well as a small boutique up front selling off-brand beach attire and tanning products—all of it, housed under a shedding, thatch-stapled ceiling, with surfing posters, plastic leis on the walls, and a faux tiki hut up front, which is where Rowena could be found, four days a week, manning the counter.

And after three weeks on the job, Rowena pretty much had the routine down pat, along with its clientele. There were the schoolgirls, of course—they were the tanning world's bread and butter—who popped in before every big social event for that extra glow that would get the boys to notice them. Then there were the gay guys, always tan and stylish no matter the situation or season. There were crossover customers, too, from the mall's other shops: buff fitness freaks from the vitamin store, haggard-looking housewives from the dry cleaners, pimply teens from the dermatologist's office. And, finally, there were the newly-divorced of both genders, who had been thrown back into the dating pool for the first time in way too many years, only to find it was more difficult than they had remembered, and that the pickings were slim, and who thus were now looking for any possible edge they might find for themselves.

In the end, Rowena decided, the only thing that linked this group was vanity, and lots of it. After all, why else would anyone willingly lie in a bed of their own pooling sweat? Not to mention the discomfort. Or the claustrophobia. Or the skuzzy bottles of "sanitizing spray" Rowena and the other girls used to haphazardly wipe those beds down.

But even Rowena couldn't deny the results. You go in looking sickly, and you come out—bam!—looking like you just spent the day at the beach. And even though Rowena knew that all those UVA rays were dangerous and cancer-causing, after two years at the Vittles plant, working under the sizzle of fluorescent lights and hunching over mountains of "home-style" mystery meat, it was a risk she was willing to take.

Yes. The fact was, Rowena had never looked better, and never felt better, either. Her date with Wade was tonight, and better still, she had just received another letter from Lyle Pettigrew, her favorite new pen pal from Vacaville State Prison. In one of his notes, Lyle had requested a picture, so she had Estelle take one of her, right there in the salon, and he wrote back saying he looks at that picture every night before he goes to sleep. What a sweetie. If only Randy had been that devoted. Of course, if he were in lockdown twenty-two hours a day, he might have been, but that's another issue. And anyway, screw Randy. The important thing was, between Wade and Lyle and her new job, Rowena felt wanted again. Needed. And with her new tan, plus her new halter top and low-rise jeans—the outfit she had already laid out to wear tonight—by God, she felt downright sexy.

She checked the clock: still two more hours to go. Time was moving slow, and business was even slower. September was not a big month for tanning. Or at least, that's what Estelle said, claiming that people were tired from all the summer sun and needed a break before coming in for holiday parties and winter trips and such. And since she'd worked there almost five years now, Estelle would certainly be the one to know. Rowena was closing up tonight. Maybe, she thought to herself, she could cut out a few minutes early. Give herself a little extra time to get ready before Wade showed up.

Ding.

The bell over the door rang out. Rowena sat up as a large man entered, older than most she saw in here, and from the looks of it, a straight guy to boot. A walk-in, apparently, as there were no appointments on the books. He actually reminded her of her father, Eddie, in a way—rugged and manly, with a hitch in his stride and a bit of a paunch. Overall, a good-looking guy for his age. And as he lumbered ever closer, he started looking more and more familiar.

"Hi. I, uh, haven't been here before. Wanted to get a little color on my face, so, umm ..." The man lowered his eyes, his skin flushing already from his obvious self-consciousness. "Anyway, here I am."

"Well, we've got beds and booths, UV and spray. Take your pick."

"Huh. I don't know." The man was at a loss, looking as if he couldn't possibly be any more out of his element. "What do you think's best for a guy like me?"

"You say you just want the color on your face?"

"Well, heh heh, you know ... long as I'm here ..."

"Right." Rowena muffled a smirk. *The guy's more vain than he wants to let on. It's kinda cute, actually.* "Okay, then. How about we try one of the spray-on booths. The tan'll go on even, and you won't have to worry about burning your first time out."

The man said this sounded good enough, and Rowena gave him the membership application that all new customers had to fill out. When he turned it back in, she finally realized how she knew him. "Hey! You're that tuxedo shop guy, right?"

The man mumbled an affirmative, then snuck a furtive glance back at the door, as if he was worried about getting caught in the act.

Rowena rechecked the name on the application, "Todd Tisdale. Sure, I remember now ..."

Rowena then proceeded to tell a still-fidgety Todd about the time they had met, many years before, when she had gone to his shop with her prom date to help him pick out a tuxedo that would match her dress. As soon as she mentioned her date's name (Lance, the juiced-up football star), Todd laughed and—suddenly seeming far more at ease—told her that he had attended the same high school she had! This led to a lengthy discussion about Pioneer Prospector football teams past and present, especially the 70s-era squad Todd himself had captained.

Off this lively revisiting of his glory days, the newly-emboldened Mr. Tisdale proceeded to purchase a full, five-visit "St. Tropez Package." Rowena then escorted him back to the booth and showed him how to operate the machine before leaving him to it.

Back in the tiki hut, Rowena congratulated herself on her salesmanship. The salon's owner, Dimitri, gave each of the girls a bonus for every deluxe package they sold. She had just cleared an extra five bucks. And it wasn't even that tough. Truth was, talking to old Todd the Tuxedo Guy for a few minutes was actually a pleasant diversion from the monotony of her otherwise empty workday. Heck, she even hoped that whomever he was trying to look good for would appreciate it. Like her, he seemed like someone who deserved a little appreciation for a change.

From in back, Rowena heard the whoosh of the tanning-spray jet-nozzles kicking on. She paused to listen and see if Todd would remember to turn in a slow circle like she told him to do, so that his tan would come out even. Sure enough, she could hear a pair of big feet clomping rhythmically to and fro on the industrial carpet. Good boy.

She turned back to the clock. Her face fell. Still another hour and a half to go. Damn.

Driving home from the salon, Rowena sang along to Destiny's Child on the radio, feeling positively giddy. Dimitri had made a surprise visit at the shop a little after eight, and when she told him how dead it had been, he decided to let her close early. Of course, he wasn't *paying* her for those last fifteen minutes or so, and the way he followed her around while she was shutting all the machines down, staring at her ass when he thought she wasn't looking, made it perfectly clear that he had some designs on how that time might otherwise by spent ("Those tanning beds sure look nice and toasty. Just enough room for two, heh heh." Ugh! What a creep!). But now, at least, she would have the time to do her hair and get her makeup right before Wade came to pick her up.

On that note, Rowena made the turn onto her trailer park's gravel drive, the path ahead of her illuminated by her Tercel's headlights. But to her dismay, what she saw at the end of the road, parked right outside her trailer, was Wade's truck, recognizable even from afar owing to its custom paint job (flames on the hood, mermaids on the hatch) and jacked-up, monster-truck suspension. Rowena clicked off the radio in a panic. What was he doing there already? She parked and hopped out, trying her best to poof out her hair and straighten her skirt as she went.

"Wade?"

Wade was sitting on her stoop with a tall boy of Schlitz malt liquor. He looked annoyed. "You're late."

"Late? No! I'm early. Dimitri let me close early."

Wade wasn't buying it. He crossed his arms, giving them a little warning-flex as he did so. "You said 8:30"

"I said I *got off* at 8:30."

"Yeah, and ...?"

"And the date was for nine."

"Nine o' clock? A nine o'clock date? Damn, Rowena! Some of us got to get up and work in the morning. Saturdays are our busiest day. Shit."

Rowena whimpered apologetically. How had things gone so wrong so fast?

"Well, whatever. You're here now. Let's get moving. Here, these are for you."

Wade handed her a cheap, convenience-store bouquet, which was already wilting from the day's heat. Rowena gushed. "Oh, thank you, Wade! They're beautiful!"

Casting a quick glance over to her trailer, Rowena wanted desperately to run in, put the flowers in some water and, more importantly, change into the special date-night outfit that she had laid out.

But Wade was clearly in no mood for any more delays. It was now or never. She kept her mouth shut and hopped in the truck.

Not long after, Rowena found herself at Rattlers, a cavernous Country-and-Western dance club located on the far edge of town. This was no big surprise. Wade loved country music. It suited him. In fact, with his tight Wranglers, feathered hair, five o'clock shadow, and cowboy hat, Rowena thought he looked just like John Travolta in *Urban Cowboy*—a resemblance Wade was no doubt quite aware of as well.

Inside the club's main dance hall, a local band, Jimmy D. and the Junkyard Dogs, was already up on stage, playing loud enough to doom any potential conversation. Rowena was relieved. It gave Wade a chance to cool down and catch a little buzz, and her a chance to regain her composure and apply a little lipstick and eyeliner on the sly. They both sat there at their Old West-style saloon table, silently drinking and bopping their heads along to the music.

After five songs, three Pabst Blue Ribbons, and a double shot of Jack Daniel's, Wade finally turned her way, as if just now realizing she was there, having apparently decided that he had ignored her long enough. "You wanna go on out there?"

It was more a demand than a question, but Rowena acted flattered anyway. Whatever it took to get back in his good graces. They headed out onto the dance floor and Wade wasted no time strutting his stuff. He had the moves, all right. Every girl on the floor was watching him, as they and their own dates struggled through largely hapless versions of the two-step and the electric slide. As for Rowena, she tried her best to dance along, although she had no idea whether she was supposed to try and keep up with Wade or simply step back and let him have center-stage all to himself.

Mercifully, the song ended soon after, the band went on break, and the DJ put on a slow-dance golden oldie, "Looking for Love" by Mickey Gilley. The words to the song might have held some special meaning for Rowena (*"Looking for love in all the wrong places, looking for love in too many faces"*), but she was too busy trying to read and respond to the signals of her moody beau. Finally, Wade pulled Rowena close, his embrace so tight she could tell for a fact that all had been forgiven.

"Sorry I was in a bad mood. Shitty day at work. Had to run around all goddamn day patching leaky roofs."

Rowena hadn't even been aware that it had rained. At Golden Child, the weather was always sunny and clear. "It's okay. I'm just sorry I couldn't get ready for you first. Had a special outfit all picked out, too."

"That right?"

"Uh huh."

"Maybe you could try it on for me back at your place." Wade's hand slid down to her ass. "And then, try it *off.*" He fired up one of those trademark toothy grins of his and pulled her closer still—a full-body caress.

It didn't take a mind reader to know what he wanted. He wanted what every other guy wanted, ever since Rodney back in junior high. And the shame of it was, she knew she would give it to him, too, even though she had vowed to try and take things slower for a change. But after their debacle earlier in the evening, Rowena also knew that she would bend to his desires to try and make things up to him. And heck, why not? It had been over a month now for her as well. She heaved a sigh over his shoulder, where he couldn't see it, then pasted on a flirtatious smile, knowing he wanted that, too.

That's all the invitation Wade needed. "We done enough dancing for tonight. Let's get out of here."

10
MASSIVE MISSY

After her dream-crushing encounter with Richard Block over the Schwarzenegger account, Missy had stayed in her office the entire rest of the day, not emerging for lunch or dinner or even to go to the bathroom. When she finally came out, the only people left on the premises were the cleaning crew, a collection of weary-faced washerwomen who rarely spoke and didn't make eye contact, and would likely never be able to buy a house or even so much as a studio apartment from her or anybody else.

But Missy had no time to ponder these women's sorry tales, for she had one of her own. She knew there had been talk. That she hadn't fooled anyone by putting on a brave face for Richard and then ducking away like a turtle in its shell. But while she hated the vague cowardice of her actions, at least she hadn't had to pretend that it didn't hurt. That she didn't have feelings. That she was some kind of machine. Bad cop? Screw them. Screw every last one of them, especially Jolene Wyatt. She worked the hardest and closed the most deals. They were just jealous. Right?

But then, her mind flashed back to what her matchmaker Heidi had said. And her latest date, Steve. And her guilt-merchant of a mother, Mamie. Even her power-of-positive-thinking mantras had been feeling a bit hollow lately. Maybe they were all right about her. Maybe she was too severe, too demanding, too bossy.

"You want me to clean in there?"

Missy turned to a shriveled cleaning lady standing outside her office door.

"I don't smoke."

The blue-smocked worker looked confused. Missy sighed impatiently. "I don't smoke and you smell like cigarettes. You literally reek of them." Missy took in the old crone, suddenly wondering if she had perhaps been a bit too abrasive. "Besides, I keep my office spotless anyway. There's nothing to clean." Though said in her most conciliatory tone, the cleaning lady looked no less put out. She gave a defeated nod, then continued on her rounds.

Missy watched her go, shuffling down the hallway, looking even more beaten-down than before. She muttered under her breath, "My God." Then, with a little flip-wave of the hand: "You there. Excuse me." The old lady turned. "Go ahead, do whatever you want. It's fine." The old woman stared at Missy as if she were crazy. Missy clarified, "In my office. Don't let me interfere."

The woman tilted her head. "You just said it was clean."

"I ... yes. But maybe I was wrong. Go on. Do your worst. Or best, I mean." Missy smiled, as if she had just performed her good deed for the day.

But this reaction just made the previously submissive cleaning lady—whose faded blue smock had a name, Bertie, stitched on the pocket—even more upset. Her brow furrowed with confusion, bordering on anger. "You messin' with me now, is that it?"

Missy's smile evaporated. Her mouth opened to speak. But for the third time in a single day, nothing came out.

As she lamented over this troubling incapacitation, the silence only fueled Bertie's ire. With her face puckered up even further, and her bloodshot eyes narrowing, she added: "You think I like cleanin' up y'all's shit? You think I like this job? You think I enjoy gettin' minimum wage and workin' the graveyard shift? You, in them fancy clothes, fancy hairdo, probably got a fancy car, fancy house—you don't know nothin'!" She threw down her duster. "You want it clean, clean it your own damn self. I had enough of this shit. I quit."

With that, Bertie stormed off.

Missy turned beseechingly to the other member of the crew, a timid black woman who had toiled there for years, yet whose name Missy nevertheless could not quite recall. She wanted an eyewitness to this affront, and some corroboration of her own innocence. Instead, the black cleaning lady quickly looked away, as if she hadn't heard a word, like it never even happened—but not before Missy caught the trace of a wicked smile curling up on the woman's mouth.

Missy left as fast as she could, straight to her front-row, Realtor of the Month parking space. She hopped into her spotless gold Lexus, slammed the key in the ignition, and sped off. She was steaming, her face flush with humiliation. Talked down to, and laughed at, by a pair of cleaning women now? It was the final indignity.

Missy started to tear up again, telling herself that no one understood. That no one knew the real her. She had gone through so much and worked so hard to make it to this point. To become a success.

Improbable as it might seem, when Missy was a little girl, no great things had been predicted for her. Not even close. Right from the start, her life had been one struggle after another. Born to a pair of high-school dropouts who were themselves the offspring of illiterate Okie farmhands, lured west to California by the hope and promise of golden opportunities that never materialized, Missy was the product of an extremely limited environment and means. As a child, she was exposed to no art, no literature, no music— indeed, no culture of any kind, aside from the ever-present TV. Her clothes were hand-me-downs, and her food was the kind that poor people ate: heaping plates of casseroles and frozen dinners filled with starch and fat and little or no nutritional substance. Coupled with her family's complete lack of physical activity, Missy quickly developed a severe weight problem. No bones about it, little Missy Carver was a real porker. And many girls in such circumstances would have seen this and simply resigned themselves to their sorry fate. "It's in my genes. This is who I am. Pass the Cheese Whiz, please."

But not Missy. Because while she might not have been as worldly as some of her peers, or as privileged, Missy nevertheless was smart enough to realize how little chance there was for poor, fat girls in this cruel world of ours. Mocked by the boys, avoided by the other girls, and viewed as unpromising by the teachers and staff—it was like a death sentence. And once she grasped this, she became determined to do something about it.

Determination, however, is easier when there is at least *some* support for it. Missy had none, absolutely zero. Not from her blissfully obese father, who continued to revel in his usual fatty feasts and snacks, and looked askew at any morsel left on his daughter's plate as if it were a waste of his hard-earned money, even though more often than not that money came from welfare. Not from her mother, who took any effort Missy made to skip a meal or mend her clothes or touch up her home-cut hair as a personal slight, and who inevitably responded to any such effort with a lecture on the sins of pride and vanity. Not from her teachers, who (at least initially) seemed put out by her efforts, too, as if they were in direct contempt of their earlier assessments of her. And, finally, not by her classmates, either. Indeed, they were the worst of all, openly taunting her at every opportunity, from her daily attempts to swap her own greasy lunch bag of calorie-laden delights for something healthier like a fruit cup or a salad (an effort which helped develop her current sales expertise), to her afterschool exercise regimen of speed-walking, chosen because she could do it without subjecting herself to the sadistic rituals of the girls' locker room, but which also left her exposed, in plain sight, an easy target for yet more afterschool hazing ("Thar she blows!," "Moo!," etc.).

Oh, yes. It was a slow and grueling process, indeed. In order to survive it, young Missy had no choice but to build psychic walls of defense around herself a mile high. She became a virtual human fortress. And those defenses kept her going, through all the tough times, as she struggled mightily to improve not only her outward appearance, but also her mind, by making an extra effort in all her classes, and her soul, by engaging in a variety of extracurricular activities that not only enhanced her resume, but fed her self-fueled ambitions for a brighter future.

Eventually, all those efforts began to pay off. Over the space of three long, hard-fought years, Missy kept with the program. Her grades improved, and the clubs she started, for Entrepreneurs and Young Republicans, slowly began to flourish. And her body, well, that went through a transformation that was nothing short of miraculous. Bolstered by a hearty double-dose of puberty, Missy found herself morphing into someone who was no longer a blubbery laughingstock but rather a well-toned beauty with a remarkably mature and curvy figure. And suddenly—practically overnight, it seemed—all the kids who used to mock her now found they couldn't keep their eyes off of her.

Still, though the scars remained hidden, Missy never forgot all the slights she'd suffered. So while she secretly enjoyed the fact that the boys now ogled her, and the girls secretly envied her, she never let it go any further than that. After all, how could she share her hard-fought victory with the very people who had tried their best to defeat her? That would be almost as bad as letting them win in the first place. But while this was completely understandable, at least from Missy's point of view, it led to yet another wave of taunting. No longer a cow, she was now deemed to be a snob, or a brainiac, or a bitch. Remarkably, she had leapt directly from outcast status to a new, equally damning label as an elitist, without ever bothering, even for one single sweet moment, to taste the nectar of belonging in between.

Yet throughout the remainder of her schooling, and even beyond, Missy somehow remained impervious to this. To her, the way she presented herself, and the way she addressed the world at large, was merely a byproduct of her own successful sense of discipline. She never really thought that any of this might off-putting; indeed, it was the only way things had ever worked for her. It was something to be admired. If she hadn't comported herself in this manner, she'd no doubt still be living well below her potential, just like her parents, under-educated, unemployed and miserable. And, worst of all, fat. Fat, fat, fat. Looking at it this way, Missy felt justified. And proud. And empowered.

But not today. The convergence of so many shameful encounters in so short a time had shattered Missy's protective shell of self-worth. Suddenly, everything she thought was right about her life felt wrong. She felt like a failure again. A laughingstock. Had all her hard work only served to bring her right back to the point where she'd started, being sad and shunned and destined for a life of despair?

Missy stopped at a red light. She realized that her Tony Robbins motivational tape, the one that she listened to on the way to work every morning to psyche herself up, was still playing on the stereo. She clicked it off with a bitter snarl: *Fuck you, you big fire-walking phony! What do you know, anyway?*

Her eyes looked away, gradually lured across the street by the garish neon lights of a Gas N' Sip. Missy had always considered such stores to be dens of iniquity, impulse-buy havens filled with sugary, preservative-packed poisons that only led to fat and sloth—the exact kind of place her mother frequented, sating all her unhealthy habits with sodas, cigarettes, lottery tickets, and any other junky fare that she might stumble upon.

But now, Missy suddenly saw it with different eyes. She saw it as an answer to her sorrows. A balm for her soul. A way to put all her troubles behind her, at least for a little while.

Cranking the wheel, Missy zipped across two lanes and parked right out front. She headed in, her eyes dancing around the brightly-lit emporium, delighted, like a kid in a candy shop. And to her, that's exactly what it was. Wasting no time, she made a beeline for the confections aisle and grabbed a box of her old childhood favorites, Milk Duds. She ripped open the box and let the chewy morsels pour into her mouth like a fountain. My God! She forgot how delicious they were! The chocolate and the nougat and the—

But wait! Her eyes alit upon a display of Skittles, the sour fruit chews that she had also loved. She grabbed some of those, too. And Twizzlers! And Twinkies! And Twix bars! The delights grew exponentially with every fresh glance, and every newly-discovered aisle (Chips! Dips! Slushies! Nachos!).

Amid all this ecstasy, she finally looked up, only to notice to her utter horror that she was being stared at, gape-jawed, by the two other denizens of the store. One was a mangy, orange-smocked counter clerk with a constellation of angry zits across his forehead. The other was an older man with a fake tan and a flouncy belly, precisely the kind of big-man-on-campus-gone-to-seed type she had been avoiding like the plague ever since she was in her teens. To her disgust, she noted he was buying breath mints and Magnum-sized condoms. Ugh. Some things never changed. It was enough to quell any residual self-consciousness she might have felt and draw her back to the task at hand: acquiring ego-soothing junk food, and lots of it.

With her chin held high and a cornucopia of munchies clutched to her chest, she strode up to the counter and asked the pimply clerk, her voice trembling with feverish anticipation, "Do you take American Express?"

11

SPENCER GETS INSPIRED

It had been a busy week at the *Bee*. With less than a month to go until the planned special election, its fate remained up in the air. The courts were still deciding if the recall was a legal and valid process, and appeals were being loudly threatened from all sides. All the while, the Secretary of State had officially certified a record 135 candidates for the race, a number that now included stand-up prop comic Gallagher and paraplegic *Hustler* publisher Larry Flynt. Coupled with previously announced candidates like Gary "What'chu Talkin' 'Bout, Willis?" Coleman and porn star Mary Carey (*Thumpin' Melons, Rub the Muff IV*, etc.), it threatened to turn the entire election into a perverse version of *Hollywood Squares*... or, perhaps more accurately, *The Gong Show*.

And this was not even to mention the biggest star-participant of all, Arnold Schwarzenegger, whose widely heralded declaration was beginning to make the rest of the campaign season look like a drawn-out victory lap, even though he had yet to make a stand on any of the substantive issues, or face any of his challengers in a debate. Rather, he just projected the image of a guy who could swagger in and get things done for a change. And in the end, that's really what it's all about, right?

However, just as it had pretty much seemed like a done deal, even to capital insiders, some of the skeletons from Arnold's past had begun to creep their way out of his undoubtedly extensive closet. They came in the form of several unnamed female sources, who had spoken to the tabloids about their claims of his sexual harassment. The offenses in question were mostly verbal in nature and largely puerile in intent, but they were also distinctly unstatesmanlike. Even worse, there were rumors of more women who had yet to come forward, with even more sordid and physically aggressive tales to tell. Despite any proof or proper corroboration as of yet, it already had the whiff of a real game-changing scandal, and all the city's reporters were eager to get a piece of it for themselves, even if they were hard-pressed to name another candidate they liked better for the job.

All but Spencer Brine, that is. A registered Democrat, he already planned to cast his ballot for the current lieutenant governor, Cruz Bustamente, for better or (more likely) for worse. Moreover, he also knew that no matter how big and juicy the Arnold scandal got, he wouldn't be sharing in its bounty. He was, and still remained, a minor cog in the system. A drone. A peon. An obituary writer.

But despite all this, Spencer was now also a toe-tappingly happy guy. He went through his daily paces with a smile on his face and a lively spring in his step, typing out his three items per day with an ease he had never before experienced. And while the subject matter of these items had, in the past, cast a pall over the proceedings, Spencer now saw the obituaries he wrote as a chance to celebrate life and all its wondrous possibilities, not just for the deceased and their loved ones but for the community at large.

Not surprisingly, the root source of this new, vigorously upbeat attitude was his budding romance with Nikki. Spencer had never felt this way before about anyone, and the pulsating warmth he felt in his heart emanated into his thoughts, in his actions, and out onto the written page. Nikki wasn't just his object of affection, she was his muse, his siren-song Erato, and her seductively posed head shot (which also included a generous helping of body), with the disco ball from the ShowBar's center stage glittering halo-like in the background, held court over his tiny desk, casting its goddess glow over every keystroke Spencer made.

Before long, others began to notice this newfound inspiration. Case in point was a requiem he'd composed for the city's beloved birthday-party clown, Bopsy, a.k.a. Lenny Feinberg. At the time of his tragic demise from liver failure, Bopsy had been entertaining the local kiddies with his funny faces, pratfalls, balloon animals, and magic tricks for nearly three decades. It was a duration which meant that many of the city's current civic leaders, as well as Spencer's colleagues, had themselves experienced Bopsy's show at least once, and often more, and that veneration was justly saluted in Spencer's piece, entitled "Tears for a Clown." ("... *but Bopsy wouldn't want us to weep, or mourn, or even offer up a sad face. Oh, no. He would want us to remember the good times, the party times, to laugh and smile and pull rascally rabbits from our hats.*")

Off this story, Spencer had, for the first time, been receiving congratulations from his colleagues on the quality of his work, and the eloquence of his prose. It made him feel like maybe he mattered after all. Like he might actually be able to see his ambitions through one day. And while this was an unexpected turn of events, to be sure, Spencer knew whom to thank for it. It was Nikki. She was his lucky charm.

Spencer's supervisor Morris Sutphin noted this metamorphosis, too. But unlike the others at the paper, who fawned briefly and then moved on with their days, Morris viewed the development with grave suspicion. Was Spencer after his job? Or worse, was he aiming even higher, yet another dagger in the soul of his own long-thwarted ambitions?

Morris had always known this moment would come. With Spencer's fancy-pants Ivy League education (Morris had attended night school at Long Beach State) and upbringing, and his youthful good looks and preppy clothes and polished manners, it was inevitable. He was the kind of guy the publishing honchos liked. Spencer always met his deadlines, misspelled no words, ruffled no feathers, and kept resolutely to the straight and narrow. He was "one of them," a bottom-line, play-it-safe, haircut-every-two-weeks Face Man, rather than a down-and-dirty, in-the-trenches news hawk like himself. Hell, Morris thought, Brine might as well be a goddamn TV anchorman!

That said, when Morris stopped by Spencer's desk and his eyes alit upon Nikki's alluring photo, the slow-boiling envy he felt toward Spencer mutated into something far more primal and potent. He didn't know Nikki, didn't know her name, had never even so much as caught a fleeting glimpse of her, but he knew the type all too well. She was the kind of genetically-blessed alpha babe that Morris had yearned after his entire life, who in turn had never once even given him so much as a second glance, much less offer up the kind of lusty bedroom-eye gaze that was on display here.

Morris had taken this wholesale rejection to heart, and as a result he had married the first real girlfriend he ever had, a far humbler variant of the species named Wilhemina Wiggins, the daughter of his mother's bridge club partner, an apprentice spinster who worked as a guard at the local female juvenile detention center. Wilhemina, or Minnie as she was called, was named after the famous fashion model of the same name. This was a cruel twist of fate, as Minnie herself was no great beauty, and had no fashion sense, either. Rather, she was a big-boned woman with mannish features and a wardrobe comprised mostly of no-nonsense trousers and unfussy polyester tops. It was an appearance, and a style, that was perfectly suited for her position at the detention center, lending her a don't-fuck-with-me aura that served her in good stead, especially in dealing with the wave upon wave of wiseass, inner-city, gang-groupie girls who invariably got sent there.

And so, while Morris left work every night for another ho-hum evening of TV reruns with Minnie-the-Mountainous-Prison-Guard, whose sexual appetites (at least, with him) were so meager it made him wonder if she wasn't actually a lesbian, Spencer was off gallivanting with some red-hot harlot who no doubt banged his socks off every night and awoke him every morning with a blowjob for breakfast. Damn him! Morris felt the bile building in his throat.

"You need something, Morris?"

Morris snapped to, realizing he had been making weird noises under his breath. Did he need something? Of course he did, and Brine undoubtedly knew it, the bastard. Morris stared at Spencer, loathing him now with an all-consuming passion.

"No, Brine. But you do. You need to shape up your act. That's why I came by. That clown piece was a bunch of bullshit showboating. You want to write that kind of flowery crap, shovel it someplace else. You hear me?"

"But, sir—"

"I don't want to hear any excuses, Brine. You may think you're irreplaceable, but you're not. I run a tight ship here, and anybody who doesn't abide by the rules gets put out to sea, but fast. Start doing the work the way it's supposed to be done, or else."

With that, Morris turned on his heels and scurried off, refusing to give Spencer the satisfaction of even so much as a parting glance at the saucy little minx in the frame.

Spencer watched Morris go. What was that all about? He was pretty sure it wasn't the story. Morris had approved the Bopsy piece himself. Spencer even thought he'd seen a lone dusty tear come to the wizened man's eye. But now, pure vitriol.

Had he offended Morris somehow? Violated some unwritten obituarian's rule of etiquette?

Just like Morris before him, Spencer's eyes turned uncontrollably to Nikki's photo. It was amazing the power even the *image* of a pretty woman could wield. And it got Spencer thinking: Did Morris know her somehow? Had he seen her perform? Had he perhaps even gotten a lap-dance from her during some depressing nadir in both their lives?

Spencer forced himself to put such thoughts out of his mind. And not just for the obvious reasons. The fact was, even though he and Nikki had gone on several dates now, and exchanged many verbal intimacies and lingering kisses in his Volvo and at the door to her apartment, it had gone no further than that. She had not invited him in, and he had not invited himself—even though he wanted to, desperately. And she surely must have known this, too, for his body had not been able to play things as coolly as his brain would have liked; the signals were there. Still, Spencer's instincts told him that what had set him apart in the first place was his gentlemanly manner, and any change in strategy, particularly at such a crucial juncture, might have disastrous results. Thus, he had to force himself to keep playing it cool, and let the magic happen naturally.

Meantime, there was work to do. With another quick glance over to Nikki's photo for inspiration, Spencer reached for the next item in his box. Frederick "Fritz" Underwood, 84, former city alderman, Kiwanis Club treasurer, and church usher, died of congestive heart failure, six weeks after his wife of sixty years, Mitzi, had passed away quietly in her sleep. It wasn't flashy, but Spencer knew he could work with this. Play up the public service angle, the Kiwanis' charitable causes and volunteer work, and add in the church duties to tie it all together—the man was a pillar of the community. And Fritz's photo helped. The guy looked like a pillar, posing ramrod straight and sober in his navy blazer, starched shirt, and perfectly-knotted tie. Indeed, he was the kind of man who went through life without pause or waver, doing the right and noble thing at all times because that was the way God would have wanted it.

But while all this was impressive in an onward-Christian-soldier kind of way, that wasn't the thing that affected Spencer the most. Rather, it was the fact that Fritz had died so soon after his wife. Some might say it was simply his time to go, or that he didn't take care of himself well enough after Mitzi passed, but Spencer had a more romantic take on the scenario. To his way of thinking, Fritz died because he dearly missed his wife and that loss quite literally broke his heart. Oh sure, the doctors probably attributed it to faulty valves or some such thing, but Spencer felt matters of the heart were often beyond the ken of simple textbook medical explanations. Community pillar or not, the doctors had spent a sum total of a few hours with old Fritz. He and Mitzi had shared a bed and breathed each other's air for sixty years. Sixty years! Who stays married for sixty years anymore? That alone was worth commemoration.

Spencer started in on his story, determined to do Fritz's life justice. As he found a proper rhythm for his little tale to unfold, his thoughts bounced back and forth between the Underwoods' sixty years together, and the three weeks he had spent so far with Nikki. Sixty years equates to a little over three thousand weeks, so he and Nikki were nearly one-one thousandth of the way there. And the more he thought about it, that was kind of a milestone, wasn't it? It put them on the chart, so to speak. Gave them direction and a goal to shoot for.

Spencer reached for the phone to share this with Nikki, then caught himself, his finger hovering over the speed dial. He was a sentimentalist, he knew, and he knew she wasn't—not that he could detect so far, anyway. What if she took it the wrong way? Thought he was pushing too hard? Or worse, began to perceive him as "needy." He knew what would happen. It would be game over, just as it had with the two coeds he fell hopelessly in love with back at Cornell. One even said, when she caught him reading *Leaves of Grass* by Walt Whitman (unassigned, no less), "You're such a woman." And though it was meant as a joke, he knew there was some truth to it. He was in touch with his feminine side, more so than most guys, something he attributed to his artistic sensibilities but which also, he knew, had something to do with the fact that his mother had taken to her role as parent so much better than his Wall Street finance-guru father ever had. And while he was able to keep this side of him largely in check while hanging with his male friends, drinking beers and doing manly things, something about being in love brought it out in full bloom. Thus, he found himself getting overwrought at odd times, like a woman, and over-analyzing his loved one's every small comment and gesture, like a woman, and finding beauty and romance in everyday things, like a woman. And maybe that wasn't such a bad thing. It certainly helped his writing. But it also left him vulnerable in a way that he knew was dangerous, especially with a rough-and-tumble babe like Nikki.

Spencer returned the phone to its cradle and got back to work. 3 p.m. already. Time to get cracking. He could talk to Nikki later, tonight, at the club. And when he did, it would be as Manly, Take-Charge Spencer, not sensitive, poetry-spouting Spencer.

Oh, yes, Spencer thought, as he clacked away with a smile, seemingly blind to the fact that he was now taking a drastic, 180-degree turn off his previously-exalted strategy, *it's time for "The Brinester" to start calling the shots!*

12

LOOKING GOOD

Todd stood in front of the mirror, naked save for a towel wrapped rakishly around his midsection, staring at himself. Not just the usual quick once-over this time, but a real honest-to-goodness, head-to-toe physical self-evaluation.

The upshot: not bad. Not bad at all. Though he'd packed on a few pounds over the years, he was still tall, his shoulders broad, his chest barreled. He still looked like the athlete he once was. Striking a pose, Todd took a total measure. He was 54 years old, but he told people he was 52, and with his strong features, newly-tanned skin, a decent haircut, and some Grecian Formula, he figured he could pass for 45. Okay, maybe more like 47 or 48—but a *damn good* 47 or 48.

Turning to take in the profile view, Todd had to admit that his belly was not nearly as sleek as he would have liked. Depending on the light and the angle, he may have been sporting an extra chin or two as well. But hey, Todd told himself, it's not like he spent much time slaving away in the gym or denying himself pleasure. He loved to eat and drink. And, he loathed exercise purely for exercise's sake. Oh sure, he bowled, and played the occasional round of golf, but he was certainly no fitness nut. No, the fact was, Todd told himself, he looked like a guy who enjoyed life, and that's what he was, and that's what he planned to keep right on doing, which was why he was doing this now.

Todd ducked into his closet, and emerged wearing a brand-new Brioni tuxedo. It was black, with a satin shawl collar, from his own shop, which he had gotten tailored to fit him specifically—yet another hidden cost of this whole Czech-Mate thing, since it was unlikely he'd be unable to rent it out later. But in the big scheme of things, it was a wise investment. Noting how it helped conceal the aforementioned flaws, or at least distract from them, Todd thought he looked—with the aid of some new wingtips and a silk scarf wrapped jauntily around his neck—like a real international player. Maybe not quite up to James Bond's caliber, but certainly slick enough to pass as one of 007's buddies from the baccarat table. By his estimation, that was more than good enough to get the job done. He felt ready. He took off the tux and started to pack his bags.

Packing his bags, already? It was hard to believe, even for Todd. It had been less than two weeks since he had met Andrei in San Francisco, but that time had been a whirlwind. A mere two days later, Andrei had called him from Moscow, and said they were moving up their next Berlin Wall Party to accommodate the crush of eager clients and pretty Russian ladies they had found to place. The party was set for that following Saturday, and Andrei said he knew it was short notice but that Todd should really try to make it. The women this time were incredible—the best he's ever seen!

Though Todd deemed himself to be a pretty spontaneous guy, he had never done anything like this, never even considered it. After all, this was a lot of money, with a lot riding on the outcome. Still, with little hesitation, he found himself agreeing to go. In for a penny, in for a pound, right? That's what Angie always used to say, God love her. And even though Andrei's staff handled all the travel arrangements, Todd still had to scramble and find someone to fill in for him at the shop, get a passport, and figure out what to bring and what to wear and even what to say. Would the ladies speak Russian or English or what? Todd didn't know for sure and in all the rush he had forgotten to ask, so just to be careful, he had been studying a Russian phrasebook ever since.

But that wasn't all he had to do. He also had to figure out which ladies he wanted to meet. After his check had cleared and his reservation confirmed, Andrei had sent Todd a thick file on all the women that were slated to attend. Todd's "Deluxe Courtship Package" granted him two "priority picks," who he would get to meet before any of the other men, and three more ladies for his "special reserve list," which meant he would get a chance to speak with them in an intimate setting on the night of the party but before the party officially began, at which time all the guests would become "fair game," as Andrei put it. This put a lot of pressure on Todd. All he had to work off of for each candidate was a single photo and a brief bio. How was he supposed to choose?

Fortunately, one woman stood out for him, right from the very first moment he laid eyes on her: Svetlana Arsov, a sexy, statuesque Ukrainian blonde in her mid-thirties.

"Lana" (the nickname he had already chosen for her) looked like a model, she really did, with long legs and high cheekbones and pale, icy-blonde hair, just like Linda Evans in *Dynasty*. True, she was a divorcée and mother to a seven-year-old son, but these were factors that Todd actually found appealing—*and* encouraging. If Lana had left her previous husband despite having borne his child, Todd reasoned, it likely meant the guy had been abusive, or a cheater, or at the very least a total scumbag. The upshot was, it would make him look even better by comparison. And as for her son, he might have told himself all this time that he didn't want kids, but the fact was, that was more Angie's doing, and having a little guy around might be pretty great, actually. With his willingness to play daddy, plus having no brood of his own to compete, Todd figured this would make him look to a woman such as Lana like a damn fine catch, indeed.

Oh, yes. It all seemed so perfect. Sitting there, Todd started to drift, imagining the future with he and Lana and her little boy, Alek, as if it were already a done deal. This, even though the other women's photos and bios were still spread out like a deli platter on the table in front of him. But Todd didn't see any of them. He only saw himself and Lana, attending Arnold's inaugural black-tie ball. Arnold patting him on his back and telling him what a lucky rascal he was. The sex, of course, which was sure to be mind-blowing. And finally, there was little Alek. He could teach the boy things, and show him things, and coach his little league teams. That would be great, too.

The phone rang, jolting Todd back into the moment. He went to the kitchen and grabbed the receiver, his voice a bit brusque owing to the interruption. To his surprise, the voice at the other end of the line was soft and feminine. It caught him off guard. It was Rowena, the girl from the tanning salon.

"Hope I didn't catch you at a bad time," she said apologetically.

"Oh, no. I was just, you know, catching up on some paperwork. You know how it is." Then, realizing that he was speaking to a tanning-salon employee who might not be familiar with such rigors, he quickly added, "Anyway, what's up?"

"Well, I just noticed that you were scheduled to come in today for a session, and you never showed up. Normally, I'm supposed to dock you for it, but I figured maybe you just forgot, so if we put something else on the books, I could probably let it slide."

What a sweetheart. She was cute, too. Todd paused a beat. *Wait a minute! Is she flirting with me? Am I missing the signals?* It had been so long that Todd wasn't sure he even knew what the signals were anymore.

"Mr. Tisdale?"

Todd slumped a bit. No, of course she wasn't flirting. Girls don't flirt with guys they call "Mister." She was just being nice. Todd winced at how pathetic he must seem, and he suddenly realized that he'd probably been giving off a needy loser vibe all along without even knowing it. He made a mental note not to do that anymore.

"Mr. Tisdale, are you still there?"

"Yes. Yes, sorry, Rowena. I was just checking my books. It looks like I'm going to be out of town for the next few days. I have to go on a little business trip to Moscow."

"Moscow? Wow. That's pretty cool." A beat, as they both grappled with the seemingly faulty logic of this claim. "But I thought you ran that tux shop."

Todd scrambled. For some reason, he wanted to impress her. He also realized that he needed a good cover story for his little junket, anyway. "Well ... yes, Rowena. Yes, that's right. But I also have other investments. And as you know, there's a lot of opportunity over there right now."

"Oh, yeah. Right. So you might open a shop over there, too?"

"That's one possibility. We'll see."

"Wow. Well ... okay. Good for you. Guess I'll see you when you get back."

"It's a deal."

The two said their good-byes, and Todd hung up.

After he did, Todd lingered there by the stove for several seconds, gazing thoughtfully at the idle receiver in his hand. And as he did so, he didn't think about Lana or Alek or any of the other Czech-Mate bachelorettes even once.

But then, he caught a glimpse of Svetlana's photo in his peripheral vision and quickly snapped out of it.

He still had important decisions to make, and a lot of packing to do.

13

SPENCER'S BIG MOVE

"Ready for another drink, Nik?" Spencer asked, gesturing to her still half-full margarita.

"No, not yet, but it sure looks like you are. What's with you tonight?"

Unbeknownst to Nikki, the "Brinester Plan" that Spencer had devised earlier that day was already well underway, and that plan demanded the aid of liquid courage, which was why he had been pounding margaritas like Kool-Aid from the moment he had arrived.

Like always, Nikki had worked from four to midnight, the club's premium shift, reserved for only its top dancers, who got to perform during its busiest hours, for its best-tipping customers, without having to endure the drunken, desperate gropes and excesses of last call.

Spencer always met her for a cocktail after she punched out, and in order to accommodate this, he went straight home from work for a nap before heading over to meet her around midnight. But tonight, he had arrived early and downed three margaritas before she even sat down. With two more now under his belt,

Spencer was feeling no pain, and no anxiety whatsoever about what he had in store for the rest of the evening.

Spencer shrugged. "In a good mood. Felt like cutting loose a bit."

Nikki raised an eyebrow. "Is that right?"

"What do you say we get out of here?"

"I'm supposed to stick around."

"The other girls can handle it. Come on. Let's go have some fun."

Without waiting for a reply, Spencer grabbed her hand and pulled her up off her barstool. Nikki obliged, actually seeming to like it, the forcefulness of it.

"What do you have in mind?"

"More than a lousy kiss goodnight for a change."

"My, my, aren't we being a naughty boy?" Nikki grinned.

Spencer grinned back, a bit woozily.

Score one for the Brinester.

Twenty-five minutes later, Spencer and Nikki were at the door to his condo. Fumbling with his keys, Spencer struggled to stay focused on his primary goal, which was getting Nikki into his bachelor's lair so that he could work his magic on her.

Alas, the cheap strip-club tequila was really kicking in now, with the vengeance of an angry mule. His head was pounding, his hands wavering, his eyes playing tricks. The simple task of opening his own front door threatened to become a fiasco. Only by a sheer stroke of luck did the key finally stumble into the lock and the deadbolt give way.

Nikki entered first, bounding about the space, absorbing the scene. "Wow! Nice place! It's big. You live here all by yourself?"

Safely through the threshold now, Spencer was, like a blind man, taking comfort in the spatial awareness of his own abode. "Yep. Just me."

Cautiously traversing the room's wall-to-wall shag carpeting, dodging the sofa and bookcases, Spencer wanted more than anything to flop down on his sofa, click on the tube, and stare dumbly at some late-night talk show, basking in the buzz that was flooding over him like a tsunami.

But no. He was a host, a suitor, a man with a plan.

"You want anything? I could make some coffee."

Nikki settled onto the plush sectional, only adding to its heavy gravitational pull. "Coffee? I don't think so, tiger. I just got off work. How about that margarita?"

More tequila? Spencer was queasy just thinking about it. He had clearly overestimated his own capacities. Another margarita now would send him plummeting into a deep, stuporous abyss from which he might never emerge.

But—and Spencer was lucid enough to grasp this much—to allow Nikki to witness that weakness would be a death knell as well. No woman likes a lightweight. This was a stone-cold fact, dating all the way back to the caveman days. The weaker sex, as they are so deceivingly referred to, liked their men strong and capable, no matter the task or prey or alcoholic beverage at hand.

With that in mind, Spencer headed off to the kitchen to prepare the cocktails. And that is when, to his great delight, he stumbled upon a devilishly shrewd solution to his little problem: With himself as mixologist, how could Nikki possibly know how much tequila his own drink contained? Indeed, how would she know if there was any liquor in it at all? A-ha! She couldn't!

Pleased by this timely ingenuity, Spencer pulled out the requisite bottles and a pair of whimsical, cactus-shaped goblets (bought that very afternoon, because he knew Nikki loved margaritas and wanted to be prepared—bravo, Brinester!) and started concocting the beverages. Into Nikki's glass, the tequila was poured freely. Into his own, the bottle was barely waved over the rim. When the deed was done, it was impossible to tell the difference. Voila! Two margaritas, coming right up!

As Spencer returned to the sofa, Nikki was burrowed into his cherished corner spot, channel-surfing with an adorable abandon. Seeing her there, as innocent as a lamb, he immediately began regretting the deceit. This wasn't right. He was better than this. It was a cheap trick, and he knew it.

On the other hand, upon surveying the flash of ripe, bountiful cleavage peeking out from her silky camisole, he also surmised it might be just the thing he needed to close the deal.

The latter hand won out. "Here you go, Nik. One margarita, just the way you like it."

Nikki beamed. "Oh! Look at the little cactuses! How cute! I love those!"

Despite his staggering intoxication, Spencer nevertheless had to struggle to refrain from correcting her (*No, no: cacti! It's cact-I!*), but as he did so, and before he could even sit down beside her, Nikki grabbed one of the goblets and gave it a lusty guzzle.

"Mmm! You should be a bartender. These are yummy."

Spencer offered up a woozy grin, until it suddenly dawned on him: Had she taken the right glass? He looked back and forth between the two. He wasn't sure anymore, not at all. And since he couldn't just come out and ask her if her drink had any alcohol in it, he realized with great dismay that there was only one way to find out. He lifted the other goblet and slowly hazarded a small sip of his own. Then, he reeled back, as if his finger were caught in a wall socket.

Aye caramba! His drink was so chock-full of tequila, it was practically toxic.

"Cheers!" Nikki clinked her glass (meant to be his) against his own (intended for her—damn it all!). Spencer mustered a beaten smile and a weak cheers of his own and then raised the glass cactus for another sip, allowing more of the evil Mexican liquor to enter his already-sodden system.

And with that, everything suddenly started to change.

The room started spinning, and Spencer found that his eyes could no longer focus, or his mouth form words, or his brain otherwise gather itself in any useful way whatsoever.

Unaware, Nikki scooted closer and nuzzled his neck and friskily changed the channel to Cinemax where a soft-core porn movie starring Shannon Tweed as a psychologist specializing in sexual problems was playing—a perfect choice, were it not for the fact that Spencer's mouth was watering now, not from thirst or hunger but rather as a dire warning of some acidic crisis just now beginning to brew elsewhere in his body.

And though he struggled to stave it off as best he could by keeping one foot on the floor and remaining quiet and concentrating all his energy on swallowing, this in turn only made him look weird and sickly, so much so that Nikki noticed and asked him if he was okay, which he most decidedly wasn't, and which—as she leaned over and sat on the remote and the TV flashed over to press footage of Arnold Schwarzenegger waving and smiling at some star-struck political rally down in San Diego—made Spencer finally realize with a grave resignation that his final destination laid not in the master bedroom, which he'd adorned with scented candles and 500-thread-count sheets bought specifically for this highly-anticipated occasion, but rather in the bathroom, splayed helplessly across the cold, marble-tile floor, where his body would be violently and repeatedly purged of fluids other than the ones he had so greatly been hoping for.

14

BLACK SUNDAY

Rowena and her mother Connie went to church together every Sunday morning. It was a ritual for the two of them, one they had broken only rarely over the years: twice, in the weeks after Eddie died, when Connie was in mourning and couldn't get out of bed, and once, when Rowena had spent the previous night in jail for disturbing the peace (long story, long night) and needed to catch up on her sleep before work the following Monday. Outside of that, their record was nearly perfect, and they were both quietly proud of it. It was a lone thread of consistency in their otherwise scattershot lives.

Still, some Sundays were more difficult than others, a test of faith often in direct correlation with the amplitude of the Saturday night's festivities that had preceded it. This particular Sunday morning was an especially trying one for Rowena. She had been out late the night before with Wade ("That boy can sure drink himself some beers!" Estelle had noted admiringly), and they had remained up and "at it," so to speak, even later back at her place.

Wade had an unquenchable zest for carousing that Rowena could only marvel at. He lived his life in big gulps, just like her father had, and she was drawn to that like a moth to a flame. But how he managed to do all that and then get up to work twelve-hour shifts at the various construction sites he was employed at was beyond her. He never seemed to have even the trace of a hangover. She, on the other hand, always felt like she had one, especially now that she was spending more and more time with him.

Today was no exception. She awoke to find Wade already zipping up his jeans and sneaking out the door, which he always claimed to do so she could get her "beauty rest," but which she was never sure she completely believed. After the usual awkward good-byes, it took Rowena another fifteen minutes to tumble out of the sack herself and stumble to the bathroom to choke down a handful of Advils. Those took about ten minutes to kick in, at which point she began her daily morning routine of coffee and cigarettes, which in turn gave her the boost of energy she needed to get in the shower for a quick cleanup, throw on some clothes, and finally walk out the door with her darkest sunglasses to face the day.

From there, it was into the Tercel and onto the freeway, headed for Connie's house, where Rowena prayed that her mother would be actually ready to go for once. Lately, there always seemed to be something holding her up: hair's not right, makeup needs another pass, where the heck are my heels? Connie had only just recently turned sixty-five, but she moved a lot slower than she used to, looking, acting, and even *sounding* older than her age, despite the flaming-red dye jobs she still got every month at the local Beauty Box hair salon. What a shame, too; she used to be such a firecracker. It was tough to watch, this premature decline, especially for Rowena, who couldn't help but glimpse her own future in her mother's actions.

Every once in a while, though, there would be a glimmer of the Old Connie. She would suddenly be up and about and moving like a whirling dervish—cleaning, dusting, dancing, singing, and laughing, her ever-present cigarette waving through the air like a Fourth of July sparkler. Her mom was a hoot during these stretches, and Rowena always hoped they would last longer than they inevitably did. These brief but colorful glimpses of the Old Connie came at a cost, though. Afterwards, Connie would often go to bed and stay there, not just loafing but completely out cold, dead to the world, for stretches lasting as long as a full 24 hours.

But—thank heaven for small miracles—not today. As Rowena pulled into the driveway, she could already see her mom rumbling about inside. Sure enough, before Rowena could even make her way up the front walk, Connie flung open the door, slightly winded but looking dynamite. "There you are! I've been waiting and waiting!"

"I know, Mom, sorry. I was—"

"You look tired."

"Well ... yeah. I was with Wade again last night, and—"

"Lordy, where'd my purse get to?"

Connie turned and vanished back inside the house, slamming the door in a manner that suggested the search would likely be a lengthy one. Rowena rolled her eyes. No doubt about it; they were going to be late again. And in their church, that was a sin almost as grave as not going at all.

Just like Connie's daddy and his daddy before him, who ventured west from Biloxi, Mississippi back in the 1940s, Rowena and her mother were Southern Baptists. As such, despite all the raucous singing and dancing and speaking in tongues, they were dead serious about their faith, and their Sunday worship, and also about the Good Book, which like most Baptists they accepted as word-for-word literal truth from the hand of God himself.

That's not to say the two women had completely toed the line through the years. There had been transgressions. Both had a history of sexual relations outside of marriage (Fornicators!).

They also drank, smoked, ate meat on the Sabbath, and, at times of great weakness or despair, used the Lord's name in vain. In addition, Rowena had become friendly with several of the gay men from the salon (Sodomites!), who she refused to believe were damned to all-eternal hellfire just because they liked other guys—and unlike her mother, she was pretty sure there was some merit to the whole evolution deal, too.

Quite a list, it was true, and it was by no means comprehensive. Then again, as Rowena often told herself, nobody's perfect. You live a full life, and the sins seem to stack up, no matter who you are or what you believe. To her mind, the Pickett ladies had both done pretty doggone well in light of the hands they had been dealt. Yes, indeed. They were good Christian women.

But they were also late again, just as she had known they would be. By the time they finally arrived and got through the door, the clergy were in place and the choir was already into its opening hymn, which happened to be one of Connie's all-time favorites, "Nearer My God to Thee." Connie wasted no time joining in, singing at the top of her lungs, which spoiled Rowena's plan to duck into a back pew without their tardiness being noted by the rest of the congregation.

Unfortunately, this was not the only problem with Connie's performance. Because, as Rowena quickly realized, her mother, while marginally in tune, was not abiding to the lyrics of the hymn at all, but rather was belting out the words to Elvis Presley's "In The Ghetto." Making matters worse, Connie didn't pick up on this miscue in the slightest—not even under the disapproving glare of the service's many black parishioners—until they were seated themselves and the song was nearly over. And even then, her voice merely faded off, as if she had simply lost interest.

A troubling mistake, to say the least. And it wasn't the only one. Later on, during the sermon, Rowena happened to glance over and notice that Connie wasn't wearing a brassiere.

In fact, on second glance, it appeared her mother had on no undergarments whatsoever. And while this possibly could have been written off as simply being "weekend casual" if they were in a House of Pancakes rather than a house of worship, it wasn't, and they weren't, and Connie didn't seem to have any clue about any of it. Rowena was worried. It wasn't like her mother, not at all. She seemed ... off.

Things got even worse after the service was over. Connie went through the receiving line to pay her respects to Reverend Philbert, and when it was her turn, she told him what a nice sermon he had given and remarked that Eddie was "sorry he couldn't make it." The Reverend managed a graceful reply, but Rowena was mortified.

Back in her Tercel, she confronted Connie. "What the heck is going on, Mom?" Connie had no idea what Rowena was talking about. Rowena spelled it out: "Well, for one thing, you're not wearing any underwear!" Connie took a peek for herself. "My word! Look at that, you're right. What a sight I must have been!" She tittered nervously. "I didn't flash the Reverend or anything like that, did I?" Rowena said no, and Connie sighed with relief, seeming ready to write the whole thing off. Rowena then moved onto the issue of her singing, but Connie dismissed this, too, claiming it was an easy mistake to make. Finally, as a last resort, Rowena had no choice but to bring up the matter of Eddie, and Connie's referring to him as if he were still "with us." Connie's face suddenly darkened with anger. "Rowena Mae Pickett, I want you to apologize right now!" Rowena's mouth opened to reply, but before she could say anything, Connie charged on. "And when we get home, you're gonna apologize to him, too. Your daddy may be a rascal, but he would never leave this family! Never!"

Rowena sat with Connie in the lobby of the Mercy General emergency room.

It was the first time she'd been inside the hospital, *any* hospital, in years—to her recollection, the first time since her mom had brought her in with a wicked case of the chicken pox back in the third grade.

And Connie didn't like it, this turning of the tables. She complained incessantly, swearing up and down that she was perfectly fine, all the while insisting that she had to get back home because there were "people waiting for her," though she now wisely omitted the actual use of Eddie's name in doing so.

At the outset, this resistance and denial only made Rowena even more determined to stay. After all, where there's smoke, there's usually fire. But after two full hours of maternal indignation and filling out forms and being otherwise ignored, she began to grow impatient. Apparently, if you're not bleeding like a gusher or in full-on cardiac arrest, the "mercy" at Mercy General is doled out rather stingily.

Desperate for some attention, and some answers, Rowena finally managed to flag down a harried nurse. Before she could ask any questions, though, the nurse, without even breaking stride, offered a terse apology and said she and the rest of the ER staff had to attend to more "high priority" patients first.

This only opened the door for more doubts to creep in. Was she really doing the right thing? Did her mother truly need to be there? These doubts only grew when Connie, in her unceasing claims of perfect health, fired off a list of marginally credible mitigating factors, including extreme hunger, thirst, and hot flashes, as well as a dire need to catch up on her scrapbooking.

Thus, when her mother finally leveraged a request to go to the bathroom into a full-on sprint out the side door to the parking lot, Rowena wasn't nearly as vigilant about stopping her as she otherwise might have been. After all, with Connie's vociferous claims of mental fitness, no further signs of any distress, no corroboration of her earlier actions, and no known disease for which a lack of panties was the primary symptom, what could they really do, anyway? It was almost as if it had never even happened.

Walking out to the car, Connie had a new bounce in her step, appearing joyful and triumphant. Rowena trailed by several yards, shaking her head and mumbling. She was a jumble of emotions, far darker than her mother's, angry and scared and lamenting of the fact that they had wasted a whole Sunday afternoon without a single damn thing to show for it. And why would Connie lie unless she knew something was wrong, too? Or maybe, she didn't even *know* she was lying. Was that even possible? It was all too much for Rowena to figure out on her own.

The thing was, when she had a problem, she usually went to her mother for advice on how to handle it. Now her mother *was* the problem.

"You want to go to the Dairy Queen and get a sundae?" Connie smiled girlishly, as if she didn't have a care in the world. "My treat. I haven't had one in the longest time."

Rowena appeased her mother with this request, having a scoop of soft-serve vanilla herself to be polite even though she knew she didn't need it. Fortunately, this little snack appeared to sap Connie of her last gasp of manic energy. She fell dead asleep in the passenger seat on the way home, and barely roused at all as Rowena lifted her out, carried her into the house, hoisted her up the stairs, changed her into a nightie, and tucked her into bed—the same bed she had slept in with Eddie (and still did, according to her).

Rowena stayed with her mother for a while longer, making sure she was going to stay asleep, stroking her hair and listening to her breathe. When it was clear that all was well, at least for the time being, Rowena locked up the house, hopped in her battered car, and made a beeline for Estelle's apartment. Estelle's was like a clubhouse for Rowena and the other gals from the salon. As such, Rowena hoped to land a sympathetic ear or two, and maybe score a little weed as well, to help calm her jangled nerves (Estelle was known to have a joint or two laying around for just such occasions).

Sadly, repeated knocks on Estelle's door produced no reply. So, Rowena got back behind the wheel and made a drastic of course, headed now for Wade's place. This was done with no small amount of trepidation. Rowena knew that, in paying Wade a visit of this sort—"letting him in," Oprah's pal, Dr. Phil, had called it—she was implicitly taking their relationship to a higher level. Up until now, she and Wade had only been about having fun. With this, she was saying that she looked at him as being more than just a short-term partner for some laughs and a few no-string rolls in the hay. And that was a risk. She was laying her heart on the line. But, the fact was, she had nowhere else to turn.

Heading up Wade's front walk, Rowena waffled between feeling vulnerable and empowered. She chose to focus on the latter. The time spent with her mother had already exhausted her other emotions, and she needed a change for the better. She hoped Wade would provide it. Heck, a little afternoon romp in the hay might be just the ticket to help turn things around and provide a little perspective, maybe even better than Estelle's weed would have.

Wade's screen porch was wide open, and the entry door was open, too. His house had central air, but he rarely used it, instead relying on windows and ceiling fans to keep things cool during what was proving to be a longer than normal Indian summer. Of course, he was used to the heat, plying his trade on rooftops and I-beams year round. Thinking of Wade up in the sky somewhere with no shirt, power tool in hand, the sweat glistening off his tanned muscles, got Rowena feeling a little toasty, too. She gave the door a quick tap-tap-tap and headed right in.

"Wade?"

No answer, but there was a TV on somewhere in the house. Tuned to football, of course. Rowena rolled her eyes. Why did every guy love football so much, even the ones who never played the game themselves? Was it the whole macho thing? Were they trying to prove something? Or, perhaps, *compensate* for something? Whatever the case, Wade was a fanatic, same as the rest, watching games and then watching the highlights on ESPN and then checking the scores and standings in the next day's paper as if he didn't already know everything there was to know.

Rowena headed back to the master bedroom. The game noise grew louder. Wade had a big-screen Sony perched right at the foot of his bed; she was sure that's where he was. In her mind, she could already see him there, splayed dead-center on the mattress, head perched up with a pillow, one hand clutching a cold can of beer, the other burrowed deep inside his boxers as if making sure everything was still there and in proper working order. Enjoying a perfectly lazy Sunday, in other words, which is precisely what she would have liked to do herself if it weren't for this crazy business with her mom.

The door was open just a crack, but it was enough to let her know he was in there. Rowena eagerly popped her head in. Sure enough, Wade was on the bed, in the exact position she had predicted. The only problem was, he wasn't alone. And moreover, it wasn't a hand, much less his *own* hand, that was affixed to his crotch.

"Estelle?"

Rowena's best friend looked up with a gasp and tumbled off the far end of the bed to try and hide and also—as long as she was down there—locate some of her clothing.

"Rowena! Ro, honey! It ain't how it looks!" Estelle cried out. This was a flimsy effort on her part, to be sure, but one that might have been excused for the duress under which it was concocted were it not for the fact that she was pulling a pair of crotch-less panties out from under Wade's bare ass while saying it.

Wade, meanwhile, didn't move, not an inch or a hair. He was far too cool a customer for that. Or perhaps just far too stoned off the pot Estelle had apparently brought with her, which was still clouding the air with its aroma of calculated treachery and betrayal. "Uh ... hey, babe. Thought you were hanging with your mom today."

Rowena gave neither of these pathetic parries the dignity of a response. Instead, she simply offered up a single, heartbroken whimper and ran for the door.

15

THE BRINESTER REVISITED

Spencer woke up in his own bed.

That would have been all perfectly well and normal, save for the fact that he had gotten so thoroughly obliterated on tequila the night before that he couldn't recall with any certainty, or even foggy hypothesizing, how he had gotten there.

And that was, indeed, only one piece of a larger mystery that needed to be solved. Looking down, Spencer also saw that he was now clad in pajamas, the flannel ones his mother had sent him for his birthday the year before, which he never wore because they featured a book-and-quill print that made him look like a dorky kid at some kind of nerdy summer arts camp.

He then noticed, too, the towel draped across his bedside, and the large acrylic mixing bowl on the floor directly below, spattered with an indefinable organic matter in a wide jet-spray pattern that, on closer inspection, shared a disturbing resemblance to the spaghetti Bolognese he had eaten for dinner the night before.

This explained the bowl. It also clued Spencer in to the cause of the sickly, road-kill taste in his mouth and the raw, flagellated soreness of his throat, a condition he hadn't suffered since the sadistic rituals of his college fraternity's Hell Week.

Yes, Spencer realized, he had drunk way too much, and he had paid the price. And as he tried to sit up and his brain banged against the inner walls of his skull, he realized that he was *still* paying the price, and would continue to do so for the next several hours.

MAN VOMITS, DREAM DATE VACATES.

That was the headline, one which begged the ultimate, unanswered question from the previous evening's storyline. Namely, what had become of Nikki? Had she witnessed this pathetic display? Had she selected his embarrassing attire and helped him through his ensuing gastro-eruptive calamities? And if so, had he just blown his best, and perhaps only, chance with her, by revealing himself as a weak beta-male with no capacity for alcohol and no capability to carry through on his intended plans for seduction? The more he thought about it, the worse the jackhammer pounding in his head got.

The day was not starting well.

Spencer looked at the clock. It was already 8:30 a.m. Unless he tore ass out of there right this very second, he would be late for work, with Morris hovering over him like a vulture and questioning his devotion to the job and the good people of Sacramento whose lives he was memorializing. Spencer resigned himself to this ghastly fate. He was in no shape to tear ass anywhere other than to the medicine cabinet for some aspirin.

He made a second attempt at sitting up. This one was only slightly less painful, but enough so that he was able to maintain an upright position. Progress.

But then, from this elevated perch, he became aware of an additional, unexpected phenomenon. Indeed, one that was unprecedented in the annals of Spencer's Sacramento experience thus far. It was the presence of another body in his bed, a body whose lavender scent and hourglass silhouette were undeniably female. With the added telltale clues of the tawny hair and tan, silky skin that were peeking out from under the sheets, it appeared to be none other than the woman whose actions and whereabouts he had just been pondering.

Just to be sure, Spencer carefully slid over to take a closer inspection. And, yes—it was her, all right. His darling Nikki Balodouris. And she was soundly, blissfully, beautifully asleep. Spencer was flabbergasted. It was a miracle. And although he would have loved to linger and continue gazing upon her lovely shrouded form, this was a second chance, a shot at redemption, that he had absolutely no intention of wasting. Forgoing any and all concern for his own pain, he leapt out of bed to start setting the stage for an unexpected, but far from unpondered, morning after with his dream girl.

The Brinester Plan may have fallen short, but Plan B was now in full effect.

Under the circumstances, Spencer was truly amazed at how much he was able to accomplish in a single half-hour. He had showered and shaved and brushed and gargled (repeatedly). He had rid the premises of any remaining traces of regurgitation. And finally, he had whipped up what he deemed to be a damn fine-looking breakfast, with scrambled eggs and bacon and buttermilk pancakes and hash browns and toast with jam, complemented with two different kinds of juice and milk.

The timing couldn't have been better. Just as he finished scouring the iron skillet, Nikki appeared from the bedroom in a pair of his boxers and an old diaphanous V-neck T-shirt, tousling her long blond hair in a sleepy-eyed, bodice-thrusting way that looked more like a scene from a music video than it did anything in Spencer's life up until now. It was, to say the least, a sight to behold. And indeed, Spencer realized, it was a sight that would linger in his mind long after the actual events had passed. Frozen in time, burnished by fond recollection, it was one of those fleeting quick-flash images that would, on some subconscious level, serve as a comparison point to anything and everything else in his life that might come after it.

Nikki yawned, crossing her arms with a little wake-up shiver. Her eyes turned his way. "You're alive."

"Just barely," he muttered, a tidal wave of shame sweeping over him. "Thanks for staying. I'm sorry. I didn't mean to get like that."

"Yeah, I figured." Nikki chuckled. But was it with fondness or pity or contempt? Spencer was dying to know.

"You were kind of cute, actually. At least, for a guy barfing all over the place."

"Yeah?" Spencer flushed and beamed all at once, accepting this meager bone of a compliment as if it was the Pulitzer Prize of his dreams.

"Like a lost little puppy," Nikki said, making a sad-faced whimpering noise that Spencer might have found amusing were it not for the fact that it was meant as an imitation of him during his weak-kneed hours from the night before.

With that, Nikki moved closer, sashaying past the sectional, her bare legs displaying the same leonine grace he had witnessed so many times before on stage ... *and he blew it! God! How could he have let himself get so—*

"What are you doing in there?"

Spencer snapped back. *Stay in the moment. Forget last night. Stay in the moment.* "Making you some breakfast. Hope you're hungry."

Nikki stopped her forward progress and tilted her head, seemingly confused—like an encore of her lost puppy routine, perhaps, or like a robot that had just encountered something utterly foreign to its database. "You cooked breakfast? For me?"

"Well ... yeah. Nothing too elaborate. I figured it was the least I could do."

"That's so sweet," Nikki cooed, and Spencer tried his best yet again to decipher its underlying meaning: Fondness? Pity?

Or perhaps, it was just plain old-fashioned hunger. Spencer prepared a heaping plate for her, and she sat at the little country-style table in his breakfast nook and dug right in. Spencer ladled up a plate for himself and sat directly across from her, doing his best to generate some conversation unrelated to the previous night's foibles, as he wisely concluded that it would be best to let sleeping dogs lie. Nikki responded to these efforts, laughing at his self-deprecating humor and wry observations, seeming to be in surprisingly good spirits despite all that had transpired (and *not* transpired—dammit!).

When they were done, Nikki helped him wash the dishes, and their bodies brushed against each other, not once, but three times. Spencer made a note of each. The first was when they reached for the same dishtowel and their hands grazed one another's. The second was when Spencer passed her a plate to dry, and she gave him a friendly little "Go, Team!" bump with her elbow. And the last, but far from least, was when Nikki bent over to put the forks into the dishwasher and her ripe derriere perched itself up against his left thigh for support.

And while that was all perfectly well and good and even vaguely encouraging in an at-least-you-don't-thoroughly-repulse-me kind of way, when all the cleaning was done, it left things at an awkward crossroads: *What now?* Spencer knew he had to get to work, he was already late, but Nikki was offering up no signals as to what she wanted to do, or what she wanted *him* to do, and even though she was likely just being polite, he didn't want to make a mistake when it seemed he might finally be making up some lost ground.

"So what else can you do?"

Spencer turned. Nikki was rubbing her belly with an inscrutable Buddha smile. Was it possible she was still hungry?

"Excuse me?"

"You said cooking breakfast was the least you could do. So what else can you do? For me?" Nikki's hand slid down her belly, her fingers vanishing into her commandeered pair of boxer shorts.

Watching this, Spencer dropped his scrub brush onto the linoleum floor and gulped. While he was a notoriously conservative judge of other people's body language, it became jaw-droppingly clear, even to him, what Nikki's body was saying now.

Nikki grabbed him by the hem of his pajama top and led him out of the kitchen and through the living room and into the master bedroom. And Spencer made no move to stop her, or alter the course of action, or indeed assert any kind of control over the situation whatsoever. He was like putty in her hands; a grateful recipient of whatever kindnesses she might be willing to show him, and an eager participant in whatever activities she wished to engage in. He was a sex slave. A concubine. A eunuch. He was exactly whoever and whatever she wanted him to be.

The next seventy-five minutes were like something out of some top-secret, Jedi-level Kama Sutra instruction manual. Nikki was a sexual dynamo unlike anything Spencer had ever before seen or experienced or even read about. Backwards, forwards, up, down, wet, dry, sitting, standing, sideways, hanging. When the two had exhausted every possible position and prop and orifice, and both of them were physically spent and in dire need of multivitamins and IV drips, sweaty and gasping and scratched and chafed and bruised and burned, Spencer was so utterly mind-blown that he genuinely doubted whether he was even the same person anymore.

Nikki seemed pleased as well. Satisfied. Impressed. "Not bad, tiger," she said. She gave him a little peck on the cheek, then reached down to put her panties back on.

This was a cue for Spencer to begin dressing as well, so that is what he did. But the fact was, it seemed pointless. He was a carnal being now, like her, and clothes were superfluous. He wanted to stay in bed and continue to mine the primal pleasures of the flesh that they had just shared and spiritually bonded over.

Nikki, completely dressed now, noticed that Spencer was still in his Jockeys.

"Don't you have somewhere you need to be?" she said.

"Oh. Right. Yes. I mean, I don't really want to, you know … not now, but—"

"Aww." Nikki smiled, eyes gleaming. "My little puppy has to go to work at the big bad office." With that, she went to the door. "I'll see you tonight, won't I?"

"I wouldn't miss it for the world."

Nikki smiled again, knowing this was so, and sashayed out the door.

Spencer arrived at the *Bee* a little before noon, his mood a volatile blend of ecstasy and resignation. On the one hand, he felt like a god, a conquering god, looking down upon mankind with the wisdom of the ages and lightning bolts in his hands from some mythical Olympian summit. On the other, he felt like a drudge, punching in and trudging his way down into the basement catacombs for another fluorescent-lit, soul-sucking shift in the confinement of his dreary cubicle.

It was with these mixed emotions that he found himself coming face to face with Morris, who spied him from across the room and came charging over to spew invective his way, the words to which he had been undoubtedly rehearsing in his unenlightened mind for the last hour, if not longer.

"Think you can just stroll in here anytime you want, Brine?"

"No, sir."

"Sure looks like it. This is a daily paper, you know. Not weekly. Not monthly. Daily. That means we show up here and we write our pieces and we print the news, *every single day.*"

"I know that, Morris."

"That's Mr. Sutphin to you, Brine. I deserve that much. I was here at 8 a.m. sharp, like I always am, and I was collecting material and piecing together a Metro section, like I always do, and there was just one little problem and that was I was missing the person who was supposed to be writing the obituaries for that section, of which there are already two submitted, with another on the way. And guess who that person is?"

"The dead person or the person who's supposed to be writing the obituaries?"

"Is that sass? Are you sassing me, Brine?"

"Not intentionally, sir, no."

"Mister Sutphin."

"Mister Sutphin. I'm sorry. It was unavoidable. I'll get right on it, and I won't leave until it's done. You don't have to worry."

"Oh, I'm not worried, Brine, but you should be. Now get to work."

Spencer continued on to his cubicle with his head held high, past coworkers who cast pitying glances his way before ducking down to avoid any direct eye contact. This kind of public upbraiding would have crushed the old Spencer. Humiliated him. Made him quiver. But Spencer was a changed man now. He felt it in his head and in his heart and, perhaps most of all, in his loins. Morris Sutphin may have been his superior, quote-unquote, and he fully planned to do as Morris demanded because he had a respect for his work and for the job he was hired to do, but he also knew now that he was capable of far more, and far better, and that such overlording would never again work its wicked magic against him the way it once had. He was not just a cog in the machine, a monkey with a typewriter, to be pushed around at will. He was a talented writer and a force to be reckoned with.

At his desk, Spencer pulled the first fax from his in box. Read it over. Looked up to Nikki's photo for inspiration. And with that, he dove right in. He was determined. It would be the best damn obituary he had ever written.

16

FORTRESS OF SOLITUDE

On the morning after her late-night Gas N' Sip munchie bender, Missy Carver called into work sick for the first time in years. The next day she did the same. By the third morning, she had informed her bosses at Eureka that she needed to work from home for another day or two in order to take care of some "family matters." These couple of days soon stretched to a full week, and that week into two—and during that entire time, Missy never stepped so much as a toe outside the 2950 square feet of her house. Not for work. Not for food. Not for anything.

However, there was nothing at all wrong with this, or with her personally, as Missy made abundantly clear to anyone who asked or was willing to listen. Oh, no. While it was true that she had suffered some minor setbacks of late, there was no correlation between the two whatsoever. This was merely an elective personal retreat, a healthy respite from the hustle-and-bustle of the outside world. And she had served proof of this, at least to the temporary satisfaction of her bosses at Eureka Realty, by diligently working the phone, fax and computer to continue plying her trade, albeit now with the aide of other realtors to actually show the properties and erect the ubiquitous *"Open House"* and *"I'm Beautiful Inside!"* signs that were mainstays of their business.

The truth was, in this technological age, it was remarkable how much one could accomplish in this manner. Missy quickly discovered that she could still drum up new business, offer home loan and investment advice, place new listings on the MLS database, match buyers with sellers and vice versa, negotiate deals, and even close them—signed, sealed, and delivered—all without the need for any office visits or client interface. It was almost as if nothing at all had changed. Like it was business as usual.

Of course, despite her repeated assertions, Missy knew this wasn't true. Not even close, actually. But when Missy made up her mind on how she wished things to *appear*, she wasn't about to let any cold, hard realities get in the way. Thus, aside from reveling in how smooth the transition to her new stay-at-home work schedule had been, she also actively sought out more ways to demonstrate how and why her new self-quarantined lifestyle was so fulfilling that she was reluctant to give it up, even after the initial two week period of her retreat had expired.

The first and most important breakthrough in this regard was that there actually was no *need* for her to venture outside the home. As Missy quickly discovered, anything a person might possibly require was just a phone call or mouse click away. It all came right to you. This was true of the mail, of course, and the office messenger service. But the conveniences didn't stop there. She also had her groceries delivered. And her household supplies. And her dry cleaning. Even her new color print cartridges from Staples.

It was all so easy, and efficient to boot, that it led her to seek out even more items to have sent. She bought a chocolate leather desk chair from Pottery Barn. A brushed-titanium blender from Williams-Sonoma. A cerulean sweater set from Talbot's. She even splurged on a rare first-edition copy of *The Fountainhead*, her favorite novel, which espoused many of her own personal beliefs and credos, on eBay. In just the first week alone, it had already came to pass that, because she ordered so much, so often, and in such varied and seemingly random ways, she had no idea as to what might be coming next. Every day brought a new surprise. It was like a Christmas that had no end.

This new arrangement had other fringe benefits, too. With no need for commuting, as well as the elimination of other pointless time-wasters like hair-styling, makeup application, and idle interoffice chit-chat, Missy found that she now had time to finally tackle a variety of long-delayed home improvement projects, as well as pursue some healthy, mind-expanding hobbies. She repainted her kitchen. She refinished her cabinets. She replaced her faucets. She read books, ranging from classics like Tolstoy and Joyce to more current fare like O' Reilly and O' Rourke. She explored chat rooms and blogs on the Internet. She studied Pilates and tai chi and tantric breathing. She played on-line chess and poker and solitaire. She even—in a fit of crazed, late-night whimsy—learned to do the Macarena.

However, her favorite new recreational pursuit was one from her past, which she had divested herself of for nearly twenty years but had now come to embrace again with a renewed passion. That was eating. And not just eating in her usual, food-as-fuel way, mind you, but outright gorging, the more sinful and gluttonous the fare, the better.

It had all begun that night back at the Gas N' Sip. Starting at the check-out counter and continuing into her car and then back home on her king-size bed, Missy had feasted upon so many different varieties of junk food and sugary treats that she lost track. She had been crazed that night, on the verge of a total emotional breakdown. The food had served as a salve, a sacrifice, a way to forget. And so, when that frenzied feeding ended with her body rejecting this overabundant offering en masse, it seemed fitting. Indeed, for Missy, who had always kept herself in such top shape that she rarely got sick and never gave in to the excesses of drink, these bile-spewing spasms had felt evil, and inhuman, like something out of *The Exorcist*. Hovering over the toilet bowl in between heaves, she swore that she would never subject herself to such a thing, ever again.

However, when she woke up the next morning, Missy was pleasantly surprised by how *good* she felt. Rubbing her stomach, still just as tight and trim as ever, she realized that there was virtually no residual discomfort and, better still, absolutely no bloating. It was as if the purging had provided her a Get-Out-of-Jail-Free card. Do the crime, but don't do the time. Recalling the unbridled bliss of digging into all those delicious goodies, Missy grew giddy at the thought. After denying herself for so long, this was a trade-off that she was willing to make, especially if it continued to offer that same elevated feeling of gratification and control. And so, she wasted no time in repeating the process again that very day, with home-baked cookies. And chicken pot pie. And Moo Goo Gai Pan. It was such a simple and elegant solution; a fleeting bit of misery for a full, heaping helping of epicurean delight. And better still, no one was the wiser, not even her merciless, Swiss-calibrated bathroom scale.

So this was Missy's daily routine now. And in her own humble estimation, it was all working out quite well, thank you very much. In fact, she had never before experienced a period of time that had gone by so pleasantly and productively.

There remained, however, one nagging reminder of the previous chapter of her life, the one colossal disappointment that had wounded her so deeply that she had been unable to face the light of day since its reveal: that was, Arnold Schwarzenegger. Or rather, what Arnold Schwarzenegger represented. To Missy, he was a powerfully painful symbol of her own failure to excel at the high levels of which she felt both capable and deserving. To connect with people and make them like her and admire her and want to work with her. To feel, in one simplistic but largely accurate word, complete.

Thus, when Missy happened to turn on the TV, on one of those rare occasions when no other task or project took precedence, she was dismayed to find that she had stumbled upon a live telecast of the one gubernatorial debate in which Schwarzenegger had deigned to take part.

Like a lemming drawn to the cliff's edge, she sat down to watch, and in doing so, came face to face with precisely what her own life was sorely lacking. What Arnold had in spades. And it wasn't the obvious things, the ones that people of lesser depth might covet, like the stardom, or the wealth, or the famed physique. No. What Arnold had that Missy desired most, and lacked most, was that intangible "it" factor. The seemingly effortless charm and charisma and magnetism that made the moderator and even the other candidates turn his way and defer to him and laugh at his jokes and literally glow in his starry presence.

And with all that came the fact that he was so obviously going to win, just as she had always predicted. Which, in turn, meant that her nemesis, Jolene Wyatt, would be finding him a house. And earning the big, fat commission check. And the glowing kudos in the local papers and trade rags. And last but certainly not least, all the years of lucrative follow-up business that would come her way simply because she was the One Who Had Helped Arnold ("if Jolene Wyatt's good enough for the Terminator, she's probably good enough for the Timmermans, too, hahaha!"—idiots!).

The bitterness of all this drew Missy out of her shell, just long enough for her to briefly question her current state of affairs. It also made her question the dictionary-sized tray of lasagna she had in the oven, which she planned to devour in full and then forcibly expel from her body later in the evening. It made her wonder if maybe she wouldn't be better off just trying to be happier with herself the way she was, and be happier with others the way they were, and be happier with life and the world the way it was. Hmm. Maybe, just maybe...

Ring, ring, *ring.*

Missy's train of thought was interrupted by the telephone. Not her work line, mind you, but her home line, the number to which was unlisted and known to only a handful of people. Missy checked Caller ID and groaned, rolling her eyes and waiting another two full rings before finally gritting her teeth and reluctantly picking up.

"Did you see it? Wasn't he great?" Like some kind of mind-reading ninja, Missy's mother, Mamie, wasted no time going right for the jugular. "I especially loved it when he told that one woman off. Can't remember the name. She kinda looked like you, though, baby—all button-down in a suit, hair done up and such."

"You mean Arianna Huffington?"

"Right. Boy, that was good, telling her she belonged in *Terminator 4.* I about lost my supper on that one." Mamie cackled, then fell into a lengthy coughing jag, followed by a long, Darth Vader-ish drag off a cigarette. She then added: "He sure was smooth, all right. Heh heh. Put that bossy old girl right in her place."

"And what place is that, Mom? According to you."

"No need to get all huffy."

"Well, I mean, you compare her to me, and then you talk about how hilarious it is that she gets just totally humiliated on live TV."

"Oh, now you're being ridiculous!"

"And you know how much I wanted that contract with him, too, and so why you would choose to throw that right in my face—"

"Stop being so touchy! I was doing no such thing!"

"Yes, you were."

"No, I was not, but as long as you brought it up, Missy, did you ever stop to think that maybe that other gal got the job cause she was just better for it? Maybe a little more, you know ... inviting? I seen her signs up, you know, and she just looks so sweet, with that big smile and all. You might learn a trick or two; wouldn't be such a bad thing."

The wound was deep now. Missy was gasping. And in her pain, she lashed out. "Why would I do that, Mom, when I already have such a great role model like you? Smoking Salems all day and watching soaps and collecting welfare checks? Yeah, that's a real inspiration. Why didn't I think of that?"

Mamie gasped. "Melissa Louise Carver, you always could be spiteful, ever since you were a little girl, but I never—"

"You never *anything*, Mom. That's the problem."

A heavy beat of silence. "So that's it, huh? That's what you think of your old mother, the woman who birthed you and fed you and clothed you and raised you the best she knew how. Gave you the best years of her life. That's what you think."

"That's not what I said, Mom. You're twisting my words again."

Missy meant to stop there, she really did, but Mamie had got her dander up, had hit her when she was down, and as a result she wasn't feeling particularly charitable or forgiving, so before she could censor herself, she added the words that had been playing through her mind: "But, since you asked ... what am I *supposed* to think?"

"Well, then, I guess I'll just hang up."

"Right. Just quit. That's your answer for everything, isn't it, M—"

Click. The line was dead. Mamie had done as threatened. And while Missy felt some lingering guilt over the harshness of her words, another part of her thought it might be just what her mom needed to hear. Who else was going to be so honest with her? It wasn't too late. Her mom and dad could still turn things around, get jobs (and, more importantly, keep them for a change), save up some money, move out of the ramshackle place they called a home, stick with their diets, maybe even quit smoking those cancer sticks they were both so fond of. Look at what she had been able to accomplish, coming from the same exact set of genes and circumstances. So, it wasn't impossible.

The fact was, too, that her mom was notoriously cruel, in her own, signature passive-aggressive way. She would never admit it, but Missy knew that Mamie was jealous of all the things her daughter had accomplished, and envious of all the things she possessed. This was so, even though Missy had gone out of her way to be as generous and helpful as possible over the years. She'd even paid off their mortgages, all three of them, so that they wouldn't have to worry about the payments that were otherwise inevitably in arrears. But for some people, no matter how much you give, it's never enough.

Missy got on her elliptical and started pedaling furiously, trying her best to sweat out all her excess emotion while the lasagna continued to bake. The previous self-reflection was gone. Mamie's call had driven it clear from her thoughts. Instead, her mind was now focused on clearing away all the remaining distractions in her life, which were still tormenting her and plaguing her with self-doubt, Arnold and Mamie included. As for Arnold, she would simply stop watching TV and reading the paper. No media, no Arnold—done. Her mother, however, might be a tougher nut to crack. Mamie was nothing if not persistent. But Missy recognized her for the negative influence that she was, and knew that if she was going to see this period of personal growth and cleansing through to its natural and intended conclusion, she would have to make a clean break.

Ding.

The oven buzzer went off, signaling that the lasagna was ready. Missy did one final sprint on the trainer then ran, gasping, into the kitchen to retrieve her dinner. After all she had been through, a heaping trayful of gooey meat and cheese was precisely what she needed. And when she was done, there would not be so much as a crumb or a spatter left as evidence. This was how Missy planned to conduct all her affairs from now on. Fast and clean and thorough. She grabbed a fork and dug right in, the heat of the food burning the roof of her mouth while its flavor tantalized her taste buds and left them begging for more—the mix of sensations, good and bad, pleasure and pain, reminding her once again that she was alive and well and in complete, undisputed control of her own destiny.

17

TO RUSSIA WITH LOVE

In the days preceding his trip to Moscow, Todd had done everything he could to prepare himself for what lay ahead. Studying the pictures, ranking the prospects, packing his bags, reading his Russian phrasebook.

However, nothing could have equipped him for the actual flight, which proved to be the longest and most arduous by far of his entire life. In fact, as arranged by the crackerjack Czech-Mate travel coordinators, it was actually three separate flights on three different airlines, passing through twelve time zones, over a total travel time of nearly twenty-four hours. As a result, Todd not only traveled a greater distance from home than ever before, but he racked up several other personal bests along the way: most in-flight movies watched (5), most naps taken (6), most meals and bags of nuts eaten (7 and 8, respectively), and most Bud Lights drunk (11 ... no, make that 12 ... or was it 13?).

But despite these rigors, from the first boarding call to the very last can of beer, Todd's faith in his mission only grew. Indeed, by the time his final flight finally touched down at Moscow's Sheremetyevo International Airport, Todd was more certain than ever that it was all going to be worth the effort. That he was truly on the golden path to success.

The reasons for this were many, the first being the reaction he got from his fellow travelers. In every case, when he told them he was from Sacramento, the person would start talking about Schwarzenegger. It was almost as if Arnold had not only already been elected (the vote was still two weeks away), but also as if the two—Sacramento and Schwarzenegger—were already etched into people's minds as a matched set. And while some found this prospect more appealing than others, Todd chose not to dwell on the negatives and the naysayers, instead embracing the visionary words of his final seatmate of the trip, a charming Turkish textiles exporter named Ahmed.

As it turns out, Ahmed knew all about the recall, and Arnold, and indeed, about the state of California as a whole. He said it was Arnold's destiny to rule; that it was only the beginning of what would become a great Golden State dynasty. And though Todd was rather embarrassed because, in comparison, he knew almost nothing about Ahmed's homeland, much less its politics, and in fact wasn't even entirely sure where Turkey was on the map, the conversation nevertheless reinforced everything that he had come to believe about the transformative effects a Schwarzenegger victory would have, on his town and his own business. It was exactly as Ahmed said. It was destiny. Just like this trip was destiny. And meeting Svetlana was destiny.

It was with this sense of dreamy vindication that Todd stepped off the plane and into the Moscow terminal, where he was greeted warmly, right at the gate, by his Czech-Mate sponsor, Andrei. "Are you ready for your great adventure, my friend?" Andrei asked, in a vigorous tone that precluded any answer but "yes."

And to be sure, that sense of being ready, of being on the path of the righteous, only grew when Andrei turned and introduced Todd to two of his other clients who had apparently been on this same flight. The first potential rival—and they *were* his competition, Todd made no mistake about that—was a short, jug-eared Scotsman, Ned, whose gin-blossom nose and limp handshake served as signal to an underlying weakness of character that Todd was confident he could trounce if the need arose. The second man, a fellow Californian named Phil, had a gigantic head, a tragic comb-over, and a bulky cell phone holster clipped to the high waistline of his unfashionable "dad jeans." Nerd alert! Todd caught Andrei's eye and it was clear that he was thinking the same thing. The early odds seemed to be well in Todd's favor.

This feeling of jaunty optimism stayed with Todd throughout the ensuing customs and baggage-claim processes, and all the way into town, to the Sputnik Savoy Grand, a boutique hotel right off Red Square, where he and the other Czech-Mate bachelors would be staying. There, Andrei helped them get checked in, then accompanied them up to their adjoining "international luxury suites"—which, in truth, proved to be far from luxurious, and not really suites, either, instead having the sterile feel of an Iron Curtain hospital ward. Nevertheless, it provided Todd the opportunity to show up his fellow competitors yet again, much to their obvious envy, with some well-timed parries from his Russian phrasebook ("I like it here! Thank you! Where's the mini-bar?").

Once that was done, and Andrei bid his farewells, the men each had the afternoon free to either sightsee or catch up on their rest before the scheduled "private preview dates" later that evening. Thinking of Svetlana (and beyond), Todd was too anxious to snooze, and too antsy to stay cooped up in his room, so he took a quick shower, then headed out to soak in some of the local culture.

Unfortunately, the "culture" at hand didn't prove quite as captivating as Todd had hoped. Sure, the Kremlin was okay to look at, with all the bright colors and kooky-looking towers and such, but once you got inside the place, who really wanted to hear about all that ancient history, all the tsars and Bolsheviks and blah, blah, blah. The museums weren't much better, at least by Todd's estimation, with just a lot of old religious paintings and statues and jeweled ceramic eggs that all looked pretty much the same to him, anyway.

After an hour or so of trying to fake being as fascinated as everybody else seemed to be, Todd finally gave up and set off to find a place where he could catch some ESPN to find out the scores of the games he'd missed en route, and maybe also grab a drink or two to slake his thirst from all the walking he'd done.

Luckily, it didn't take long to find one. There was a whole row of restaurants and bars just around the corner from the square. The one that caught his eye was the Hungry Bear, a quaint little joint with twinkling Christmas lights hung on the walls and old-school American rock and roll playing on the jukebox, which reminded him of his own favorite bar, the Dog, back in Sacramento.

Walking in, Todd took a seat at the bar, front and center, and called out for a beer. The bartender repeated his order—"Boodviiizherr?"—in a way that actually made it sound exotic, then rushed off in search of same. He returned from the cooler with a frosty longneck, and Todd took a long pull off the bottle and felt right at home.

Alas, this illusion was short-lived. When he asked this same snaggletoothed barkeep if the TV mounted over the bar could be switched over to ESPN, the Russian simply stared at him, utterly lost. Speaking slower and louder, while also pantomiming a forward pass to accentuate his point, Todd repeated his request. Again, the man appeared dumbfounded.

As Todd reached into his jacket pocket and began rifling through his phrasebook to find a comparable Russian term for "sports highlights," a stocky gentleman with a shaved head sitting a couple stools to his left leaned over to him with a knowing smile. "No cable here, no ESPN. Sorry. Maybe I help. What game you want to know?"

"Niners," Todd mumbled, still poring through the phrasebook's pages.

"You are in luck, my friend. Your team, they beat the Chiefs, 20-10."

Elated by this news, Todd finally turned to the man, who smiled and offered his hand in introduction. "Anton Chekhov, at your service."

Todd's face brightened in recognition. "Like on *Star Trek*, right?"

Anton met this with a good-natured laugh, and the two men fell into a friendly chat. As it turned out, not only did Anton know the score of the 49ers game, he knew all the scores, and many of the stats as well. Before long, Anton had scooted his stool next to Todd's, and the two were talking football and trading toasts over shots of chilled local vodka. Anton spoke of his love for all things American, and in turn, asked what brought Todd to his country. Self-conscious, Todd lied at first, just as he had with Rowena, claiming that he was there on "business." But as the vodka flowed and the conversation flourished, Todd's tongue got looser until he finally came clean.

Much to his surprise, Anton did not look down on Todd or belittle his objective. Rather, he saluted Todd's initiative and offered him a hearty vote of confidence. "You are a smart man," Anton said. "Russian women, they are tired of the hard life and the old ways. They want to go to sunny California, where the movie stars live. For a successful man such as yourself? They will fall all over themselves. Trust me, I know this."

Todd was happy to hear it. While it was true that Andrei had offered these same sort of assurances, that was his job. Since Anton was on the home team, so to speak, his encouragement meant more. And Anton, being a good sport, didn't stop there. He insisted on buying Todd one last shot of premium vodka and serenading him with an old Kamchatkan courting song to wish him good luck on his date. Todd was deeply touched.

Soon after, Todd looked at his watch and saw that he had to run. He wished Anton a fond farewell; in their brief time together, they had really bonded. He raced back across the square to the hotel to get ready, thinking that if the ladies he met were anywhere near as nice and welcoming as Anton, this would be a fruitful trip indeed.

Back in his suite, Todd took another quick shower to fight off the jet lag he was feeling (okay, maybe it was partly the vodka, too). He re-deodorized, splashed on some cologne, and put on his "lucky shirt," a fancy silk number that Angie had bought for him the Christmas before she passed ("Go get 'em, tiger," she had said, God rest her soul). It was only when he threw on his jacket and did a final inspection in the bathroom mirror that he sensed something was amiss. It was his jacket; it felt light. Todd patted his chest and checked all the pockets and was puzzled to discover that his wallet was not there. He looked around the sink, in the bed, and under the rug. It was nowhere to be found.

Retracing his steps, a bitter realization slowly came to him, as all roads led back to the only possible culprit: his new Russian "friend," Anton. Todd realized it must have happened during those brief, convivial moments when Anton was singing to him, his arm draped over Todd's shoulder like an old Army buddy. The wallet would have been right there for the taking. Just to be sure, he tried the phone number Anton had given him. No surprise, it was disconnected. Todd sagged onto his bed, feeling like a chump. He had played right into the man's trap. And now, what was he going to do? All his money was in there. His credit cards...

Ring, *ring*, ring, *ring*.

Todd answered the phone. It was Andrei, down in the lobby. "Where are you, my man? The limo is here. Time for you to meet the lovely ladies!" Andrei was infectiously cheerful, but Todd was in no mood. It all seemed like a big con game to him now. He almost hung up with a big eff-you to the whole deal.

But then, he caught a glimpse of Svetlana's photo on the bedside table. It gave him pause. And the fact was, he had already paid up front, so if he didn't go, that would just be more money down the tubes. Bucking himself up as best he could, Todd mumbled an apology and told Andrei he'd be right down.

In the lobby, Ned and Phil were already there, dressed in ill-fitting suits and looking like they were on their way to job interviews. Phil was quizzing himself on a series of dating-chat flash cards, while Ned was pacing and fretting, wiping the sweat off his forehead with a monogrammed hankie. When they saw Todd, they both stopped what they were doing and tried to play it cool, as if they were just three buddies getting ready for a big night out on the town. These efforts were futile, of course, but they were also so pathetic that they offered Todd some solace, at least for a moment. *I may have problems*, he thought to himself, *and I may be a rube, but I'm still way better off than these two sad sacks.*

Soon after, the group piled into the limousine and journeyed through the capital city's gritty cobblestone streets to a nearby restaurant, The Golden Tchotchke.

The Tchotchke was a plush, dimly-lit place, decorated in shades of red and gold like a bordello, its mood set by a puffy-shirted pianist offering up a multilingual, airport-karaoke-quality rendition of Frank Sinatra's "Strangers in the Night" in the far corner.

As the men's eyes adjusted to the lack of light, Andrei led each of them to private, curtained booths that had been reserved for their respective dates. Todd took a seat in his booth's burgundy-leather banquette and quickly ordered a tall Stoli on the rocks. Still beating himself up over the lost wallet, he grabbed a menu and started trying to decipher the list of unfamiliar offerings, when a tall blonde with bee-stung lips slinked through the curtain and offered up a cautious smile.

"You are Todd, yes?" The voice was sultry. Todd had never heard his own name sound quite so delicious before.

"...Yes." Todd cleared his throat and lowered his own voice to sound more manly and self-assured. "Yes. I'm Todd. Todd Tisdale. You must be Svetlana, right?" Svetlana nodded. "You look beautiful. Even better than your picture. Please, sit down."

Todd scooted over to let her in, painfully aware of the fact that it was impossible to seem manly *or* self-assured while doing so. Accessing the cozy banquette, Svetlana demurely hiked up the hem of her already short skin-tight skirt, exposing several inches of shapely thigh, which Todd couldn't help but notice and admire and extrapolate upon. And with that, the entire tenor of the evening changed, as whatever reservations or regrets he had been clinging to about the events that led him up to this moment quickly vanished from his mind. It was, for him at least, love at first sight.

From there, things proceeded swimmingly—especially for a blind date in which the parties spoke different languages, came from different sides of the globe, and had nothing from which to operate other than a shared desire to find a suitable mate. For Todd, the toughest part was trying to act like he wasn't completely blown away by how smoking hot Svetlana was, and ignore the fact that if this were any of the nightclubs back in Sac Town, he wouldn't even stand a chance with her. Crooked teeth aside (which reminded him of the bartender, which reminded him of Anton, which reminded him of his wallet again—dammit!), she looked like a supermodel, and not that Todd had ever actually met a supermodel before, or even a *non*-super model, but he was pretty sure that if he had, she wouldn't have been nearly as sweet and down to earth as Svetlana was.

This, as Todd learned, was largely a product of Svetlana's humble beginnings. As she told it, she had been a poor country girl from the Ukraine who moved to the big city with big dreams, but instead got lonely and married the first guy who was nice to her—a guy who turned out to be not so nice, after all. This husband, Yuri, was around just long enough to get her knocked up before he was arrested and hauled off to prison for a litany of charges including, but not limited to, arson, extortion, and assault with a deadly weapon. And with that, Svetlana found herself on her own again, but now with a baby to care for, and no means or skills to do so. It was a time of hard work and tough lessons. Her parents were too poor to help her, nor could they welcome her back home without the fear of disgracing the family name. Svetlana was thus forced to take whatever menial work she could find, and making ends meet was difficult. She soon found that her beauty could curry her some favor with her male employers, though that came at a cost. But she had little Alek to think of, so ...

It was a heartbreaking story, to be sure, one that revealed Svetlana to not only be beautiful, but also noble and proud and selfless. However, for Todd, the whole situation seemed almost too good to be true. It was like the instant sense of fellowship he felt with his friend-cum-pickpocket, Anton. After that experience, he was wary. Was this just another trap for the naive American? A lie? A ruse?

On that note, Svetlana asked Todd to tell her about his own life in America. Reticent at first, Todd started with the nutshell version, but grew ever more expansive as she responded with genuine interest to the mention of his early athletic achievements, and to the college scholarship he had earned (though, in fact, it was only a partial scholarship, and actual "scholarship" had little or nothing to do with it). She was even more impressed to learn that he owned his own business, especially one as glamorous as selling tuxedoes, and touched that he attributed its founding and success to his late wife, Angie. Additionally, she made flattering remarks about his big, strong arms, his boyish smile, and his warm, hearty laugh ("You almost sound Russian!" she exclaimed).

So much for Todd's wariness. He was won over all over again. And soon, with his skepticism cast aside, he and Svetlana had transcended this usual first-date chatter and moved on to deeper, more intimate issues. Which, after all, was a necessity. While still trying to maintain a low-key approach, the fact was, both of them had motives for more than just a casual date, and the rigid timeline of Todd's visit demanded that they get everything on the table quickly so that decisions could be made.

It was in this spirit that Todd finally came clean about his own ill-advised first marriage, to Katy Kapowski. It was a black mark, a youthful mistake in judgment, one that they had in common, and Todd told Svetlana all about his experiences with the scheming Tupperware temptress to prove it. Digging for other such potential bonds, he also found that they were both hard workers, and no strangers to hard luck—and yet, they both had the grit to stand up and make a change for the better. Both of them loved sports, although Svetlana was more of a basketball fan herself. And, both also agreed that *True Lies* was Arnold's best movie. On top of this, Svetlana loved California (Anton was right about this much), and Todd was in love with the idea of becoming a father figure for Alek, whose school picture revealed a scrappy little rascal with rosy cheeks, his mother's blonde hair, and a lovable tough-guy attitude.

There was also, last but not least, the matter of sexual chemistry. In Svetlana, Todd saw a drop-dead exotic beauty who could satisfy all of his wildest Bond-girl fantasies. He was sold from the get-go. With Lana, the sense of attraction may have been less visceral, and less immediate, but Todd could tell he was winning her over. She even said, at one point, "You are like a big teddy bear," and threw her arms around his neck to prove it. So there was a spark there. Todd felt it. It was undeniable.

At the end of the night, Svetlana asked Todd if he wanted to spend more time with her the following day, before the big party. Todd wanted nothing more than this, but he was too embarrassed to tell her about his stolen wallet, which left him with no cash and a pressing need to spend time canceling credit cards and procuring replacement IDs. He instead deployed his trusty "business obligations" excuse, and promised he would do everything in his power to "get the deals done fast" and get a hold of her before the party. Svetlana accepted all of this stoically, her poker face far better than Todd's.

Walking her out of the restaurant, Todd gallantly insisted that she take his limousine home. As she slipped into the back seat, Todd kissed her on both cheeks (à la Bond), and Svetlana reciprocated with a tender smooch of her own, a kiss that resonated throughout his body and left a scent of apricots in its wake. And even though it was all quite chaste and proper in form, Todd had to use every ounce of his willpower not to jump in after her, while also contorting his body to hide the telltale tumescence that was lurking deep inside his pleated Docker chinos.

As he waved a final good-bye and the car disappeared into the night, Ned and Phil emerged from the Tchotchke with their own dates. Phil, the flash-card guy, was with Ludmilla, a woman also on Todd's short list, whom he was slated to visit with at the next evening's big party. Seeing her in the flesh, Todd was happy to note that, even though she was reasonably attractive in a Soviet-gymnast kind of way, she couldn't hold a candle to his Svetlana. He smiled, once again congratulating himself on his decision. His comrades, however, were not smiling at all. In their faces, and the faces of their dates, he saw only dejection and disappointment.

But while this may have been true, there was more to it than that. "Hey!" Phil called out. "Where the hell is our car going?"

Only then did Todd realize the error of his actions. Apologizing profusely, he immediately took charge and flagged down a stray cab, all five of them cramming into the backseat for a crowded and painfully awkward ride home that was made even worse by the fact that the ladies lived out in factory-district housing, and the cabbie seemed determined to bilk the foreigners for as large a fare as possible. As if this weren't bad enough, Todd—whose actions had necessitated this alternative transport in the first place—had to sheepishly inform the other guys that he had no cash with which to cover the tab, or even contribute to it. Ned and Phil were forced to split the extortive sum themselves, and although Todd apologized profusely yet again once they reached the hotel, he sensed that the guys, Phil in particular, held a grudge.

Back in his room, Todd immediately launched into the task of making all the calls necessary to safeguard his credit (what there was of it) and his good name, and get proof of his own identity for the return trip home. Because of time zone and translation issues, this was not an easy thing to do. However, Todd was determined, not only because he wanted to keep his promise to Lana, but also because he feared what might happen if he was to fail. Visions of KGB agents smashing down his door, and years spent on an icy, wind-ravaged gulag as a suspected spy, haunted his thoughts.

Three hours later, he had finally managed to cancel all his cards, but not before the wily Anton—if, indeed, that was even his real name—had used those cards to go on a lavish spending spree, buying several expensive suits, an evening with a pricey call girl, and a fancy seven-course dinner for two, ostensibly for himself and the aforementioned lady friend. Thank God for theft insurance.

As for the IDs, however, Todd was unable to accomplish anything via telephone. For that, he needed to speak to someone at the American embassy, on-site and in person, and they would apparently receive no visitors, save for the gravest of emergencies (gulags, KGB thuggeries, etc.), until nine the following morning.

Todd got there promptly at 9:45. While the intention had been to get there right as the doors opened, with no money for a cab he was forced to go by foot. With the combination of some wrong turns, and the need to stop for a rejuvenating cup of coffee and a croissant (he found a couple bucks in his pants pocket en route), it was a delay that was unavoidable.

As a result, however, Todd found himself at the end of a long line of fellow—but far more punctual—travelers and émigrés in need of assistance. A lengthy, back-aching wait thus ensued before Todd finally reached the head of the queue, granting him audience with some low-level clerk, whose sole power was to hand him reams of paperwork to fill out, which in turn led to an even *more* interminable wait as this paperwork was shuffled through the rusty cogs of the bureaucratic machine.

Four hours later, Todd's name was finally called. Led into a windowless inner sanctum, he underwent a rigorous vital-stat recitation and signature analysis to prove that he truly *was* Todd Terrell Tisdale Jr. of Sacramento, California, before a pasty-faced factotum took his photo (crooked smile, bad lighting, multiple chins) and laminated it onto a temporary-issue passport, good for the remainder of his stay. Todd was also able to procure five crisp new hundred-dollar bills, wired from his dwindling account back home, which the factotum strongly urged him to exchange for traveler's checks as soon as possible. Todd thanked the man for this advice, but now that his KGB fears had been quelled, his biggest concern was to reconnoiter with Svetlana right away, and get their budding romance back on track.

Unfortunately, this did not prove to be nearly as easy as Todd had hoped. By the time his "meeting" was done, it was already mid-afternoon. Racing to the nearest phone, Todd dialed up Svetlana's number, hoping that she would be there, eagerly awaiting his call. Instead, his effort was met only by an outgoing message in hurried Russian, which he was unable to decipher save for her name and a single word: "good-bye." Todd had no choice but to leave a message of his own, explaining in his best American Industrialist's voice that "negotiations had taken longer than expected" and that he would try her again later. But even as he did so, an unspoken fear was building up inside of him, that his opportunity might have already been lost; that Svetlana was *already* "back on track," but with someone other than him.

The rest of the day did nothing to allay this fear. Todd tried phoning Svetlana two more times. Both calls were met by this same inscrutable recording. Worse still, Todd wasn't even able to leave a message after the second call, as an annoying beep cut him off, signaling that her tape was already full with messages from what he was now certain were other ardent suitors, whose wallets had not been stolen, and who thus had the upper hand in winning her affections.

This was a crushing blow for Todd, who had been so certain that this trip was destined, despite all his travails, to be a success. With instead an abject failure staring him in the face, Todd proceeded to do what any red-blooded American alpha male in his situation would do: he began to drink, heavily.

Two hours later, the mini-bar was decimated, a swarm of empty cans and sampler bottles littered the room from end to end, and it was time to get ready for the big party.

"Whoop-de-fuckin'-do!" Todd growled to himself, as he stumbled out of the bathroom and started fumbling with the studs on his tuxedo shirt.

The alcohol had done little to help Todd's spirits. Resigned to the suspicion that Svetlana was now in the company of another man, he had adopted a rather dangerous, devil-may-care nihilism about the proceedings to come. He was a ticking time bomb, a man with nothing to lose, one who had no intention whatsoever of going quietly into the night. Oh, no, not by a long shot. If he had anything to say about it, and he did, the Czech-Mate contingent, male and female, master and servant, would all know goddamn well that Todd Terrell Tisdale Jr. had been there.

On that note, Todd threw on his jacket, patted his pockets to make sure his cash and new passport were there, and staggered out the door.

18
MAXIMUM SECURITY

After the shock of walking in on Wade and Estelle together in bed, Rowena had turned right back around, headed straight out Wade's front door, and never looked back. This was true, even when Wade came running after her, hopping down the driveway with his jeans at half-mast as if it were some sort of hillbilly sack race, showing off the crack of his ass to anyone who happened to be passing by. And it remained so when he tried calling her, starting that afternoon and continuing on for the next several days. She refused to pick up, no matter how often or how hard he tried. What was the point? Whatever he might have to say, Rowena knew, would be a total lie. He was a dog, just like she always knew he was, and she should have known better. Hell, she *did* know better, but she just went right ahead and did it, anyway.

As for Estelle, that was a more painful split. The two had been best friends for as long as she'd care to remember, and even though it was true that they were attracted to the same type of guys, and indeed had dated some of the *same* guys through the years, neither one of them had ever gone and done anything nasty like that before. It was like an unwritten rule, and Rowena was hurt, especially seeing as how it was Estelle who had set them up in the first place. If she had wanted him so bad, Rowena reasoned, she should have just gone right ahead and taken him that first night, without getting her caught up in the middle of things and ruining a perfectly good friendship in the process.

Needless to say, she had quit her job at Golden Child as well. The only reason she had worked there in the first place was Estelle. When she told the story to Dimitri, he sided with her completely, writing her a nice letter of recommendation and consoling her the best he knew how, while also making one last attempt to score with her himself. Ugh. Good riddance. Good riddance to him and her and that whole sleazy situation.

But while Rowena had taken the high road, the result was that she was back to square one again. Square zero, actually; with no job, no boyfriend, and no best friend, either, she had managed to wipe out her employment *and* her social life in one fell swoop. And with her mother still acting out of sorts, too, she realized that, in many ways, she was more alone now than ever before.

At a crossroads, unsure what to do next or where to turn, Rowena had suddenly recalled a flyer that she had seen posted on the church bulletin board, announcing available positions for the annual Halloween stand that went up every fall next to the mini-golf place out by the freeway. It was a seasonal gig, lasting only a month or so, but it started immediately and paid a decent wage for what was actually pretty easy work. It would also allow her to spend a part of every day out-of-doors, a welcome change of pace after her last two jobs. On top of that, employees got to pick out one free pumpkin and get a costume at half-price. Not a bad deal, Rowena thought. With Dimitri's letter in hand, she went down first thing the following morning and got hired on the spot.

While it wasn't exactly her dream job, Rowena was pleased, nevertheless. It gave her the fresh start she needed, right at the moment when she needed it most. And better still, she had made it happen, just her, without any help from anybody.

And in fact, this wasn't the only way in which Rowena found herself quickly getting back on her feet. While it was true that her weekends were likely to be rather quiet at first without her old posse from the local bar scene, Rowena had instead turned to, and found tender solace in, her favorite pen pal, Lyle Pettigrew.

As it so happens, in the whirlwind weeks that she'd dated Wade, Rowena had lost touch with many of her inmate friends, largely because her own correspondence time had been so greatly curtailed. But not Lyle. He had kept writing, reliably and faithfully, his notes continuing to arrive every two to three days, even though Rowena was lucky if she could churn out one per week. This had not gone unnoticed, either, as Lyle had repeatedly voiced his concern in his letters, asking if she was all right and if he had done anything to offend her. Such a gentleman. After her destined-to-fail fling with Wade, it was refreshing to find a man who clearly knew how to treat a lady right for a change, even if he was currently residing in a maximum security prison for his role in an armed robbery.

Lyle had come clean to Rowena about this, it's worth noting, and without any prompting whatsoever. Over the course of his last two letters, he had confessed, in great detail, exactly why he was there, what led him to do what he did even though he knew it was wrong, and what he had been doing to rehabilitate himself so that he could get a fresh start upon his release. It was all very sad and touching and sincere, and Rowena believed him when he said it was a mistake he had learned from and would not repeat.

As Lyle told it, he and his buddy Lonnie had been laid off from their jobs at the herbicide factory down in Chino, just two weeks before Christmas back in 1999. Having suffered a similar fate not so long ago, Rowena empathized with Lyle's anger, as well as his lingering sense of betrayal over it. She was less won over, however, by his and Lonnie's ensuing plan to regain their self-esteem by purchasing shotguns and robbing the factory's payroll offices. But it was a desperate time, and Lyle's letters made it clear that it was precisely that desperation that made him pursue such a drastic course of action.

The crime (and that's what it was, no matter how remorseful Lyle was; Rowena made sure to keep a clear head about this) had unfolded on, of all nights, New Year's Eve, which was also the millennium's eve, and—due to all the Y2K scares—also, to their ultimate dismay, perhaps the most heavily secured night of the year. With a set of gate keys that they had copied off a security guard friend, the two had snuck in through the rear of the facility, with no break-in or brandishing of weapons required. Lyle emphasized, in fact, that they had no intention of firing their guns at all. They were just for show. Lyle was not a violent man. He stressed this repeatedly. He would not so much as hurt a fly.

Anyway, not surprisingly based on Lyle's current place of residence, the plan hit a snag. Sneaking in, Lyle and Lonnie had noticed the inordinate number of guards on duty. But, being already on site and emotionally committed, they continued on anyway, in their all-black clothes and masks, to the payroll office, back by the chemical silos. There, Lyle was able to pick the lock and jerry open the door when, all of a sudden, the lights came on and they found themselves facing a roomful of armed guards, standing there with party hats and noise makers, bottles of champagne at the ready.

As fate would have it, one of the guards, Ernesto, had been assigned a graveyard shift even though it fell on his thirtieth birthday, and his buddies on the force had hatched a scheme to brighten up the night with a little surprise party for him—a party that Lonnie and Lyle had obviously not been aware of, much less invited to. The fact that they were both carrying shotguns, and dressed precisely like the thieves they had intended to be, only made matters even worse.

Since the two would-be burglars were outnumbered and outgunned by a vast margin, rendering any chance for a daring Butch-and-Sundance-type escape out of the question, they both simply threw their hands up and surrendered peaceably. A couple of the guards, sympathetic to the situation, even poured them each a glass of the bubbly before hauling them off.

The bitch of the thing, as they learned after being cuffed and shoved into the back of a paddy wagon, was that there was no money in the office anyway; all the petty cash accounts had been drained to help pay for Christmas bonuses and holiday decorating expenses. Ho ho ho. Happy fucking New Year.

Rowena felt for Lyle, she really did. He seemed like a good guy who simply got pushed too far at the wrong time and made a horrible mistake before he got his right mind back. And she could tell from his letters that he had learned from his mistakes. He talked of his love for mechanics. He could fix just about anything, he claimed, and had earned some status among his peers on the cell block for doing just that, repairing everything from TVs and clock radios to prosthetic limbs and toilet stills. Rowena figured this would prove to be a valuable skill once he got released, one that would allow him to find gainful employment despite his criminal record. She was encouraged that both his intentions and his prospects seemed genuine.

Thus, when Lyle closed his latest missive with an invitation to come up to Vacaville for a visit sometime, Rowena had a big decision to make. The timing wasn't great. She was still reeling from the whole mess with Wade, and she had just started her new job. On top of all that, she was reluctant to stray too far from her mom, at least until she got a better sense of what her problem might be. During her last visit, Connie had suddenly started talking about the flowers she wanted to plant and the hedges she wanted trimmed, and it finally dawned on Rowena that her mom thought she was speaking to her neighborhood lawn boy, Pedro.

On the other hand, Lyle had been honest with her, and true-blue all the way, and that ought to be supported, or else how does anybody *ever* get rehabilitated? And the fact was, she had a good feeling about Lyle. He may have done a bad thing, yes, but he was no bad boy like Randy or Wade; that much was clear from his letters. Rather, he was a sensitive soul, not unlike herself, and maybe that was what she needed in her life right now, just as it seemed that he needed someone like her.

Weighing all the pros and cons—no pun intended—Rowena's choice suddenly became crystal clear.

Two days later, on her first day off from the Halloween stand, Rowena hopped in her Tercel with a tattered Northern California road map by her side and hit the road, headed for Vacaville State Prison.

Just a quick ninety minutes from Sacramento on a straight shoot up Interstate 80—in all honesty, a far more pleasant drive than Rowena had ever expected—the city of Vacaville was tucked into the heart of an idyllic, pine-wooded dale, just one hill over from that world-famous Mecca of wine making, Napa Valley. Much to its credit, Vacaville had an ample supply of rustic charm, too, its tree-lined streets populated with all sorts of cute shops and cafés and parks. Thus, it was hard at first glance for Rowena to believe that the quaint little burg, billed on banners and park benches as "The City with a Small Town Heart," was also home to a sizable population of the western United States' most hardened and recalcitrant felons. But, indeed, that's what it was.

Rowena faced that reality head-on as she followed the State Prison signs—which were far less conspicuous than those trumpeting the area's "Small Town Heart"—to a daunting barbed-wire perimeter on the community's seamiest outskirts, passed through an armed-guarded gate, and drove onto the grimly desolate grounds of the prison itself. From there, it was more of the same, as she was led through a series of rigorous security checkpoints, which helped assure to the satisfaction of the prison staffers that her car, clothes, purse, shoes, and body cavities were all free of any contraband materials.

Once this gauntlet was run, and Rowena was sufficiently traumatized in a *Scared Straight* kind of way, she was escorted to her ultimate destination: a narrow concrete-block-walled room, divided neatly into more or less equal halves by a wall of thick metal and bulletproof plexiglass. It was there that she was to finally meet Lyle, her ardently devoted pen pal, for their first-ever face-to-face visit.

And while this visit may have been entirely voluntary on her part, the fact was that the longer it was delayed by all the checkpoints and invasive procedures, the more anxious Rowena became about it. The reason for this was simple, and perfectly understandable: while Lyle had been in possession of Rowena's photo for the last several weeks now, he had never returned the favor and sent a picture of himself to her. And although she had tried to convince herself that it didn't matter what he looked like, the fact was, she knew in her heart of hearts that it did. The question then became, *how much* did it matter? And where exactly would she draw the line?

Take, for instance, the issue of tattoos. Rowena didn't mind a tattoo here or there on a man; she'd even found them pretty damn sexy on occasion. But what if Lyle was one of those guys with hissing serpents coiled around his biceps and a huge horned demon on his back? Or, what if he was one of those weightlifter freaks that prisons always seem to attract, with a bunch of jagged scars and unexplained rashes and acne pits on his face and a crazed gleam in his eye? Or, worse still, what if he had that pasty, weak-chinned child molester look? Ugh. Rowena couldn't even bear to think of it.

But while Rowena's mind went over the grim rubric of possibilities, the one image she refused to even acknowledge as a possibility was that he might actually turn out to be tall and handsome. She knew that to hope for such a thing would not only set her up for yet more disappointment, but it would also be unfair to him. He had written those letters, the letters she had come to cherish, and so at the very least he deserved one visit from her in which she expressed her appreciation not only through her words, but also through her reactions, which thus demanded that she exude nothing but goodwill and admiration for both him *and* his appearance, whatever the case may be.

Tick. Tick. Tick. Tick.

The bolted-down clock on the wall kept counting off the seconds. Rowena sat on her stiff-backed metal chair, also bolted down, trying her best to look at ease, while other prisoners and their guests conducted visits on all sides of her.

To her left, a pony-tailed defense attorney conferred with his dead-eyed client, whispering, "Tell me the truth, Vincent. Did you give that old lady a roofie or not?"

On the other side, a harried young wife with straggly, prematurely gray hair juggled a colicky baby while trying her best to talk dirty through the voice box to her incarcerated hubby, who was moaning, eyes closed, his hands moving rapidly under the table. "Oh yeah, oh yeah, oh yeah!"

Oh, Lord! It was enough to make Rowena, already on edge, go fleeing for the door. But then, of course, there were the stone-faced guards, positioned at all corners of the room, hands perched on the butts of their guns and Tasers, on alert for any kind of sudden movement. They would not, Rowena realized, respond kindly to any such door-darting actions on her part.

Just as she realized that she had no choice but to go through with this thing, a buzzer sounded beside the far door, the one that accessed the inmate holding area. And not a moment later, a non-felonious-looking white male, six feet in height, with short strawberry-blond hair and a neatly-trimmed goatee and only one visible tattoo on his well-muscled arms, stepped through the door and entered the space, his cuffed hands making him look penitent and his kind, sensitive blue eyes staring right at her, looking altogether better than she would have ever allowed herself to even imagine. And so, as he kept approaching, and the guard stepped forward with a large ring of keys to unlock his cuffs and whisper the usual rote warnings, Rowena held her breath and hoped upon hope that he was the one, until he finally took a seat directly across from hers and uttered her name, "Rowena," with a deep, soothing voice and a warm, welcoming smile. And only then, *only then*, did Rowena allow herself to exhale and accept the fact that God had finally smiled down upon her. That this indeed was the same man who had written her all those sweet letters. This was Lyle. Her Lyle.

With her body visibly relaxing and her face melting into an easy smile, Rowena offered up a warm, familiar, and brazenly flirty greeting of her own, "Hey, you," and the two began to chat away like old friends, just as they had done in their correspondences. And despite all her previous reservations and their far-from-idyllic surroundings, Rowena suddenly found herself feeling safer and more hopeful with Lyle than she had with any other man in her entire life.

19

AND THE WALL COMES
TUMBLING DOWN

In the back of a black stretch limousine, en route to the
highly-anticipated Berlin Wall party, Todd Tisdale sat
mired in a deep, funereal funk. While the occasion should
have been a cause for raucous celebration, instead an air of
impending doom hung over the ride. On top of Svetlana having
gone missing, Andrei, the group's organizer and cheerleader,
was also absent from the scene, ostensibly owing to other party-
related responsibilities, and so was Phil, the flashcard-wielding
Californian. It sent a Grim Reaper chill down Todd's spine to
think that it might actually be that insufferable egghead, of all
people, who had swooped in and usurped Lana's affections in
his place.

With these unexplained absences, the only other person
in the limo with Todd was Ned, the short, hapless Brit who
had so clearly crashed and burned with his date the night
before. To his credit, Ned had pulled himself together for the
night's festivities as well as could have been expected. With
his Scottish tartan vest and Union Jack lapel pin trumpeting

his British citizenry, a status clearly intended as a major selling point with the ladies, he even looked vaguely distinguished—especially since he was now sans the toilet-paper, razor-nick bandages that had graced his visage the night before. Perhaps there was a sliver of hope for him after all.

As for Todd, his tuxedo looked quite dapper on him, too, and he had accessorized it well, all the way down to a snazzy set of pearl cufflinks and studs. Alas, the excessive mini-bar plundering he'd engaged in prior to the ride detracted greatly from this sartorial splendor and its intended suave 007 effect, lending him instead the debauched air of a drunken ne'er-do-well uncle at a family wedding.

However, Todd was in no frame of mind to notice or even care about such trivialities. Instead, he stewed in the juices of his own bottomless remorse, revisiting all the myriad things that had gone so horribly awry during his short time abroad, while also taking a full and fairly honest accounting of his own role in these woes—including, among other transgressions, gullibility, deceit, selfishness, and sloth.

In so doing, he was the one to finally break the awkward silence, offering Ned a slurred but sincere apology.

"I got your money, by the way. Wasn't trying to stiff you."

Ned turned, his brow furrowed in confusion. It took him a moment to realize what Todd was trying to say. Then, with the kind of gentle smile one might offer a child: "Oh. From last night, you mean? Think nothing of it, laddie. We're all a bit out of sorts here. Just trying to find our way, right?"

Todd nodded—or perhaps it was just a toxic spasm—and endeavored to offer some platitude of his own before a vicious belch got the better of him. Indeed, even he now seemed a bit taken aback by how thoroughly blotto he had gotten in so short a time, which in turn reminded him to add "gluttony" to his list of sins.

Ned took this as a cue to keep speaking. "Got your sights on anybody special tonight? I saw you with that one bird. Quite a looker, she was."

Todd froze a beat. Then, he looked up to the limo's moonroof. To the heavens above. Shaking his head, over and over. "Svetlana ... oh, God ... Svetlana ..."

Off the bitter melancholy in Todd's voice, Ned averted his eyes and scooted farther back on the limo's leather seat, suddenly seeming quite leery of what this hot-headed American might be capable of next. To be sure, Todd's demeanor suggested it was wiser to tread lightly.

Todd continued to gaze up to the heavens, as his hands guided their way blindly toward the complimentary bottle of vodka on the rail. He proceeded to pour a glass up to the rim, still not looking, like some sort of parlor trick. When the pour was complete, Todd plopped a single cube of ice into the mix and then delicately hoisted the vessel to his lips as if it were a communion chalice. Upon fully draining the glass, a look of wounded introspection came over his features. He turned to Ned, huddled now against the exit door, warily watching this display out of the corner of his eye.

"Weaker sex? My ass! Look what they do to us! Just break our hearts or bust our balls, every single time! And we let 'em do it! Why? Why do we even bother?"

Todd refilled his glass. Ned, clearly stricken by the plainspoken truth of Todd's words, withdrew momentarily into painful recollections of his own before adding, with an uncharacteristic boldness, "The bloody bitches!"

He then reached for the vodka himself, pouring a glass that matched Todd's in its vigor, all the way down to the rakish addition of a single icy cube. It was a meeting of the minds for a pair of sad, love-hungry souls that needed no further words. The two spent the rest of the ride self-medicating themselves into a blissful oblivion.

***

The Pavlova Ballroom, in the Karapov Palace, situated on the fashionable east end of Gorky Park, was a lovely place to throw a party. Indeed, it had been home to an endless swirl of formal balls and charity galas and lively Politburo torture-interrogations for well over a century now. But if one was looking to really cut loose and perhaps don a lampshade or two, which was the direction in which Todd's fate now seemed to be steering him, it was not nearly so ideal. Filled with Chippendale furnishings and Tiffany chandeliers and other such finery, it was like a museum, which Todd had already taken a disliking to, and which, by placing him once again in its midst while in his current state, was like throwing a lit Molotov cocktail onto a towering pile of dry leaves.

This danger became apparent from the very first moment that Todd staggered out of the limo's back seat and up onto the curb, his arms wrapped around the equally intoxicated Ned. As a matronly hostess from the party's welcoming committee stepped forward to hand the men their nametags, Todd grabbed his and immediately slapped it onto the seat of his trousers, with an uproarious Ned quickly following suit.

Andrei, who was already on-site and thankfully close at hand, quickly swooped in to suss out the source of this unruliness. "Hello, gentlemen. Is there anything I can help you with? Any problems?"

"No problem, boss. Just having a few laughs with my little buddy Ned here."

Todd tried to ease past, his eyes already locked on the bar set up in the palace's grand entrance hall. But Andrei blocked his path. "You do not seem well, my friend. Why? I do not understand. I hear from Svetlana that your date went quite well."

"Yeah? Well, if you did, you got one on me. Now if you'll excuse me, I think I see a bottle with my name on it."

Todd again tried to move on, but Andrei persisted. "Todd, if there has been any *difficulty* with Svetlana, this I do not know. But I worry that you are maybe too quick to judge. The night is young. And Ludmilla, she is here too already, waiting to see you."

"Ludmilla, right. Okay, why not? But first things first."

With this, Todd made another end run for the bar, his grizzly-bear grasp still guiding Ned along with him. Andrei chose not to try and stop them. Todd had the right of way. Nevertheless, he stayed close by their side.

"I must ask that you be a little cautious with the drinking, Todd. Like I say, the night is young, and it appears you and Ned may have already had a cocktail or two, yes?"

"Guilty as charged, brother." Ned snickered again, as Todd barged his way up to the unwitting barkeep. "Two of those, Der Kommissar, and don't hold back. Fill 'em all the way to the top."

But Andrei was not so easily dismissed. He had other clients to consider, and the last thing he wanted was some vulgar American vomiting all over them.

"Yes, yes. Your drinks will be exactly as you wish," he insisted, all the while signaling the bartender to dilute the drinks and steering the men clear so the deed could be done. "In the meantime, allow me to show you where you will be meeting your lady friends."

By the time Andrei was finished, the deceit was a fait accompli as well. Todd and Ned grabbed their glasses and took healthy slugs, their taste buds already too numbed to tell the difference. "Now *that's* what I call a drink, right, partner?" Ned laughed and the two clinked glasses, happy as larks. Andrei looked on silently, acting none the wiser, then guided them away from the booze and farther into the palace.

"The ballroom is this way, gentlemen. And the private sitting rooms where you will meet the ladies are immediately adjacent. Oh, and Todd, I happened to notice that your name tag somehow got misplaced ..."

Not long after, Andrei guided Todd into one of the parlors, where Ludmilla was already waiting for him. It was yet another chintz-filled space that left Todd cold, everything about it appearing overly delicate and on the verge of imminent collapse—including Ludmilla herself. She was a tiny woman, thin as a rail, whose physical fragility carried over into her facial features, especially her large, saucer-shaped eyes. She looked trapped, like a rabbit in a cage. Thus, when Todd swaggered in like Foghorn Leghorn, drink in hand, greeting her with an overzealously firm handshake and immediately asking if she wanted to go do some shots while they chatted, it was, for her, a rather jarring start to their visit. Ludmilla was not much of a drinker, as it turned out, and not much of a sports fan, and she knew next to nothing about Arnold Schwarzenegger. Rather, she preferred bird watching, and Victorian architecture, and snuggling up with a good book. Todd nodded and mmm-hmmed to all this, as politely as he knew how, then let loose a yawn and once again posited the notion of doing shots. Ludmilla again demurred. Silence ensued.

It was, needless to say, not a love connection.

As the silence thickened like old soup and the sound of music began wafting in from outside their increasingly tomb-like room, the two quickly agreed to forego the rest of their allotted time and join the party instead. Racing one another for the exit, they both burst out to find that the party was now in full swing. Men and women were mingling, and the dance floor was aswirl with couples waltzing. But while this was what captured Ludmilla's attention, Todd instead zoomed in on the bar at the far corner of the hall, where his buddy Ned already queuing up.

Surmising from Ned's slumped shoulders and gallows stare that he had gotten shot down yet again, Todd felt genuine pity for the sweet if slightly trollish man. And from that pity sprang an idea.

"Milla, follow me. I got a buddy over here I want you to meet."

After her time with Todd, meeting one of his pals was likely the last thing Ludmilla wished to do. She tried her best to beg off. "I don't know. I should probably, uh ..." She looked all around, searching for some plausible excuse to flee.

Todd took this hesitation as his cue. "Oh, come on! He's British. He wears bow ties. He talks like a professor. He does all sorts of fancy shit. You'll love him."

"I really don't think, uh ... I think I see a friend ..."

As Ludmilla gestured vaguely toward a gaggle of owlish spinsters with whom she might or might not have been actually acquainted, Todd grabbed her elbow, refusing to take no for an answer. "This'll just take a sec."

Todd dragged Ludmilla over to Ned and made hearty introductions. While both were wary of Todd's judgment, especially in his present condition, once they laid eyes on each other, it was an instant alchemic reaction. Within moments, they were chatting away about books and birds and other such "fancy shit" as if they had known one another their entire lives. Todd slowly inched away to let them continue on their own, pleased by the successful outcome, but also eager to replenish his glass.

And that is when he saw her. Standing at the door in a white chiffon dress, looking incandescent, like a princess from a fairy tale. It was Svetlana. And it was impossible to know how long she had been there, but she was staring right at him, and he stared right back, full of desire and longing and regret.

Indeed, it would have been a magical moment, one which Todd could have used as a centerpiece for the "whirlwind romance" story he planned to share with Arnold and the others back home—save for one thing: Phil (a.k.a. Flash-Card Phil, Pocket Protector Phil, Badly-Balding Phil) was at her side.

Breaking eye contact with Todd, Svetlana whispered to Phil, who crossed his arms and leveled Todd with an icy glare, full of nerdy malevolence. But as Lana continued to prevail upon him—and God bless her for it—Phil finally acquiesced.

As she broke away, Todd headed straight for her, weaving through the crowd, all the while keeping one eye on Phil, who had turned his back on the scene and was now pretending to be riveted by the less-than-enthralling art on the walls. It was almost as if the weaselly bastard didn't even view Todd as a viable competitor anymore. And Todd, who was nothing if not competitive, took this not only as an insult but as a challenge. He wanted Svetlana back, and he knew with all his heart that he was better for her, and she for him. That it was destiny. And thus, Todd vowed to make Phil rue the day he ever underestimated him.

On that note, he finally reached Svetlana, at the center of the dance floor. He took her hand and achingly uttered her name: "Svetlana."

"Hello, Todd," Svetlana replied, her voice a bit cooler in tone.

"I missed you today."

"I miss you, too. You do not call like you say."

"No, no! I called! I did! I left three messages."

"I was there. No calls."

"No, I did, you can check! It was late, I know. But I had that meeting to go to, and, and—"

Todd stopped himself, his eyes no longer able to meet hers. He hung his head in shame. "Ah, fuck it. No, I didn't. It's all bullshit. The truth is, my wallet got stolen, okay? Last night, before I saw you. It had all my money and credit cards and IDs. I had to go to the embassy to get it fixed and it took forever, so I didn't get a chance to call you till almost four o'clock. But you were gone already. And with him, right? With Phil."

"Yes. He call me. He get my number from the Czech-Mate people. He say he see me at the restaurant and want to talk."

"Yeah, I bet he did. Did he bring his flash cards?"

"His what? No. But he is ... very nice man. Very sweet man. He meet my son. They seem to get along ..." Svetlana bit her lip and looked over to Phil, who turned from the naked-cherub fresco he was idly perusing to catch her eye.

Todd scowled and scooted sideways to block Phil's sightline, a trick he learned from his days blitzing quarterbacks. "So what are you saying here? I thought you and me ... I thought we really hit it off."

"Yes. I think so, too. But Philip, he really talk to me. Tell me how lonely he is. How he make so much money at his job in the Silicone Valley and have such big house and no one to share it with. He say he want us to come live with him. To be with him."

"But I want that, too. That's all I want."

"You did not say, so I do not know."

"So, what? He did? He said all those things, already?"

"Yes."

"So did he actually propose to you?"

"Yes, I did," came the answer from a smarmy voice directly at his back.

Todd turned to Phil, who was at least four inches shorter, which normally would have given Todd the upper hand but which, under the circumstances, only made him feel like even more of a sap.

Phil seemed to sense this. Worse, he appeared to be reveling in it. "It was a little spontaneous of me, I know, but I learned in business that when something feels right, one should always—"

"Yeah, yeah."

Todd resisted the urge to punch Phil, and instead turned back to Svetlana.

"And what did you say? You didn't say yes? Tell me you didn't say yes."

"She said—"

"I asked *her*," Todd growled, eyes still on Svetlana.

"I say I need some time."

"So you didn't."

"Not yet, but—"

"Butt out for a second here, Phil, okay?"

"I will do no such thing! I have just as much a right—"

"Right, and you said your say, and she said she'd think about it, so scram already. Go get a drink. You look like you could use one."

Phil started to protest again, but then he saw the look in Todd's eyes, a look made especially fearsome because his pupils were dilated and his eyes bloodshot from all the vodka he'd consumed. It was a look that flashed Phil back to his traumatic school days, when he was mercilessly taunted for his inability to play handball or kickball or indeed childhood games of any sort that didn't involve joysticks or advanced algorithms.

Phil took a step back. "This isn't right. It's not right. I'm going to get Andrei."

"You do that."

Phil cast a final begging glance to Svetlana, hoping she might somehow step in to solve this problem for him. When that didn't happen, he instead scurried off to locate Andrei, much as he had gone in search of gym teachers and principals for protection back in the day.

Todd turned back to Svetlana. Her poker face was on. "That was not so nice."

"I'll apologize later."

"He is a good man."

"So am I."

"You are drunk."

"I've had a few, yeah. I was upset. I wanted to see you again."

"Is that so?"

"You know it is. How could you not know? Look at me."

"So, you are seeing me now. We are here, just the two of us. What is it you want to say?"

Todd suddenly found himself completely tongue-tied. There was too much to say with too much at stake and too much pressure to get it exactly right. It was all on the line, right here, right now. He didn't want to make a mistake. Looking around the room for inspiration, he finally managed to blurt out, "Dance with me."

"That is all? After all that? You want to dance?"

"It's a start."

Todd grabbed Svetlana's hand and they started to move along with the couples all around them. The fact was, he wasn't much of a hoofer and never had been, particularly not when it came to this fancy ballroom stuff. But it was crucial now that he do his best to at least fake it. And with his tuxedo and her white dress, they certainly looked the part. Better yet, they moved well together, just as he knew they would. And with the gods seemingly, once again, looking out for him, he didn't trip or stumble or step on her toes, not even once.

As they twirled around the room, Svetlana seemed to be enjoying herself, and Todd basked in this pleasure right along with her. Until, that is, they both caught a glimpse of Phil reappearing, with Andrei in tow. The two men stood on the sidelines, not wanting to cause a scene but ready to pounce as soon as the song was over. Todd took this in, his eyes narrowed, ready for a fight. He wasn't sure what Phil had planned, or what Andrei could do to intervene, or what rules he may have broken, but he didn't care. This was his moment, and he planned to make the most of it.

"So Phil's been making all sorts of big promises, I guess, huh?"

"He say he want to take care of me, yes. Me and Alek."

"Yeah? Is that so? I don't see a ring on your finger yet."

"No. There is no ring." Svetlana's eyes gravitated to her unadorned left hand, perched atop Todd's right shoulder.

She then gazed up at Todd, her longing laid bare. And with that, Todd—realizing he'd found his edge, his open seam, as it were—offered up a big, game-winning grin.

"So, do you want one?"

Svetlana pulled back and stared at Todd quizzically, and Todd merely nodded to confirm what she likely already knew. And with that, Svetlana laughed and cried and did a little hop and hugged Todd tight. And while the tears of joy began to flow and Todd breathed in her lovely scent and pulled her even tighter, and it became clear to everyone around them what had just happened, including a disgruntled Phil (who was already whining to Andrei and wheedling him for a refund), it also became equally clear to Todd what he would soon be doing with the five crisp hundred dollar bills nestled safely inside his jacket pocket, and indeed with every other spare nickel and ounce of credit he could get his hands on.

III

MANIFEST DESTINIES

20

ELECTION DAY

The entire town of Sacramento was abuzz. It was unavoidable, like a plague of locusts, and this was true no matter who you were or how you lived or what your level of political awareness was. After a year of blackouts and budget crises and price-gouging scandals, followed by months of Gray Davis bashing and calls for his dismissal, leading to several *more* months of debate and appeals and editorial dissection, and culminating in a whirlwind two-month, three-ring-circus of a campaign season, it was finally here. October 7, 2003. The day of the first-ever California recall election.

However, as the day began, it was already abundantly clear who the big winner would be. Having successfully fended off a Fellini-esque assemblage of opponents, as well as the nagging rumors and accusations of illicit hanky-panky that still nipped at his heels, all the polls agreed that muscle-bound mega-star Arnold Schwarzenegger held a lead in the race that was all but insurmountable.

And to be sure, Arnold did not seem very worried, as he made a swaggering early morning appearance at his local upscale Brentwood, California, polling place, taking time to stop and joke around with the reporters about how he would be casting his vote for "whomevah hass da lonkest lass name."

But while things were all fun and games and breezy punch lines down in Brentwood, the approach up in the capital was a different thing entirely. This was the city's big moment in the sun—its chance to be, for once, the center of attention not just for the state, but for the entire planet. And indeed, despite the election's forgone conclusion and the notable absence of its main star attraction, the media had assembled there from all four corners of the globe to report on it. Thus, while one might question why people in such hard-luck outposts as Djibouti or Bulgaria could possibly care about the absurd travails of the Californian political landscape, they were represented, nevertheless, along with hundreds of others, all staying at the same hotels and chasing the same leads, speaking a polyglot swirl of different languages and dialects that would make even a Berlitz instructor's head spin, while in the process making downtown Sacramento seem far more exotic and worldly than it would have otherwise.

And this was a good thing. A *great* thing, actually. It not only brought some much-needed excitement to the proceedings, but it also brought the first ripples of what was perceived to be a new wave of sustainable energy for the city as a whole. Streets were crowded. Restaurants were full. Conversations were lively. Plans were hatched. Todd Tisdale's pie-in-the-sky predictions of a downtown renaissance seemed to be not just feasible, but actually coming to fruition, and it was all beginning right here. Right now. Today.

Of course, despite all the hullabaloo, time did not stand still, and people still had their own everyday lives to lead. For Spencer Brine, Election Day was one of both civic duty and career opportunity. He voted, of course, casting his ballot for the leading Democratic candidate, Cruz Bustamente, as he had planned all along, because he honestly felt that Cruz, although clearly not the most charismatic candidate, was the most qualified for the job.

The bigger challenge was getting Nikki to vote, too. She was of the mind that her vote didn't matter, and that making the effort was just a waste of her precious time, when she could instead be resting up and getting ready for her shift at the club, which was expected to be an unusually busy one, especially for a Tuesday. Spencer responded with what he felt was a rather stirring lecture on the rights and privileges of living in a democratic society, accompanied by examples of important elections that were decided by the slimmest of margins in which, indeed, every vote truly *did* count.

The result was that, after staging one last-gasp attempt to stall matters with a morning quickie—which worked, by the way; Spencer wasn't crazy—Nikki got out of bed, got dressed, and got in Spencer's Volvo to join him down at the nearby junior high school cafeteria to cast her ballot. And while Spencer made no effort to sway Nikki's decision in any way, thinking it best for her to apply her own mind and conscience to the situation, he was nevertheless a bit dismayed to learn after the fact that she had voted for Mary Carey, the porn star, who had befriended Nikki one night when she'd made a guest appearance at a club where Nikki was also on the bill. Still, Spencer convinced himself, it was a step in the right direction. She had made the effort. Her vote was counted. Her voice was heard.

From there, it was on to work at the *Bee*, and that's when the day truly took an unexpected turn. Just as Spencer was arriving, the press corps was assembling in the newsroom to receive their assignments on this most important of days. Though the city was swarming with outside news teams, it was expected that the *Bee* would have the hometown edge, particularly with regard to any juicy local-interest pieces, and damn if the editors weren't feeling the pressure to deliver on those expectations.

It was because of that, and because of the paper's stretched-thin resources, and because Spencer happened to step through the door at just the right moment, that he finally got the big break he'd long been hoping for. Turns out, one of the front-section editors, a former OC surfer boy named Paul Hoying, had been a fan of Spencer's Bopsy the Clown obit. Noticing Spencer as he walked past on his way to the basement, Paul caught his eye and hailed him over. The deal was, Paul had too many open assignments and not nearly enough reporters to fill them. He needed extra hands, and bodies, ASAP, to help close the gaps. Would Spencer be interested in pitching in?

Paul needn't have even asked, and he certainly didn't have to ask twice. Of course Spencer was interested!

The assignment was to attend some of the rallies being held around town for long-shot fringe players like Larry Flynt and Green Party candidate Peter Camejo. All Spencer had to do was accompany a staff photographer, help him select a few colorful crowd shots (i.e., overzealous sign bearers with painted faces, campaign T-shirts, and hope-filled eyes destined for crushing defeat), and capture in words some of the piquancy of these events, along with a few choice quotes from supporters of the various parties. The results would then be folded into a bigger piece, in which Spencer would get a shared byline. It sounded like a pretty fun way to spend the day, to be honest. Better yet, it was an opportunity to finally show what he was capable of. And he planned to take full advantage of it.

***

Rowena was also caught up in this election-related swirl, albeit more tangentially. At the highway-interchange Halloween shop where she was now employed, she had noticed a huge upswing in sales of their Arnold-as-Terminator masks, as well as people wanting to carve and festoon their porch-bound gourds in similar fashion. Indeed, Mr. Schwarzenegger seemed to be the main topic of discussion almost everywhere she went, and with almost everyone she bumped into. Where would he live? Where would he eat? Where would he shop? What would he do for the local economy?

As a result, Rowena wasn't too surprised when she received a call from Connie, saying she wanted to go cast her vote for "that handsome Hollywood fellow." Rowena promised that she would stop by after work and they would both go. Truth was, Rowena hadn't followed the situation very closely, but she was pretty much like everyone else she knew, thinking it would be pretty cool to have a big-time Hollywood celeb like Arnold living in town. Maybe his famous friends would come and visit; maybe, they would even film their movies and TV shows up here. It was exciting just thinking about it. And she had read somewhere, too, maybe in *People*, about how he had helped those poor Special Olympics kids. Why not give him a shot? He sure couldn't do any worse than the last guy.

Rowena got off at five and went to pick up her mom. For once, Connie was ready to go, her scarf and purse and glasses all close at hand. Counting her blessings, Rowena noted that her mom seemed fairly "with it," too. She had even remembered on her own accord that it was Election Day. Things seemed to be looking up. Maybe, Rowena told herself, that whole mess at the church was just a one-shot deal, a simple case of emotional overload, something we all suffer from time to time. True, there had been a few other little slip-ups, but maybe they were just jokes. Connie always was one to exact a little sweet revenge, after all, and her humor was pretty dry...

"Who you voting for, Rowena?"

"Same as you, Mom. Isn't everybody?"

"The actor, you mean."

"Right."

"Well, good. That's good. I like him."

Connie's eyes glazed over as she turned and stared out the window, humming some old ditty Rowena vaguely recognized but couldn't place. There was no denying it— her mom was still acting a little goofy. But there was nothing wrong with that. She had lived a tough life. She had buried a husband. She was entitled.

The rest of the drive proceeded smoothly. With surprisingly light traffic, they made it to the Shriners' Hall polling place in ten minutes flat. At that hour, there were no lines and no waiting. The two went in and signed up, lickety-split, no troubles. Connie had even brought her driver's license, just as Rowena reminded her to do.

But then, Connie ducked into a voting booth and just stayed there, for five, ten, going on fifteen minutes. Rowena waited patiently, not wanting to rush her—maybe she was just reading over the propositions—but after a while, even the Shriner volunteers in their little velvet, tasseled fezzes began to wonder what the problem was. Rowena finally sidled up to the curtain and gave her mom a gentle verbal nudge to try and speed it up a bit in there.

"But ... I don't see it," Connie cried.

Rowena rolled her eyes. "You don't see what, Mom?"

"The name of that actor. You know."

"Well, there's a lot of names, Mom, I know. Look down near the bottom."

"I have. I've looked and looked, and I can't find it."

This seemed unlikely. "You can't find *Schwarzenegger*?"

"I can't find what?"

"Schwarzenegger. The list is alphabetical, you know."

"Schwartza-what? What on earth are you talking about, Rowena! I'm looking for that actor's name, just like I said. Ronnie Reagan."

Rowena's face fell. There was no denying it now. This was no fluke, no passing phase. Something was wrong with her mother, something seriously fucking wrong.

"Poor thing. She's got the Alzheimer's, don't she?"

Rowena turned. It was one of the volunteers, who had apparently overheard this exchange. He nodded sadly, his tassel dangling off his fez like a flag at half-mast.

"I seen it before, too many times. Good people, smart people, and they just can't keep none of it straight no more. You go on and help her, do what you need to do."

The elderly Shriner shuffled off, giving Rowena and her mother their privacy. Rowena just stood there, frozen, in a state of shock. She'd heard the term "Alzheimer's" before, and had a vague notion of what it entailed, but had never put two and two together and associated it with her mother's situation. But now, it all made sense, in some deep and darkly disturbing way, while at the same time it made absolutely no sense at all.

With an additional, approving nod from the sympathetic poll worker, Rowena finally stepped in to help Connie fill out her ballot, then quickly ushered her out of the lodge and into her car. But from there, she wasn't quite sure what to do next. She only knew that it was just the beginning of what would likely be a long and arduous journey, both for her mother, and for herself.

***

With the polls about to close, Missy Carver had not voted yet. Nor did she plan to, even by absentee ballot. She had also abided by her vow to avoid any reminders of a certain unnamed, Bavarian-born leading candidate, who had played such a painful starring role in her earlier tribulations. Oh, no, there would be none of that for Missy. Here in the confines of her home at 2928 Sunnydale Drive, behind the thick curtains and locked doors, she was safe from such annoyances. None of the anxieties and disappointments that her dealings with other people inevitably led to could follow her here.

However, no matter how rigidly one attempts to control their environment—and Missy had hers virtually vacuum-sealed—problems still do arise. In Missy's case, it began when she noticed the blood in her vomit.

This was troubling for Missy, of course, although not for the reasons one might suspect. The fact was, it bothered her because she truly felt as if she had been performing her rituals proficiently enough to avoid such harms. The trick, as she had quickly discovered, was to wait long enough for the food to get broken down, but not so long that the calories can get absorbed—that would defeat the whole purpose of the exercise—then, you simply insert a couple well-trained fingers down your throat to trigger the gag reflex and bring it all right back up. Presto.

Alas, it seemed all those gastric acids were more virulent than she thought. What had started as a mere trace of blood had grown increasingly more pervasive. Missy guessed that it was from her esophagus, which she could tell had gotten abraded from the workout she was giving it, now up to three or four times a day. But if her throat was bleeding, she realized, her stomach was likely suffering some damage as well. Plus, the headaches were getting worse. And with these various irritations, it was getting harder and harder to sleep at night. Which, in turn, affected her ability to focus on her work during the day. She knew all of this, and she knew she should do something about it. But the truth was, she didn't want to have to leave the house to do so.

The reasons behind this were only reinforced when she tried to correct the situation by reaching out to her longtime family physician, Dr. Stankowski. She had hoped that he might be able to suggest something to help her sleep, and maybe ease the pain she was experiencing. This did not seem to her like an unreasonable request. But to her dismay, despite her long standing as a model patient and her track record of perfect health, the good doctor refused to prescribe her even so much as an extra-strength antacid without seeing her for a checkup first. Missy was outraged, and even more so when he began lobbing all sorts of intrusive questions at her. She had already told him exactly what the problem was, more or less, and even provided the solution. What was the point of all of this, other than to waste her precious time and line his own pockets?

Not surprisingly, Dr. Stankowski failed to yield to this argument.

With her throat hurting worse than ever from the yelling, Missy had hung up the phone, furious. The call had only confirmed her instincts. If something were to be done, she would have to handle it herself, in her own way, on her own terms. And so, she instead turned to her ever-reliable computer for answers. And there, it took almost no time at all to find a helpful, well-stocked online pharmacy that would satisfy her needs without all the unnecessary fuss and expense. Indeed, after typing in her symptoms, the Canadian-based entity whose services she chose to engage, JiffyDrug.com, not only filled her order on the spot, but also suggested other related medicines that might be of benefit. Feeling thoroughly vindicated, Missy took the advice and stocked up with a full month's supply, confident that the cure to all her various woes was now just a doorbell ring away.

Sure enough, the package arrived just two days later. And the sleeping pills she ordered, coupled with the pain medication the website suggested, helped her fall asleep much faster and easier than she ever had before. Indeed, it was almost like falling into a coma—perfect bliss.

Alas, the mornings after still proved trying. In this regard, the pills did not seem to help at all. No matter how much sleep she got, or how deep those slumbers were, she remained drowsy the next day, the fog refusing to clear from her thoughts. And for someone like Missy, who was accustomed to drill-sergeant efficiency, this simply would not do. She thus turned again to her friends at JiffyDrug for suggestions as to a little morning pick-me-up. The site spit out its recommendation for an energy-boosting "wonder pill" that she had never heard of, and she took a leap of faith and ordered some.

And boy, those little suckers really did the trick! For the next few days, Missy had the afterburners firing full blast. She worked and she phoned and she wrote and she read and she tinkered and she exercised and she cooked and she ate and she threw up, and then she started all over again. It was awesome.

Unfortunately, this initial power-burst of effervescence proved short-lived, as did the pill's maximum effect. Day by day, dose by dose, Missy mourned its gradual waning. It had felt so right, like she was on the verge of a real personal breakthrough. And with the old nagging pains returning, too, she was desperate to replicate that feeling as soon as possible. But how does one do that? How does one get that sense of transcendence back? Missy tried approaching this dilemma from a variety of different angles—exercising more, working more, eating more, purging more—but the only method that seemed to work was to take more of the pills, and to take them in increasing combination. Addicts call this "chasing the dragon." It is the oldest and hoariest cliché of the drug-taking world. But Missy would not have known that; she had never been a drug user. Indeed, these were prescription medications, so to her mind they really didn't even count. And so, she followed in the steps of millions of others before her, and started steadily increasing her intake.

And before she knew it, this insidious cycle began to take over her life, occupying more and more of her waking thoughts and actions, her other activities and interests all gradually growing less urgent, less appealing, less relevant—including even the realty work that had so recently been her lifeblood—until all that remained was the food, the cleansing, the obsessive exercise and, last but not least, the ever-growing panoply of pills from an ever-growing array of shady, foreign online pharmacies that made it all possible.

Though it would not have seemed possible just a few short weeks before, to her or anybody who knew her, Missy Carver had transformed into something even she might not have recognized: a ghostly, bulimic, shut-in pill junkie. And there was no one around to notice, or flag it, or stop it. She was a hamster in a gilded cage, running in a wheel that just kept right on spinning, faster and faster, with no end or destination in sight.

***

As for Todd Tisdale, his focus never wavered, never strayed. He was a rock of purpose, indefatigable. But while he was thrilled that Election Day had finally arrived, he of all people wasn't even around to bask in its giddy glow, nor in the seemingly swami-like accuracy of his related prognostications. Rather, he was still in Moscow, trying to untangle all the miles of red tape necessary to close the deal and marry his newly beloved, Svetlana.

As it so happens, when Lana had accepted his proposal that night in the ballroom, Todd had rather naively assumed that the tough part was over. In fact, it was just beginning. Yes, he had staved off Phil's attempted coup and won Svetlana's hand, and that had been thrilling. But then, he had to buy an engagement ring for that hand, a big one with a big rock that emptied his pockets and maxed out his MasterCard, so that it was official. Then, they had to go tell young Alek, who proved to be a pretty tough customer in his own right. And since the boy's approval was a crucial part of the deal, Todd had to spend time and effort winning him over, too, with ice cream and toys and sports equipment and father-son play of all sorts, which maxed out yet another credit card and left Todd's body so stiff and aching that he barely had any energy left for the nightly bedroom romps with Lana which he had been so greatly anticipating.

And sadly, that aspect of the relationship had presented some unexpected hurdles as well. For while Lana's first husband, Yuri, was safely ensconced in some dank prison cell out in the foothills of the Ural Mountains, the specter of his less-than-gentle conjugal touch pervaded Todd's own amorous efforts. The fact was, Yuri had been rough. He had been abusive. And although Lana was loath to come out and actually admit it, he had likely been pretty damn sadistic to boot.

But Todd, to his credit, was none of these things. He was a big man, bigger even than Yuri, but more of a gentle giant—a "Toddy Bear," as Svetlana had come to affectionately refer to him. And so, as Todd's sweet and tender nature gradually won her over, the walls began to come down. They kissed. They cuddled. They fondled. And eventually, after the proposal and the ring and a week of slowly escalating foreplay, they made love. Nothing at all like how Todd had imagined, however. Rather, it was tentative, and awkward, and quite frankly, unsatisfying. Lana's wounds might have healed, but they had clearly left behind some deep psychic scars. Todd realized that he had his work cut out for him, and that it was a situation that wouldn't correct itself overnight. It was going to demand all the support and patience that he could possibly muster.

Speaking of patience, there was also the matter of getting the official approval for Svetlana and Alek to actually leave the country with him. He and Lana would have to get legally wed, of course. And, procure the proper passports and visas. Then, Todd had to provide documentation to prove to the government officials of both countries that he could financially support both mother and child for a period of no less than three years. And all of these things demanded paperwork, reams and reams of it, in two different languages, as well as not-inconsiderable processing fees, which drained Todd's dwindling resources even further. When all was said and done, and Todd's hand was so cramped it looked like a claw, he swore he would never fill out another goddamn form for the rest of his life, and he meant it.

In the meantime, all that was left to do was wait, and spend more quality time with his gorgeous fiancée and soon-to-be-adopted stepson. And when his thoughts turned to them, and their triumphant return to Sacramento, with Arnold at the helm and business booming like never before, the smile would return to his face and all would be right with the world again.

***

By early evening, the networks were already calling the election. Arnold had won handily, as expected, by a two-to-one margin over his closest opponent, Cruz Bustamente. His percentage of the total vote was just a shade under fifty percent, which was less than half, but still fairly impressive when you stopped to consider that there were 134 other candidates vying for those votes.

In his acceptance speech later that night at his campaign headquarters down in Los Angeles, Arnold thanked the voters for their trust and support, and vowed to balance the state's out-of-whack budget, while also promising "no more borrowing and no new taxes." It was a tall order, to say the least, one which most pundits felt was impossible, but Arnold swore to the crowd, "*I will not fail you*," and coming from a proven action-hero like him, not just another rank-and-file politico, it was a promise which many Californians took to heart. They had faith.

Meanwhile, in the race-within-the-race, several other celebrities of wildly varying repute also finished near the top of the tallies. Leading the way in fifth place, with one percent of the vote, was Arianna Huffington, whose academic credentials and oratorical skills made her a legitimate-enough candidate, but who was likely better known to most people as a talk-show regular whose wealthy husband had came out of the closet as a gay man shortly after losing a costly self-funded state election of his own. Next, in seventh, with a tally which rounded down to a humbling zero percent of the total, was Hustler publisher Larry Flynt, and hard on his heels in eighth was Gary Coleman, of *Diff'rent Strokes* fame, also with zero percent.

Finally, rounding out the top ten, was Nikki's choice for governor, Mary Cook a.k.a. Mary Carey, still just twenty-two years old at the time, who went straight from her press conference concession speech, which she gave in a dubiously patriotic stars-and-stripes bikini, to her 9 p.m. call time out in the flats of the San Fernando Valley to shoot the thrilling climax of her latest XXX-rated cinematic opus, *Boobsville Sorority Girls*.

And with that, the 2003 California recall election season was truly complete.

21

TRICK OR TREAT

The morning after the election, Rowena was back to work at the pumpkin patch. Spotting a copy of the *Bee* left behind by a harried mom with too many kids to wrangle, she grabbed the front section to see that Schwarzenegger had indeed won. Underneath a marquee-style headline reading "*GOVERNATOR!*" a large color photo showed Arnold in a perfectly-tailored, GQ-Goes-to-Washington pinstripe suit, beaming like he'd just had a great night's sleep and a spa treatment or two, while giving a victorious thumbs-up to the crowd and the cameras at his victory celebration. Rowena smiled at the picture, sharing in Arnold's triumph in some small way since her vote, the very first of her adult life, had added to his winning tally.

In this same article, Rowena's eye also caught on the name of Ronald Reagan, mentioned as being the last actor-turned-politician to hold the office, back in 1975, nearly thirty years earlier. She noted in the election summary that he had received no votes this time around, not even one, which of course made perfect sense under the circumstances. Still, it made Rowena sad, because it dredged up memories of the previous day's debacle with her own mother.

After the scene at the Shriners Hall, Rowena had driven Connie back home. Throughout the ride, the elder Pickett had remained upset—not over the whole "Vote for Reagan" snafu, mind you, but rather because she had a vague sense that she was forgetting something. Rowena thought to herself, *No shit, Mom,* but Connie was thinking more along the lines of something tangible, like her purse or a pair of mittens. She kept checking her pockets and around her seat as if there were something terribly amiss, and none of Rowena's entreaties could stop her from wanting to go back and retrace their steps. Rowena finally pulled over to the side of the road by a 7-Eleven and went through every possible item that Connie might be missing (purse, by her feet; scarf, in her purse; glasses, perched on her head, etc.) before she finally allowed Rowena to continue on— but only after, per her request, they each got cherry Slurpees for the drive.

Back on the road, Rowena watched her mother delighting in her icy treat, eating it with the tiny, spooned end of her straw while bopping her head and humming that same elusively-familiar tune from the day before. The whole thing gave Rowena the creeps. It was like she and her mom had switched places, with Connie now being the little girl and Rowena being the young, awkwardly nurturing mother. Taking into account the potential ramifications, it was not just unsettling, but also downright terrifying.

This, in turn, begged the question of how to proceed from there. On the one hand, Rowena at least had a name now for her mother's apparent affliction, so that was something. It wasn't just some mysterious kookiness anymore. But that only led to more questions and concerns. For starters, based on what had happened thus far, there was concern over what Connie might do when Rowena wasn't around to fix it. And if Connie was already this bad, was it going to get worse? Was it treatable? Was it, God forbid, fatal? Rowena choked up at the mere thought. Connie was all the family she had left. Her mother was too young to die. And she was too young to be left all alone.

No, Rowena told herself, *don't think like that. Don't.*

However, even putting such grim prognoses aside, one unavoidable realization still loomed large in her mind: her mother simply couldn't, and shouldn't, live by herself anymore. There were too many ways she could get in trouble, wandering off and forgetting who she was or where she lived being just one such potential disaster. And since Rowena could barely afford to pay the bill from her mom's recent boondoggle ER visit, much less for any kind of extended stay at some hospice or retirement home, the only available remedy to this situation was painfully obvious. She was going to have to move back home again, even though it was something she swore that she would never do, no matter how dire the circumstances became.

This time was different, though. Her mother was the needy one, not her. And indeed, keeping in mind her incarcerated swain Lyle as well, Rowena was suddenly feeling needed more now than ever before. Despite all the inconvenience and demands on her time, which would only grow in the coming days, it felt good. She felt like she mattered, like she actually made a difference, which was a feeling she had never gotten from any of the other jobs or relationships she'd cultivated through the years. After all, what good does a deeper tan or a few extra cans of Cat Vittles truly matter in the big scheme of things, anyway?

So there it was. On top of working forty hours a week at the pumpkin patch, at least until the end of the month, and writing to Lyle every day and visiting him every week, and trying to find another job starting November 1, Rowena was now committing herself to the full-time, live-in care of her ailing mother. It was a lot of responsibility for one person to take on, much less someone like herself, who had never really been much of a go-getter to begin with. But that was the situation, and so that's what had to happen.

Rowena continued to ponder this throughout the day—the costs, and the logistics, and the sacrifices. She even realized there was one hidden benefit to her plan, which was that by moving back into her mother's place—the mortgage of which had been paid off years earlier with the money from Eddie's life insurance policy—she would be able to sell her trailer and cash out the equity. Not a fortune, to be sure, but a decent sum of unaccounted-for funds that might actually allow her to avoid living paycheck to paycheck for once in her life. And for Rowena, that was a luxury so great it almost made the whole thing worthwhile. But, before she could go any further with this:

"Spency, look, she's reading your story!"

Rowena looked up from the bale of hay she was sitting on to see an attractive but wildly mismatched young couple standing in front of her. The man was clean cut and well dressed, in pressed khakis and an Oxford shirt—a bit too buttoned-down for her taste, but attractive nevertheless. The girl was a different story. Low cut top, low-rise jeans, boobs and tattoos and piercings on full display for everyone to see. Rowena knew the type, and knew it well. She was the kind of brazen hussy Rowena had butted heads with and lost boyfriends to ever since back in junior high with Rodney Stanzler and that diabolical slut-in-training, Debra Hartwig. On closer inspection, Rowena was pretty sure she'd crossed paths with *this* one, too, at Teasers or some other similar environ.

The girl clapped and laughed like a seal, nearly causing her boobs to burst out of her woefully ill-equipped top. That clinched it. Oh yeah, Rowena had seen her around, all right. And she had a sneaking suspicion that her old rat-bastard of a boyfriend Randy had, too.

"He wrote that!" the girl barked, still clapping and jiggling. "He wrote that story, right there on the front page! Didn't you, Spency?"

"It's a shared byline. But yeah, I wrote a part of it."

The man, who Rowena guessed was not normally referred to as Spency, blushed at being put on the spot, which only added to his aw-shucks likability. But it made Rowena even more bewildered as to how a seemingly sweet, put-together guy like him would end up with a white-trash skank like her in the first place.

"Oh, Spency, so modest," the floozy chided, flagrantly rubbing her enormous fake boobs all over him while doing so. *Well*, Rowena thought, *that explains that*.

"So you're a reporter, huh?"

"Well, sort of. I'm trying. I mostly just write the obituaries for now, but still—"

"Covering the election's a pretty good start."

"Let's hope so. Thanks."

Spencer and Rowena shared a smile that made it clear they both understood the pain of unfulfilled ambitions. The strumpet made a note of it, too, and wasted no time in breaking the moment up. Cocking her bony hip, she heaved an impetuous sigh. "So we need a pumpkin. Are you the one who helps us or what?"

"I can be, sure," Rowena replied.

"Okay, then. Let me show you. I know just what I want."

Despite this claim, the fake-titted dimwit wasted nearly an hour of Rowena's time before finally settling on two pumpkins, a big one for the porch and a small one for the mantel. She then picked out two costumes, too, a pirate ensemble for him (hat, eye-patch, parrot, sword) and a genie outfit (low cut top, low rise pants—pretty much like what she already had on) for herself. Spencer paid for it all with a credit card, and when Rowena rang it up, she made a note of his name, although she wasn't exactly sure why.

Then, they were off, with "Spency" struggling to lug all the goods by himself as his shameless harlot walked ahead, applying more lip gloss and blabbing away on her cell phone, easy in the knowledge that she had the poor sucker fully wrapped around her trampy little finger.

Watching them go, Rowena couldn't help but smile, basking in the recognition that her lifelong problem with misguided romance was apparently not one exclusive to her. Nor, to women like her. Oh, no. It was pretty obvious, at least from where Rowena was sitting, that Spencer Brine, Preppy Boy Reporter, had himself quite a little bad-girl problem of his very own.

A few pumpkins and fright wigs later, Rowena clocked out for the day and headed straight over to her mother's to face the inevitable. In between assisting customers and ringing up sales, she had continued giving a lot of thought to the matter of Connie and how best to approach her. Remembering all the delusion and denial following the church incident, she decided the soundest course was to just bite the bullet and pretend like *she* was the one who needed the help. Most likely, Connie wouldn't put up a fuss, as long as Rowena promised the move back home would only be temporary—and after a while, she likely wouldn't even remember that. Why create any unnecessary drama?

Pulling into the driveway, Rowena found herself face-to-face yet again with the kind of scenario that made her concerns so justified. Connie was out on her front porch, clad only in a threadbare nightie and a pair of Eddie's old size-twelve boots, brandishing a mop and yelling a stream of curses at Pedro, the beleaguered lawn boy, who was just trying to trim the hedges as usual and suddenly found himself under siege.

With a sigh, Rowena hopped out of the car and rushed over to try and defuse the situation. "Mom! Mom! What do you think you're doing?"

Connie's head whipped in Rowena's direction, her temper immediately ebbing. Suddenly, she looked as befuddled as Pedro. "I—he—I..."

Connie went silent. She knitted her brow, then turned back to the cowering lawn boy, who still had his hands up in surrender. "Pedro, is that you?"

"Yes, ma'am, Mrs. Pickett. I was trying to tell you."

"What are you doing here today?"

"It's Wednesday. I always come on Wednesdays."

"Oh. Yes. You certainly do. Didn't recognize you with that hat on."

The fact was, Pedro always wore a hat, and in fact always wore the *same* hat, the exact same one he had on now. Mercifully, he was as eager to drop the subject as Connie was, so he just let it go. "Yes, ma'am."

"Thought you were some kind of vagrant or something."

"Sorry about that, Mrs. Pickett. Didn't mean to scare you."

"Well, then, all right. You get back to it."

Pedro nodded and scurried off to work at the far edge of the yard, clear of the line of fire. Connie turned to her daughter with a haughty smile. "Well, that's that."

"That's what, Mom? Jeez. You nearly took the poor kid's head off."

"He shouldn't go creeping around like that."

"He wasn't creeping. He was doing his job."

"Oh yes, he was! Or wasn't, that is to say. Or ..."

Connie suddenly found herself confused by her own line of reasoning and quickly changed tack. "Besides, Rowena, you weren't around, anyway. How on earth would you know?"

There was the opening Rowena was looking for. "Okay, Mom. Maybe you're right; maybe I wouldn't. I know I haven't been around much lately. I was kinda hoping to talk to you about that."

Connie's brow raised in guarded concern. "There something I should know?"

"Well, I don't know. It's just, what with losing my job and all, the bills kind of piled up on me. And with the mortgage on my trailer, too ..."

"You in some kind of trouble, hon?"

"A little bit, yeah." Rowena replied, with an Oscar-worthy quaver.

"Oh, baby, come on up here and tell your mama all about it." Connie spread her arms wide like a faith healer and summoned her daughter up onto the porch and into her motherly embrace.

Guiding Rowena into the kitchen, Connie poured them both some coffee, set an ashtray and a pack of Kools on the table, and let her baby girl spill it all out. Rowena told her all about Wade, and Estelle, and the bills, and everything else that had been going on, exaggerating a bit here and there for effect, while excluding touchier subjects, such as Lyle and his current residential status, so as to make sure that the conversation didn't accidentally veer off course.

By the end of their chat, Connie was fully in support of Rowena moving back home for as long as she needed, and Rowena was relieved at how smoothly it had gone. Even with the lies, the omissions, and the underlying ulterior motive, it had felt good talking like that again. It was just like the old days, when her mom was always there to mend a broken heart or lend a little extra cash under the table.

Then, as Rowena was ready to head to her trailer and start packing, Connie added, as if it were just plain common sense, "Of course, we'll have to run it by your daddy first, just to make sure."

And that's the moment Rowena finally realized with a sobering certainty that the good old days were gone for good, and that the real work had just begun.

22

SWEET HOME SACRAMENTO

Todd and Svetlana's wedding was held on a rainy Friday afternoon in a local Moscow magistrate's office. Todd wore his tuxedo. Svetlana wore her white chiffon dress. Ned, back from Glasgow for another visit, acted as best man, with a beaming Ludmilla by his side as witness, and young Alek serving as ring bearer. The ceremony was conducted in Russian, and the magistrate gave Todd a little nudge on the shoulder whenever it was his turn to nod and say "da." Aside from that, Todd had absolutely no clue what was being said. For all he knew, he could have been agreeing to buy black-market nuclear warheads. Nevertheless, when the vows were complete and the magistrate signaled for the two to kiss, Todd found himself sobbing like a little girl. It was the culmination of a dream come true.

After the nuptials, the wedding party headed to the site of the couple's first meeting, The Golden Tchotchke, for a small reception dinner. Todd had asked Svetlana if she wanted any of her family from back in the Ukraine to attend, and he'd offered to do whatever he could to help facilitate it. Svetlana tersely declined this offer. Her parents had shunned her in her hour of need, and she apparently felt that they deserved the same treatment from her now. It was time for a fresh start.

And the fact was, Todd was relieved. It wasn't that he didn't want to meet his new in-laws; he did. Or at least, he was willing to give it a shot. Rather, it was more an issue of finances. In jumping through all the hoops necessary to reach this point, he had already tapped every possible source of funds he had at his disposal. Until he got back to Sacramento and began implementing what he now referred to as his "Team Arnold Plan," he was pretty much flat broke.

But Todd refused to let that or anything else spoil the festive mood. He and Lana and little Alek were a family now—or at least, they would be, as soon as his adoption of Alek was officially approved. As for the rest, it would work itself out in due time. Echoing this sentiment, Ned picked up the tab for the entire dinner, proving himself to be a standup guy after all. The piano man did his part, too, playing only American music in honor of the occasion, although his repertoire was limited to the same Sinatra standards he always played, a handful of Billy Joel tunes, and, strangely enough, "Whip It" by Devo. Despite this, the two happy couples danced all night long, with little Alek boogying right by their side.

The next day, a whole new chapter for the Tisdale clan began. With the big plane trip to California just a little over twenty-four hours away, it was time to tackle the daunting task of packing up to leave Mother Russia and Svetlana's cramped one-bedroom tenement flat behind for good. For Todd, this was easy. He just jammed everything back into his two suitcases, sat on top, zipped them up and, voila!, he was good to go. For Svetlana and Alek, it was a different story. How do you decide what to bring? What do you leave behind? How do you presume to separate a past from a future that holds so many facets yet to be revealed?

Todd tried to help as much as he could in this regard, telling them all about Sacramento and its environs. He even offered to make room in his suitcases for more of their things. In the end, though, Svetlana decided that they would each take as much as they could fit into the two pieces of luggage they were permitted by the airline to take, plus a smaller carry-on, and then leave the rest to fate. A clean break.

The following morning, the three piled into a taxi and headed out to the airport. Svetlana and Alek were both visibly nervous, eyes darting all around, fingers and toes tapping out anxious beats. On top of everything else, neither of them had ever been on an airplane before, much less one flying over a vast, storm-tossed ocean. Noting this, Todd tried his best to act like a suave veteran air traveler. But the truth was, he was rather green-gilled at the prospect himself, which is one of the reasons why he had consumed so many alcoholic beverages on the flight out (the other, of course, being that they were free).

Now, however, he had a duty as head of the family to provide comfort and support. To be the fearless leader. This meant booze was out of the question; or at least, until his little flight crew finally went nighty-night. It also meant he had to keep them distracted and entertained in the interim, which he endeavored to do by regaling them with his vast arsenal of colorful tales from his shop and his glory days as a varsity sportsman.

Sure enough, this seemed to do the trick. Listening to these stories, both mother and child were lulled into a trance-like state as they made their way into the terminal, through customs, to the departure gate, onto the plane, and into their seats in coach. From there, Todd's duty to distract was greatly eased by the discovery of seatback TVs, which Lana and Alek both wasted little time in gleefully accessing. And while Todd was happy to see them both put at ease so quickly—a job well done, he thought—in a sense it was a shame because he still had so much more he wanted to share with them.

***

Many movies and meals and naps later, the Tisdale clan's jetliner touched down safely in the good old U.S. of A. at San Francisco International Airport. Svetlana and Alek emerged from the arrival chute and, even before clearing customs, were already wide-eyed and giddy, looking all around and basking in the sparkly, bigger-is-better American-ness of it all, with a vast Aero-Mall of shops and restaurants all conveniently located within a short walking distance. It was love at first sight.

This was tough for Todd. He could tell how enthralled they were, and he would have loved nothing more than to indulge them in a celebratory purchase or two. As it stood, he had to empty out his pockets simply to buy them each a small Frappuccino with which to merrily toast the occasion: "Cheers! Nostrovia! God Bless America! Here's to the Tisdales!"

From there, the trio traversed another seemingly endless corridor, surrounded on all sides by even more pecuniary temptations, before taking an escalator down into that traveler's purgatory known as Baggage Claim. It was only then, watching his appointed carousel's empty track go round and round, that Todd remembered he had left his Ford Bronco in the airport parking structure, and that he had undoubtedly racked up a rather sizable tab during his unexpectedly lengthy debarkation—a tab which, post-frappe, he no longer had the cash or the available credit to pay.

Though he kept a smile pasted on for the sake of his little clan, still happily sipping away on their icy treats, the situation gnawed at him. Not only was retrieving his Bronco without undue embarrassment a problem now, but it was also a bellwether for other such crises that would surely be rearing their ugly heads in the days to come. Back on American soil, it was only now finally sinking in for Todd how deep the financial hole he had dug for himself truly was. All he could do now was reach for his checkbook—an action that truly brought the trip full circle—and hope for the best.

Fortunately, these prayers seemed to work. The narcotized parking lot attendant accepted Todd's check without so much as a question or a qualm. Of course, had he been able to inquire as to its cashability, the outcome would have been quite different, and Todd knew that better than anyone. Stepping on the gas, he offered a timid, no-look "thank you" and burst clear of the gate before the lackey could change his mind.

Once beyond the airport's stark concrete boundaries, however, Lana and Alek's hunger to experience all that their new homeland had to offer only continued to grow. Every new Technicolor vista and passing billboard seemed to present yet another new wonder to behold. Wineries! Resorts! Water parks! Casinos! Naturally, they wanted to see it all, and they wanted to see it all *now*. Todd understood this, and he appreciated the enthusiasm, but for now he really just wanted to get back home, so that he could regain his bearings and start figuring out how he was going to pay for it all. Thus, he found himself doling out a stream of breezy promises, just like a seasoned politician: "Yes, we'll go to the outlet mall! Can't wait! Parasailing? Absolutely!"

And the truth was, on some level, he meant these things, just like a road-weary politician believes the things he says on the campaign trail. But the bottom-line purpose of these promises was to avoid losing momentum. To just damn the torpedoes and keep moving forward at all costs. And, as is often the case, the plan worked, at least in the short term. Svetlana and Alek were both sufficiently sated by these dangling-carrot affirmations, and their thoughts turned instead to the city of Sacramento— the name of which meant "blessing," after all—and their new lives there.

Alas, this scenario wasn't without hazards, too. While Todd loved his hometown dearly, he knew that it did not exactly square with the fun-in-the-sun California lifestyle his new family was familiar with from music and the movies. When the

Beach Boys sang about "California Girls," those girls may have been blessed, all right, but they were not from Sacramento.

Landing in San Francisco hadn't helped matters, either. Although not a beach town, per se, it was still one of the most majestic seaside cities in the world, its timeless postcard views on full display as their jet circled in over the bay and the Golden Gate Bridge for a landing. Staring out her porthole window in a swoon, Lana had exclaimed "Oh, Todd, it is so beautiful!" as if it were the view from their own back porch that she was seeing.

Overall, then, it was safe to say that the bar for expectations had been set exceedingly high. But to his credit, Todd was ready for this, acting the part of enthusiastic tour guide, and painting everything they saw in the best possible light. On that note, he took the most scenic route into town, over the trestled Tower Bridge and across the American River (a great name, which Todd employed to maximum advantage), which provided a panoramic view of the downtown skyline, as well as the futuristic Arco Arena where the Kings played (Todd knew how much Svetlana loved hoops).

From there, he drove through the quaint Old Sacramento district, then into an idyllically wooded dale of large homes and sprawling estates, the very picture of upper-middle-class American suburbia, before they ultimately segued into a somewhat less shady, less idyllic, less upper-middle subdivision of 50s-era tract homes called Farmer's Dell, which was where Todd's own humble abode was located.

And humble it was, even though Todd himself had never before seen it that way. To him, it was a castle. But the sad truth was, after Angie died, Todd had lost much of his motivation and zeal for upkeep. What was left, then, was a rather sad-looking two-bedroom ranch that an upbeat realtor like Jolene Wyatt might charitably describe as a "fixer-upper."

Pulling into the crack-webbed drive, Todd saw it all anew, through Lana and little Alek's eyes. He saw that it was in dire need of a fresh coat of paint, preferably in a shade other than its current peachy hue. He saw the screen windows, caked with years of dirt and grime and kamikaze mosquitoes. And the yard, filled with mangy bushes and dead leaves and weeds, in need of a good threshing before a mower could even get through it. And the dated architectural flourishes and lawn ornaments, which looked tacky at best, and tasteless at worst. And the porch and sidewalk, littered with newspapers and fliers like the aftermath of a wartime bombing run. And that was only the exterior.

Todd pulled the Bronco to a halt. "Well, here we are." He turned to Lana and saw the glimmer of disenchantment in her eyes. "I know, it's kind of a mess right now, but we'll fix it up in no time. Don't you worry."

Then, turning to Alek in the backseat, "And hey, sport, you'll have your very own bedroom. How about that!"

"Kull."

As in "cool," Alek's favorite American word, which he used incessantly. To him, everything was cool. The wedding was cool. The gifts and treats that Todd lavished on him were cool. The plane ride was cool. And the seatback video-game player was *way* cool. Thus, his rote, monotonic utilization of the term in this case gave Todd even more room for concern. What did they expect, a mansion?

Todd then recalled his own grandiose descriptions of his business and plans for expansion, and realized that that may have been *precisely* what they had expected. He lowered his eyes in a mixture of anxiety and shame. "Come on. I'll show you around the rest of the place. We can grab the bags later."

Then, he added, as if to help convince himself as well, "You're both gonna love it here."

23

GENIE IN A BOTTLE

"God, I love it when you're here," Spencer muttered to Nikki late one night, in a state of dreamy post-coital bliss, as she nimbly dismounted from his sweaty, spent body.

"I love it, too, baby," Nikki cooed, flashing a delectable wedge of taut flank as she wiggled her way back into her silky pink panties.

"We've gotta find a way to spend more nights together like this."

"I can think of one," Nikki offered.

"Whatever it takes. Let's do it," Spencer countered absently.

A beat. Nikki spun around, thunderstruck. "Oh, my God, do you mean it?"

"Yeah, absolutely," Spencer said, still basking hazily in the afterglow.

And that was all it took. Before Spencer realized what was happening, Nikki was on the phone with her best friend, fellow ShowBar dancer Roxy, shedding tears of joy and making arrangements to borrow Roxy's pickup truck, so that she could pack up her things and haul them over the very next morning.

Perhaps this was a simple case of miscommunication. Or perhaps, Nikki merely intuited Spencer's true desires, the hidden meaning behind his words, and acted in a manner she deemed necessary to best make it a reality. Whatever. The various interpretations and theories were irrelevant now. The fact was, after only a handful of "dates," with that term being given its loosest possible interpretation, Nikki had moved in, and she and Spencer were now living together as a couple.

This was a daunting prospect for a number of reasons. Chief among them was the fact that Spencer had never shared a domicile of any kind with any woman aside from his own mother, much less one of Nikki's caliber. While he had, by this point, managed to attain some level of ease while in her company, the reality of her being at such close quarters at all times, especially when he had to do anything of an unseemly personal nature, was another matter altogether. He had enough insecurities to grapple with without her being witness to any of that. And truth be told, he wasn't particularly eager to see any such fantasy-shattering displays on her part, either. In fact, Spencer had almost convinced himself that she, as a goddess-like being, was exempt from these kind of earthly flaws and foibles. Alas, the gargantuan box of tampons she stowed under the bathroom sink on day one quickly dispelled that myth.

There was also the matter of their vastly different lifestyles. Spencer worked in a cubicle from nine to six, Monday to Friday, every week, without fail. Nikki worked on a strip-club center stage, usually from happy hour until midnight or so. When they were just getting to know one another, Spencer had made a special effort to seek Nikki out at her workplace. To see her in all her scantily-clad, sexily-choreographed glory, and worship at her mirror-bedecked altar. And in doing so, he had always made it a point to present himself in the best possible light as well, playing the role of the well-dressed, well-behaved reporter-on-the-rise to the very hilt, thus distinguishing himself from the other drunken, leering, heavy-breathers in the crowd. It was a dynamic calculated on both sides of the equation for maximum impact, one that made them both stand out in ways that were inevitably going to be hard to sustain over the long run and upon closer inspection.

That said, sharing living quarters only accentuated this problem. In lieu of "best possible lights," Spencer and Nikki's time together now often came in passing, with one party getting ready for work while the other was getting ready for bed, or sitting on the toilet, or squeezing a zit. Laundry and cleaning and cooking became central topics of conversation, with the related issue of who was responsible for what following right on their heels. Romance, the air of mystery and longing, began slowly seeping away. Sex came in logistically preplanned or hurriedly stolen moments, and while it was still pretty damn terrific, at least as far as Spencer was concerned, he nevertheless noted a downward trend in both its frequency and its fervor.

But it wasn't just the proximity that was causing problems. Other minor conflicts, which during the honeymoon period of their relationship they had overlooked or underestimated, had now begun, like a small rash exposed to the sun, to grow and fester and thus take on greater cause for concern.

In Spencer's eyes, Nikki's lack of education and her accompanying disinterest in cerebral self-betterment of any kind was the standout. While he had always been aware of this issue, its presence had in the early going been largely confined to the occasional malapropism, like when she referred to his work as "writing the mortuaries." These were harmless enough, and Spencer actually found them rather endearing in a way, at least coming from her. However, as this knack for misspeaking continued, its charm waned in direct proportion to the increasing ignorance of the statements in question, such as her repeated assertion that the war in Iraq was "all caused by those crazy towel-heads," a claim made even more troubling because Spencer was fairly certain that Nikki herself had some of this same accursed Persian blood coursing through her own veins.

All the while, Spencer kept trying his best to gently, lovingly nudge her in the right direction, exposing her to all the art and literature that he admired, as well as helping her develop a keener sense of the world at large. Alas, these efforts were largely in vain. Unless Nikki could dance to it, or eat it, or achieve an orgasm with it, it fell outside of her range of interests, the limits of which she had no apparent desire to expand upon or even question. She was what she was.

In the interest of fairness, it should be noted that Nikki had developed some complaints of her own. Chief among them, appropriately enough, was Spencer's "professor complex," as she came to call it. While there was no doubt that Spencer had way more formal education than she did—something which she'd admired about him at first, along with the air of sophistication that came along with it—Nikki now found it annoying how he always had to remind her of this, in ways both big and small, and treat her as if she were some child or pet he was trying to train. After all, if she wanted to know who Picasso was, or how to pronounce cacophony, or which fork to use at dinner, she could ask. She wasn't stupid. And besides, if he was so smart, why was she making so much more money than he was? Sure, maybe he was paying his dues, and maybe showing off was just his way of feeling better about himself, but if she wanted to take a frigging pop quiz every damn second of the day, she would have stayed in high school, thank you very much!

It was also insulting to Nikki how little interest Spencer seemed to have in learning about *her* interests. Case in point was the local club scene, a world she held near and dear, as it allowed her to bone up on her dance moves, hear the hottest new music for her routines, and court new customers in the process. At first, Spencer had tagged along, although his enthusiasm for it even then had been meager, and his efforts on the dance floor even less so. Typically, he would hold out for a slow song, hold her tight, offer some sweet caresses that soon morphed into gropes, then beg her to leave as soon as the song was over so they could go home and have sex. And for someone who loved dancing as much as Nikki did, that grew pretty tiresome.

Nevertheless, Nikki reminded herself, it was the effort that counted. And it was precisely this odd-couple give-and-take that had provided their relationship its spark—its sense of being special.

Lately, however, Spencer didn't even seem to be trying. Instead, he was always begging off, claiming to be too tired from work, wanting only to stay at home and order a pizza (and if that's what he wanted, maybe *he* should try having to work in the nude for a change) or read a boring book or watch some artsy-fartsy movie where everybody was dying or drugged-out or miserable. And *then*, after that, he'd inevitably want a little "snuggle time" before she headed off for her own evening's labors.

But that wasn't how it worked. Uh uh. Not for Nikki. She wasn't just some sex doll, there for the taking. She needed to dance and sweat and flirt and feel desired, and feel her body, get in touch with it, get it tuned up and juiced up and running on all cylinders so that any ensuing lovemaking would be loose and wild and climactic. The culmination of something. Something meaningful. Not just some final, rote, ritual thing to do before turning off the lights or walking out the door.

Despite her best intentions, though, Nikki couldn't seem to find the words or the occasion to explain any of this to Spencer. He, in turn, remained equally unable to air his grievances with her. Maybe it was because it was so early in their cohabitation. Maybe they both figured a little patience and understanding would help iron it all out. Or maybe it was because they both realized they had made a terrible mistake and neither of them knew how to fix it. Whatever the case, the result was that the two just kept going through their paces, crossing paths and sharing a bed, trying not to step on one another's toes, trying to pretend like the issues occupying all their waking thoughts didn't even exist—that they were both as happy as clams with things just the way they were. Even though that could not have been further from the truth.

This unspoken truce, or grace period, or whatever one might choose to call it, finally came to an end on the night before Halloween, a night often referred to as Devils' Night. Paul Hoying, the front-section editor who had drafted Spencer into duty on Election Day, was throwing a big costume party. Spencer, who had been moping over the lack of any follow-up opportunities, was delighted to receive an invite. It meant he was still on Paul's mind, still on the rise, still in favor; that he might just make it out of that dreary basement hellhole someday, after all. And with perfect timing, too: Schwarzenegger's inauguration was only a couple weeks away. Big stories were sure to follow. As such, he was in a great mood.

Nikki was excited, too, both at the prospect of a night out on the town with her man, and for a party that would allow her to finally meet his coworkers and play dress-up in the process—another of her absolute favorite things that Spencer and his apparent lack of imagination had somehow still failed to take advantage of. Maybe, Nikki thought, tonight would be the night.

With all these combustible hopes and emotions at work, the night started off on a high note. As soon as Spencer got home from work, he and Nikki both changed into their costumes (pirate and genie, respectively) so that they could get into the proper mood and do a little pre-partying. Spencer whipped up a batch of frozen margaritas, Nikki put some old-school hip-hop on the stereo, and as they drank from their favorite cactus glasses, she belly-danced around the den while Spencer chased after her with his plastic saber and spouted salty pirate lingo.

It was fun, and spontaneous, and playfully sexy. It reminded both of them why they had been attracted to one another in the first place.

Driving to the party, the buzz from the margaritas continued to cast a glow over the couple. Nikki swayed to a TLC CD on the stereo, and Spencer hummed along, while also running over all the things he planned to say to Paul and the other editors when and if he got the chance. Nikki grabbed his hand and held it tight. It was an important night for both of them, and they both sensed it, felt it, *knew it*, without having to actually come out and say it.

However, their perspectives on what that importance entailed, and how best to achieve it, were vastly different, as was made painfully evident from the very first moment that they arrived at the party.

"Hello, hello!" Paul said as he opened the door to greet them, clad in a doctor's costume and hoisting an oversized martini.

Sensing a guard-down attitude he planned to fully exploit, Spencer started to offer up a pithy line about pirate-crew HMOs. Before he could get the words out, however, Nikki beat him to the punch, cooing to Paul in her sexiest voice: "Hello, Doctor. Can you help me? I've been in my bottle for ever so long, and I'm in desperate need of a checkup."

Naturally, Paul ate this up. "Well, I'm sure we can accommodate you, little lady. Why don't you step inside my office, take off all your clothes, and we'll get started right away," he said, arching his eyebrows like Groucho Marx and chasing after her with his toy stethoscope. A funny bit, yes, but not exactly how Spencer wanted the night to start: getting overshadowed by his date, while she, in turn, got eye-fucked by his boss.

And soon enough, it wasn't just Paul who was blatantly ogling her. With the combination of her skimpy costume, her sexy looks, her flirtatiousness, and her overall *aura*, Nikki stood out like a sore thumb among the other females at the party.

While several of these women were attractive in their own right, it was in a far more staid, respectable, country-club-wife kind of way. As a result, they were jealous, and their male dates were envious, and all of them were watching Nikki out of the corner of their eye and wondering, *Who is that chick?*

Nikki didn't disappoint. No wallflower, she was as outgoing and gregarious as usual. She continued her genie routine, tossing off more lines about being "out of her bottle for the night" and granting wishes (wink, wink), and even doing the *I Dream of Jeannie* blinking head-bob when she asked the bartender to conjure up another margarita for her. All the while, her comment about being a "working dancer" got all the women murmuring, and all the men lathered up to see some of her dance moves, up close and personal.

But Nikki resisted this temptation, largely because she saw in Spencer's eyes that he disapproved. This disappointed her at first, then made her angry. It was a party, after all. Who was he to tell her not to dance? What happened to all the fun they were having? And why was her Spency being such a total buzzkill all of a sudden? Off this, she started to sulk—and also to imbibe far more freely than she should have.

Meanwhile, Spencer was still trying his best to network, but the only thing the other *Bee* staffers wanted to talk about was the smoking hot babe he was with. Nikki, right? Was she a stripper? That was the rumor going around. Spencer, to his credit, refused to lend any credence to those allegations, or parlay them into any frat-boy backslaps. But, he quickly realized, any attempts he might make to impress his superiors didn't stand a chance with Nikki in the room. She was the star attraction, not him. And while the fact that he was her date earned him some associative kudos, it wasn't the sort of attention he was looking for. He wanted to be taken seriously, as a smart, ambitious young reporter who was ready for bigger and better things, *not* as the guy from the basement who scored with the babe-a-licious stripper.

On that note, just as Spencer finally seemed to be making a little headway, chatting up his "matey" Paul in his best Yo-Ho-Ho accent and telling him how what he really wanted was to "plunder more front-page booty," it was Nikki's booty that suddenly became the party's focus. Turns out Ham Trammell, a jackass sportswriter in a lumpy Arnold "Pump You Up" weightlifter costume, had managed to locate a CD dance-mix of Christina Aguilera's "Genie in a Bottle." Hearing this was too much for Nikki to resist. Before Spencer knew what was happening, she was on top of the dining room table, doing a Seven Veils dance routine as all the men chanted "Go Nik-ki!, Go Nik-ki!," and all their dates huddled in a corner and shot deadly laser beams from their eyes in her general direction.

Spencer sprinted to the table to try and quietly coax her down. But Nikki, now six sheets to the wind and four veils to the floor, ignored any and all such efforts, kicking him away with her stiletto heel and playfully giving him the finger. The men all laughed, hooting along as if it were just another part of the show. Seeing that things were quickly going from bad to worse, Spencer rushed to the stereo, located the power cord, and yanked it out. The males in the crowd booed at the interruption, while the party's disgusted female contingent seemed greatly relieved. In their eyes, at least, Spencer had earned a few brownie points.

But then, the men—Spencer's bosses, for god's sake!—took up the chant again, "Go Nik-ki!, Go Nik-ki!," and she responded with more music-free bumps and grinds and dropped veils. Spencer saw now that it was beyond the point of no return. He stood in the back of the room and watched along with the others, helpless to stop it.

When the last veil finally dropped, Nikki bowed to the hoots and whistles like the pro that she was. Thankfully, all her private parts remained covered, but the damage had been done. If there were any doubts remaining as to the identity of Nikki's dancing career, they were now vanquished. Spencer thanked

Paul for inviting him, grabbed Nikki's hand and, holding onto it with a vise-like grip, ducked out the door before anyone thought to yell out for an encore.

Back in the safety of Spencer's Volvo, the chants echoed over the stone silence. Nikki was slowly beginning to realize that she had perhaps gone a bit too far. Spencer was furious, his face red under the wiry pirate beard, his one patch-less eye wide with indignation.

"What was that? What the *hell* was that?"

Nikki, in a meek voice: "I was just trying to have some fun."

"Oh, you had it, all right. At *my* expense! What were you thinking?"

"It was a costume party."

"Right! A party! Not a damn strip show!"

"I was a genie, I was just being a genie!" Nikki yelled back, growing tired of the lecture. "They played the song—"

"Just one problem, Nikki. Genies don't strip!"

"I wasn't stripping! I was dancing!"

"*On top of my boss's dining room table? With everybody watching?*" Spencer groaned and shut his eyes to block out the vision.

Nikki started to weep. "You didn't say anything—"

"Did I have to? Did I really have to? Come on!"

Nikki sniffled, crossed her arms and looked away. "Bastard. Take me home."

"You bet I will."

The sex that night was amazing. Beyond amazing. It was better than ever. In the middle of the night, Nikki scooted over to his side of the bed and started playing genie again, but now just for him, with a passion and a desire to please—and, to make amends. Spencer got his three wishes and then some, in ways he hadn't thought humanly possible. And all the while, Nikki kept spurring him on with sexy whispers about how she'd been in her bottle all by her lonesome and hadn't enjoyed any earthly pleasures in so, so long. "Take me! Plunder me!

Pillage me! Rub my magic lamp! Rub it, baby! Rub it hard!"
Needless to say, despite whatever lingering ill will Spencer
may have been harboring, his Little Buccaneer reported for
duty immediately.

By the end of hour two, with the sun already rising in the
east, Spencer was feeling pretty well pillaged himself, and for
the first time in his life he realized how truly incredible makeup sex could be. Their first fight. Hell, if this was what it was
like, he and Nikki would have to fight more often. He'd even
be happy to fake them if necessary. He collapsed into a dreamy
slumber, a thoroughly sated smile on his face.

When he finally woke up, it was late Sunday morning. He
yawned and stretched and smiled, remembering the previous
night's rendezvous, with him as the marauding pirate-ship
captain and Nikki as his helpless genie wench. The notion of
role-playing opened up a whole new realm of sexual fantasy
and fulfillment for Spencer—and with him as scenarist and
Nikki as his ready, willing, and *supremely* able co-star, there was
no shortage of arousing options to explore.

It was then that he remembered today was Halloween.
Beautiful. They could perform another round of costume-party
theater that very night. Indeed, his fertile mind had already
drawn up a headline for its review: WRITER LEARNS NEW
TRICKS, GETS MORE TREATS. And as for *last night's* party
and the fiasco that ensued ... well, nobody's perfect, right?

On that note, Spencer turned to Nikki's side of the bed, only
to find that she wasn't there. This was a bit of a surprise, as he
assumed she would have needed to catch up on sleep as much
as he had. However, it wasn't so unusual. Sunday mornings,
Nikki usually went to the gym, then went shopping. That's
probably where she was. Fair enough. It just meant he had
the place to himself for a few hours, so that he could read the
paper and order some food and watch some football—and, most
importantly, rest up for what would surely be a memorable
encore performance that very night.

As Spencer got up to start his day, his mind swam with juicy potential vignettes: the tutor and the naughty schoolgirl, the pool boy and the frisky housewife, the rock star and the fawning groupie. All sounded equally excellent. Spencer couldn't wait to get started.

But then, as he stepped into the bathroom, he noticed something else that was unexpected and decidedly *not* usual—all of Nikki's perfumes and toiletries were missing. On further inspection, he discovered that some of her clothes were gone from the closet as well. He looked in the other bathroom, and the guest bedroom, and checked the hallway washer-dryer as well. No sign of her, or of any of the other missing items. Worried now, he dialed her cell phone. There was no answer.

And that is when he saw the note, taped to the refrigerator door, in Nikki's big, loopy handwriting. As he read the note, which opened with the ominous phrase *"Dear Spenser,"* his face fell, and his knees nearly buckled.

It was Halloween, but Spencer Brine apparently would not be getting any treats, after all.

24
HOME FOR THE HOLIDAY

Despite all the precious little ghosts and goblins and Disney characters roaming the streets all over town, and indeed all across the country, Halloween night at the Carver house unfolded pretty much like every other. Missy didn't go out. She didn't let anyone else in. She didn't answer her door. And, in a more recent development, she didn't answer the phone, either—not even her work line.

In her one nod to the holiday, Missy had left a basket of miniature candy bars on her doorstep, with a printed message for all the children to "Please, Take Just One." Perhaps not surprisingly, this request was ignored. The first kids who came to the door, a crew of hulking pre-teens in ghoulish Freddy, Jason and Arnold masks who were all a bit too old to be trick-or-treating in Missy's estimation, dumped the entire basket of goodies into their own bags, then raced off like hyenas, chortling and swapping high-fives. The other, younger, more deserving kids would get nothing.

What a shame, Missy thought. She wished there was something she could do about it. But the fact was, the final bag of Snickers bars that she still had lying on her kitchen counter was already earmarked for her, and her alone.

On that note, Missy reached for the bag, ripped at its thin plastic sheathing, and dug right in. The pills she was taking now by the handful had her riding a roller coaster of hyper highs and head-hanging lows all day long, but there was nothing like a good, old-fashioned sugar buzz when push came to shove. Bag in tow, she hopped on her elliptical, turned on MTV, cranked the volume, and started munching and churning, munching and churning. The paradoxical nature of these two activities didn't faze her in the slightest. She was calling the shots.

Forty-five minutes later, the bag was empty, the floor was littered with wrappers, and Missy was basking in the endorphin high from her workout. She had just burned almost five hundred calories! And once she ran to the toilet and jammed a finger down her throat to expel all the chocolate and nougat she'd just snarfed down, she felt even better. She caressed her abs, preening with delight—still just as trim and tight as ever.

Of course, if Missy *hadn't* raced back out of the bathroom, as if denying that the purge even happened ... if she'd instead turned on the lights (Missy rarely turned on lights anymore; they hurt her eyes) and taken a good long look at herself in the mirror, something she hadn't done in weeks now because, well, what was the point? ... if she had seen the deadness of her eyes and the dark rings that framed them, the prison-like pallor of her skin, the blotchiness of her complexion, and the limp stringiness of her hair ... if she had seen those things, and stopped long enough to contemplate their source, perhaps they might have collectively provided her the dose of bitter, ugly reality that she so sorely needed.

But she didn't. Instead, she headed straight back into the kitchen to grab another handful of pills and pour a big glass of white wine to wash them down with. The effect of this registered so quickly one might surmise it was largely Pavlovian in nature. The drugs couldn't possibly enter her system that fast, especially in light of the insanely high tolerance she had built up. Nevertheless, for just a second or two, it allowed Missy to look almost like her old self again: a world-beater, with fire in her eyes.

It was also enough of a boost for her to confront her dusty, ignored answering machine, and push the play button on the "Message Center," her lone receptacle to actual human voices from the outside world. The button was flashing, its meter indicating that she had two new messages. For former Master-of-the-Universe Missy, this tally would have been shockingly low. In the old days, she'd return to her office from an open house and find a heaping stack of messages waiting for her, many marked as "urgent," all in the space of a single hour. Now, it had been a good four or five days since she had checked, and all she had to show for it was two lousy calls. And of those, one if not both were likely to be unsolicited telemarketing calls. Or perhaps, bill collectors. They were even worse.

Of course, none of this would have even been an issue was it not for a call she had received a couple weeks before, from Richard Block and the other senior partners at Eureka Realty. In their cloying, faux-concerned voices, they claimed that they had no choice but to reassign her remaining accounts and let her go. "Undetermined suspension," they called it. It seemed the other realtors had been complaining, and secretly lobbying against her. They apparently didn't like sharing their clients and commissions with someone who never even bothered showing up in person to acknowledge a sale or collect her checks. It was poor etiquette, and bad for office morale, and kind of creepy to boot. Who did she think she was, anyway?

Missy had thought about making a surprise appearance at the office and showing all those petty ingrates how wrong they were. To give them a piece of her mind in the formidable style they apparently deemed as being a "bad cop." But then, even though she still stood by her belief that she could do her job perfectly well from home, she decided it wasn't even worth the effort. Truth be told, there was very little related to her work or to Eureka Realty as a whole that she had felt was "worth the effort" for quite a while now. They would miss her, though. That much she was sure of.

On that note, Missy still clung fondly to one little nugget of secret office info that she had managed to cull from her former assistant, Jerome, prior to her dismissal, which kept a smile on her face and allowed her to keep believing that she was fully in the right on all that had transpired. That was, Jolene Wyatt had lost the Schwarzenegger account. Turns out, Maria had chosen to keep their family anchored in Brentwood, and as for Arnold, he would stay in a downtown hotel suite whenever he was in town. While Missy was sure that Team Player Jolene and the other partners all simply wrote this off as being, sadly, "one of those things," Missy knew that if *she* had been steering the deal, that never would have happened. Arnold and Maria would have toured and been made privy to so many appropriate, well-protected estate properties that they would have inevitably seen at least one that they simply couldn't pass up. After all, it wasn't as if they didn't have the money. And certainly, too, a politician of Arnold's stature needed a place to call his own, better yet a *showplace*, something far more intimate and inspiring than any old office or hotel room, where he could forge alliances and hammer out deals and entertain dignitaries. Not to mention the fact that being governor of a state, *any state*, much less California, and not at least keeping a part-time residence in the city where he held office was downright tacky. These were things she would have told Arnold and Maria, point blank, no minced words. And they would have listened, too. She knew they would have.

But enough of that. It was in the past now. It was out of her hands and out of her life. She turned to the answering machine again and pushed "play," before the pills wore off and she started second-guessing herself again.

The first message began. Much to her surprise, it was neither a telemarketer nor a bill collector whose voice emerged from the machine. It was her mother, Mamie, who she hadn't heard from since their nasty spat after the debate.

"Hello, Melissa." The voice was curt and yet overwrought at the same time. "I know you don't want to hear anything from me anymore, your nagging old mother, but I thought you should know that Cliff—your *father*—had a heart attack. I'm with him at the hospital now. I don't know if he ..."

The voice cut off. Missy couldn't be sure, but she thought her mother might have been crying. Not the crocodile sobs she used so skillfully to elicit guilt and pity, but real tears.

"Anyway, I thought you should know."

A beat, then the second message played. There was no voice, but she thought she heard a heartbroken whimper, with the words "doctor," "ER," and "stat" faintly audible in the background. The line went dead, and the machine beeped to signal that the playback was complete.

Missy quickly dialed her parent's home number. No answer. And, of course, neither of her parents had a cell phone. That would be far too logical.

She stared at the receiver in her hand for several seconds, as if waiting for it to offer up a solution for what she should do next. Then, she looked to her spice rack, filled not with rosemary or oregano, but rather an arsenal of prescription pill bottles. But no answer was forthcoming there, either. Finally, she turned to her front door, with a look of pure dread, as if it was a direct portal to the deepest bowels of hell itself.

Despite that fear, written boldly across her wan, haggard face, when she finally moved from her spot by the phone, it was not to her trusty stash of pills but rather to the kitchen table, where the jacket to her black Donna Karan power suit had laid untouched for over two months now, ever since that first night when she returned home from the Gas N' Sip and shut herself away.

Like a superhero donning her cape, Missy grabbed the jacket and threw it on, around her shoulders and over the dingy cotton pajamas she had been wearing for more days in a row than she cared to remember. Then, scooping up her car keys with a determined swipe of her hand, she went to the front door and—before she could talk herself out of it—flung it open for the first time in weeks and dove off into the dark of the night.

Trick or treat, indeed.

25

TEAM ARNOLD

As soon as he got back home to Sacramento, Todd had, as promised, immediately dove into the implementation of his Team Arnold Plan.

However, despite its grandiose title and vast touting, this plan—at its launch—consisted solely of Todd tracking down a glossy still photo of Arnold in a tuxedo from the movie *True Lies* and taping it up in his store's front display window.

It was only upon successful completion of this initial task that Todd's thoughts finally turned to the notion of what a "step two" for his bold scheme might entail. After much deliberation, what he ultimately settled upon was a grassroots marketing campaign, based out of his shop and spearheaded by himself, to build awareness and generate excitement around Arnold's inauguration and the swirl of elegant balls and gala celebrations that would inevitably surround it.

The perceived benefit of this, aside from the goodwill it would engender, was the likelihood that at least some of the lucky invitees would have to rent formalwear in order to attend. As such, Todd started scouring the *Bee* religiously, every day, looking for a schedule of inaugural events that he could post in the window alongside Arnold's picture. This, Todd reasoned, would add incentive for shoppers while also lending the impression that his store, Todd's Tuxedos, was an official, if not *the* official, formalwear supplier for these events—and by extension, for the Schwarzenegger regime as a whole.

It was only after a full week of feverish anticipation and paper scanning that Todd finally came upon a lone related item, hidden deep in the *Bee*'s Metro section. Sadly, though, the information it offered was not of the sort Todd had hoped for. In the article, written by some jerk-off named Brine, it claimed that there would be no galas or balls or celebratory events of any kind. The story quoted one party-pooping official who said that, in light of the circumstances, involving both the state's calamitous fiscal condition and the nature of the recall itself, such celebrations simply wouldn't be appropriate. The organizer went on to claim that Arnold had approved this cost-cutting measure personally, and would instead greet legislators and other local representatives at a couple of low-key gatherings yet to be announced.

Todd was despondent at first. Then, he became defiant. He refused to believe any of this downbeat liberal propaganda, particularly the part about Arnold's role in the decision-making process. If anybody knew the value of some well-orchestrated hoopla to get the ball rolling, it was a big Hollywood star like Arnold. No, Todd was convinced that this mandate was being forced upon him by the capital's small-minded, back-room number crunchers. Weasels like that only understood the cut and dry, the bottom line; things that could be neatly reduced to a fixed number and logged into their beloved spreadsheet programs. The intangibles that a heroic figure like Arnold offered, like glamour and pizzazz and star power, were beyond them.

Firm in this belief, Todd waited for Arnold to come to his senses and overrule the decision. To announce to one and all that he was hosting a big black-tie kickoff bash of epic proportions, one that would let the people of Sacramento and everyone else in the state know that there was a new sheriff in town, and that he knew how to party. After all, wasn't that how JFK had done it? Sure, there was a Cold War going on at the time, and all sorts of ugly racial tensions, but that was the whole point: you throw on a tuxedo, drink a little bubbly, smile for the cameras, and what does that do? It makes people think you're not worried, that you have everything under control. And as crazy as that sounds, it works. Before you know it, everybody's feeling better about things because, hey, if you can look so happy and relaxed when the pressure's on, things must not be as bad as they seem. And if that's the case, then people inevitably want to hop on the bandwagon and be a part of it. That's how Camelots are made, dammit!

But despite all of Todd's wishful thinking, Arnold never changed his mind, and neither did the number crunchers. The inauguration schedule was set in stone, and it was to be an informal no-frills affair all the way around. For Todd, this was a cruel blow. He had counted on a big bump in sales figures to help him catch up on his bills, and pay off some of the crushing debt he had accrued while in Moscow. Without that, he was doomed to fall even further behind—and his plans for showering his new family with gifts and good times would likely be delayed as well.

To his credit, though, Todd did not dwell on these disappointments. Like his old high school football coach always said, when the going gets tough, the tough get going. He wasn't going to let this temporary setback get him down. Oh, no. It just meant he had to work that much harder, and reformulate his strategy to make it that much stronger. That way, when it all paid off, the taste of victory would be even sweeter.

On that note, Todd stepped up his efforts even further. He worked longer hours at the shop, every day, Monday through Saturday, not even skipping out for the occasional happy hour cocktail like he used to. He missed no opportunity to talk up

Arnold with customers, hyping the fiscal upturns and glitzy social events ("Might as well buy your tux now!") that were sure to come. When not at the shop, he turned his attention to the home front, where he labored mightily on the house and the yard, tackling projects one after another, painting, sanding, sweeping, and spraying. He made sure to spend quality time with Lana and Alek, too, cooking burgers on the grill, basking with them in his pride-and-joy redwood hot tub, watching early-season Kings games on the tube—anything they wanted, so long as it didn't cost much money or take too much time. His budget and his schedule were too tight to do otherwise.

Alas, when Todd sat down during the first week of November to go over his books again, he found that, despite these renewed efforts, it wasn't enough. He was still operating at a deficit.

But while this was tough for Todd to accept, the truth was, the reasons behind it weren't tough to pinpoint. For starters, he now had two extra mouths to feed, and clothe, and house; it's hard to tighten the belt when that belt suddenly has to hold three people. There was also the cost of all those home improvements he had been undertaking—but again, he had others to consider now, and he felt he owed it to them to make their new place of residence look as nice as possible. And as for the shop, well, he felt like he was pretty much doing all that he could there, too. It's not like he could *make* people rent more tuxedoes.

In the final analysis, though, it was those damn credit cards that were the real killers. As if the interest payments weren't bad enough, the credit card company number crunchers (them again!) had jacked up his rates, and tacked on penalty charges to boot, all because he'd missed a single payment while he was out of the country. Even worse, this little slip also doomed him to some sort of bad-debtor's file, so he had bill collectors hounding him at all hours, asking in their faux-courteous tone if he'd like to "make an easy payment right now over the phone," even though if it were so damn easy, he would have already done it, thank you very much. But that didn't matter to these vultures. The calls kept coming, and the debts kept mounting.

So there it was. Todd was in a real jam, one that was only getting worse by the day. And he quickly deduced that there was only one way to correct the situation: the Tisdale clan needed to generate more income. Since he was already working his fingers to the bone, the obvious answer was for some other family member to step up to the plate and contribute. Alek was in school, spoke halting English, and was only seven years old to boot, so the obvious choice was Lana. To Todd's way of thinking, this was not an unreasonable request. She had worked in Moscow, so why not here in Sacramento, too? For the last five weeks, she had been witness to the sweat of his labors. That was how the American Dream was built. Brick by brick, bill by bill, tux by tux, hour by hour. It was time for his wife to join the effort.

But while this was simple and obvious in theory, execution was a different story. The truth was, Todd was concerned how his wife might receive this little proposal. Since arriving, Svetlana had slowly eased her way into a sort of scattershot domesticity, but she remained rather touchy whenever the issue of household duties came into question. This included their sex life, which was still infrequent, and—being brutally honest—lackluster. But, it *also* counted among its numbers the more mundane day-to-day matters of cooking, cleaning, washing clothes, doing dishes, and buying the groceries on a tightly-fixed budget ("clipping coupons" was apparently not a concept in his wife's current lexicon).

Nothing, in fact, was ever easy with Lana. Maybe it was that hot Slavic blood of hers. Maybe it was the hardships she had endured in her previous marriage. Whatever the case, Todd decided it was best to step lightly when broaching the subject—to frame it as nothing more than a hoot, a lark, something that might help her get out of the house more and broaden her horizons and meet new people. It would be fun! It would be a blast! She would probably love it!

Or maybe not. Todd finally found a golden opportunity to chat, after a dinner that he had strategically helped cook and clean up after. He and Lana were kicking back with a glass of wine while Alek was playing in his room. Lana seemed relaxed. It was time to strike. Todd rubbed her shoulders and asked if she liked it here in sunny California. Lana nodded yes. He asked her if she wanted to get out more, do more, see more, meet more people. She nodded again, and turned to him with eyes aglow.

"Oh yes, I would very much like that!"

"Well, then, you should. By all means, do it. Get out there. Heck, I bet you could find a job around here in no time."

Lana's smile vanished, and her eyes narrowed. "A job?"

Off her dagger-like glare, Todd proceeded cautiously. Clearly, it was no time for doomsday tales. "Well, yeah. Heck, Lana, what better way is there to meet people? You tell me. And hey, if you bring home a little money, too—"

Nostrils flaring, Lana cut Todd off. "Do you know what I do back in Moscow, Todd? Do you? I scrub toilets. I clear tables. I sweep, I cook, I clean, I polish—"

"Lana, come on, you can't—"

Lana cut him off again. She was on a roll now. "*Twelve hours a day* I do this, Todd. Every day. Then, I must make boss happy, to keep job. Then, I go home and do more of same for Alek. Then, it start all over again. Again and again and again!"

"Hey, look, Lana, I didn't mean—"

"No. I know you don't. That is why I tell you. I am here now. I make good home for you. I cook your food. But no job. No more job."

It all became clear to Todd now. Lana had her own vision of the American Dream, and it did not, in any way, involve seeking gainful employment. As a result, Todd started checking the help-wanted ads the very next day … for himself. That is how he ended up with a part-time second gig as, ironically enough, a telemarketer, for a local home remodeling firm.

When the shop closed at six, Todd would stay another two hours and work the phones, cold-calling local residents at dinnertime (something he hated when it was done to him) to see if, by chance, they might be looking to add a bathroom or update a kitchen or re-shingle a roof. It was a straight commission gig, so Todd had to deliver signed contracts in order to actually get paid, but it was the only thing he could find that would fit into his already-hectic schedule. And better yet, he could do the job without anyone knowing about it, thus allowing him to keep his lion-king pride intact, and keep secret from his little family how bad his financial troubles truly were.

The fact was, Lana's approval meant more to him than anything. While it was true that their relationship had its up and downs, he chalked that up to the swiftness of their courtship. They were still getting their feet as a couple, getting to know one another—their moods, their rhythms, their habits, their quirks. But being with Lana offered him something no local woman could have. She offered him a clean slate. A chance to start fresh and be the man he saw himself as in his dreams; the man he'd always wanted to be. And to be sure, being married to a tall, exotic, drop-dead gorgeous woman like her was a pretty good start. That was why he worked so hard all the time, harder in fact than he ever had in his entire life. He wanted to prove that he was worthy of her.

And that was what was foremost in his mind when, despite all the adversity he'd encountered, Todd forged ahead with his Team Arnold Plan, laying the groundwork for its most crucial step thus far.

Consulting his raggedy Rolodex, he scrolled through the tumbler until he found the card he was looking for, then quickly punched in a local number.

"Hello! Todd Tisdale for Denny Wagstaff, please," he opened eagerly.

He waited, hopefully, until the reply came back.

"No? Too busy right now?" Todd's face collapsed into a grimace. This was his best shot. His *only* shot.

But then, tapping his pencil hard against the desk's surface, he suddenly decided that he was through taking "no" for an answer. It was time for action.

"No. No message. Just do me a favor and go ask your Mr. Wagstaff there if *I* was too busy when his son puked all over himself on the way to prom and needed a new tux that matched his date's dress and could be delivered to the alley behind the American Legion Hall. And at ten o'clock on a Saturday night, no less. Ask him that."

There was a pause on the line. A moment later, Todd smiled triumphantly. "Hey, Denny, how's it goin', partner? Good, good! Glad to hear it. Well, yeah, there is, actually. Remember how you always said you owed me one, or maybe even two? Well, it's been a while, I know, but ol' Todd here finally needs to call in the favor. Big time."

Denny, as fate would have it, was a bigwig at the local Chamber of Commerce. Thanks to his chits in the favor bank, as well as some well-timed pleading, Todd was able to wangle a pair of tickets for the inauguration and a reception at the Convention Center to follow. The reception, Denny assured, and *re*-assured repeatedly, would be small enough, and intimate enough in scale, that Todd would be able, if he so desired, to get up close and meet Arnold personally.

Todd was ecstatic. With his back against the wall, in desperate need of a break, he had created one for himself. He had made it happen. And if he could just take advantage of that, and seize the moment, and meet Arnold, and tell him about his store, and introduce him to Lana, he knew, *just knew*, that they would hit it off. And once that happened, everything was going to fall neatly into place, just as he had always predicted.

And from there? From there, Todd told himself, the sky was still the limit.

26

THE CARVER FAMILY REUNION

Missy sat in the Mercy General emergency room, waiting for news about her father, surrounded by mummies and vampires and other freaks of the Halloween night. Although not in costume, she was paler and deader-looking than all of them, even the young zombie couple making out in the corner. But Missy was not of a right mind to notice this. Her latest salvo of pills was quickly wearing off. Her head was pounding from the withdrawal pains. And truth be told, she was already a wreck simply from being out in public again.

Bouncing her knees and bopping her head, Missy's glazed, bloodshot eyes slowly crept over to the ER's adjacent pharmacy window. Through the glass, she could see them there, all the little helpers and healers, deliciously lit, row upon row and shelf after shelf. Missy licked her lips. It was so late, there was only one person manning the booth. His back was turned; he seemed tired, distracted. It was almost too easy. She wondered what it would take to—

"Miz Carver?"

Missy bolted up in her seat, looking wired and shifty. "Yes? Yes! That's me. I'm Missy Carver."

A squat black nurse that matched the world-weary voice perfectly stood there, giving her a long, hard, dubious look before finally turning her attention back to the medical chart in her hand.

"... Okay. So you were inquiring about your father, I believe? A Mister Clifford Carver?"

"That's right. How is he?"

"Well, he came through here earlier this evening, all right, but we dismissed him a little over two hours ago."

"No."

"Yes, ma'am. I checked him in and out myself."

"Oh, you have *got* to be kidding me," Missy replied, her voice turning to venom.

"No, Miz Carver, I am not," the nurse replied, equally sassy in her tone. "When your father came in, he was clutching at his chest, saying the pain was so bad he *must* be having himself a heart attack. Well, we checked his vitals and it didn't seem likely, but he was so all-fire sure of it, we went ahead and ran all the tests, anyway. And just like we thought, they come back negative. Every last one of 'em."

"So ... I don't understand. What was wrong with him?" Missy asked.

"Well, that's the funny thing," the nurse replied drolly. "Wasn't till we was done with everything we could do that he finally came clean about the big ol' spicy sausage pizza he had just ate, and the 2-liter bottle of Mountain Dew he polished off, and that scary movie he'd been watchin' from that big 'ol recliner of his—"

"Wait a minute. You're saying all he had was *indigestion*?"

"I expect that's pretty much the sum of it. Yes, ma'am."

Missy reeled back in her seat, ready to kill somebody, preferably her parents.

"Sorry you had go to all the trouble."

"So am I. Jesus. I can't believe this." Missy shut her eyes tight, shaking her head, willing it all to be just a nightmare. But then, a wave of nausea swept over her. She bolted back up again.

"Where's your bathroom?"

"You all right?"

"Just tell me where the bathroom is."

"Down the hall and to the left."

With a nod, Missy raced past the nurse and down the hall, ducking through the door and into the closest stall just in time to let the second wave of partially-digested Snickers bars, pain pills, porterhouse steak, and her own clotting blood erupt from her stomach, out into the toilet bowl. Thankfully, it was now so late, she had the space all to herself. She was able to finish retching and tidy up after herself, and no one else saw or heard a thing.

When she emerged, still a bit unsteady on her feet, Missy stood at the door, looking out upon the waiting area she had just left and the smattering of costumed people still hanging around for news of their friends and loved ones. In this setting, they all looked utterly foolish. But, in truth, Missy felt like a bigger fool than any of them. Mamie had done it to her again, creating misplaced guilt and false alarm and making her waste her time and effort for nothing. It was just like her, and it was enough to send Missy fleeing back to her house for another go-round of blissful binging and isolation.

Before this re-retreat could be successfully launched, however, Missy's eyes caught on a bank of pay phones. Most likely, the same phones that Mamie had used to summon her. She raced to the closest one and punched out her parents' home number, determined to give her mother a dressing-down so scathing that she would never forget it.

The phone rang four times before Mamie finally picked up. Hearing her voice, so calm and composed now, with a singsongy cheerfulness to its enunciation of the word "Hel-looo," as if nothing at all of any direness had transpired, made Missy even angrier.

"Good to see you're home, Mother. At least one of us is."

However, before Missy could go any farther, Mamie's brave facade gave way. She began to choke up and sob, thanking Missy over and over for caring enough to call. "Oh, Missy, it was awful. Your poor father, he said he couldn't breathe. And he's such a big man, you know. I didn't know what to do, so I called 911. And those paramedics, they said he had to go to the hospital, that it looked like he might be having a heart attack. Oh, honey, I thought we were going to lose him for good this time!"

Mamie proceeded to recount the entire story, somehow managing yet again to neglect mentioning the pizza, or the two liters of highly caffeinated soda, or their failure to alert the medical staff of the same. Also excluded from this retelling were the messages that Mamie had left, which made it sound as if last rites were being administered and Cliff was already seeing angels. When Mamie finally got to the end of her tale, explaining how this had been a real wakeup call for both her and Cliff, and how they were determined to change their ways once and for all, a thoroughly maddened Missy could hold her tongue no longer.

"Mother, please! You've said the same thing a million times."

"I know I have, honey, but I mean it this time, and so does your father. The doctor told him that with all his bad habits, he already has one foot in the grave, and if that's true, I can't be far behind. We need to make a change."

"That's what I've been saying to you for years now! But you've got to really do it this time, Mother, and stick with it. You can't just try it out part time, or halfway, or when it's convenient. You need to make a full-on commitment, or else it's just another wasted effort, and you'll be right back where you started."

"I know, baby. But what choice do we have? We have to try. We have to."

Choice. It's a funny thing. Even when a person chooses, acts under their own free will, they still often end up with something far different from what they actually wanted. In Missy's case, when she chose to confine herself to her house, she certainly had no intention of becoming such a total recluse—it just *evolved* that way—and she certainly never had the intention of getting hooked on the various medications she was taking, either. So, when she offered to support her parents in their plans, it wasn't with the thought of having them move in with her while doing so. However, the more she and Mamie talked, and the more Missy thought about it, the more she came to realize it was the only chance they had to succeed.

Missy presented this theory to Cliff and Mamie, face to face, later that morning. She looked awful, and her parents noticed, assuming it was from her late-night/early-morning hospital vigil. Missy offered no amendment to this theory. Her problems were her own; she was there to talk about theirs.

The three sat in the wood-laminated den of the Carvers' home, a dilapidated little bungalow resting in the deep shadows of a giant electrical tower, whose looming, monstrous presence and incessant hum helped bring power into Sacramento and the rest of the Central Valley. The Carvers listened from the plush confines of their matching, side-by-side La-Z-Boys, which were framed by display cases featuring Mamie's cherished collection of Franklin Mint *Manifest Destiny* plates and figurines.

With an army of hand-crafted gold rushers, railroad barons, and coolies staring down at her, her dad Cliff hawking up gobs of phlegm and constantly reaching for the remote, and Mamie swatting his hand away and asking if anybody was hungry, it was difficult to maintain a train of thought, but Missy somehow managed, and she minced no words: "See, this

is exactly what I'm talking about. Dad, you sit in that chair
all day; it's a wonder you still know how to walk. Mom, you
cook all day, which enables you to *eat* all day, too. You both
smoke like chimneys. Your diets are horrible. Neither one of
you has worked in months. You don't get any exercise. Dad,
you have a beer in your hand every time I see you, and Mom,
you drink those wine coolers like they were fruit juice. Both
of you are bad influences on the other. Even this *house* is a bad
influence; it literally reeks of tobacco and fried foods and stale
beer and—"

ZZZZtt, ZZZZZtt, ZZZZZZZZZZtttt.

From outside, an eerie buzzing, not unlike the ray-gun
sound effects from some old Buck Rogers movie.

"Power lines must be really juicin' today," Cliff opined
casually.

"Yeah, and I'm sure *that's* doing wonders for you, too!" Missy
paused, taking a deep breath to calm herself and gather her
wits for her big closing argument.

"Look, you two, here's the facts: if you stay here ... if someone's
not around to watch you every second of every day ... one of
you is going to slip, and the other will happily follow suit. It's
hopeless, and I think, deep down, you both know it's hopeless.
The only chance you have is to make a complete change, leave
all this behind, and move in with me. That's the bottom line."

This impassioned pitch was met with silence. Mamie turned
to Cliff for a reaction, but he just coughed and stared forlornly
at the darkened TV screen. His favorite show, *Bass Masters*, was
on, and he was missing it.

Mamie finally spoke, a selfless martyr sadly resigning
herself to her fate. "I don't know, baby. If we're really as hopeless
and horrible as you say, why would you even want us in that
lovely house of yours? We certainly don't want to *intrude*."

The acid in her mother's tone was unmistakable, but Missy
let it go for once. She was trying her best to stay on point, an
effort which was growing ever more difficult as the last couple

Golden State   231

of stray pills she had found stuck to the bottom of her purse wore off and her head began to feel like it was expanding and contracting along with each new wave of withdrawal pain she was experiencing.

"If you're serious about this, I want to help. And if it works, it'll be worth it, for all of us. You'll get back on your feet, and I won't have to worry. It's a win-win."

Mamie bit her lip. Missy had taken her best salvo and kept right on coming. She turned again to her husband. "Cliff? What do you think?" Cliff sighed and looked away, tired of all the drama and disruption of routine. Mamie upped the intonation of her voice another several decibels—*how much more must I endure to keep this family going?* "Cliff, Missy wants an answer, and you know how she gets."

Cliff finally turned to his wife, exasperation shooting from his sagging, bloodshot eyes. "If I just say yes, can we turn on my damn show already? It's nearly half over."

"If that's what you want."

"That's what I want. Now give me back my remote."

And that was that. The decision was made. The TV was turned back on. The bass were biting. And Missy's parents were coming to live with her, full time.

Needless to say, this transition was destined to be neither a smooth nor an easy one for anyone involved. To her credit, Missy realized this, and she also knew that if they were ever going to do it, they had to do it right then and there. To strike while the iron was hot, as it were, before the old excuses and delays and delusions began to set back in. Thus, as soon as Cliff's show was over, she pulled him up and out of his chair, got her mom away from the stove (where she was already well underway on a frosted Bundt cake), and led them both into their small, cluttered bedroom so they could each pack a bag of clothes and toiletries for the move. Both stalled and complained incessantly. However, Missy knew that the key was to get them out of their comfort zone before it fully dawned on them just how drastic the changes were going to be. It was an intervention, and that was how interventions worked. Grab the targets while their guards are down and their minds and bodies are pliable, and then push, push, push, until the desired results are achieved.

Ironically enough, the same thing could be said for Missy, too. She never would have left her house voluntarily. The previous weeks had proven her mettle, and steeled her resolve. Only a life-or-death emergency, such as the one she had been led to believe had occurred, was enough to induce a hair-trigger response from her and break the cycle. And now that it was, Missy was pushing herself even further, reaching out to her parents and inviting them into her dysfunctional biosphere of a home so as to hopefully broaden the long-range prospects for all of them. It was a noble effort, even if Missy herself had not yet grasped its full ramifications.

Those ramifications started to become clearer, however, as soon as the Carvers, *en famille*, piled into her Lexus for the drive over to her place. Mamie and Cliff had wanted to drive themselves, but Missy insisted they ride with her. Not only did she fear they would stray off-route and head for some fast-food drive-thru or liquor store for one last fix, but she was also afraid that, owing to the condition of Cliff's rusty, tool-strewn pickup and their *Hee Haw*-esque attire, her neighbors might mistake them for yard workers and try to hire them. That was an indignity she simply could not bear.

This, in turn, only exacerbated her parents' suspicions. Why was it so important that they ride with her, anyway? Missy blurted out what she thought was a clever excuse relating to community restrictions on overnight street parking. However, her parents knew that her house had a two-car garage, and she only had one car herself. Why couldn't they park in the extra spot? Missy spun another tall tale, involving storage and garage door remotes. But Cliff, who loved his old truck like the son he never had, fired right back yet again: "Why not the driveway, then, huh? What about that, Missy?"

On and on it went, throughout the entire twenty-minute trek across town, all the way into the driveway itself, where Cliff noted yet again that his pickup would have fit on there just fine. And with that, Missy finally realized that it wouldn't be only her parents' behavior that would be held under the microscope—hers would be, too. This, in turn, made her realize how much she had come to rely on lying and deception as her go-to weapons to get her way and avoid unwanted detection.

Just like a junkie, she realized soberingly.

On that note, the Carvers got out of the car and grabbed their bags from the trunk, Cliff still muttering bitterly about the truck.

As he and Mamie started up the front walk, Missy burst to the head of the pack, not just to unlock the front door but also to assure that, upon entry, she could get in first and tuck away any potentially incriminating items from clear view. Looming largest in her mind was the cornucopia of painkillers she had scattered all over the kitchen. And for more than just propriety's sake; she was also dying to knock back a few of those bad boys, ASAP, just to take the edge off.

However, once they were through the door, she quickly realized how much there was to hide—far too many things, far too spread out, for her to do so in any sort of stealthy manner. And in viewing the musty, murky space through an outsider's eyes, she finally began to grasp how perverted her existence had truly become.

"My Lord, Missy, this house is like a morgue! Clifford, turn on some lights, I'll open the drapes. And what's that *smell*? It's like something died in here!"

The notion of her mother accusing anybody of household odors was one of the most ludicrous things that Missy had ever heard, and she opened her mouth to say just that—but then, she caught herself. She had far more pressing needs.

"Maybe I left something on the stove. I'll go check."

Missy sprinted into the kitchen and grabbed a handful of whichever little helpers were closest. Purple and blue and pink, round and ovoid and square, she began choking them down indiscriminately, as fast as humanly possible, to speed their effect.

"Well? Did you find it?" Mamie bellowed from the foyer.

Missy forced the last couple of pills down her bone-dry gullet. "No. No problem here that I can see." Hands shaking from the feverishly anticipated rush, Missy swept all the remaining pills and bottles into a side drawer, buried them under an assortment of delivery menus, and then raced back out. "Are you sure it's not from outside?"

"I know a stink when I smell one, young lady. And it *stinks* in here!" Mamie wrinkled her nose, her beady eyes wandering over the room like a GI on border patrol in the Baghdad Green Zone.

"Well, I'm sorry, Mother. I'll spray, okay? I'll use incense. I'll order flowers. It'll smell like a friggin' bed of roses in here if that's what you want."

Missy paused a moment. Took a deep breath. The pills were kicking in. Inhale, exhale, aaah. She felt at peace again with the world.

"Why don't I show you two the bedroom you'll be staying in?"

"Well, I certainly hope it's in better shape than out here," Mamie countered.

"The room is perfectly fine, mother. It's bigger than the one you have at home. It has fresh sheets and towels. It's all brand new, in fact. You're the first overnight guests I've had."

"Oh! Well ... *that's* nice! Cliff, isn't that nice?"

"Yep, uh huh, real nice." Missy's father's focus was elsewhere. "Big TV. That a plasma screen?"

Missy nodded absently. She suddenly seemed troubled again.

But Cliff had found nirvana. "Must be a forty-incher, at least."

"Forty-two, Dad."

"Hoo, boy. You got cable?"

"Umm, yeah. Sure, Dad. The works. Surround sound, too."

"Surround sound? Damn. Well, that's nice, Missy. That's real nice."

Cliff smiled for the first time all day. While he had yet to learn what hardships lay in store for him, he knew his television viewing experience would be top notch, and that was enough to make him content.

Missy, however, remained distracted by the disturbing realization that her parents, who she could barely tolerate on the best of days, were her first-ever overnight guests. She'd been in this house for nearly four years. And no guests? None at all? How was that even possible?

And yet, it was. Not one houseguest, ever. She suddenly realized how totally alone she felt. How she'd felt lonely at her core for as long as she could remember. But why was she only realizing this now, after having done everything in her power to avoid human contact of any kind for the last two months? What was wrong with her?

"Missy?"

Missy blinked. Her mom was standing there, arms held out to her sides, her face contorted into a look of suffering worthy of Joan of Arc herself. "Missy, baby, I can't hold these bags much longer. Can we go see that bedroom now?"

"Sure, Mom. Whatever you want. Let me help you with those."

Missy grabbed one of the bags and led her parents off toward the guest bedroom, determined to make the most of the situation, to try her hardest to be civil and friendly and engaging. And more importantly—*most* importantly—determined to do whatever it took to never again feel as utterly alone as she felt right then and there, at that very moment.

27

A MOMENT IN THE SUN

On Monday, November 17, 2003 at 11 a.m., Arnold Schwarzenegger was sworn in as the thirty-eighth governor of the great state of California. Vanessa Williams, Arnold's sexy co-star from the hit action movie *Eraser*, kicked things off by singing the National Anthem, providing the touch of Hollywood showmanship that Todd knew Arnold just couldn't resist. State Supreme Court Justice Ronald George then administered the oath of office, as Arnold placed his meaty paw on an old King James Bible, the same one used for Reagan's swearing-in, this time held by his own beaming wife, Maria Shriver.

With a sprinkling of celebrities in attendance, like Danny De Vito, Tom Arnold, and Rob Lowe, as well as a number of toothy Kennedy in-laws from back east, it was the first view of the "New Camelot" Todd had been so eagerly anticipating. Better yet, Todd was there to see it all for himself, live and in person, with a clearly dazzled Svetlana sitting by his side. And best of all, he and Lana were witnessing this starry history in the making, *not* among the looky-loos huddled forlornly behind hurricane fencing several hundred yards back, but rather up close and personal, in the ticketed VIP section, where they had assigned seats, and from which Todd was fairly certain he spotted the back of muscleman Lou Ferrigno's head just two rows ahead of him.

Arnold did his part, too, in stirring up the magic of the moment. First of all, by somehow—as if through sheer strength of will—summoning the sun from out of the clouds as he approached the podium to speak. Then, in his booming address, when he said, "I will not rest until our fiscal house is in order... I will not rest until the people of California come to see their government as a partner in their lives, not a roadblock to their dreams."

For Todd, it was as if Arnold were speaking to him personally. As if he understood all of Todd's troubles, and all his wishes for the future. Todd clapped and whistled and his eyes welled up with tears of joy. It was everything he could have hoped for, and more.

Spencer Brine was there, too, part of the team covering the inauguration for the *Bee*. He had been getting a lot of these choice assignments lately, while also continuing his usual obituary beat for Metro. But while he would have liked to believe that it was all because he was so bright and swift of pen, that his performance on these pieces was so uniformly strong it could not be denied, he actually had a strong suspicion that it had a lot more to do with Nikki's performance at Paul Hoying's Halloween party.

As fate would have it, Nikki's little tabletop genie-dance hadn't been perceived by Paul and the other staffers to be nearly the atrocity that Spencer had feared it would be. Rather, it had become something of a legend. Spencer, who had previously been seen as just another well-educated white boy trying to make a name for himself, now found his previous bland, milquetoast-y image being vastly upgraded. The newsroom gossip mill worked overtime, churning up the rumor that he was actually a rogue of the highest order. A rake. A ladies' man. As Paul himself said, brimming with admiration, "It's always the quiet ones who surprise you." Other editors now sought him out, too, and took an interest in his work. They asked him along for drinks, and included him in their late-night poker games. He became "one of the guys."

And Spencer basked in this newfound status, accepting every invitation and extra assignment that he could, knowing that this golden boy moment likely wouldn't last long and that he had to build up a network of allies and a body of work while it was still being made so readily available to him. In return, he gave them exactly what they wanted. Oh sure, there was his journalism, of which he was justly proud. But, Spencer realized, what his new friends at the paper were really after were some vicarious thrills. They wanted to know about Nikki, and any other women Spencer might know who were like Nikki, and what it was like to be with women like that. To walk on the wild side, as it were.

Spencer understood this, and indeed, even empathized with it. After all, it was a big part of what had drawn him to Nikki, too. And even though, in truth, his "wild side" experiences were rather limited, he did his best to deliver the goods. While refusing for reasons of discretion and good taste to offer up any graphic details, he would often toss out a tantalizing tidbit or two, such as the fact that Nikki liked playing dress-up (nudge, nudge), and that she should could really "work a pole" (wink, wink). Needless to say, these kind of vague innuendoes were highly enticing, and left all his new pals begging for more.

But the truth was, while Spencer managed to keep a brave face on at work for the sake of his new rep as a playboy, deep down he was nursing a heart so badly broken he thought it might never heal. When he woke up on that overcast Halloween morning to find Nikki missing, with a "Dear Spenser" note (yes, she'd misspelled his name, and that made it sting even worse) left behind on the fridge in her stead, it was the last he had seen of her. It had been over two weeks now. He had tried to track her down, to somehow make amends. He went to see her at the club, but his old bouncer pal Ivan had been given explicit instructions not to allow him in. He tried calling her at Roxy's apartment, where he had correctly surmised that she was staying, but she refused to come to the phone. He even used his skills with the pen to write her long, heartfelt letters, which eloquently expressed his regret and remorse and deep, deep longing for reconciliation.

Alas, none of these efforts were rewarded with a reply of any kind. It was as if he didn't even exist anymore. As if their time together had never even happened. And so, all that remained for Spencer to do was read her brief farewell note, over and over again. In it, Nikki apologized for her behavior at the party, and for causing him undue embarrassment. But perhaps it was for the best, she went on to say, because it had become clear to her that she wasn't making him happy anymore ("Untrue!" Spencer found himself calling out, to the lonely void of his empty condo), while he hadn't been making her feel particularly great, either (ouch). It was a mistake, obviously, for both of them, and it was best if they just both moved on with their lives, "seperitly." She wished him the best, signed her name, sealed it with a luscious good-bye kiss, and that was all she wrote, both literally and figuratively. She was gone, and she had stayed gone ever since.

But while Nikki was gone, she was far from forgotten. Thoughts and memories of her haunted Spencer at every turn, and he found himself dissecting every single moment they spent together, trying to figure out where it had all gone wrong.

Oftentimes, he could only find himself to blame. It was he who had started their fight that final night, after all. Hell, with his shortsighted oafishness, he had practically pushed her out the door. What an idiot he was! She was a goddess, a dream girl, and he had blown it! He had totally blown it!

On other occasions, when a cooler head prevailed, he would see things differently. It was she who had walked out on their relationship, not him. She hadn't even tried to make it work. She had just thrown their love away, like it was nothing but a misbegotten fling—like it was *worthless*. And in a way, this was even worse, because it meant this was yet another soul-crushing instance of Spencer's fate being controlled by someone else's actions. It made him feel like a puppet, a human puppet, being played with and then tossed aside at other peoples' whims.

As these ebbs and flows of loss and despair washed over him, Spencer's wounded ego would occasionally rise up to try and make him see that it was *Nikki* who should really be feeling the pain of the break-up. After all, when was she ever going to meet someone as smart and sensitive and loving as him? Never, that's when! If she knew what was good for her, she would soon come crawling back. And because he was a good and caring person, and a believer in second chances, he would forgive her, and they would resume their romance right where it had left off.

But, inevitably, this would lead to another wave of doubt. What if she didn't? What if she never came to appreciate what she had left behind? What if he never again saw her face, or felt her touch, or rejoiced in her embrace?

In that case, Spencer vowed—trying his best to convince himself at the same time—that he would simply have to show her what a horrible mistake she had made. It would be tough, but he would heal and move on, better than ever. And he would prosper, too. Oh, yes, he would prosper. And then who would have the last laugh? He would, dammit! It would be him, and only him.

All of a sudden, though, what Spencer heard all around him was not laughter, but rather applause—*inaugural* applause, for the new Governor Schwarzenegger, whose speech had apparently just ended. Spencer realized he hadn't heard even so much as a word of it. It was just background noise, running low and inconsequential over his own internal diatribe. He turned to his fellow reporters in the media pool, trying to look jaded and wise, all the while knowing he would have to beg a transcript from somebody before he could even start to work on his piece, which also required him to attend both the luncheon and reception to follow. It was going to be a long day.

Yes, indeed. A long, lonely day.

***

"Where is Arnold?"

That was the question on everybody's lips. Todd and Lana were at the Convention Center, standing around the reception hall and waiting along with everybody else for the scheduled meet-and-greet to truly begin.

Apparently, Arnold had been unavoidably detained at a luncheon for campaign insiders being held in the capitol's Rotunda Room, a lunch that Todd hadn't been aware of, much less invited to. Instead, he and Lana had supped at a Sizzler en route, where Todd toasted the new regime with a Surf and Turf and a Diet Coke, while Lana opted for the salad bar and an iced tea. The bill, it should be noted, came out to nearly thirty bucks, plus tip, which was more than Todd had planned to spend. Money was tighter than ever for him. In light of the circumstances, however, he was willing to splurge. This was a special day.

On that note, a buzz suddenly began to build from the front of the room, followed by a flurry of murmurs and applause, swelling until an eddy of synchronized movement was detectable up near the dais. Todd looked all around, standing on his tippy-toes to see what all the commotion was about.

And finally, there it was. Indeed, there *he* was, the man himself, in the flesh, Arnold Schwarzenegger, headed right for him, not more than twenty feet away. Todd was thrilled. Lana was agape. How could it get any better?

Todd knew. It was time for Team Arnold Plan step four. Grabbing Lana by the elbow, he made a weaving dash through the crowd, on a beeline for the white-hot center of the action. Arnold, bigger and taller and tanner than most politicians, was easy to spot, in the center of a group of pasty-faced apparatchiks who clung to him like remoras.

"Arnold! Arnold, hey!"

Arnold turned. He and Todd, very likely the two biggest men in the room, locked eyes. A silent acknowledgement of physical superiority passed between them—or at least, that was how Todd later recalled it. The fact that Todd was the only man wearing a tuxedo, save for the catering staff, may have also played a role.

Nevertheless, Arnold paused just long enough for Todd to reach out a hand in greeting. "Todd Tisdale, Todd's Tuxedos. Glad to have you aboard, Arnold."

Arnold shook his hand. "Thank you for coming. Nice tuxedo."

Todd beamed. "You like it? Well, hey, like I said, I have my own shop, and ..." Todd reached into his wallet for a business card.

"Fantastic." Arnold smiled, giving Svetlana an approving once-over as well.

"Yeah. You know, you should come by sometime. It's right there on G Street. I'm always there. I could put you in one just like it."

But by the time Todd looked back up, card in hand, Arnold was already being ushered up to the dais by his entourage. At the rear of the pack, one of the posse's junior members saw the proffered card and took it. "I'll make sure he gets it. Thanks again for supporting the Governor."

"You got it! Yes! Thank *you*!" Todd watched the clean-cut young man walk off and join the others, waiting for him to hand the card to Arnold. Instead, he simply pocketed it. But that was okay. This wasn't the right time, anyway. Better to wait, until it could receive Arnold's full and undivided attention. The important thing was that he and his staff now knew about Todd's Tuxedos. Team Arnold Step Four was a success!

Todd turned to Lana. She was beaming, too, basking right along with him in the afterglow of their starry encounter. It was exhilarating. They were both short of breath. The sweet smell of success lingered in the air.

But there was something else, too. It was the look in Lana's eyes, one he hadn't seen since the night back in Moscow when he had proposed. It was a look of genuine admiration. No, better: of adoration. Even of ... could it possibly be? ... lust. Lana's panting suddenly took on a new and urgent meaning for Todd, one which he had no intention of ignoring.

"I think we're done here, baby. Time to take you home."

Todd's words were laced with libidinous intent, and Lana didn't resist. She took his hand and off they went, back through the crowd, man and wife. And if Todd had anything to say about it, that bond would be consummated repeatedly and spectacularly for the rest of the afternoon.

As the couple rushed for the exit, Spencer watched them go. He could tell they were both elated by their little brush with celebrity, and he was happy for them. But from his point of view, it was a disappointing exchange. Arnold had been given a golden opportunity to interface with one of his new constituents, an appealing local with a story to share, which could have allowed Arnold to flex some of his own high-wattage charisma in a sound bite-friendly way. But rather than take advantage of this chance to shine, like he routinely did on talk shows, Arnold did the bare minimum. He shook the man's hand, offered up one of his lame trademark retorts, and then quickly retreated to the safety of the podium. It was as if, when confronted with a common citizen's simple desire to connect on a human level, without an agenda or a script or a pre-rehearsed set of parries and gag lines to work off of, he wasn't quite sure what to say or how to react.

Fortunately for the new governor, the rest of the reception was extremely well choreographed. Arnold made a brief, perfunctory speech about "uniting the parties on both sides of the aisle" for the "important mission" they were facing. He followed this by taking a handful of pre-screened questions from the crowd, which was comprised largely of fellow state legislators—none of whom Arnold seemed to recognize in the slightest— wondering which way the wind might be blowing as regards their own personal agendas and pet projects. He then grandly descended onto the arena floor to offer up a few more photo-ops and backslaps, with his aides close at hand to whisper in his ear and let him know ahead of time who he was favoring with his presence, and what interests they represented, before he was whisked away to his waiting Town Car.

Spencer, who was determined to pay far better attention to the proceedings than he had at the inauguration, stayed as close as possible to the big man, watching every action and hanging onto every syllable, hoping to capture any kernel of new information, some clue as to what Arnold's specific plans for the sweeping reforms he'd promised during his campaign might be.

Alas, no such scoop ever emerged. Aside from his vow to repeal a universally reviled car tax that Gray Davis had pushed through as a last-gasp attempt to refill his depleted coffers (not exactly a maverick move, by the way, and one that stood in direct contrast to his larger goal of fiscal accountability), Arnold continued to speak in hazy generalities. In fact, when considered objectively, Arnold sounded even dodgier than the career politicians who had preceded him in the office. It was almost as if he had showed up on the set of a new movie, but hadn't been given a script yet.

And actually, Spencer suddenly realized, that was *precisely* what it was like: the Governor, still waiting for his script. With a wry smile, he quickly jotted this down, knowing it would make the perfect tag line for his story.

However, at the same time, he also noted, with no small amount of irony, that with his own life in such total disarray, he was feeling the exact same way.

29

BACKWARDS, FORWARDS

The house where Rowena Pickett grew up hadn't changed much over the years.

In fact, since her father had died nearly a decade before, it hadn't changed at all, not even in the slightest, from the furniture and the paint colors all the way down to the pictures on the walls and the knickknacks on the mantle. From the moment Connie had gotten word of Eddie's Rocky Mountain trucking accident, she hadn't touched a single, solitary thing. It was like a shrine.

Rowena's old bedroom was no exception. It was just as she had left it on the day she moved out, back in the summer after she finished high school. It was still painted purple, her favorite color at the time. It still smelled like the patchouli she used to burn, to cover the smell of the cigarettes she used to smoke, sitting by her small bay window. Her old Aerosmith and Metallica posters were still on the walls, and her old clothes still in the closet. Even her old high school yearbooks were there, lying exactly where she left them, stacked front and center in her room's lone bookshelf, as if they were the only books in the entire world that truly mattered. Indeed, it was, all of it, perfectly preserved, down to the smallest detail, as if not a single day had passed since that time—a time capsule to her beloved and largely misspent youth.

However, Rowena *had* changed, and she was continuing to change, moment by moment, day by day, week by week. She could feel it, like a fetus, growing inside of her. It was an awakening to the world beyond her own inconsequential microcosm of it. And with that came the realization that life was about more than just herself, and her own petty problems, and her own transient stabs at happiness. And for a woman who had never before demonstrated a particularly vast intellectual or philosophical curiosity, this was truly an epiphany of the highest order.

Ironically, all of this had started with her *last* epiphany. Her Oprah epiphany. And it had begun to truly spread its wings the day she drove out to Vacaville to meet her ardently devoted pen pal, Lyle, for the first time. Rowena had never been inside a prison before, nor had she been exposed to the vast array of sad characters and even sadder tales contained within its walls. She suddenly grasped, through Lyle and others she met, how easily one could slip into a life of bottomless despair and crime. It made her look at the lockup's denizens with a greater sense of empathy, while also viewing her own life and its relatively tame obstacles with a deeper sense of gratitude—there but for the grace of God go I.

It was this new frame of mind that allowed her to take on the challenges of tending to her poor mother. Connie had Alzheimer's; there was no doubt about it now. Their family physician had confirmed the diagnosis, as well as Rowena's suspicion that her mother's condition was rapidly deteriorating. And even though Rowena was living with her now, making sure she ate right and took her vitamins and went on daily walks for exercise, it was to the point now where Connie forgot and misplaced and misspoke far more often than she remembered.

And this is where the Old Rowena likely would have lost patience and bailed out, cursing her mother for all the problems she was causing. But the New Rowena had a broader perspective on things. Connie didn't want to be like this. She didn't want to be a burden. And she surely didn't want to be incontinent, which was a recent development that had caused them both a fair amount of distress and discomfort. Connie had been a good wife to Eddie, and a good mother to her, and she had devoted much of the last thirty-five years of her life to taking care of both of them. Now, she was incapable of taking care even of herself. It was time to pass the baton.

And the truth was, overall, Rowena liked taking care of her mother. Sure, there were times, when Connie just stood there like an impartial observer to her own condition, that Rowena would have preferred to be anywhere else, doing anything other than what she was. But overall, she enjoyed the process, and the proximity. Better yet, she thought she was pretty good at it; not only at addressing the various ails that arose, but in anticipating them and averting them and ameliorating them. It just felt natural and right, like something she was born to do.

Since Rowena needed a new job, anyway, she decided to look around and see if there might be some kind of position out there for her that would relate to this new sense of purpose—or at least, be more rewarding than selling pumpkins. The logical place to start was Mercy General, the city's best hospital, and also its biggest, a fact Missy soon discovered firsthand when she went down to try and apply. With no clue where or how to begin, Rowena wandered Mercy's maze-like corridors, asking questions and receiving a lot of misguided advice, before she finally ran into a kindly old custodian who took her by the hand and led her personally to the office of the hospital's Staffing Director, Hal Quackenbush.

Entering, Rowena quickly realized what a big-shot Quackenbush was, as his outer office was manned by not one, but *two* secretaries. Both of them were bright-eyed and attractive, and they smiled welcomingly as she approached with a shy, hopeful smile of her own.

"Hi, my name's Rowena Pickett. I'm here to apply for a job?"

One of the women handed Rowena a form to fill out, and as she did so, Rowena made a point to be extra nice, asking about their work and if they liked it there, hoping an upbeat attitude might play in her favor when a decision was made. The ladies seemed to respond to this, and to her, and so, by the time Mr. Quackenbush finally beeped in to say he was ready, Rowena felt optimistic about her chances.

Alas, those hopes were quickly dashed when she laid eyes on Mr. Quackenbush himself. Despite the whimsical surname, Hal was no barrel-of-laughs kind of guy. Rather, he had all the markings of a dry, no-nonsense, toe-the-line bureaucrat. His office walls were white and unadorned, his desk was lined with reams of white paperwork, neatly arranged in like-sized stacks, and he was dressed to match, in a white, short-sleeve button-down shirt with extra starch in its blade-like collar. The coup de grace was his face, shaped like an axe, his mouth set into a grimace, his "smile lines" aimed resolutely downward. He looked like an assassin.

"Ms. Pickett, take a seat and we'll get right to it."

Rowena's own face settled into a sober grimace. Quackenbush was all business, so she thought it best to act the same.

"Application, please." Quackenbush extended a hand without even looking up. Rowena meekly handed over her form and took a seat, as requested, in as crisp and professional a fashion as she could muster.

Then, she waited, sitting with her legs crossed just so, as he stared down at the document she had just handed him, silently consuming it. No words, no gestures, no utterances or indications of any kind. After nearly a minute of pin-drop silence, Rowena couldn't take it anymore.

"Look, Mr. Quackenbush, I know I haven't done this kind of work before, but I think you'll find that I'm pretty flexible—that is, adaptable—to just about any type of work situation. I mean, I've done just about every kind of job there is to do. In plants and factories and stores and restaurants. I've worked at the counter and on the line. I've done manual types of jobs, too. Waitressing, busing tables. I work real well with people. Good people skills. I pride myself in that. And I'm pretty sure that would be true here, too. And there's another thing, something that doesn't show up on that piece of paper, which is that I've been taking care of my mother. She's got Alzheimer's, and her husband, my daddy, is passed on, and so it's just me and her, you see, so I moved back home a few weeks ago and ..."

In short, she rambled. And Quackenbush let her, nodding along and muttering "mm hmm" occasionally while continuing to make only minimal eye contact. When she was finally done, or at least temporarily at a loss for words, he finally spoke up himself.

"Well. It seems you've had quite a run up to now, haven't you?"

Rowena wasn't entirely sure what he meant by this, so she simply nodded and kept her mouth shut.

"Unfortunately, that doesn't qualify you for the type of position that you're seeking here. Our nurses are trained professionals. They went to school to learn their craft. They studied and interned and apprenticed. And once they did, they took a job and stayed the course. Do you understand what I'm saying here?"

"I believe I do, Mr. Quackenbush. Yes, sir." Rowena nodded grimly, realizing this was meant as a sharp critique of her own work history. As such, she grabbed her purse and scooted to the edge of her chair, ready to offer a crisp "thank you for your time" and head out the door. She knew a rejection when she heard one. She didn't have to be told twice.

Then, much to her surprise, Quackenbush added a single word: "But."

Rowena knew what that meant, too. She kept still and sat back to listen.

"*But*, there are a shortage of trained professionals available in the district right now. And moreover, the union has been threatening to strike, which would leave us all in a hell of a bind. And on top of that, I can tell—despite your resume—that you're truly passionate about this. A sickness in the family will do that. So, under the circumstances, I *might* be willing to give you a shot. On the very bottom, ground, entry level, mind you. And strictly on a trial basis. But if this is what you really want, it's a start."

Hal leaned back in his chair and looked at Rowena, really looked at her, for the first time. And he smiled, the lines on his face magically turning upward. Not such a bad guy after all. "So, what do you say?"

Of course, Rowena said yes. In fact, she said it several times. She even gave Hal a big hug over that gray fortress of a desk of his, which based on his startled reaction was his first intimate physical contact of any kind in far too long a time. She then bounded her way out the door to share the news with the secretaries.

"I got it! I got the job!"

And even though it wasn't quite the nursing job she had actually been applying for, their giddy cries of shared happiness made even Hal crack a smile.

From there, Rowena couldn't get out of the hospital fast enough. She wanted to get back home, so she could tell her mother. She knew Connie would be so proud. She also knew that she would most likely forget soon after, which meant Rowena would be able to tell her about it over and over again, like a gift that keeps on giving. And in return, Rowena planned to give right back, tending extra closely to Connie and her needs in preparation for her new job—better yet, her new *career*—in the health care field.

The next day, as part of her plan to coddle her mom as much as possible, she and Connie stayed home all afternoon and held an *Oprah* marathon. Rowena had missed a lot of episodes during her shifts at the pumpkin patch, but she'd taped them and was anxious to catch up. Connie was a big fan, too, and even though she had already seen the shows—she was in front of the TV every day at 3 p.m., religiously—she'd also forgotten most of them already, so the two were able to enjoy them together as if they were all brand new.

Five episodes and a gallon of Breyers Rocky Road later, Connie fell asleep in her chair. Rowena tried to rouse her for one last tape, a special one she had set aside, Oprah's annual "Wishes Come True" show, but her mother was snoring now, and even if Oprah herself had appeared in the living room, Connie wasn't waking up.

With a sigh, Rowena carried her mother up the stairs and tucked her into bed. Then, she went back downstairs to watch by herself. But it just wasn't the same.

So instead, she put on some clothes, hopped in her car, and headed down to the hospital. Her first on-the-job training wasn't scheduled until the following Monday, but Rowena was eager to get started, and she figured it might not be such a bad idea—based on her trials simply locating the staffing office—to get the lay of the land first. To see how things moved and operated.

And the upshot was, they moved *really* freaking fast. Watching all the gurneys being wheeled around, and all the machines and buzzers and intercom systems going off, and the attendants racing from room to room, Rowena realized that it was a lot different from just looking after one absent-minded old woman. As for the nurses, she marveled at the work they did and at the variety of patients and procedures they took part in. It was almost like being an actual doctor.

Daunted, she decided to return again the next night, too, after her mother had gone to bed, hoping that she might absorb some of what she witnessed, so that when she officially reported for duty, everyone would see how serious she was about the job, and maybe think she had some aptitude for it, too.

This time, however, her observations didn't go unnoticed.

"Who do you belong to?" a squat black nurse, built like a wrecking ball with a personality to match, asked her, as Rowena sat in what she had thought was a subtle manner near a floor desk, listening in on the nurse's conversations.

"Me?" Rowena replied, caught off-guard.

"Yes, you. Are you visiting someone? I saw you here last night, too."

"I ... no. Not really."

"Because visiting hours are over."

"I was just watching, that's all."

"Watching? Watching what, exactly? Ain't no TV here."

"I know. I was just watching you ... the nurses. And the doctors, too."

"What kinda person hangs out in a hospital and does that? And on a Saturday night, too! Shoot, girl, your social life must be even sorrier than mine."

"It probably is, but that's not why. I just got a job here. I start on Monday."

"For real?"

Rowena nodded anxiously.

"Well, aren't you the little eager beaver! What for? You a nurse?"

"Not yet. But I think I want to be."

The nurse laughed good-naturedly. "Wait till you finish your first shift and I'll ask you that again. What's your name, anyway?"

"Rowena. Rowena Pickett."

"Well, Rowena, my name's Pearl. Welcome to Mercy General. Long as you're here, let me show you around. Save me or somebody else the trouble come Monday."

And so, Rowena got her first official hospital tour, and found her first official hospital friend, which was a good thing, because Monday and the days and weeks that followed proved to be rigorous, indeed. Though her official title was nurse's aide, all she really did during this trial-basis period was clean up the nurses' messes, and their patients' messes, and any other messes that might happen to spring up. It was grunt work, plain and simple. But with the help of Pearl and her own heightened conscience, she was at least able to see that it was grunt work in the name of a greater good.

And that greater good cut both ways because, even at this menial stage, working at the hospital opened up a whole new world of possibilities for her. Not only to learning the ropes of a worthy profession she loved and admired, but also for meeting a better class of professional people who could offer her advice and support and maybe even friendship—and who, it went without saying, would never stoop so low as to sleep with any of her boyfriends. After years of false starts, false hopes, and dead ends, Rowena basked in this opportunity, soaking up all the camaraderie and information that she could. She was like a sponge; a sweet, malleable, eager-to-please sponge. And it wasn't long before her coworkers, like Pearl before them, started responding to that, including her in their conversations, pointing things out to her, remembering her name, and greeting her in the hallways. She felt like she was making progress. She felt like she belonged.

That is why, on top of everything else, Rowena had gone ahead and signed up for night classes at the local Cal State campus, starting in January, with the goal of meeting all the prerequisites necessary to apply to nursing school.

Oh, sure, she knew it was crazy. Where would she find the time to study, much less attend class? She also knew how tough those classes were going to be, even before Pearl and the other nurses started chiming in with their own night-school horror stories. Heck, even the names of the classes were scary; things like anatomy and physiology and biochemistry—and those were just the classes she had to take to qualify for the program. If they were anything like the science classes she suffered through in high school, Rowena knew, they would all be full of words and theories that would leave her brain aching night after night.

But Rowena was determined. She knew that, if she could somehow muster the willpower necessary to see it all the way through, she would be the first one from her family to ever achieve such a thing, the first one ever with a professional degree (her father Eddie's trucking school diploma aside). And that was a milestone accomplishment that would allow Rowena to hold her head up high, no matter where she was or what kind of company she kept.

And in fact, Rowena was already holding her head up higher. Lyle noticed it first thing when she stepped into the Vacaville Visitors' Room that very next day. It was a confidence that comes from knowing you are finally on the right path, even if that path runs for miles ahead of you. And he could see it grow in her even more as she sat down and told him all about her week, and the progress she'd made. It was a wonder to behold, and it gave him inspiration. If she could find her way, perhaps he could, too.

However, while Rowena appreciated this sentiment, and might have on a different occasion luxuriated in it, her thoughts on this day centered instead on Lyle. While on first glance he had looked like his usual handsome self, on closer inspection Rowena had seen that his left eye was cut and badly swollen. When asked about it, Lyle had tried to write it off as nothing, claiming it was just a silly accident—that he hadn't been looking and bumped into the corner of his bunk. But Rowena knew better. She'd gotten a couple of black eyes herself over the years, and she had lied about them, too, and she knew that you didn't get an eye that bad by just "stumbling" into something. No, someone did this to him, and they did it on purpose.

And so, Rowena was worried. Not only because of the eye, though that was certainly bad enough, but also because Lyle had felt the need to lie about it, and because he was acting so skittish, which was completely out of character and suggested that her concern was more than justified. The worst part of it was that he was in there, she was out here, and even though only a couple inches of plexiglass separated them, they might as well have been on opposite sides of the globe as far as her ability to help him went. She felt helpless.

And it was just then, with Rowena's sense of distress in full flush, that another inmate, Joe Luther Grimes, entered the room. Standing a solid 6 feet, 4 inches tall, Joe Luther was a menacing looking black man with rippling muscles, a simian stride, and long Medusa-like dreadlocks that made him seem even bigger and scarier than he already was. Walking past in Hannibal Lecter-like restraints, Joe Luther's dark, deep-set eyes locked onto Lyle, then Rowena, before "accidentally" bumping Lyle's chair, nearly knocking him to the ground as he made his way to a cubicle and a visitor of his own.

This was no accident. Rowena was sure of it. And she was also pretty sure there was some link between that incident and the one that caused Lyle's blackened eye. It was written all over Lyle's face. He looked fearful.

Rowena couldn't hold her tongue any longer. "Lyle, what is going on here? Talk to me, baby."

Lyle tried his best to act as if he didn't have a clue what Rowena was referring to, even though his feigned indifference was as transparent as the glass that separated them. "What are you talking about?"

"You know perfectly well what I'm talking about! Is it that man? Did that big black man do something to you? Is he the one who hit you?"

"That ... what? You mean the guy who just walked by? Joe Luther? No."

"I don't believe you."

Joe Luther was seated now, talking to a heavyset woman in church clothes and an Easter bonnet who looked like she might be his mother. Big, too, with wild scruffs of gray hair on her lip and under her chin. She was almost as daunting as he was. They both turned in unison and stared at Lyle. Lyle pretended as if he didn't notice.

"Ro, I know you mean well, but there's nothing to worry about. Let's talk about something else now, okay?"

"Lyle, he's looking right at you, *again.* Don't tell me—"

"*Just drop it, okay?*" Lyle's cracking voice betrayed his true emotions. He tried to temper it with a little laugh, but this only underscored his obvious fear.

Ro lowered her voice to a whisper. "Don't tell me it's nothing. It's not nothing."

Lyle leaned as close as he could to the glass, his voice barely audible. "Look, Ro, this is a prison. There are bad people here. People test you. All you can do is give them their space and show your respect and do your time. That's what I'm trying to do. Don't make it any tougher for me. Now, can we talk about something else now? Anything ... *please.*"

Rowena finally grasped the situation in full. Joe Luther was a jailhouse thug, a bully who threw his muscle around to stake his turf and make others fear him. Lyle was doing the smart thing and giving him a wide berth. Not that this made Rowena any less concerned, but at least she understood now. As such, she did what Lyle asked, and changed the subject, albeit grudgingly.

"Okay ... well ... you remember I told you I was gonna try and sell my trailer?"

Lyle did, nodding vigorously, his show of enthusiasm for the topic far exceeding its actual entertainment value. But again, at least Rowena now knew why. And so, she dove into her little story, milking it for all it was worth even though all she really wanted to do was reach across and wrap him up in a big, mother-bear hug.

As it so happened, once Rowena had gotten settled back home with Connie, and it had become clear that her stay there would likely be a lengthy one, she had forged ahead with her plan to sell her mobile home. Because she wanted to maximize the sale, she had swallowed her pride and called the best real estate person she knew—namely, her old Pioneer High classmate, Missy Carver.

But that's when things got surprising. When she finally got up the nerve to call, the receptionist at Eureka Realty informed her that Missy was no longer employed there. Rowena found this so hard to believe that she repeated the name, thinking perhaps the woman hadn't heard her correctly. But no, the woman had heard her, all right, and in a bilious tone, she added that the departure had been rather contentious, and "not by Miss Carver's choice, either, believe me." The implication, of course, was that Missy had been fired. But how was that even possible? The Missy she knew was too reliable, too focused, and just too totally *on-the-ball* for something like that to ever happen.

Yet, it had. And, as fate would have it, Missy probably couldn't have helped her, anyway. Apparently, Eureka Realty only represented "fixed foundation" properties, a fact that once again allowed the snotty receptionist to adopt a superior, patronizing tone, even if all she did there was answer the freaking phone.

With her meager tale now pretty much complete, Rowena struggled to make more of it than there was, for Lyle's sake. Surely, there had to be a lesson in there, somewhere. And Rowena wracked her brain to come up with it in a timely manner so that she could share this little kernel of wisdom, and maybe offer Lyle some solace and hope for his own situation.

Alas, the best she could come up with is that "nothing is ever as good or as bad as it seems."

"So, baby, hang in there," she added desperately. "You can do this. You're going to get your early parole, just like we talked about, and you'll get out of there, and I'll come pick you up, and you'll stay with me for as long as you need to, and we'll get you a job, and it's all gonna be just fine, you'll see. Okay?"

Lyle nodded, and thanked her for caring, and sticking by him, and he told her he never would have gotten through these weeks and months without her. Rowena put her hand to the glass, and Lyle put his up on top of hers.

But while it was lovely moment, the air between them charged with emotion, Rowena couldn't help but notice, out of the corner of her eye, that Joe Luther was still watching them.

29

CRACKING THE WHIP

"What is this?!"

On the warpath about something or other, Mamie Carver had emerged like a raging bull from her daughter's guest bedroom—a room she still didn't feel comfortable in, by the way, owing to its stark modern lines and Spartan décor. ("None of these tables have doilies—totally impractical ... Who sits in a chair with no pillows? ... And would it have killed you to use a little color in here?")

In the kitchen, Missy was chopping lettuce for a salad as Mamie stormed in. Noticing the sheet of paper clutched in her mother's doughy paw, Missy replied, ever so calmly: "Oh, that. Good. So you've seen the new house rules."

"Rules? They're more like tortures at some Nazi prison camp!"

"You're exaggerating again, Mother."

"Am I? Look at this. No food after six? No caffeine? No bread? One hour of exercise *a day*? As if what we've been through already isn't bad enough! Why don't you just put us on a chain gang and be done with it?"

"I got those guidelines off a website for the top health spa in Palm Springs."

"For sadists?"

"For people who say they want to get healthy and *actually mean it*, Mother."

"Well!" Mamie turned back to the sheet of rules, crumpled up in her hand. "And no cigarettes? None at all? You expect us to just quit cold turkey now, is that it?"

"Cold turkey is the only way, Mom. I've got the patches and the gum all ready to go. And you know it has to be done. You said so yourself."

"This is just crazy. It's crazy! And since you bring up the issue of turkey, have you forgotten that next week is our national holiday of Thanksgiving?"

The truth was, Missy *had* forgotten about Thanksgiving. Days and dates had become far less important to her in the last several weeks, particularly after she lost her job. But that didn't really matter. Mamie was just using it as an excuse, and Missy knew it.

"So? We can still give thanks. And we can have a turkey, too, if that's you want. But no dark meat. And no Yorkshire pudding, no candied yams, no booze—"

"This is crazy! It's crazy! And it's evil. Your father will hit the roof. You know that. He won't abide by this nonsense, and neither will I."

"If that's what you think, go get him and let's discuss it."

"Your father is resting right now."

"Wake him up, then. It's the middle of the day. He shouldn't be sleeping, anyway."

"Missy, you know how your father loves his naps."

With that, Missy's face darkened. It was her bad cop look, and it was not to be denied. "Go get him, Mother. Right now. Or else I will."

"Well, I never!" Mamie started to argue. But then, she took another look at the hard set of her daughter's face and decided against it. Instead, she muttered a curt little "hmmph" and waddled out of the room.

Ten minutes later, the Carvers were all gathered in Missy's living room. Neither of her parents looked happy to be there. Cliff's hair was standing on end from his aborted nap, while Mamie's beefy arms were crossed in a pose of sulky defiance.

"So I trust by now you've both seen the rules I drew up."

"Yes, we have, young lady! And let me tell you—"

"No, Mother, let me tell *you*," Missy interrupted, stopping Mamie dead in her tracks, "and *show* you why I made them. And why you're going to follow them."

With that, Missy produced a Hefty garbage bag from behind the sofa, filled to the rim with bags of chips and cans of soda and a veritable smorgasbord of snack cakes.

Cliff and Mamie both went pie-eyed.

"Now. Maybe one of you would like to tell me where this came from?"

Gathering herself, Mamie quickly whipped up her best false indignation. "How would we know, Missy? You don't let us have any of those things. Your rules, remember?"

"If you were following the rules, you'd both be losing weight, which you're not. Which is why I went looking around in the first place and found this stuff. It was in my gardening shed, by the way. Ring any bells?"

A pause. Cliff and Mamie traded a quick glance, but they kept their mouths shut.

"No? Okay. Maybe this will."

With that, Missy grabbed the remote and hit play. A blurry image appeared on the screen. Cliff leaned closer to see, hoping it was a sporting event of some kind.

"What is this?"

"Just watch and you'll find out."

They did, and what Cliff and Mamie saw—much to their horror—was themselves, committing a variety of crimes against the health and fitness regime that Missy had laid out for them. Sneaking food and stealing smokes like thieves in the night. Shirking workouts like grifters. Watching TV at verboten times. On and on.

Mamie was indignant. "You taped us? Who gave you the right?"

"I don't need to be given the right. It's my house. And my time, that you've clearly had no problem wasting. And you both agreed to follow the rules when you came here. Rules, I might add, which you have flouted at every available opportunity."

Missy turned back to the screen. "I especially like this one."

On the tape, Mamie was lying on the floor, a pair of throw pillows under her head, munching on a Ho Ho and lazily operating the pedal to the exercise bike with her hand while watching *The Jerry Springer Show.*

Missy chuckled. "Pretty clever, I have to admit. I even checked the odometer."

Mamie fumed. "Oh, you think you're so smart, young lady."

"No, I don't. If I did, I would have caught you earlier. Because even though you think you've been getting away with things, all you're really doing is buying yourselves a one-way ticket back to the emergency room. But it's not going to happen anymore. Not on my watch. You're going to follow these new rules. All of them. And to the letter. Or else."

"Or else what?" Mamie fired back.

"Or else I quit, Mother. I quit." Missy threw up her hands, her voice softening, though not her resolve. "In which case, you're both perfectly free to leave anytime you want. But just know that if you do, I won't listen to any more of your complaints, about any of this, ever again. Not one."

Missy turned off the tape. Set the bag of treats on the sofa, temptingly close.

"The choice is yours."

The room was silent. The gauntlet had been thrown.

"Okay, okay," sighed Cliff.

"Cliff, honey, no! We're the parents here," Mamie countered, her eyes locked on a golden-caked Twinkie peeking out from the rim of the bag. "She can't tell us—"

"Mamie, dammit, will you just shut your trap for once in your goddamn life!"

Mamie closed her mouth immediately and sank back into the cushions.

Cliff turned to his daughter. "Missy, baby, I'm sorry. We were weak. I ran out to the Gas N' Sip while you was asleep the other night. Mamie snuck out the week before. But don't give up on us just yet, baby. Please. We'll do better, I promise."

"What about her?"

"I'll watch her. I will. She'll toe the line."

"Will you, Mother?"

All eyes turned to Mamie.

"I suppose I could try," Mamie offered grudgingly.

She then turned to Cliff, her eyes narrowing. "And if you think you're gonna spy on me, Mister, you better know I'm gonna be all over you, too. Like a hawk!"

Missy remained stone-faced, staring down at her parents as if deciding whether or not to trust them, and give them the second chance neither of them, especially Mamie, actually deserved. But the truth was, her mind was already made up. Because, deep down, she knew that if they failed, her own failure was sure to follow. Missy didn't want to be alone anymore, this much she knew. But she also knew that she wasn't ready, physically or emotionally, to emerge full-bore back into the outside world again. Her wounds were still too raw. She needed baby steps. A beta test. A trial run. And who better to do so with than her own readily available and equally needy parents?

That said, standing there, she still had to make them both believe that she was truly ready to toss them out. She also had to be sure that neither of them could detect even a trace of the satisfaction she was feeling about seeing them like this, nor allow even an inkling of how totally wired she was from the heaping handful of pills she had wolfed down just minutes before, when both Cliff and Mamie had still been in their room.

"Okay, then," Missy said, in her most magnanimous tone. "I guess we'll give this one more try. But this is it; do you understand me? Now, why don't you go get on the exercise equipment and I'll join you in a little bit. I just have to finish making our salad for lunch first."

"Okay, baby," Cliff mumbled, looking like a beaten dog. "Will do."

Missy watched them go, shuffling off as if to the gallows. And the fact was, beneath the tsunami rush that was sweeping over her and making the whole world seem good, she felt a bit guilty. She knew it was unfair to be so strict with her parents about all their bad habits when she herself was still secretly feeding her own. It was hypocritical, and there was nothing Missy hated worse than a hypocrite.

But Missy also knew that she had everyone's best interests at heart. She would quit the drugs, and address her own food issues. But first, she had to focus on them, and getting them on track, and get past all the whining and moaning and denial and dysfunction that was, inevitably, coming right along with it—things that could easily lead to a colossal relapse on her part if she didn't wait and tackle things in their proper order. So, until then, Missy was allowing herself a grace period on the pills and trying to binge and purge only when it was of an utmost necessity. And that was a deal that, for the time being at least, she was willing to live with.

Still rushing from the successful encounter, Missy went to the kitchen and started chopping again, humming to herself, her hand and the knife moving at a samurai pace. While her affairs and her behavior weren't fully under control again yet—indeed, they had been completely *out* of control for far too long; she could see that now, with a crystalline clarity—she had nevertheless turned a corner and made a stand. Now, it was only a matter of keeping focus and staying the course, and these were goals she knew she could meet. Sweeping the lettuce into a serving bowl with an assortment of other freshly chopped vegetables, she could feel it already, swelling up inside of her, fighting its way through the drugs and the denial and the doubt.

The old Missy, Master of the Universe Missy, was on her way back!

30
STORMING THE CAPITOL

Hot off their Inauguration Day close encounter with Arnold, Todd and Lana rushed straight home and enjoyed the best sex of their marriage thus far. It was celebratory sex. Joyous sex. Sex imbued with the belief that all their hopes and dreams might actually come true. Lana was unusually affectionate and playful, even going so far as to refer to Todd as her "Toddy Bear" for the first time in weeks. She laughed and teased, and her body responded to his touch in ways it never had before. For once, it didn't feel like she was simply fulfilling some kind of dreaded obligation. It felt like genuine, from-the-heart lovemaking. She was happy, and she wanted to make him happy.

And for Todd, that happiness extended far beyond the sex itself. To him, it seemed to be a sign from God above that the hard part, the struggle, was finally over; that his large investment of time and money was finally starting to pay off. From here on out, it would be a smooth and steady ascent up the ladder of success. Todd was sure of it.

This ebullience lingered over the next several days. Todd got into the shop early, to tidy up and do his inventory work, and he stayed late, to make his calls for the remodeling firm and get things organized for the following day. In between, he bounced around the store like a host at a fancy nightclub, entertaining his customers with his usual joie de vivre and telling them in whispered confidence about his burgeoning relationship with the new governor, who'd be dropping by any day now to purchase a new tuxedo, just like the one Todd had gotten for himself. This association with power and celebrity lent a frisson of excitement to the daily comings and goings at the shop, and Todd was confident it bolstered the foot traffic as well. Clearly, it seemed, the buzz was spreading.

Back home, Todd shared all of this with Lana and Alek, assuring them how well things were going. That it was just a matter of time now before the gravy train really started rolling in. While Alek was too young to understand, Svetlana joined in the excitement. Though she had never truly grasped the parameters of her husband's big plan, and Todd had never been forthcoming with any specifics, she could tell from his mood that everything seemed to be headed in the right direction. After all, if he was important enough to actually speak with the Governor, he must be doing *something* right.

Unfortunately, like all big ideas built solely on wishful thinking, the weakness of its foundation slowly began to be exposed. While Todd continued to drop his connection to Arnold into every possible conversation, the longer the Man Himself failed to actually appear, the more Todd began to look and sound and even *feel* like the Boy Who Cried Wolf. One of the managers from the motor-scooter dealership up the block—a total douchebag, it was true, but still—even had the audacity to interrupt Todd mid-story and say, with a long roll of his eyes, that he'd "already heard *all* about it, thank you very much."

Meanwhile, the cost of all of Todd's quixotic efforts continued to haunt him at every turn. The bill collectors, who called incessantly asking for their "easy payments." His landlord, Leona, stopping by with increasing frequency and decreasing civility to ask when she might be receiving a rent check. The customers, who Todd had to lie to, over and over, all day long, to make it seem as if everything was going perfectly to plan, in the hope that, by doing so, perception might somehow magically become reality.

Even at home it was like this, as Todd found himself fending off all the various good-time promises he'd made. It was enough to make him feel like a con. A fake. A failure. And Todd felt like he was working too hard to feel that way. That he deserved better than that. That he *was* better than that.

So, with many of these variables spinning out of control and others sure to follow, Todd came to view the next step in his Team Arnold Plan as being absolutely crucial. If he could just get Arnold to stop by, Todd reasoned, even for nothing more than a quick photo op, he felt confident that it would redeem him in the eyes of his friends and customers, and go a long way toward solving his other problems as well.

However, after three long weeks, there had been no sign of him, and nary a peep from his people. Todd began to wonder if Arnold, in the swirl of duties and obligations his new position undoubtedly entailed, had somehow forgotten about him. Or worse, if that young aide from the reception had failed to even pass along his card. Maybe Arnold didn't know who to call, or where to go. Maybe it was all just a big mistake.

Todd thus decided he had to take matters into his own hands. Dialing up the Capitol and asking to speak with the Governor, who he claimed to be "friendly with," Todd got passed around by a series of receptionists and underlings until he was finally, through sheer persistence, put through to Arnold's chief executive assistant, Lloyd Chew, who explained that Governor Schwarzenegger was a very busy man these days, but that he would look into the matter and see what he could find out.

Todd was initially satisfied with this. Despite his nasally voice and terse manner, Lloyd sounded like a man who got things done. After all, he worked for Arnold, right? Arnold wouldn't hire a slacker. But when another week passed with no word, Todd thought it wise to check in again, just in case. This time, however, Lloyd was not available to come to the phone. Instead, Todd left a detailed message, to assure that Lloyd would remember him and the situation at hand, and have all the information necessary to prevail upon Arnold and get the job done, as promised.

Alas, despite its specificity and tone of urgency, this message did not elicit a return call, either. And with pressure mounting from all sides now, Todd felt he had no choice but to become an even *more* proactive advocate for his own cause. So, that very next day, during a slow lunch hour, Todd donned his lucky tuxedo yet again, closed his shop, and boldly marched across the city's pedestrian walkways to Capitol Avenue, which he then followed all the way to its ultimate terminus at the Capitol Building itself.

Standing at the base of the majestic building's grand marble entranceway, Todd paused for a moment to wipe his sweaty brow, take a deep breath, adjust his cummerbund, and summon his courage.

"Showtime," he muttered to himself, drawing curious stares from an elderly churro vendor and the group of Japanese tourists taking pictures of his cart.

Then, he was off again, taking the stairs two at a time, just like in *Rocky*, the theme song of which was playing loudly in his head. This time, he swore to himself, he was not to be denied.

Bursting into the building's grand lobby, Todd's arrival quickly drew attention. Perhaps it was the determined look in his eye, the sense that this was a man who meant business. Or, perhaps, it was the rumpled, sweat-stained tux and Todd's heaving gasps from the ill-advised sprint up the stairs. Whatever the case, a perky blonde in a state-seal-emblazoned blazer wasted no time stepping out to greet him.

"Good afternoon, sir. How can I help you today?"

"Yes. Can you tell me where the Governor's office is?"

"Well, it's down the main corridor—"

"Down there? Great." Todd gave the girl a nod and strode on, sweat-drenched and purposeful.

The blonde followed. "Sir? If you'd like to join a tour—"

"No need," Todd said, waving her off. "I'm here to see Arnold."

"Do you have an appointment?"

"No. But he knows me. We met at the inauguration. He has my card."

The blonde's pretty face soured. "Sir, I'm sorry to tell you, but the Governor isn't in his office presently."

"That's okay. I'll wait. Is it down here? Ah, yeah, there we go, I see it now," Todd said, taking off yet again.

The perky blonde managed an obliging smile, but her hand nevertheless went to her wireless earpiece. Moments later, she was joined by three members of the capitol's security staff, a wrecking crew of buzz cut Neanderthals in blazers just like the blonde's, although exponentially larger.

Todd was undaunted. "Hey, fellas. Looks like you work out, huh? Boy, Arnold must love that. You know, I actually do a little—"

"You must leaf now," interrupted the biggest of the three men, a Teutonic heavy with an accent startlingly similar to Arnold's. "Come vid us, please."

"Come on now, fellas. No need for the bum's rush. I just want to say hi, maybe leave another card, that's all. Not like I'm a terrorist or anything."

Todd laughed, but no one else did. The situation was deteriorating rapidly. The second guard, with a more Mafioso-like mien to him, grabbed him by the shoulder. "Time to go, big guy. You heard the man. We don't want to cause a scene now, do we?"

"I'm not causing a scene. *You're* causing a scene. I just want to—"

Suddenly, as the guard's vise-like grip got even tighter, Todd saw something. It was a young bespectacled nebbish, heading into Arnold's office. And if a face ever matched a voice, Todd prayed that this was it.

"Hey, Lloyd! Lloyd Chew? That you, buddy? Todd Tisdale here! Lloyd?"

A beat. The young man slowly, grudgingly turned Todd's way, reacting as if someone had just let loose an egregiously loud fart. "Uhhm ... yes?"

Miraculously, the man in question was, indeed, the elusive Mr. Chew. And thanks to Todd's shot-in-the-dark identification, what had been quickly escalating into an ugly scene was peaceably averted. That's not to say Lloyd was a sport about it, though. Rather, he just seemed annoyed by the whole situation, as if the fact that he hadn't done what he'd promised, or at the very least returned a damn phone call, was somehow Todd's fault.

"Look, Mr. Tisdale, you really shouldn't have come down here. I logged your messages. But the Governor and his entire staff, myself included, are extremely busy. We have a budget to draw up, legislative agendas to attend to. Pressing state issues, you understand. Social calls, meet and greets, they're pretty low on the totem pole right now. That's just the way it is. I'm sorry."

Todd nodded, as if weighing the relative merits of all this.

"Okay, Lloyd. Fair enough. Just tell me this: when are things going to clear up enough so that we *can* schedule something?"

Lloyd sighed. "It's too early to say."

"Okay, then. Any idea when you might have a better idea? Because I can—"

"Look, Mr. Tisdale. I don't know, okay? And I don't know means just that: *I don't know.* If and when an opportunity arises for the Governor to pay a brief visit, you'll be the first to hear about it, I can promise you. But until then, there's really no need to discuss this any further. Do we, *I hope*, understand each other?"

"Yes. I see. All right."

"Good. Thank you," Lloyd said, giving Todd's hand a brusque shake.

"And thank you, too, gentlemen," he added, to the humorless guards, still hovering nearby, who in turn responded by employing the same robotic gravitas as the Terminator himself in showing Todd the fastest and most direct way out of the building.

Walking back to the store, shoulders slumped, his bow tie off and collar loosened, Todd replayed the entire chain of events in his mind and came away with one sad but undeniable conclusion: it had all been a big blow-off—and a rather rude one at that. It made Todd wonder why Arnold would hire such unpleasant people in the first place. It made him lose respect.

It also made him lose hope. Todd had made his big play, and taken it as far as he could, but it had yet to bear any fruit, and he wasn't sure how much longer he could hang on. Despite all his efforts, the Governor remained a no-show. The *True Lies* poster in the window remained unsigned. The inaugural thrill was gone. The stories had grown tired. The big prom and wedding seasons were still months away. The debts were mounting. And while the upcoming holiday season promised a slight uptick in business (ties and hankies are perennial gifting favorites), it was not nearly enough.

Adding insult to injury, a sign had just gone up at the frozen yogurt shop next door, Frogey's, announcing its imminent closure. Todd knew the lease was coming up, and he'd always expected the place to shut down—but what he had wanted, more than anything, was to take over the space himself. Of course, he didn't have the funds to do so, much less add the costly inventory that would be required to make such an expansion effort worthwhile. But still, that had been the dream. Or one of the dreams. Or part of a bigger, all-encompassing dream.

Whatever the case, it wasn't happening. Not now, and very likely, not ever.

Ironically, then, if there was any shred of salvation to be found, it was coming from Todd's part-time phones-sales gig for the Benitez Brothers remodeling firm. While the local tux biz seemed to be hibernating for winter, its home-improvement sector was booming like never before. With house prices on the rise, people were nesting, and feathering those nests, at an unprecedented rate. Thus, while his shop was still operating at a steady deficit, he had actually managed in his spare time to land a couple solid leads for remodeling jobs, and better yet, one of those—a driveway and patio-paving gig—had actually been booked.

The commission check that resulted from this was like pennies from heaven, a tidy sum of unexpected cash right when he needed it most. But while the prudent thing to do would have been to use that money to help pay down credit cards or catch up on back rent, Todd had other plans.

With the bitter derailing of both his expansion hopes and his mighty Team Arnold Plan, Todd had finally come to see that the one *real* joy in his life, the only thing he could count on in the pinch—indeed, the only thing that truly mattered in the big scheme of things—was his wife and soon-to-be-adopted son. And with all the craziness of the recent weeks, he was aware that he had not devoted as much time and energy to them as he should have; that his priorities, however well-intentioned they were, had been misguided of late. He thus determined to make a change. And with that change came a new plan—maybe not as broadly visionary a plan as his Team Arnold Plan but a plan, nevertheless—with a goal to show Lana and Alek how great life as a Sacramento Tisdale could be, whether they were rich or poor or anywhere in between. And with the holiday season right around the corner, Todd realized that he had the perfect platform to bring this new plan to full fruition.

Oh, yes. Todd could see it all clearly now. It was going to be a great Yuletide for the Tisdales. And if Todd had anything to say about it—and thanks to God and the Benitez Brothers, he did—it was going to be even *better* than great. It was going to be the best damn family Christmas ever!

31

THE BIG SCOOP

"Where is she?" Spencer stood out in the pouring rain, outside the ShowBar, asking the question that had become the constant refrain in his life, to Ivan, the bouncer who had once been like a friend, but who now guarded the door to the club's inner sanctum like a vicious bit pull, a keeper of secrets.

"Sorry, bro. Not here."

Spencer nodded sadly at the likely deceit of this reply, as the opening strains of "Santa Baby" by Eartha Kitt, the only strip-worthy Christmas song ever recorded, drifted out from the cozy confines of the club itself.

"Not here, as in she's really *not here*, or as in, you're not supposed to let me *know* she's here?"

"Either way, answer's the same."

"Yeah." Spencer hung his head, his shoulders hunched against the cold.

"Maybe you should just give it up, man. You got your shot. Probably had some fun. Hell," Ivan paused to cackle, in a way that made Spencer loathe him, "I know Nikki, you probably had *lots* of fun. But it's over now, you know? Time to move on."

"I just need to see her. Just for a minute. To talk."

"Talk, huh?" Ivan cackled, seeming less than convinced.

"To clear things up. Apologize."

"And where's that gonna get you?"

"I don't know."

"And neither does she. And that's why it's probably not gonna happen."

Spencer looked up, a glimmer of hope in his eyes. "So you've spoken to her?"

"Hey, man." Ivan heaved a heavy sigh of disgust, realizing he'd said more than he should have. "Yeah. Okay. I heard some things, like, second hand. But, whatever. I doubt it's anything you don't already know."

"Does she—"

"Just go home, dude. Okay? Go home. There's nothing for you here. Not tonight. That much I know for sure."

The truth was, Ivan was right. And deep down, Spencer knew it. But that didn't make it any easier to accept. He had hoped, despite all evidence to the contrary, that whatever problems existed between him and Nikki were reparable. And he had gone to great lengths to make that happen. It made him feel better somehow, knowing he was putting forth the effort, even when those efforts were only met with resistance and rejection. He had become a persona non grata in Nikki's world, it was true, and that stung. But at least he had refused to bow to the shame of it all. He was standing up for what he believed in. There was a respectably naked honesty to his desperation.

The same could not be said for his experiences at work. There, the Nikki legend lingered on, even though she had been out of the picture for weeks now. Spencer had done his part to keep it alive, too, both out of hope, and also out of fear of what would happen if the truth of his abandonment were known. He had kept her picture up in his cubicle. He had continued to relate stories involving her, in a manner that suggested they were still together. He had even, on one occasion, pretended to speak with her on the phone, for the sake of his patron, Paul Hoying, who remained her most ardent fan. This ruse had worked, but its success only made Spencer feel more empty-hearted and pathetic.

It was at home where the reality of his loss hit Spencer the hardest. Free from all the lies and rejections, and surrounded by reminders of Nikki's former presence, it was where he felt the most alone. There was her perfume, which still clung stubbornly in the air. There was the pair of panties that she had left under the bed, in her rush to clear out while he was still asleep. There was her note, which he had now memorized, all 65 words and 332 letters of it. And finally, there were the memories, of the good times, and only the good times.

Spencer turned the key and entered his living room. There was no alluring waft of lavender greeting him on this day, only the piney scent of his little Christmas tree, perched in the corner and bought on the slim hope Nikki might return to see it—its slow, inevitable death now creating a pandemic of needles all across his beige wall-to-wall carpeting. It reminded him that, even as a non-Christian, he still needed to buy gifts and send cards and do other such ostensibly merry seasonal activities. But the fact was, he lacked the energy or the enthusiasm to do it. Instead, he sidled up to his bookcase and grabbed the cherished tome he always turned to for a little emotional healing when he needed it most, *Leaves of Grass*.

Plopping down on his sectional sofa, Spencer cracked the book and began to read at whichever random page the well-turned volume opened to, allowing it to divine the message it most wanted to convey. And the book did not disappoint. The first line Spencer's eyes laid upon was "Do I contradict myself? Very well then, I contradict myself. I am large, I contain multitudes." The message of this verse, and its relevance to his own current state of mind, eased Spencer's troubled soul. He wasn't alone. Whitman felt it, too, this internal hypocrisy, and in fact promoted it as a necessity of the human condition.

Spencer kept reading, devouring the venerated poet's wisdom. A page or so later, he came upon the book's most famous line: "I sound my barbaric yawps over the rooftops of the world." This image stirred Spencer. It inspired him. It got him up off the sofa, intent upon creating his own barbaric yawp, of a sort that could no longer be ignored by the woman he still loved with every fiber of his being.

Ready to compose his most lyrical and heartfelt plea yet, Spencer dashed into the kitchen in search of pen and paper. But before he could access these items, something else caught his eye: a golden key, affixed to a magnetic clip on the refrigerator door. More specifically, it was a key to his condominium, one that could have only been left by the only other person who had ever possessed such a key, which was Nikki herself.

The cutting symbolism of this gesture immediately sapped Spencer of all his poetic zeal, the resulting gloom only further aggravated by the discovery of a small note clipped to the magnet along with the key.

As with Nikki's previous note, Spencer found himself drawn to it, even though he knew before opening it that its contents would likely displease him. However, even he could not have possibly anticipated the crushing finality of its message. Spencer stared at it, reading it over and over, in a state of shattered disbelief:

Dear Spenser,

Hear is your key. I am sorry if I have hurt you. You are a sweet guy, just not the one for me. Randy and I are getting married tonight in Reno. He is the only one who has ever understood me, and appreshiated me for who I am. Please be happy for me.

Love, Nikki

Spencer didn't sleep that night, not a wink. Every time he came close to drifting off, his mind conjured up another image of what Nikki might be doing at that very moment: exchanging vows, eating wedding cake, granting sexy wishes. It was all too much for him to bear. And it left in its wake one bitter, unsolved mystery: who the *hell* was "Randy," anyway? Where did he come from? What did he do? How did he rate such a swift and utter victory? It made Spencer's blood boil to even think about it.

This sentiment carried through to the next morning. Spencer hunched over a bowl of stale Cheerios in his cramped breakfast nook, imagining the bountiful feast of food and flesh that this Randy character was now surely enjoying in his stead. It made him recall his own first morning with Nikki, and how she had gently nursed him back to health and then carnally cleansed him, body and soul. It was a feeling that seemed far distant now.

This sense of loss loomed over Spencer as he emptied his bowl and completed the rest of his pre-work routine. It stayed with him, like a storm cloud, as he drove to the *Bee*, trudged into the newsroom, and retreated down the stairs to his dank cubicle workspace where, to his dismay, he found Morris all-too-eagerly awaiting his arrival.

"Morning, Brine. On time this morning, I see. That's something."

Spencer heaved a heavy-hearted sigh. "Can I help you, Morris?"

"Yes, you can, actually. It's a busy day today, as you can see." Morris gestured to the stack of submissions in Spencer's in-box—three more mundane-lived locals who needed overly praiseful epitaphs written in their honor. "And frankly, I need you to get your head back in the game. Your work has been, I have to say, pretty shoddy lately. And these people deserve better. George Upshaw was a personal friend of mine, the best ombudsman this city has ever seen, and I want your efforts to reflect that. Step it up, do you hear me?"

"Yes, sir."

"All right, then. Get to it." Morris rapped the cubicle wall and strode off.

Spencer took off his jacket and sat down. He stared at his in-box. Its contents did nothing to improve his mood. The cloud remained, dark and dense and ominous. He dug through and found the file on Mr. Upshaw. Sure enough, the man was a dinosaur, his heyday coming a full three decades before his eventual passing. There was nothing really to mourn here, in Spencer's opinion. The man had spent the last twenty years simply marking time and waiting for the inevitable. He was divorced. His kids all lived several states away, as if purposefully distancing themselves. What was the point?

Spencer pored over the file, trying to find a respectful angle on the situation. At least he *had* a heyday, Spencer thought. A bright shining moment when his existence actually mattered. What about the rest of us? What about me?

A grim headline suddenly flashed before his eyes: WRITER SPURNED BY STRIPPER, COMMITS HARA-KIRI IN CUBICLE. Then, in smaller type: BODY FOUND DAYS LATER.

And with that, the thundercloud hovering over Spencer's head started to rumble and spew, the start of a dark and turbulent storm that threatened to linger interminably.

Indeed, it wasn't until much, much later in the day that a loud, braying voice finally managed to penetrate this tempest's dismal boundaries:

"Well, big guy, what do you say?"

Spencer looked up with a jolt. It was Paul, standing at the cubicle's edge, in the same exact spot Morris had occupied earlier, wrapping up a query for which Spencer had no basis whatsoever to reply. He shook his head, clearing the cobwebs. "I'm sorry, Paul. Can you repeat that?"

"Hello! Earth to Brine! What's with you today?"

"Sorry. I just ... I didn't sleep so well last night."

"Oh, yeah?" At this, Paul perked up; his mind, immediately leaping to the tawdriest possible explanation. "Another late-night visit from the sex fairy, maybe?"

"It was a genie. And no. Nothing like that."

"Too bad. My coffee's wearing off; I could use a little jolt. How is our girl these days?"

Spencer shrugged, just wanting Paul to go away and leave him alone. "Ah, you know ..."

"Actually, I don't. That's why I asked," Paul replied curtly. "What's the deal? You keeping her locked up in your bedroom or something? I mean, shit, she never comes by, we never see her out—"

"Look, you said you had something for me ..."

"And I might. But first things first. What's up? When are we gonna see our girl again?" Paul's timing couldn't have been worse. And neither could his ensuing riposte: "Come on, big guy, give it up. Quid pro quo."

Paul smirked gratingly, as he took Nikki's picture and stroked it like a genie's lamp, "Come out, come out, wherever you are," thinking he was being hilarious in his usual WASP-y, frat-guy way.

But Spencer was no longer amused. Indeed, this attempt at humor felt like a knife being driven straight into the center of his already-aching heart. And so, he stood up and got right in Paul's face, adopting a tone as close to menacing as a nice Jewish boy from the mean streets of Amagansett could possibly muster.

"You really want to see her, Paul? Try the ShowBar down on Crescent. She works from four to midnight. But bring your wallet. She doesn't usually dance for free."

"Hey, now—"

"And private dances are extra, but I bet you already know that, too, right?"

"Now see here, Brine—"

But Spencer wasn't listening anymore. His censor button was off, and he was on a roll. He took Nikki's photo and slammed it into Paul's chest. "Here. She's all yours. But you'll have to hold onto your dick for a few days, because apparently she's in Reno right now marrying some clown named Randy. Now if you'll excuse me, I have some work to do, so go shop your quid pro quo bullshit somewhere else, okay?"

Spencer sat down again and, with inspiration fueled by anger, started typing up his elegy to Mr. Upshaw, as if Paul were no longer there. Paul lingered, partly because he couldn't believe what he had just heard, and also to make sure no one else did. When it seemed the coast was clear, Paul leaned down and got in the last word.

"I don't know what your problem is, Brine, but that was a big mistake, mouthing off to me, after all I've done for you. And I hope you like writing about these dead farts—I really do—because trust me, that's all you're going to be doing from now on. Adios, asshole."

Paul stormed off. Spencer kept clacking away, as if he didn't notice or even care. And the fact was, he didn't. Not anymore. That's what a broken heart will do. It slowly bleeds out, infecting the other organs until they start failing, too. He had just vented his spleen. What was next to go? Spencer wasn't sure. All he had left with any certainty was his mind and his work, so he tried to focus on that to the best of his ability while he still could.

And as he did, Morris Sutphin watched and silently took note.

32

THE BEST DAMN
CHRISTMAS EVER

O n the day immediately following his forcible expulsion from the Capitol, Todd left the shop early for the first time in weeks and headed straight home.

Entering from the garage with a warm greeting for a surprised Svetlana, reading a tabloid paper in the kitchen— "Hey, baby"—and then swinging through the hallway for a quick hello to little Alek, watching *Scooby-Doo* in the den—"What's up, big guy?"—Todd proceeded directly up the stairs and to the attic, where he immediately set about rummaging through a forest of cobwebs and random forgotten clutter until he finally came upon what he was looking for: a collection of boxes and crates that contained all his old Christmas decorations.

Those decorations had been collecting dust for the last three years, ever since Angie died. But now, they were the linchpin to his new yuletide "family first" strategy.

Dragging the boxes down the stairs, one by one, Todd felt the curious eyes of Lana and Alek on his every move, but he offered no explanation. He knew it was far too early for that.

Instead, he focused on his labors. First, by unraveling a Gordian knot of colored lights and stringing them up all around the house and yard, through the bushes and under the eaves. Then, by extracting a plastic Santa and seven bent-wire reindeer from those same boxes and lugging them up onto the roof, at which point his peculiar behavior finally attracted the full and undivided attention of his wife.

"Todd! What in the name of God are you doing up there?"

Todd spun around to face her, nearly losing his balance in the process.

"It's Christmas. Gotta have a Santa comin' down the chimney, don't we?"

Todd waved the plastic Santa through the air and playfully pranced it around the chimney stack before Lana finally broke into a grudging smile.

"You are a crazy man. Do not kill yourself. I almost have dinner ready."

With this loving admonition dancing in his mind, Todd pieced together a rooftop holiday tableau worthy of the finest department store display cases. Then, after enjoying a fine repast of burnt chicken and frozen vegetables, he adjourned to the living room to assemble his final pièce de résistance, a shiny white aluminum tree. And it was there, without any need for urging or encouragement, that Lana and Alek got involved, too, stepping in to help him put up the ornaments and place the stockings by the fire.

Todd was elated. It had been a lot of hard, back-breaking work. Indeed, he was fairly certain that hanging all those little doodads on the tree would have finished him off for good. But those efforts had been rewarded, more so than his Team Arnold efforts ever had. He could see it right there in front of him. His family, sharing their first big holiday together, united in a common goal. It felt right. It felt like a home again.

With this new, festive atmosphere in place, Todd kept his new family plan going full steam ahead, returning home early as often as he could and initiating all sorts of new family rituals, in the form of weekly game nights and TV nights and pizza nights. And while these gambits were not always as successful as his initial "decorating night"—Lana didn't like pizza, Alek had trouble grasping the particulars of Monopoly, and neither one of them liked watching "Sportscenter" nearly as much as he did—they still offered more opportunities for togetherness, which is what Todd felt was most important.

That said, the planned culmination for all these efforts had always been Christmas Day itself. And in the spirit of family teamwork that he was now fostering, he brought Lana into his machinations to make certain they secured the right presents for little Alek, to assure that the big day would be extra-special for him, too. Sneaking off to the mall one afternoon while he was still in school, the couple picked out a snazzy array of merchandise including some new clothes for school (obligatory), a big set of Legos, a Joe Montana-signature football that Todd lobbied for in the hope that the little guy might take a shine to his personal sport of choice, and finally a new Tony Hawk pro-model skateboard—the one thing Alek wanted most of all—which Todd and Lana had to charm and cajole a series of sales clerks to locate.

It was this last, highly coveted item that they left under the tree, unwrapped, so as to maintain the illusion that it was the handiwork of Santa and his elves. When Alek saw it lying there, with a big red ribbon around it and a handwritten note from St. Nick himself, he could not believe his own eyes. He couldn't even move.

"It is mine?" he asked. "The kull skateboard, it is for me?"

It was a Hallmark moment, all right, one that would have surely been the highlight of most families' Christmases. But Todd had more surprises in store. After Alek finally accepted the fact that the skateboard was actually his to keep, and he had opened all his other gifts as well, Todd turned to Lana with a grin and said, "Okay, baby, now it's your turn."

Unbeknownst to his wife, Todd had gone on a separate shopping excursion just for her, and he had secretly tucked these items under the tree when she wasn't looking. There was a pretty beaded necklace, a pink cashmere sweater, and a pair of embroidered jeans that she had admired in a store window. Lana loved all of them, just as he knew she would, but with each new present she expressed even more feelings of regret, because she hadn't gotten anything for him. Todd assured her that he had already gotten his gift when she had agreed to marry him. Hearing this, Lana was so happy, and so overwhelmed, that she was moved to tears.

Later that afternoon, the family remained gathered around the tree in the living room. Elvis Presley's rendition of "Jingle Bell Rock" was playing on the stereo. A fire was blazing in the hearth. The air was redolent of pine and hot cider. Lana and Alek were both dressed in their new Christmas clothes, and Alek was spinning his skateboard's wheels to the hypnotic rhythms of Elvis's languid crooning. Todd was sitting on the sofa with a mug of the cider, which he had secretly laced with a generous amount of spiced rum, staring down at them both, feeling justifiably pleased with the results of his munificence. The day had been a huge success.

But for Todd, mere success wasn't enough. Not this time; not after all he'd been through to get to this point. Tonight, he wanted the grand-slam home run. And so, it was at this moment that he revealed his final and biggest holiday surprise of all, in the form of a small purple and black envelope that he slipped from his back pocket and handed, silently, to Svetlana.

Lana stared at the envelope, confused. "Todd? What is this?"

With a sly smile, Todd offered no answers. "Open it and you'll see."

Lana ripped open the envelope and examined its contents with wide-eyed disbelief. Thanks to Buddy Quayle, an old Prospector teammate of Todd's who worked in concessions at the Arco Arena, whose recent shotgun wedding Todd had outfitted on unavoidably short notice, he had scored two tickets to the Sacramento Kings basketball game against the Dallas Mavericks for that very night.

Todd knew how much Lana loved basketball, so the fact that she couldn't find the words to express herself only confirmed to him that the money and effort he had spent to make this happen was well worth it.

When Lana finally *did* find her voice, it was to the matter of practicality. The game, according to the tickets, tipped off in less than an hour. "But, how? What do we ...?" She turned to young Alek, still under the spell of his new skateboard.

As if on cue, the doorbell rang. Todd smiled. "And that would be the babysitter." Getting up, he patted Alek on the shoulder. "Sorry I couldn't bring you, too, sport. Next time, okay? "

"Kull," Alek replied, nodding tranquilly, all the while keeping his eyes firmly on his skateboard, which he had yet to relinquish from his grasp even for a second.

Todd went to the door and let in the shiny-braced babysitter, Bethany, who Lana vaguely recognized from the high school bus stop down the street. "We better get going. Shall I get your coat?"

Lana looked up at Todd, once again at a loss for words, and if the sparkle in her eyes was any indication, then Todd's holiday swing-for-the-fences was heading over the left-field wall with room to spare.

Forty-five minutes later, this was no less true, as he and Lana entered the arena and found their seats. Turns out, Todd's pal Buddy really came through. Just a few rows up from courtside, right at center court, the two could see and hear everything that was happening, even in the team huddles, and they could feel the rattle in their bones when Chris Webber drove home one of his monster slam dunks. Lana got an additional thrill from discovering, via the game program, that the Kings had two players from Russia, one of whom was from central Ukraine just like herself. As such, she cheered for the Kings with an added fervor, as if they were her own, real hometown team.

The Kings were winning, too, which only further bolstered Lana's high spirits. Todd viewed this as a good omen. The truth was, he had big plans for the evening, beyond watching a mere sporting event. He wanted to show Lana a good time, yes, and he wanted to give her a taste of how fun-filled life in Sacramento could be. But more than anything, he longed for the night to culminate, back home, with a good, old-fashioned frolic in the bedroom. It had been nearly six weeks now since his and Lana's last physical intimacy. This was due in part, he knew, to his own preoccupations, but it was also because Lana had made no effort to initiate things, either, nor even signal that overtures on his part might be welcome.

But tonight was different. Todd had been attentive to a fault of late, and he had fully delivered the goods on any and all holiday wishes Lana and her son might have had. He had been a model husband and father. He deserved to reap the rewards.

Todd looked over at his young wife. She was a beautiful woman, and he was proud to have her on his arm. The clothes he had bought looked great on her, too, accentuating her statuesque build and bountiful curves in ways that got his blood flowing and his groin tingling. Lana caught his eye and smiled, rubbing his shoulder in a warm, albeit less than sensual way. That was the sole disappointment in all of this for Todd; despite her looks, Lana was far from the frisky sex kitten he had hoped she'd be.

In all fairness, though, Todd recognized that he had likely created some false hopes as well. While his posturing as a successful American entrepreneur wasn't *intended* to be deceptive, per se, it surely could have led one to believe that he oversaw a vaster empire, and lived in a fancier house, and boasted personal finances of a far more secure nature. His visions of becoming the "James Bond of Sacramento" hadn't exactly panned out, either. James Bond didn't drive a dinged-up Ford Bronco. He didn't work as a telemarketer or get pushed around by Cro-Magnon security guards. And of course, he never left his Bond girls at home all day, washing skillets and ironing underpants.

But again, tonight was different. While Todd wasn't rich, it was true, and he wasn't a licensed-to-kill international spy, either, he had nevertheless gone to great lengths to put together a decidedly VIP-style experience for the two of them. And in that regard, everything was going perfectly according to plan. Lana had loved the surprise of a night out, as well as the great seats, the exciting ballgame, and the tasty concession snacks. As if that weren't enough, Todd had also made arrangements to get a shot of them beamed onto the gigantic Magnatron over center court during half-time, just like the Hollywood celebrities she read about in all the magazines. When the appointed time came and Lana saw her image up on the big screen, she giggled and blushed like a schoolgirl.

And Todd wasn't done yet. As soon as the final buzzer sounded, he produced one last surprise item from his jacket pocket, and placed it around Lana's neck: it was her very own laminated locker-room pass on an official NBA lanyard.

When Lana realized what it was, she squealed with delight. "Oh, Toddy Bear!"

And with that, Todd began, not unreasonably, to assume that his hopes for a Holy Night bedroom rendezvous were pretty much a done deal.

As the rest of the crowd made their way out to their cars, Todd and Lana headed down to the arena floor as VIPs. There, they presented their credentials to the guards (who were a far sight friendlier than those at the Capitol, Todd noted), then walked along the court, down into the arena tunnel, and straight into the home team's locker room which, in honor of the holiday, had been specially decorated and catered for the occasion.

And there, amid a swarm of reporters and player wives and team officials, Todd and Lana made the exact kind of grand entrance he had always envisioned for them. With everyone looking their way, and likely wondering who they were, Todd played it to the hilt, acting as if he were to the arena born, a VIP all the way. Gesturing to the fancy buffet, he placed his hand on the small of Lana's back and asked, ever so suavely, "Care for anything, my darling?" Lana demurred, still basking in the moment, happy just looking around and taking it all in. But Todd himself had a hankering for another frosty beverage and maybe a finger sandwich or two, so he decided to take a casual stroll over to the table to see what they had.

A few moments later, Bud Light draft in hand, Todd returned to the spot where he had left his wife, but she was not there. Scanning the crowd, he found her nearby, talking to a lanky, mop-headed giant who he immediately recognized as the King's backup center, Drago Petronovicz—the player from the Ukraine that Lana had read about in the team's promotional materials.

As he approached, Lana turned to him with a radiant smile. "Todd, this is Drago. You know him from the game; he is the team's center! Drago, this is my husband, Todd."

A hairy hand descended toward Todd, which looked to be about the size of a casserole dish. Todd shook as much of it as his own comparatively meager appendage would allow.

"Drago was telling me he grew up in Kharkiv. The two of us, we were practically neighbors!"

"Well, boy, that's really something, huh?" Todd replied, cordially enough, all the while wondering why Lana, who had been so eager to put her past behind her, was suddenly so giddy to be discovering some tenuous link to those same forsaken roots.

Drago offered up a heavy-lidded nod. "Lana has told me how you met. You are a lucky man. The Ukrainian women, they are beautiful, yes?"

"This one sure is." Todd put his arm around Lana, pulling her close and tight. She blushed, shyly averting her eyes from both men.

A slightly awkward silence ensued. "Well, anyway, great game tonight," Todd proffered, unsure what else to say, hoping this might serve as a subtle cue to move on.

"Thank you. We are actually having a party at my house tonight to celebrate, the game and Christmas both. You would be more than welcome to come and join us."

"Tonight? Well, boy, that's sure nice of you, Drago, but uh ... wow, look at the time!" a wide-eyed Todd said, staring hard at his watch as if in disbelief.

"Maybe just for a little while?" Lana chimed in hopefully. "We haven't been to any parties, you and I. It would be fun, yes?"

Lana turned to Drago. An inscrutable glow settled over his Mount Rushmore-sized cranium, one that made Todd decidedly ill at ease. "Yes, much fun. I have pictures from home, I could show for you."

"That would be nice. Toddy? Toddy Bear, please."

Lana served up another coquettish smile. And usually, that would have done the trick. But Todd was starting to feel pressured, and manipulated. And the fact was, Todd had his own designs on the next couple hours, and they didn't involve feigning interest in a scrapbook of old photos featuring a bunch of Chernobyl-adjacent potato farmers.

"Thanks for the offer, Drago, really, but we have to be getting home."

Hearing this, Lana's whole body sagged in disappointment.

"Alek is waiting, remember?" Todd added, hoping to at least score some paternal brownie points. "He'll want to know about the game."

Drago stared down at the couple, sizing up the dynamics at play, before finally accepting Todd's decision. "Too bad. Perhaps another time, yes?"

Lana looked away, as if her spirit had been crushed. "Yes. That would be nice." Drago handed Todd a card, with the Kings logo on it. "This has my private cell number, in case you change your mind."

"Or," he added, turning now to Lana, "if you ever want to get together ... talk of the old country ... speak in our native tongue."

"Thank you, I will," Lana said, crisply prying the card out of Todd's fingers.

"Nice to meet you both." Drago shook Todd's hand again and placed a consoling paw on Lana's crestfallen, cashmere-clad shoulder. Then, he went off in search of his colleagues and, ostensibly, more party guests.

The drive home from the arena that night was a chilly one, indeed—and not because of the weather. Lana had wanted to go to the party, and there was nothing that Todd could say or do to make up for it. According to her—and she made plenty sure Todd heard her side of things, loudly, clearly, and repeatedly—this had been her one golden opportunity to get out and meet people, people who might actually understand and befriend her, and he had denied her of it, without even so much as a moment's hesitation.

Todd tried his best to defend himself. It was late, for one thing. The basketball players may be able to start partying at eleven o'clock at night, but he didn't share that kind of luxury. He had to work in the morning. There was also the matter of the babysitter, who didn't come cheap, especially not on a holiday, and especially not if she ended up working overtime. And then, there was their little guy, Alek, to think about, too.

That was what he said, and he felt it more than justified his decision. But the fact was, there was more. He didn't have a good feeling about this hulking Drago character, and he didn't like the way he'd stared at Lana, talking about their "native tongue." It all felt a bit too forward. And if anybody was going to get forward with his wife tonight, it was going to be him, dammit.

Todd kept this last bit to himself, of course. But that was the plan, and he remained committed to it, even though Lana was giving no signals of being anywhere *close* to in the mood. To his mind, the evening had still been a huge success, and whatever ill will Lana was feeling would pass in time for them to make up and let the magic happen. That was a rule he and Angie had always abided by—never go to bed angry—and it had never failed them.

But Lana was no Angie, and that Ukrainian blood of hers had an entirely different boiling point. She remained steadfast in her fury, even after they got home, and even though Todd went out of his way to play "good daddy" with Alek, recounting the game and the entire arena experience in vast, colorful detail. This ire remained undimmed all the way into the bedroom, as Lana continued to give Todd the silent treatment, changing out of her clothes and into her nightgown and getting right into bed, where immediately pulled the covers up to her chin and closed her eyes.

Todd, however, read things with his usual fuzzy-eyed optimism. The way he saw it, Lana was simply signaling that he needed to make the first move, and call the truce, and show her that all was forgiven. After all, she had certainly wasted no time getting into bed, right? And she had worn her frilliest nightie; that had to mean something. Todd thus proceeded to take off his own clothes, and spritz on some cologne to lend a little extra aphrodisia to the air. He then slid into bed, soft as a feather, and slowly eased his body closer until he was clinging to Lana's side like a remora.

For several moments, Lana didn't respond. Todd again attributed this to part of the routine. Lana would pretend to be asleep, until awoken by his amorous embrace. It had a slightly naughty feel to it that only got Todd more aroused. He accelerated his efforts, adding some slow, rhythmic thrusts to his gentle caresses, to let her know how much her presence in his bed, and his life, pleased him.

With this, Lana's body suddenly went stiff.

"What are you doing?"

Todd stopped. Lana was definitely awake now. He met her blazing blue eyes, suddenly unsure whether this was part of the act or not. "I don't know. I guess I thought—"

"You thought what? I want you to hump at me in my sleep?"

"No. I was just trying to ... relax you."

"I was relaxed. I was asleep!"

"I'm sorry, babe. It's just ... it's been awhile, you know, and we had such a great day—"

"It was a great day, until you ruined it by being so rude to Drago about his party."

"But I mean, still, it was a great day overall, right?"

"And so, what? You think that means you can just do to me whatever you want?"

"Well, no. That wasn't what I—"

"Let me tell you something, Todd—"

"Lana, no. You're taking this the wrong way. I—"

"No. You listen," Lana said, gathering steam. "You know I was married before. And you know he was a bad man. What you don't know—what I don't say to anyone, not ever—is how bad. How he treat me like some thing that he owns. How he do things to me. *Even after he go to prison*, how he does them. But I let him, because, what choice do I have? He has friends, and they are cruel, too. Maybe worse. I cannot take the chance. Not with Alek. So I let him do his things. Things I do not want. Things that hurt me inside. But I tell myself, never again. I will get away from him, from here, and never again. And I am away now, and he will never find me. And I will never let any man be like that to me again. I will never let any man act like he owns me. Like I am his property. And I won't. Not ever."

Todd listened to all of this, struck silent. The only thing he could think of to say was, "I'm sorry. I'm really, really sorry." .

"So am I. More than you can know."

At this point, even Todd recognized that any hope for a make-up, for intimacy of any sort, was out of the question. He also saw, through the bitterness of Lana's words, that the problems they faced ran even deeper than he had thought. And he knew, too, that if there any answers to those problems, they wouldn't be found in this bedroom. Not tonight.

"So ... maybe I should just go sleep on the sofa, let you have some time to yourself?"

"Yes. I think that would be best."

Todd nodded sadly, got out of the bed, and grabbed a spare blanket lying at its foot. He turned back to Lana. She looked different to him now, although he wasn't sure why.

"Well ... goodnight."

"Yes. Goodnight to you, too."

At the door, he turned back and said, softly, "I love you, Lana," hoping that might provide some solace and provoke some glimmer of hope in his young wife's eyes.

But Lana had already pulled the covers back up and turned away from him. And with that, Todd had no choice but to leave, his words left dangling there, unfulfilled, like an empty noose.

33

AULD LANG SYNE

5:05 a.m., New Year's Day, 2004. The champagne had poured, the ball had dropped, the confetti had rained down, and now most of the night's celebrants were safely tucked into their beds, sleeping it off in anticipation of the bowl game parties to come.

But at Sacramento Mercy General, it was a different story. There, the holiday and its array of revelry-related mishaps lived on in vivid, grisly detail. The car accidents. The toxic overindulgences. The injuries stemming from bar fights, lover's quarrels, and flying corks. The lonely suicide attempts.

Over the course of one hectic shift, Rowena felt as if she had seen it all, and then some. To be sure, the sight of one man staggering into the ER with his own severed fingers in a plastic baggie, as if they were some kind of macabre party favor, was one she knew she would not likely forget anytime soon. But all that was behind her now, at least until the next shift. In the meantime, there was still much to do and miles to go before she could sleep.

First stop was home. Or rather, what Rowena had come to think of as home again, which was her mother's place. And while the pre-dawn hour might normally suggest that she would return to find a dark and blissfully silent house, Rowena knew better.

Ever since she had started working at the hospital, Connie had taken to greeting her daughter at the end of every shift like a conquering hero. No matter the hour, Connie was always there at the door, pot of coffee and pack of cigarettes at the ready, eager to hear every detail of the latest chapter in Rowena's new career. And Rowena felt obliged to honor this, no matter how weary she was. For one thing, it was flattering. Connie had always lamented doing no more herself than sling hash at a series of diners and truck stops, so Rowena knew her show of pride and interest was genuine. But more importantly, it was one of the few remaining links to her mother's ebbing lucidity. Whatever the reason, Connie thrived on the routine, and was always uncharacteristically cogent, laughing and affable like her old self. Rowena thus vowed to enjoy the intimacy of these little mother-daughter powwows for as long as they lasted.

Pulling into the drive, Rowena saw that lights were on throughout the house, suggesting that Connie was still up and about, as expected. However, as she approached the door, she was surprised to find that her mother wasn't there to greet her. And once inside, there was no aroma of coffee to signal their impending klatch. Rowena's brow knitted with a mixture of confusion and concern.

"Mom? I'm home. Where are you?"

After several moments, a muffled whimper emanated from somewhere on the second floor. Rowena raced up the stairs to investigate. "Mom?"

Searching from room to room, Rowena eventually found Connie in the closet of her master bedroom, swathed in a bundle of Eddie's old flannel trucking shirts.

"Mom?"

Connie looked up. Her eyes had never looked greener, or more lost. "Your father didn't come home, baby. He didn't call.

I don't know where he is." Then, in a heartbreaking whisper, "I'm afraid something may have happened to him."

After several minutes of gentle reassuring, Rowena was finally able to get her mother out of the closet and down to the kitchen. Connie continued to fret and pace, one of Eddie's shirts still wrapped around her like a security blanket. But slowly, and with a sure hand, Rowena eased her out of her dementia and into their usual post-shift routine, telling her all about her day, albeit free of any grisly details that might have provided even more fuel for her concern.

The ploy worked like a charm. Connie began to respond, and ask questions, her pride in her daughter shining through the fog and the fear. Before long, though, she began to yawn and get heavy-lidded, the tribulations of her restless vigil finally catching up with her.

Rowena helped her mom up the stairs and into bed, and she was sound asleep in no time. Rowena calculated that Connie had been awake for over twenty-four hours straight now. Based on that timeframe, and the manic behavior she exhibited throughout it, her mother would likely be down for the next twelve hours, at the very least. Rowena was relieved. That would give her enough time to finish her homework, and hopefully get some sleep, too, before the cycle started all over again.

For the next couple of hours, Rowena returned to the kitchen to study. She was only able to do so thanks to a pot of strong coffee and the room's bright fluorescent lights, but when the work was done, she felt good about it. The classes were tough, and it was tougher still to find the time to do her reading and assignments. But it was worth it. For once in her life, she felt disciplined, and directed, and devoted to something other than seeking out the next good time. She felt like a better person.

On that note, Rowena went back upstairs to check on her mother again. Entering the room, Connie didn't so much as stir.

Her breathing was soft and steady, her body tucked under a blanket and curled protectively around a large pillow. Rowena stroked her hair and wiped a stray tear from the corner of her eye.

Assured that her mother was okay, at least for the time being, Rowena took a quick shower to wake herself up, changed into some fresh clothes, and then got back in her car for the drive to Vacaville to see Lyle. It was Thursday, not normally a visitation day for her. But since it was New Year's, a symbolic day of renewal and fresh starts, Rowena felt as though she needed to make the effort. After all, that was what relationships were all about, right?

The truth was, Lyle had been on Rowena's mind more than ever lately. Even though it would be at least another seventeen months before Lyle could get out, Rowena found herself thinking more and more about the possibility of a future with him. Like herself, Lyle had taken his lumps and learned his lessons, and now he was determined to stay on the right path. That was why she had been so worried about him lately. Lyle was clearly in some kind of trouble, as evidenced by the cuts and bruises he always seemed to be sporting. But he had refused to talk to her about it. *Trying to protect me*, she thought. But what good was protecting her if everything they were hoping and planning for was being jeopardized? As such, Rowena was determined to get to the bottom of things this time, and do everything in her power to fix the problem. In fact, now that she thought about it, that would be her New Year's resolution: to never let herself be passive in regards to her own life's course, ever again.

An hour later, Rowena pulled up to the gates of the prison. After passing through the usual gauntlet of security checkpoints, Rowena found herself back in the stark confines of the concrete-block Visitors' Room, waiting for Lyle to arrive. The room was crowded, with every cubicle filled and many others waiting for their turn. Rowena looked around at all the family members and friends, of every race, creed, and color,

there to assure their loved ones that this would be the year
that they would get out. That God and Allah and Buddha and
whomever else people prayed to would finally shine their holy
grace down upon them—that things would be different this
time.

A fresh start. It seemed everyone in the room, on both sides
of the glass, had this same fervent wish. It was pervasive, and
it made Rowena feel foolish to realize that her own hopes were
such an obvious jailhouse cliché.

It was unsettling for another reason, too: clearly, not all
these people were going to succeed. The gods were simply
not that kind. Some would never earn their release. Others
would, only to commit crimes again. What if Lyle wasn't one
of the lucky ones? What if he got caught up in all the prison's
bad influences? Or worse, what if he ran afoul of a bad crowd,
violent men with no hope left, who thought nothing of ruining
another man's life, no matter how good or handsome or loyal he
was? It made her shudder to even think about it.

As if on cue, Joe Luther Grimes appeared at the doorway.
Big as he was, he was impossible to miss, but for Rowena, it
was more than that. She just sensed, in some strangely intuitive
way, that her own fate was inextricably linked with his. That
he was the source of all her worries and fears, her own personal
boogeyman.

Entering the room, his hands and feet in chains, he lagged
behind as his guard went ahead to ready his chair. Unchecked,
Joe Luther caught Rowena's eye and held it, cold and hard. He
recognized her—that much was clear—and not in a good way.
Alarmed, Rowena tried to signal the guard. But before she
could, Joe Luther leaned down to the voice box and whispered,
"You ain't all that, bitch."

Just then, the guard finally saw what was happening. "That's
enough, Grimes! Get your ass in this chair, or I'll suspend your
privileges faster than you can blink."

Joe Luther complied with a grunt, strutting off, stealing one last menacing glance over his shoulder as he went. Rowena remained frozen, trying to riddle out the meaning behind his words. It was a put-down, but to what purpose? To further degrade Lyle? Or was it her? Did she remind him of some former love? Or, worse still, a former victim? None of the options were savory.

"Hey."

Rowena startled, to find Lyle already seated in front of her. "Happy New Year, baby." He quickly noted the deep worry lines on her face. "What's wrong?"

"I'm not sure." Rowena scanned Lyle's face for clues. No visible contusions this time. No abrasions or tears on his clothing. But he still seemed uneasy, as if something was going on that he was unable or unwilling to discuss. "Maybe you can tell me."

Lyle laughed at her directness. "Whoa. Listen to you. Somebody get up on the wrong side of the bed this morning?"

"No. I haven't slept at all. But that's not it. I want to know what's going on, and I want to know right now. If you're in trouble, I want you to tell me."

"Trouble? Boy, I'm sure starting to feel like I'm in trouble. Heh, heh."

"Stop it. I'm serious. I want to know, right now."

"Baby, let's just enjoy our time together, okay?"

"No. I made a promise to myself. No more letting things go. I'm worried about you, and I deserve to know why. How did you get those bruises? That black eye?"

"Ro—"

"Tell me!"

Rowena's voice was loud enough that it drew attention from the other visitors and inmates, as well as the guards. Lyle's eyes darted over to Joe Luther, then quickly back. When he saw that Rowena had noticed, he seemed abashed.

"Is it him?"

"No."

"I don't believe you."

"Ro, you don't understand."

"How can I understand if you won't tell me! Now either you tell me, *right now*, or else I'm going to the warden and the governor and whoever else I can find, and I'm telling them."

"Ro—!"

Before either could react, Joe Luther was up and out of his seat, dragging his chair and chains and leaping at them, fists balled, eyes blazing. "This ass is mine, bitch!"

Rowena screamed. Lyle braced against the certain blows to come. But just as it seemed Lyle was about to get pummeled, or maybe even killed, Joe Luther instead grabbed him around the neck in a hold that wasn't nearly as tight or violent as expected. In fact, strangely enough, it seemed almost ... affectionate.

Rowena's scream caught in her throat. The guards quickly moved in to separate the two. Joe Luther struggled mightily, threw one of the guards against the wall, and reeled back to unleash his fury on another when suddenly—ZZZZZZT!—a wicked, sparks-flying Taser blast sent him sprawling, spastically, to the ground. More guards quickly swarmed in to assist. Joe Luther was pulled to his feet, unsteady now, and a straitjacket was wrestled onto him. He was then summarily escorted out the door, but not before issuing one last threat: "He's mine! You mine, bitch! You mine!"

The door slammed shut. Joe Luther's screams grew ever more faint. Slowly, a semblance of order was restored to the room.

A guard came over to check on Lyle. "You okay, Pettigrew?"

"I'm fine," Lyle answered, under his breath, seeming embarrassed more than anything by the attention.

"Okay, then. Enjoy the rest of your visit. Sorry for the interruption, ma'am."

As the guard walked away, Rowena thought she detected the trace of a smirk hidden beneath the man's walrus-like moustache. She turned to Lyle. "Lyle...?"

Lyle was blushing red. "It's not what you think, Ro."

"Not what I ...?"

Rowena didn't know what she thought. She didn't even have a clue. But as she sat there, watching the guards huddle and snigger, and consuming the amused stares of the other inmates, it slowly dawned on her. Something so horrible, she could hardly believe that her own mind was conceiving it.

"No..."

"Rowena, I love you, baby."

"No."

"It's just for protection, that's all."

"No. You can't be—"

"It doesn't mean anything."

"Oh, my God, no. You can't be serious. With him? You?"

"Rowena, no, let me explain—"

"How could you?"

"I—"

Lyle hesitated, just for a millisecond, as if suddenly unsure whether she meant "How could you cheat on me?" or "How could you have sex with another man?" Either way, any answer he might have offered was poor consolation. The fact was, the man she loved, who she had been certain would remain faithful to her because, if for no other reason, he had no opportunity to do otherwise, had nevertheless found a way. The bitter truth sunk in, knocking her off her feet as surely as a Taser blast would have. She had been lied to, and betrayed, yet again.

With Lyle still pleading for forgiveness in the background, Rowena got up from her chair and raced out of the room, in tears. She continued running, all the way out of the prison and into the parking lot and to her trusty old Tercel.

As she got in the car and sped out the prison gates, she pounded the steering wheel and berated herself for the efforts she had made and the worries she'd wasted. She swore to herself that she would never come back, no matter how many letters he wrote, or how sorry he'd claim to be.

And, in an addendum to her New Year's Resolution, she also vowed to never let herself be taken advantage of by a man—any man, in any way—ever again.

IV
EUREKA!

(California's state motto, from the Latin, meaning "I have found it!")

34

NEW YEAR'S RESOLUTIONS

After Missy had laid down the law on that fateful evening back in late November, her parents, Cliff and Mamie, had struggled mightily to adjust to the new terms of their arrangement. At first, it had been tough enough to simply cope with the loss of their junk food troves and secret smoke breaks. But, on top of that, there was also all the exercise Missy was making them do, under her direct supervision now, and all the healthy, low-fat meals and snacks she was whipping up, and forcing them to at least try.

"Some snack!" Mamie had cried. "Little veggie sticks, not even any ranch sauce to dip 'em in!"

However, at the next weigh-in, Mamie was stunned to find that she had dropped nearly ten pounds. And, even more stunned to see that Cliff had lost nearly fifteen. And even if this weight loss was more a result of restricted indiscretion than any sort of truly laudable effort, the two were inspired by it.

As such, the two both began, slowly but surely, to take a more active role in their own recovery. Mamie choked down a few bites of non-fried vegetables at dinner. Cliff did sit-ups on the floor while watching his fishing shows. They both wore their nicotine patches and did the required half-hour-minimum of daily aerobics. And best of all—as threatened—they both helped Missy monitor each other's actions, figuring that if they had to make the sacrifice, the other one damn well better make it, too.

And with all of this, Missy began to get better, too. Her stress-load eased, she found her compulsion to binge and purge flaring up far less frequently. With less abuse being done to her digestive tract, the same began to be true of the pills, too. *One pill at a time,* she told herself. And that is precisely what she did, subtracting one pill from her surreptitious intake every day, until the smaller amount, the healthier eating habits, and the endorphin-boosting of her own lead-by-example exercise all led her to question whether she needed them at all anymore.

By the time Christmas rolled around, the whole Carver clan had gotten itself into a startlingly healthy new groove. The culmination of this was the first non-dysfunctional holiday dinner in Carver family history. The food was all fresh, and organic, and homemade. Mamie helped out in the kitchen, while Cliff set the table in the dining room. The TV was off during the meal, and the once-pervasive haze of cigarette smoke was absent. Even the conversation was pleasant, even-toned and spiced with the kind of sweet reminiscences that families are supposed to share on such occasions.

Among other things, the three talked about their New Year's resolutions. For Cliff and Mamie, the main goal was to simply continue what they were already doing. Although they still had many pounds yet to lose, and many hurdles to overcome, the couple felt empowered and hopeful for the first time since they said their "I do's" as jobless high-school dropouts back in the 70s.

Additionally, Mamie, having worn nothing but tent-like muumuus for as long as Missy could remember, also cited a desire to get a personal style makeover, "just like on those TV shows." And, in a delicious moment of vindication for Missy, she also noted that "something like you wear, baby; I might like to try that."

As for Cliff, he was sprier than he had been in years, walking without any sign of his previous stoop, and buttoning his trousers all the way up to the top for a change. In this spirit, he even swore that his back was feeling so good, he might be able to go off Disability. And although the prospect of him actually seeking gainful employment again would still need to be seen before it could truly be believed, the fact that he would even mention such a thing as a possibility was itself a clear sign of his progress.

Once Cliff was done, Mamie turned the question on their daughter, who had been silently basking in her parents' unexpected and heretofore-unseen glimmers of ambition. "What about you, Melissa Louise? Anything special coming up for you?"

"Yeah, baby. What does our little hard-charger have planned?"

Sitting there with her parents, both of them smiling and clear-eyed and looking better than she could ever remember, Missy nearly cried, not only because of that, and because she could tell their interest in her answer was genuine, but also because she knew they had no idea whatsoever of all she'd been through the past few months. In their eyes, she was still the same world-beater she'd always been.

But the truth was, now that she was finally beating back her demons, and thinking clearly again, she did have something she wanted to do; something she'd thought about ever since she'd started her Young Entrepreneurs Club back in high school. And it was something which she needed to get cracking on, and fast, because she hadn't worked in over three months now, and—taking care not only of herself but her parents, too—she was quickly running out of money.

"I'm going to start my own company. Carver Properties. And I'm going to build it into the biggest independent realty company this town has ever seen."

"Oh, baby. Listen to that."

"You'll do it, too," Cliff beamed.

So that was the plan, even though it was the first time she had actually said it out loud, and thus far had done nary a thing to actually bring it to fruition.

But now that it was out there, and she had something to live up to, Missy quickly applied herself to it, just like in the old days. She consulted her old client, vendor, and contact lists. She carefully gauged the various feasibilities, as to size and scope and focus. She made calls, and enlisted advice, and spread the word, and got up to speed on all that she had missed. And, with her parents still deeply entrenched at her house and not ones to go about their business quietly, she started looking for a place to hang a shingle, too.

Of course, this was an expense she could ill afford at this juncture. But on the other hand, she could ill afford not to. Working from home may have been cheaper but, Missy realized, it would not be the healthiest of decisions. On top of everything else, the place still literally reeked of her earlier excesses and delusions. It was time for a change.

So she began to search. Knowing what she wanted, what she could afford, and what the local market would bear, Missy knew she would have to get creative. And lucky. She soon narrowed her search to a handful of convenient, well-situated office spaces that could potentially suit her needs without breaking her budget.

Among them was a newly listed site on G Street, which had abruptly come up for lease when the previous tenant, a frozen yogurt shop, had gone out of business. The price wasn't bad, and Missy suspected the poor holiday timing of the listing might allow for some wiggle room on the lease terms. As such, she elected to check that one out first.

Waiting out front as she pulled up in her Lexus was the building's landlord, Leona Hornstein. Leona waved at Missy as if hailing a ship from a desert island.

"Miss Carver, there you are! Hello! You're right on time—of course, I expected nothing less. Can I call you Missy? I've seen your name around town for so long, I feel like I already know you!"

Missy smiled back. "I feel the same way, Leona."

Missy did indeed know Leona, by reputation if nothing else. Leona was a local woman whose husband, Sidney, had left her the building in his will when he choked on a chicken bone at an Optimists' Club dinner in his honor and expired right there on the dais. Leona did not share her late husband's business savvy, not by a long shot, and she had been struggling to stay afloat ever since. The fact that she was standing outside on this brittle January morning, and being so overly solicitous for what was just an initial inspection of the property, signaled her desperation.

"Well, come on, let's head inside. I think you're going to just love the place!"

Leona's claim wasn't entirely without merit. Though the space was on the small side, and still featured the gaudy neon signage and spattered, industrial-age-gone-amok machinery endemic to all frozen-yogurt purveyors, its potential was obvious. The space was open, there was exposed brick on two walls, the terra cotta tile on the floor was surprisingly tasteful and in good condition, and the large front windows allowed in a lot of bright, western-exposure light.

"Well? What do you think?"

Leona was so eager to make a deal she was practically jumping out of her fur-lined boots.

But Missy knew the game. Knew it better than anybody. The best way to a good price in these circumstances was to stall, and ask questions, and point out flaws, and appear only slightly intrigued. "This equipment would have to go, of course."

"Oh, of course! I could have it out tomorrow if you'd like."

"But even then ... it's a bit on the small side. For my needs, you understand," Missy asserted, even though, in fact, she could barely afford it as is.

"My, my, aren't we ambitious? I like that! Well," Leona moved closer, her voice lowered now to speak in confidence, "I really shouldn't say, but the tenant next door is behind on his rent, and there's a distinct possibility his space will be coming available shortly, too. If so, I'd give you right of first refusal and you could expand, no problem!"

"Is that right? Hmm," Missy purred.

Leona had again showed her hand. If she was in danger of losing yet another tenant, *of course* she was desperate to rent out this space quickly. Once a building starts showing signs of falling out of favor, of not attracting enough customers, the whole thing starts to snowball. Before you know it, you're out of business, too. Leona was no genius, but she surely knew enough to realize that.

"Maybe I should take a quick look next door, too. Just to see."

"Oh, of course! By all means! We can just pop our heads in."

The two women made the quick hop, back out into the bitter cold and then right back inside, through the door of the adjoining suite, occupied by a little formalwear shop called Todd's Tuxedos.

There, the shop's blustery overseer—Todd himself, apparently—was chatting up his lone customer, a short, mousy-looking white man, accompanied by an Amazonian black lady with a bonsai-like hairdo, who might or might not have been his girlfriend.

"I tell you, partner, you can always go for the traditional black tux, and that'll do you just fine—I have one myself—but if you like things with a bit more pizzazz, and judging by this pretty lady right here you do, I might recommend something a little more lively. Let me show you this sweet-swingin' satin number I have right over—"

And that is when he finally saw Leona and Missy, standing by the entrance. For Missy, there was something vaguely familiar about Todd. For Leona, she only saw the same hand-in-the-cookie-jar expression that Todd fell into every time she stopped by.

Excusing himself from his customers, Todd sidled over like a scolded schoolboy. "Leona, this isn't really a very good time right now, but I'll have your check by Friday, I promise."

With poorly muffled contempt, Leona replied, "I hope so, Todd. That would be a nice surprise. But I'm actually just showing Miss Carver here around. She's looking at the space next door."

"Yeah?" Todd turned his attention to Missy, giving her a shameless once-over of the sort she'd always detested. "Well, good for you. Welcome to the neighborhood."

"I'm just looking for now. But thank you." Missy forced a smile, all the while slyly casing the man's shop, realizing it would indeed make a perfect add-on to the other, if things went as planned. "Leona, I think perhaps we should get going."

"Okay, then. Todd, I guess I'll see you on Friday, then," Leona added pointedly.

"Right … Friday," Todd repeated, with far less enthusiasm.

With that, Leona and Missy left the shop, and walked back to Missy's car for the inevitable wrap-up chat. "Well? So what do you say?"

Missy looked back to the empty storefront, then to the tuxedo shop, where Todd was holding up a gaudy smoking jacket and feigning some kind of Negro-jazzman move that likely offended both the man and his African-American lady friend. Clearly, he was doomed. Putting him out of business would be doing him and the world at large a favor.

Turning back to Leona, Missy got right to the point. "Leona, I think maybe I can help you out here. But first, you're going to have to help me ..."

35

MISSING PERSONS

In the time it took for Rowena to leave Vacaville behind for good and return to Sacramento, her tears had dried, but her heartbreak remained. She felt cheated and humiliated and betrayed. But most of all, she felt tired, right down to the very core of her being. She wanted nothing more than to curl up in her bed and close her eyes and make it all go away. And with any luck, that was precisely what she going to do. By her calculations, Connie should still be asleep for another several hours, and her next shift wasn't until midnight. This left a good stretch of the afternoon for her to stay in bed and wallow in her own sorrows for a while, just like old times.

However, upon Rowena's arrival back home, the odds of this happening quickly grew slim, as it became obvious that her mother was already awake again. The den was aglow, the TV was blaring, and a pot of boiling water was whistling furiously on the stove. There was even a fresh cigarette butt in the ashtray.

Seeing all of this, Rowena tried to look on the bright side. Maybe they could have their little coffee klatch after all, she thought. Better still, maybe her mother would be alert and lucid enough to listen to her sad story and provide the soft shoulder to cry on that she had almost convinced herself she didn't need, even though she really did.

There was only one problem with this heartwarming little scenario. Despite all the signs of her mother's presence, Connie herself was nowhere to be found. Rowena searched from room to room, starting from her bed and proceeding from there, trying to anticipate her most likely path. But no matter where Rowena looked, she came up empty. It soon became a matter of no small certainty that her mother had, in fact, fully vacated the premises. No note. No trail of bread crumbs. No anything. And in light of Connie's current condition, this was a very big problem, indeed.

Trying her best to think rationally, Rowena did the logical first thing and called the police to report the situation. After just one ring, the call was answered.

"Sacramento Police Department, Officer Baines speaking," a man said, his voice deep and commanding, just the kind you want to hear from an officer of the law when he's in a position to assist you (as opposed to, say, arrest you or testify against you).

"Yes, Officer Baines, this is Rowena Pickett. I need to report a woman missing."

"Okay. And what is the woman's name?"

"My mother. It's my mother, Connie Pickett." Saying this, Rowena started to choke up, the cumulative effect of her trying day finally getting the best of her.

"And how long has your mother been missing, Ms. Pickett?"

"I don't know exactly, I just got home." Rowena grabbed a tissue, blew her nose, dabbed at her eyes. "A couple hours, maybe?"

"I see. And how do you know she isn't just out shopping or something?"

Something in the officer's tone threw Rowena off, made her momentarily doubt herself, even though she knew deep in her gut that her alarm was justified. "I ... she ... well, she has Alzheimer's, you see. Her mind, it isn't as sharp as it used to be. She may not know where she is, or what she's doing. Not exactly, at least."

"Has she wandered off before?"

"No. Never."

"So you have no reason to believe that she'd be putting herself in harm's way."

"Not on purpose. But she's been talking a lot about my father, and he's dead, but she talks about him like he's alive, and that can't be a good thing, right?"

"So there was no note, no sign of distress ...?"

"No, no. Nothing like that."

"Okay. Well. The department policy is that, without some sign of distress or criminal involvement, a person of adult age isn't considered officially missing until they remain unaccounted for, for a period of at least forty-eight hours."

"Forty-eight hours? But ... can't you at least put out an APB or something?"

"Ma'am, I can tell you're upset, but there are procedures we have to follow. If you'd like, I could send a squad car by the house. Would you like that?"

"Yes, please, anything."

"All right, then. Why don't you give me your address?"

Rowena gave the address. A half-hour later, a squad car stopped by. The two officers were both perfectly nice and sympathetic. But like Officer Baines, there was little they could do. They did offer to make a quick run past the cemetery, Eddie's final resting place, to see if she might be there—a good idea, and one Rowena wholeheartedly endorsed. Alas, that effort came up empty. No mourners, no flowers, no footprints.

All the while, Rowena's worst fears continued to mount. So did her exhaustion. Having been awake for nearly thirty-six hours now, with another graveyard shift just a few short hours away, she knew she needed to get some sleep. But Rowena also knew that with her mother still missing, the possibility of her actually nodding off was minimal, anyway. And rather than just sit there in the empty house, feeling helpless, Rowena instead took another shower, slugged down more coffee, and got back in her car to start combing the neighborhood streets herself.

She was going to find her mother, by God. Even if it was the last thing she did.

***

Later that evening, Todd Tisdale returned home from another long day at the shop to find someone missing, too—namely, his wife, Svetlana. But Todd wasn't alarmed by this absence. He wasn't even surprised anymore. He had come to expect it.

Ever since Christmas, when he and Lana's big night out ended so abominably, she had been spending more and more time away from home. Although he knew, or at least suspected, that much of this time was being spent in the company of a certain freakishly-large Ukrainian basketball player, Lana refused to confirm this or even discuss it in any detail beyond saying that it was "nice to have someone to talk to for a change."

The result was that it was now Todd who was left with no one to talk to. And this was unfortunate, because Todd needed someone to confide in now more than ever. Ever since his landlord, Leona, had come by the shop with that Missy woman, her requests for the back rent he owed had grown increasingly hostile, to the point where it looked like he might need the services of a lawyer in order to stay. Of course, he could no more afford a lawyer than he could the rent. It seemed he was left with no other recourse but to face the music, and his creditors, and—after more than fifteen years on the job—close his shop.

Bankruptcy. Divorce. Despair. Gloomy scenarios of all sorts swirled through Todd's mind as entered his darkened abode with the intention of locating whichever intoxicants were most readily available and drinking himself into a lonely stupor.

However, as he entered the kitchen and made a beeline for the liquor cabinet, his hands lunging for the nearest bottle, he discovered, much to his surprise, that he was not alone after all. Young Alek was there, too, sitting at the counter, under the dim light of a single overhead bulb, eyeing a plastic-sheathed plate of leftovers that Lana had left him for his supper, its gelatinous array of items looking far from appetizing, even from a distance.

The two locked eyes. An unspoken empathy passed between them. Alek clearly didn't want any part of the leftovers, and Todd was having second thoughts as well about the liter of cheap gin his fingers had wrapped themselves around. The situation called for a new plan. And Todd, being the adult, realized it was up to him to formulate it.

"Hey, buddy, didn't know you were here. I was just looking to fetch up some grub myself," Todd said, all evidence to the contrary, as he tried to subtly tuck the bottle back onto the shelf. "What do you say we get a pizza instead? You and me. The biggest one they got."

Alek dropped his fork and scooted away the plate, signaling his approval, and Todd reached for the phone.

An hour later, all that was left of the large Sicilian deep dish from Luigi's that they had ordered was a few crusts, a smattering of grease, and a lone disc of pepperoni. Todd had retreated to the den, with Alek following close behind, and they had turned on the TV to try and offset the awkward silence that was closing in all around them.

However, as that lack of conversation and its underlying cause became more and more unbearably obvious for both of them, Todd finally turned to his would-be son with a heavy sigh—*here goes nothing*—and began to speak.

"So, big guy," Todd ventured, in his usual gregarious tone, as if nothing at all was awry, "new semester, right? How's school treating you these days?"

"Okay," Alek replied unenthusiastically.

"Okay like good?" Todd countered, trying his very hardest. "Or okay like you don't want to talk about it with the old man here?"

"I don't know. Whatever," Alek offered, with a morose shrug, his eyes remaining glued to the screen.

Todd sighed again. With all that was happening, he knew he needed to reach out to the boy. He had hoped Alek might actually *want* to talk, so that all he'd have to do was get the ball rolling and then Alek would steer the dialogue from there. Alas, this didn't seem to be the case. The boy was keeping mum, holding it all in, just like he was. More work was clearly needed.

"Funny, I thought you liked school."

"I only say it to make Mama feel better."

A-ha, Todd thought. "Worried about your mom, are you?"

"More like she's worried about me."

Not the reply Todd had expected. It threatened to take their chat off its intended course. But what else could he do? He had to roll with it.

"Worried about you? Why's that?"

"Because she wants me to fit in."

"So? You're a good kid. Tall, smart, good-looking—"

"Not like them."

"The other kids, you mean? Why, because you're Russian? The boy snorted. *Duh.*

"And you think that's a problem?"

"They do."

"Who?"

"All of them."

"Maybe they do because *you* do. Because you let them."

Alek snorted again. "Like you know."

A defensive, smartass reply, delivered with the same mercurial contempt that had become his mother's stock in trade. But Todd fought right back: "Hey there, little man, I know more than you think. Did you know I went to Babcock, too, when I was a kid?"

At this, Alek turned with surprise, looking vaguely intrigued for the first time.

"Oh, yeah, I was a Babcock Bobcat for six years. And let me tell you, if you play it right, being Russian's the best weapon you got."

Alek was paying attention now. Todd smiled. His venerable schoolyard wisdom was winning the boy over. "See, all these other kids, the ones who act like they're so cool? Most of 'em have never been anywhere except the mall their entire life. You lived on the whole other side of the globe. You know a whole other language. You've seen things and done things they can only read about in books. Knowledge is power, buddy. You've got the advantage."

The boy leaned closer. "You really think so?"

"Heck, yeah! And the guys in your class, they may put up a front, like they know what's what. But they're scared of you, trust me. You're new, and different, and that makes you dangerous. Once you act like you know it, and stand up for yourself, they'll fall in line—I guarantee it."

For the first time, Alek seemed to be buying into Todd's theory. Testing the waters, he cited one potential example: "Some of the girls, they asked about my accent."

"See? That's what I'm talking about, buddy! It's the whole Man of Mystery thing. Girls love that stuff!"

"They do?"

"Oh, yeah. Big time."

"Kull."

"Damn straight it's cool. And long as you know that, and act like it, it's just gonna keep on getting better. Before you know it, you'll be running that joint."

Alek sat back in his chair, pondering this. After a time, the tension in his narrow shoulders finally eased, and he broke into a smile. "Thank you, Todd."

Todd beamed. "Any time, buddy. Heck, it was my pleasure."

And indeed it was. Todd felt like thanking the boy right back. The talk had lifted his spirits, too.

Another pregnant silence ensued. Alek looked at Todd, but differently now, something in his eyes suggesting Todd had broken through and earned his confidence. He thus broached a new topic, the one that had been looming all along.

"Mama, she try to help me, too, you know. Give me advice, show me what to wear, how to fit in. But she is new here, too. How can she know?"

Todd sat up in his chair. He saw where this discussion was going, and he wanted to give it the proper respect.

"Well, that's a good question, son. Not sure I can answer that one."

Alek then added, tentatively, "She's gone a lot lately."

"I know."

"She needs help, too, I think. Maybe you can talk to her."

"I've tried, son, believe me."

"But maybe you should try some more."

"I will. But I don't know how much good it'll do."

"She's older. It's harder for her."

"I expect that's right. And maybe that's why I'm not having much luck." A beat, as Todd pondered his own sense of loss. "You know how much I love your mom, right?"

"She loves you, too. She told me."

"Yeah," Todd nodded forlornly. "Just maybe not enough."

This possibility, or probability, or drop-dead certainty—Todd didn't know for sure which term best applied, and little Alek likely didn't either—lingered like a foul odor, threatening to spoil the aura of goodwill the two had been fostering between one another.

Fortunately, Todd was aware enough of this to wisely steer things back on course. "But hey, one thing at a time, right? Let's stick with you for now, and figure out how we can show these little Babcock punks who's boss."

"Okay!"

"Okay." Todd smiled, putting all thoughts of Lana aside, and turning his focus back squarely on young Alek and his ascension to elementary school greatness. "Now, the way I see it is, you're like a character from a James Bond movie ..."

36

SPENCER TAKES A STAND

On another overcast January day, Spencer sat at his cramped desk, clacking away dutifully on his keyboard. In the cubicles to his left and right, and indeed all throughout the *Bee*'s vast newsroom, other reporters did the same.

To the uninitiated, this little tableau might serve as signal that everything was just peachy. That Spencer and his colleagues were all functioning properly and up to speed. But Spencer knew better. He knew that it was a far sight different now than it had been during those glorious fall days when everyone was abuzz, and anything seemed possible. Now, people went about their business methodically, almost robotically. There was no excitement. No electricity. No air of the unexpected. It was busy work, feeding the machine, no more and no less.

Part of this dim outlook, it was true, could be traced to Spencer's own personal travails. After his meltdown with Paul, he had been banished from his former mentor's good graces, which meant no more feature assignments, and no more relief from his daily gravedigger's grind. There was also his continued estrangement from Nikki, the root cause of that meltdown, which left him in a deep funk, with no muse for inspiration, and no more rakish mystique among his peers. With all his previous ace cards shuffled out of the deck, Spencer realized, he was right back where he started—just another faceless wordsmith, toiling away in the basement, trying to spin silk out of sows' ears.

But Spencer knew there was more to it than just that. The aura of "anything is possible" that had energized the city in the days of the new action-hero governor's arrival had been slowly siphoned off and replaced by the usual murky political stagnancy. Since the inauguration, and that first burst of new-sheriff-in-town swaggering, there had been little word, much less action, from the Capitol, nor from the nearby Hyatt hotel suite where Arnold had chosen to rule the roost on those rare occasions when he was actually in town.

It was a letdown. An affront. One that made even the True Believers realize that while they had successfully elected a larger-than-life figure, it was the man behind the iconic image who would be actually holding the office. And that man was human, and flawed, and unrealistically optimistic about his own ability to affect change, same as every other person who seeks public office.

And, that man—who had likely bought into his own image as much as the rest of the world did—was also very likely sitting down in his Brentwood mansion at this very moment, wondering how he was going to manage all these new responsibilities that had seemed so eminently doable when he was just talking about them, and ruing all the bureaucratic crap he was already having to field, and the compromises he was already having to make, and regretting having to get on a plane to Sacramento and leave his home and his family, yet again, only to wear a suit all day and sleep in a shitty hotel bed at night. In short, he was very likely asking himself, *What the hell did I just do?*

And there was a story in this, Spencer realized. An important one. Perhaps even a revelatory one. One that could address head-on the issue of all the false hopes that people inevitably build around change, especially in the political arena—and how, in the end, that hope can only lead to disappointment for all involved.

But now that he was out of favor with the powers that be, he wouldn't be allowed even to pitch a story like that, much less write it. No, the only people whose tales he could tell were those who were as dead as his own fledgling career appeared to be. And perhaps, Spencer thought, wallowing in his own misery, that is all he deserved.

"Spencer?"

From somewhere close by, a female voice called out to him. And for one brief moment, Spencer allowed himself to believe that it was Nikki, having finally come to her senses, and now sweeping into the room like a repentant Tom Cruise in *Jerry Maguire* to beg for him to take her back.

You had me at hello, Spencer thought to himself.

"Spencer Brine?"

A teary-eyed female face appeared from over the cubicle wall, matching the voice but not, alas, matching his fantasy. "It is you, isn't it?"

It wasn't Nikki, but the face was attractive, and looked familiar. Why and how, Spencer was not entirely sure. Still, he felt a strange urge to reply as if he did.

"Of course. Great to see you again. How are you?"

The young woman's reply proved far more complex than Spencer had expected. Upon clarifying that she was Rowena Pickett, whom Spencer had met one day while purchasing Halloween supplies out by the highway, Rowena then launched at length into the matter of her current state of affairs, which wasn't good, not at all, due in large part to her mother, who was suffering from Alzheimer's and apparently missing.

Spencer listened patiently to Rowena's tearful tale, as he sensed that, more than anything, this was what she needed.

Once she was done, Spencer offered his heartfelt sympathies. Then, as gently as possible, he also expressed his uncertainty as to how any of this might pertain to him.

"But, aren't you a reporter?" Rowena countered, with a disarming naiveté.

"Yes." *Albeit a failed one,* Spencer thought to himself.

"So, couldn't you maybe write a story, and run a picture, and tell people to be on the lookout for her?"

"Well, in a perfect world ..." Spencer knew the rules. He knew that if the police had yet to deem a situation worthy, the paper would feel likewise.

"*Please.*" Rowena grabbed his hands and placed her mother's picture in them, pleading, desperate. "She's sick and confused and she's all alone out there." Then, staring deep into his eyes. "She's all I have."

Spencer knew the rules, all right. But looking at Rowena, and seeing how sweet and emotionally fragile she was, and realizing how desperate she must be to come to him this way, he found himself speaking against his own better judgment. "Okay, I'll do what I can."

And even though he knew that even his best efforts would very likely be met with rejection, the adoring smile that Rowena gave him, and the tender kiss she planted on his cheek as she got up to leave, almost made it all worthwhile.

"Chasing down some new trailer-trash tail, are you, Brine?"

Spencer was in Paul's office, lobbying for the approval he knew he'd never get. Paul had gotten an eyeful of Rowena, and his disdainful reply was precisely as expected.

"The woman's mother has Alzheimer's, Paul."

"Yeah, and she has a nice caboose, too, but that still doesn't make it a story."

"And what does, then?"

"Forty-eight hours and an SPD bulletin, same as always. Until then, how do we even know if she's telling the truth?"

"I'm pretty sure she was, Paul."

"And *pretty sure* might've been good enough for your college gazette, Brine, but it's not good enough for this publication. Sorry. Class dismissed." With that, Paul gave Spencer a backhanded wave of his hand to let him know he could leave, then turned his attention back to the J. Crew catalog he was flipping through.

Bowed but not beaten, Spencer left his erstwhile patron behind and headed straight to Morris Sutphin's desk down in Metro. There, he pitched the story anew, with a fervor fueled by Paul's derision. Morris listened patiently, and offered his sympathies in much the same way that Spencer had offered them to Rowena. But like Paul, he cited company policy, and said he had no choice but to say no.

With no place else to turn, Spencer slumped back to his cubicle. The effort had only confirmed his worst fears. No one cared anymore what he thought or said. He was, as far as the newspaper was concerned, a total pariah. A dead man walking.

But as the day wore on, this woe turned into indignation, and then anger. Though the story and the missing woman were merely symbols of a larger sense of futility, they also became totems to Spencer's growing desire to rebel against it. After all, if a newsman can't use his position to help out a woman in distress, what's the point of having the damn job in the first place? And with that, he started typing, with a passion that had been absent from his work ever since Nikki left him.

By 9 p.m. that evening, the only people still in the newsroom were a handful of sports columnists waiting for final scores and a skeleton crew on hand to intercept any late-breaking stuff off the national wire. All the section editors, including Morris and

Paul, were gone for the day. Spencer, waiting patiently in his cubicle, looked around and saw that the coast was clear.

As stealthily as possible, he got up from his desk and made the trek from the newsroom, over to the adjoining wing where the printing and layout departments were housed. There, unlike in the newsroom, it was still a hive of activity. This was their busy time, making final corrections and adjustments to go to press, in order to get the paper printed and ready for the following morning.

Despite having worked at the *Bee* for nearly five years, Spencer had spent hardly any time here. It was like a different world, or at least a different business, with its vast factory-like space dominated by a huge rollercoaster assembly of presses and dryers and collation machines, all of them commandeered by a platoon of blue-collar technicians in safety goggles and grimy overalls.

But for the moment, those workers and their machines remained largely at rest, although Spencer knew that wouldn't be the case for long. The clock was ticking. Breaking into a jog, he finally located an office at the back of the cavernous space, where a couple of bleary-eyed supervisors were going over spec pages and making final tweaks to the edition's layout. Spencer took a deep breath, then, as coolly as possible, he knocked and entered the room.

"Hey fellas, got a last-minute add for Metro."

The two men looked up, both clearly less than thrilled. "Nobody told us about it."

"I'm telling you now. Missing person piece. Right here."

Spencer handed over the story. The two men eyed it dubiously. The senior of the two aired his suspicion. "Who signed off on this?"

Spencer met his eyes. "No one. Morris was gone and so were Paul and Ted. But it can't wait. Woman's missing, got Alzheimer's. She might be in some real trouble."

A beat. The two continued eying the story. Did they know the 48-hour rule? Did they care? The senior man finally heaved an exasperated sigh. "Pages are locked. We'd have to bump something."

Fortunately, Spencer had anticipated this and had a solution at the ready. "We can hold the piece on the city council meeting for a day. No one will notice."

"Says you," the other man snorted. "Either way, somebody's gotta sign off on it. I sure as hell ain't doing it."

"I'll take full responsibility. I'll be happy to. Just tell me what I need to sign."

And just like that, the deed was done. The story was in.

And even though Spencer knew that there would be a price to pay for his actions, as he quickly exited the building— ducking away before anybody else could notice or object— and got in his Volvo to head home, he felt better about it than he had felt about anything in a very long time, indeed.

37

MISSY CARVER, GOOD SAMARITAN

In spite of the afternoon hour, the skies over Sacramento were dark. Clouds of varying shapes and hues clashed and thundered. Rain, and perhaps even hail, seemed imminent. The sidewalks were largely empty, as people braced for the winter storm to come.

But on G Street, in the new offices of Carver Properties, there was no such cowering. The space was aglow and bustling. The phones rang out in a constant melody. People came and went with a sense of urgency that belied the foul conditions.

In the center of all this activity was Missy herself. Forgoing any hierarchical corner office cloistering, she had instead positioned her desk out in the open, right smack in the center of the space, so that she could see and contribute to all that was happening, while also keeping a close eye on her new assistant, who went by the name of Mamie—or, in Missy's case, Mother.

Mamie had lost another twenty pounds since the New Year, and she had taken her makeover a step further by shedding her old floral muumuus for a more polished style of dress. In fact, in her white button-down shirt and no-nonsense navy suit, she fit the part in a way that had her also looking, quite startlingly, like Missy herself, a fact that gave them both an equal measure of pause and unconfessed pleasure.

But despite this smart new veneer, Mamie's workplace capabilities were still in their floral-muumuu phase. It had been at least a couple of years since she had held a job of any kind, and to her vague recollection she had never lasted in any kind of white-collar position for more than a few days.

"Mother, can you get me those flyers for the Chandler property?"

"Oh." Mamie blinked twice, as if short-circuiting. "Which one was that again?"

"The ones we printed up last night. The big Spanish Revival place."

From the vacant look in Mamie's eyes, it was clear this still didn't register.

Missy sighed. "You said it looked like a church for Mexicans, remember?"

"Oh! Yes. They're right here. On my desk. Somewhere ..."

As Mamie searched frantically, Missy allowed herself another stoic sigh. Her mother was hapless—that much was undeniable—but Missy knew she making the effort, and for that reason she had eased up on her typically rigorous standards, going out of her way to patiently train her mother, and cover her tracks, and repair her mistakes, as she slowly bungled her way up (and very often, right back down) the very lowest rungs of the corporate ladder.

"Here it is! I've got it! Right here, honey!" Mamie beamed as if she had just recovered the Rosetta Stone. Missy smiled patiently. Despite everything, it was good to see her mother display some pride in herself for a change.

"Good job, Mom. I'm going to go post these. You hold down the fort, okay?"

"Don't you worry, baby, I've got it covered," Mamie assured her daughter.

"Good. And call me if anything comes up."

"On your cell phone, right?" Then, once again scanning her disorderly desktop, "What's that number again?"

After giving her mother the number for the umpteenth time, and offering a few final reminders, Missy ducked out the door and into the worsening storm. It was dark now, not only from the weather, but also from the late afternoon hour, which was as good as night in these days of daylight savings.

Rushing to her car, shielded from the driving rain only partially by her umbrella, Missy happened to look up and see her next door neighbor, Todd, through his display-case window. As usual, he was holding court, managing to swagger even while standing still, as he ostensibly helped one of his increasingly-rare customers select an ensemble. It was a pose that had helped Missy recall precisely where she had seen him before—at the Gas N' Sip, buying condoms and breath mints, on the night of her initial retreat.

To Missy's dread, the two locked eyes. Todd smiled and waved like a Super Bowl champ on his way to Disney World. From underneath her umbrella, Missy offered a tentative little wave of her own, all the while wondering how the man could be so garrulous, as if he didn't have a care in the world, when she knew for a fact that he was sinking faster than the *Titanic*. Was he playing some kind of game? Was he an idiot? Or was he simply so used to being on the make that he didn't know when to quit?

Averting her eyes, Missy finally reached the safety of her Lexus. She disengaged the locks, shook off her umbrella, and ducked inside. Immediately, the shelter from the rain and the fresh leather smell of the cockpit put her at ease. Her car was a haven, no more so than at that very moment. She took a few seconds to bask in its Zen-like tranquility.

But as she did so, she caught sight of something she hadn't meant to. Something she wasn't supposed to. It was Todd again. With his customer now hustling down the same rainy sidewalk she had just left—no sale, apparently—Todd had retreated to his storeroom. And the cocky, carefree facade was no longer in evidence. Hunched over a workbench, head in his hands, he looked miserable. *Leona must have told him*, she thought to herself. But while Missy was an accomplice to Todd's troubles, having agreed to take over his space as soon as it became available, seeing him like this somehow took the joy out of it for her. It put a tragic face on something that she had allowed herself to view as inevitable and impersonal.

It also transported Missy back to her own struggles. Like Todd, she had tried to maintain a brave face and convince everyone that everything in her life was just peachy, all the while keeping the pain and misery bottled up so tight that it had nearly killed her. It made her view Todd in a different light. He may not be a good businessman, and his shop may deserve to go under, and he may be a bit of a pig as well, but he was still a human being, with feelings, and he was a neighbor, and he had tried to be nice to her despite the illicit maneuverings on her part.

And so, in spite of her own feelings, and her guilt, and the weather, not to mention the flyers she still had to post, Missy found herself getting back out of her car, and making her way through the rain and through the door of Todd's shop to do ... something. What, she wasn't sure yet. This was new to her. She was winging it.

Ding-a-ling.

As the bell over the door rang out and Missy swept inside, Todd startled, standing up and putting his happy face back on as best he could.

"Hello, there!"

Seeing it was her, his expression grew quizzical. "You again ... hey." Then, collecting himself, "To what do I owe the pleasure?"

Missy hesitated, realizing she wasn't quite sure where to start.

"Looking for some formalwear for that special guy, maybe?"

"No, no, nothing like that," Missy said, chuckling uneasily.

"Well, I'm not in the market for any real estate, either, so ..." Todd shrugged boyishly, although a trace of melancholy was now visible around the eyes.

"Look, I just—"

"Yes?"

"I saw you, okay. Back there." Missy pointed to the storeroom.

"Oh."

With that, Todd's whole body deflated, like the air going out of a balloon. Missy had seen behind the curtain.

For her part, Missy suddenly felt highly inappropriate, as if she were some kind of peeping Tom. "I'm sorry, I didn't mean to, I really didn't. I just ..." Missy paused, struggling to find the right words, the right tone. "I just thought it looked like you might need someone to talk to, that's all."

Todd stared at Missy. It was hard to tell how he felt about this. Was he embarrassed? Offended? Angry?

"Good Christ, lady, you have no idea."

With no further prompting necessary, Todd proceeded to offer up a detailed litany of his troubles. Through it all, Missy had to bite her tongue not to blurt out, *Serves you right, you bonehead!* After all, marrying some hot-to-trot Russian divorcee he'd only known a few days, and with her last husband in prison, no less—what did he expect? The debt he accrued in doing so was also painfully predictable.

On the other hand, his feelings for the woman's son were admirable, and when he told her about his failed Team Arnold Plan, as pathetic as it may have been, this also struck a chord. Despite his crude phrasing, he summed up the situation rather aptly when he said, "One minute it seems like the guy's gonna come barreling in and change everything. The next, it's like he barely even gives a shit—just wham, bam, fuck you, Sacramento!"

When Todd was through, it was clear how close to the edge he truly was. Leona was evicting him. He was up to his eyeballs in debt. His wife was leaving him for some hulking pro athlete, and she was taking her young son with her, even though Todd had been acting like a father to the boy and had been well down the road to officially adopting him, too.

"So. What do you think?" Todd asked meekly.

I think you're screwed, Missy thought.

"Is there anything I can do to fix all this?"

"Not a chance in hell" was the reply that leapt to Missy's lips, but Todd's plain-faced desperation started getting to her. She kicked into her old bad-cop mode.

"Well, for starters, you can stop acting like you've already lost."

"But, haven't I? Lana's already gone—"

"Good riddance. She's clearly a gold digger. You don't need someone like that in your life, anyway. Especially not now."

Todd might have normally argued this point and defended his wife's honor, but the forcefulness of Missy's tone precluded it. Besides, Lana had made her choice, and he had too many other problems to dwell on just one.

"And the debt. I mean, they're calling all the time—"

"Of course they are. They want their money. And they're not going to get it by putting you out of business, now are they?"

"Guess you have a point. But still, Leona's kicking me out. Unless, maybe—"

"Don't even go there. For one thing, you're four months behind on rent. It's a miracle you've held out this long. And in case you don't know, I'm taking over this space myself, and I need it. This isn't a good location for you, anyway."

"Excuse me, lady, but I've been here fifteen years and doing just fine for most of that time, thank you very much."

"Another miracle. Look around. What's here, aside from me? A vegan bakery. A martial-arts studio. A motor-scooter dealership. Where's the synergy? You need to be near a flower shop or a bridal boutique or a jeweler. Some place where people can kill two birds with one stone."

"Hey, that's not a bad idea, I gotta admit. Not bad at all. Not much good now, but still. Why didn't I ever think of that?"

"Do you really want me to answer that?" Todd shook his head. Missy was in the zone now.

"And then there's your inventory. It looks like most of it's just lying around gathering dust. Have you ever thought of cross-referencing with other shops in the area, or running sales on old stock to keep your merchandise up to date? And what about customer files? Do you have them on some kind of computer program, so you can send out e-mails, and updates, and invites?"

Todd's head was swimming. "Damn, lady, you're pretty good."

"The name's Missy. And I'm better than good, actually."

"I bet you *are*." Todd lifted an eyebrow, the old cockiness seeping through...

... which Missy wasted no time in shooting down. "And under the circumstances, I suggest you stick to thinking with your *other* head for a change. Okay, big guy?"

Todd laughed—really busted a gut—for the first time in weeks. Not intimidated by her like most men, just amused, and intrigued. "Damn, Missy, you are something, aren't you? Okay, old gal, give it to me straight. Tell me how to fix my screwed-up life, top to bottom."

"I'd need some coffee for that."

"I'll get you a whole pot. Whatever you need. Back rub, maybe?"

Missy had to smile. The guy was shameless.

"The coffee will do."

"Okay, then."

"And just remember, you asked for it."

And with that, Missy did as Todd asked. And Todd listened, well into the night. And as the two lingered over a second pot, one couldn't help but get the sense that not only were Missy's suggestions going to work, but that these two might actually hit it off better as a team, a pair—maybe even as a *couple*—than either one of them, or anybody else, would have ever expected.

38

GOODBYE CRUEL WORLD

The view from California State Route 89 as it winds around Emerald Bay on Lake Tahoe is truly breathtaking, with nothing but snow-capped mountains and deep, crystal blue water for miles in every direction. Unspoiled and painterly in scope, it looks like a postcard—and indeed, many have been made of it.

However, with that beauty comes no small amount of danger. The road is narrow, often slick, wickedly curved, and precipitously sloped. With entrancing panoramas on all sides to cause distraction, it has, over the years, claimed the lives of far too many cars and drivers to count. And for those reckless few who try to tackle the route on foot, the risk is—if possible—even greater still. There is no formal walking path for much of the way, the road's shoulders are steep and rocky, and its endless curves create blind spots that often leave pedestrians unseen until it's too late to change course. In the winter months, which predominate, there is also the matter of the snow and ice that clog up the road's shoulders and make footing treacherous. The whole situation is perilous.

Connie Pickett wasn't thinking about any of this, however. Nor was she asking herself why she wasn't wearing something warmer than Eddie's flimsy old "Ace Trucking" windbreaker that was getting her buffeted about by the cove's swirling winds. And it didn't occur to her, either, that she might have been tempting fate by clomping along the icy berm in Eddie's size-twelve boots rather than her own size-fives. None of it mattered to her in the slightest. Her mind was elsewhere. She was searching.

Staring out over the glacial waters far below, steel toes hung over the edge of the slippery escarpment, she muttered to herself, her brow knit in worry, "Where are you, Eddie? Where are you? Come back to me. Come home."

The only reply came from the wind, howling across the waters. But to Connie's ears, it was more than that. It contained a message, one meant only for her; the one that she had been waiting for all these many years. She smiled happily, deliriously.

"Eddie …"

The years melted away from her face. There it was, she could see it now, right there in front of her, so close she could almost touch it—the big missing piece to the life that had been so unfairly taken from her. All she had to do was reach out and grab it.

But just as her hands extended out, her feet began sliding forward, and the snow started giving way, something else grabbed her attention and, at the very last second, pulled her away from the ledge. It was a horn. And not just any horn, but the horn of a sixteen-wheel Mack Truck—the same truck Eddie used to drive, with the same battle-hymn blare Eddie used to play, to signal his arrival back home after yet another weeklong cross-country haul.

Connie turned and stared at the truck. At its tinted windshield and its spit-shined chrome grille. It triggered a fresh flood of memories. She called out to it, "Eddie?"

The driver's door opened, and a tall, rugged-looking man in a plaid flannel shirt and jeans stepped out of the cab. It wasn't Eddie, but it was close enough of an approximation that she paid heed. "You all right, lady?"

"I'm fine. I'm just ... looking for somebody," Connie replied.

"Out here?" the trucker countered dubiously.

"Yes. This is the place, I'm sure of it," Connie answered, less certain now, but still committed, staring out over the snow-caps and the deep blue water, a vista not so different from the one in Colorado that had claimed Eddie's life a dozen years before.

The driver took this in, the older, flame-haired woman with the spacey demeanor and the haphazard appearance. Something about it rang a bell. It was something he had read in the paper that very morning, while drinking his third cup of trucker-lounge Folgers and waiting for his cargo to get loaded off the docks. "Hey!" he exclaimed. "I've seen you. You're that lady who's gone missing, aren't you?"

Connie, of course, had no idea what the truck driver, Walt, was talking about, and this created even more wariness between them, which was only heightened as cars raced by at alarming proximity and horn-blaring traffic started to back up behind them. But the longer they stood there, the more it became clear to Walt that this indeed was the woman he had read about.

"Hey, listen, it's pretty cold out here. Why don't you come and hop in my truck, we'll go get some coffee or something. How's that sound?"

"I don't know," Connie replied. She still had a strong sense that she was there for a reason. The spot, she knew, had some important meaning, some relevance, although for the life of her she could no longer recall what it was.

"Come on," the trucker urged, not wanting to cause any more of a scene, or a hazard, than necessary.

Connie stared at the man, his large hand reaching out to her, looking so much like Eddie had back in the day. Different hair color, and face shape—but still, a similar core essence.

"Maybe just one cup," Connie offered, as she took Walt's hand and he led her to the passenger door. Hiking herself up, she added, "My husband used to drive one of these trucks, you know."

"Is that right? Well, I guess he'd approve then, now wouldn't he?"

"You know, he just might at that," Connie giggled, pleased by the irony despite not grasping its full extent. And with that, she hopped into the truck like a schoolgirl on a first date and put the dangers of Route 89 and the rest of her wayward journey behind her, as if it had all been just another silly mistake.

***

A mistake.

That's all it would have taken, probably, to save himself. To say it was a mistake, and to apologize. And yes, maybe grovel a little, too. That always helps.

But the fact was, Spencer didn't feel like he'd made a mistake. He felt he had done the right thing. Rules were important, yes, but some less so than others. In this case, to help locate a mind-addled old woman and calm her sweet, desperate daughter, he felt his flouting of the rules—which to his mind seemed rather arbitrary, anyway—was completely just.

And when Paul Hoying came charging down the stairs to confront him, spewing venom over his "gross insubordination," he had said exactly that:

"I'm sorry, Paul. I did what I felt I had to do."

To which Paul had replied, "Yeah? Well, now I'm going to have to do what I have to do, which is to make sure your sorry ass is out of here by lunchtime."

As a result, Spencer was now busy packing up all the personal items from his cubicle into a couple of empty cardboard boxes he'd borrowed from the copy room. And although his space and his belongings within it were rather spare, it still proved a difficult task, wrought with more emotion than he'd expected, and this difficulty was compounded by the fact that he knew all the eyes in the room were on him as he was doing it. That indeed, every single person in the room already knew he was getting fired, and knew why, even though it hadn't *officially* happened yet.

But official or not, it was inevitable. His first job as a reporter, and he'd lost it. Worse still, he'd done so in a city with no other dailies and few periodicals of note to fall back on. He would have to move. Sell his condo and leave with his boxes in his trunk and his tail between his legs like a whipped puppy.

He wondered what his family would think. Especially his father, who had offered him a position as a trader for his firm even though Spencer had never show any talent or inclination for it. Most likely, that was why he'd headed west in the first place, to stave off the nepotism and allure of easy money. And it was likely why he'd never gone back, either, aside from the occasional short visit. To wait until he'd carved out a niche of his own, one that would allow him to forgo the temptation a second time around.

But now? Where was he now? Unemployed, with no prospects, and the black-mark onus of being fired on top of it all. His future looked grim, indeed. It was certainly a high price to pay for taking the moral high road, if that's what it was—and the more he thought about it, packing away his keepsakes and avoiding people's damning stares, the more he began to have his doubts.

"Brine, I'd like to see you in my office, please."

And now it was Morris's turn to get in a few final jabs, too, before he was out the door for good. *Great*, Spencer thought to himself, *just what I needed.*

"Look, Mr. Sutphin, I'm sorry. I know what I did was wrong. I just thought—"

"Not here, Brine. In my office. *Now.*"

"Okay, yes, sir," Spencer nodded resignedly. Morris had never liked him or his work. This would be a delicious moment for the old guy, a sweet vindication of his musty skills and ethics. It was time to reap the whirlwind.

With all the room's eyes following along with him, Spencer trudged his way into Morris's little tin-can office space. There, Morris sat at his worm-eaten desk, with a little smile, hands behind his head, basking in his own reclaimed superiority.

"Saw you clearing out your desk," he opened. "Thought it might be wise to pull you in for a little chat, just you and I, before you finished the job."

Here we go, thought Spencer, fighting with all his might the urge to roll his eyes.

"First things first: about the article. There was nothing wrong with it, actually, per se. It followed the proper style: paragraph, punctuation, spelling. It contained all the vital information. Effectively appealed to the emotions. You even placed it where I would have within the section. Bravo."

Spencer gritted his teeth. The gloating was almost too much to bear.

"There was just one problem, as I'm sure you know. And it was a big one."

Boy, he's really milking it now, Spencer thought. *Just get it over with already, old man.*

"That is, I didn't agree to sign off on it for you and override the policy ... which I absolutely should have done."

At this, Spencer did an honest-to-goodness double take. "Excuse me, sir?"

"You heard me. You were right to run that piece. That woman was a lifelong local, she was sick, she was missing, and that's news worth printing, no matter how you cut it."

"Well, thank you, sir. But, I guess I don't ... where does that—?"

"I'm not done. So just listen for once. It might do you some good."

A long pause followed. Morris was testing him now. Spencer remained resolutely silent.

"The thing is, the woman was found earlier this morning, wandering around Lake Tahoe, and the man who found her, a trucker, had actually seen your story. That's how he was able to identify her. And believe me, that's a little factoid that'll garner some newsprint as well. Which, I might add, is precisely what I said to Mr. Claiborne."

"You told the Editor-in-Chief?"

"Oh, he already knew. Not all of it, but some. Your buddy Paul has apparently been on the warpath all morning."

"I think the warpath started at my desk, actually."

"Which explains the boxes."

"Yes, sir."

"Well, you won't need be needing those anymore."

"No?"

Morris shook his head. Leaned forward. Put his elbows on the desk, just like a real old-style newsman would. "The thing is, Brine, you've got talent. I suspect you know that, which is why I don't dwell on it. But it's there. And a guy with talent who sticks to his principles isn't somebody you get rid of for some minor infraction, especially when it produces such happy results, like yours did. And that's what I told Mr. Claiborne. And that's what he's decided to do."

"Mr. Sutphin, I don't—"

"Keep listening, dammit. I'm not done yet."

"Okay. Sorry."

"He also decided that your work merits a better forum, and that's why—with my blessing—he's bumping you up to capitol beat, full time."

"Seriously?"

Morris nodded. "Soon as you finish serving a paid, one-week suspension. A slap on the wrist, you understand, so people don't start getting any bright ideas."

At this, Morris leaned back in his seat again, as if it was all just business as usual, which only made Spencer even more confused.

"Well, thank you, sir. But I guess I don't understand. I was under the impression that ... well, honestly, that you didn't like me so much."

"It's my job to be tough, Brine. You should know that. But yes, maybe I rode you a little harder than the others. Maybe, in your case, I even liked it."

"Then why?"

"It was the right thing to do, for one. And I have my own reasons. Let's just leave it at that."

"Okay. Well, thank you again. But what should I ...?"

Spencer pointed to his cubicle, and the boxes, and his peers, still stealing sly glances over, waiting for the bloody outcome.

"Just leave everything right where it sits. It'll be fine. And don't worry about those monkeys. I'll let them know what's what. Meantime," Sutphin said, pointing to his watch, "you've got a suspension to serve, and it starts as of right now, so go. Leave. And don't show your face around here for a full week, do you hear me? You'll get your new desk when you get back."

Like a prisoner on death row who had unexpectedly received a pardon from the governor, Spencer broke into a huge smile, gave Morris a crisp salute, "Yes, sir!" and skipped his way out the door.

Morris watched Spencer go with a wry expression on his face, pleased by his actions and their results. Then, once he was absolutely sure that the dog-and-pony show was over and no one was watching anymore, he turned to his desk and withdrew a single glossy sheet from his drawer. "We all need our little inspirations, don't we?"

In his hand was an 8-by-10 photo. Of Nikki Balodouris. By all appearances, the same one that had once graced Spencer's cubicle. Morris blew a little stray dust off its shiny surface, straightened out a bend in the corner, and smiled contentedly.

39

A CUP OF COFFEE

Sitting in a downtown coffee shop two days later, Spencer was in full-on slacker mode. Dressed in baggy jeans, a hooded sweatshirt, and some old Converse sneakers, his face unshaven, he sipped leisurely from a tall latte while reading *Of Human Bondage* by Somerset Maugham, one of a stack of books he planned to devour over the course of his weeklong newsroom exile.

Oh, yes, it was a glorious time, indeed, feeling more like a paid vacation than anything. One which not only allowed Spencer to catch up on his reading, but also reflect on all that had happened, and prepare for the exciting new challenges to come.

The Maugham book was proving excellent fodder for this. In it, a young educated Brit falls in love with an immoral strumpet from a lower class who nevertheless spurns him cruelly and repeatedly. Despite this, or perhaps because of it, the Brit remains obsessed with her throughout his entire life, right up until the very bitter end.

Reading about this poor man's foibles, Spencer was finally able to recognize his own. In doing so, he at last reached some sort of closure on his star-crossed romance with Nikki, which he now saw was destined for failure, no matter what the ultimate causes or circumstances may have been.

In fact, Spencer realized, Nikki had done him a favor. He could now move forward into this important new chapter of his life without the onus of being involved with a stripper, something no journalist wishing to be taken seriously would ever do, unless they were going for the whole gonzo Hunter S. Thompson thing, perhaps, or in the desiccated, trophy-wife twilight of their career.

Still, Spencer did miss the companionship, no matter how inappropriate that companion may have been. And he realized too that, after having tasted those forbidden fruits, he could no longer go back to the kind of overly-proper, poodle-owning Jewish-American princesses that had previously been his stock in trade. There had to be a middle ground. A woman who had the requisite class and decorum at her disposal, but who nevertheless knew how to get down and dirty and have a good time, too.

Spencer looked around the cafe. It was the middle of the afternoon. Most people were at work. There were a couple women by the window. Attractive but older, with matching sweater sets and helmet-like hairdos, just like the editors' spouses he had met at the Halloween party. Sure enough, he saw they both had on wedding rings, with bulky shopping bags at their feet. Country club wives. Ladies who lunch. Spencer didn't want this, either. He wanted a woman with a life of her own, with her own career and interests and goals. He wanted, in short, the whole package.

But where do you find someone like that? Spencer didn't have a clue. Maybe, he thought, it wasn't something you could actively seek out, but rather was yet another thing that just happened, coming to you through fate, when the time was right.

Besides, now wasn't the right time for romance, anyway. Not for him, at least. He needed to keep his mind clear, and focus on this new opportunity he had just been given.

"Spencer Brine, Capitol Beat," he said to himself with a grin. He even liked the sound of it. And with Schwarzenegger as governor, Spencer knew he had hit the mother lode. This was to be his launching pad. He was sure of it.

"Spencer? Spencer Brine? That is you, isn't it?"

Spencer turned. It was a pretty girl in a nurse's uniform. Upon second glance, he realized it was the daughter of the lost woman.

"Hey! Rowena, right?"

"Right! Boy, I hardly recognized you without your work clothes on."

A beat, as she knit her brow, suddenly comprehending the potential significance of this. "Why *don't* you have your work clothes on?"

Spencer related the story, blow by blow, much to her great relief and approval. Then, she told him the story of how her mother eventually came to be found.

"And now," she said, wrapping up, "it's like it never even happened. She doesn't know how she ended up all the way out there, and most of the time she doesn't remember how she got back, either. But she's safe now, that's all that matters. Thanks to you."

"Hey, all's well that ends well, right?"

"I guess so." Rowena heaved a little sigh of relief. "I was really worried."

"About your mom?"

"And you, too! I mean, I call the paper and they say you're not there. And then, I see you here, in the middle of the day, looking all wrinkled and scruffy."

Spencer reddened. "Just being lazy is all."

"No, don't be embarrassed. You look cute. I just didn't know if you got in trouble or even if ... well, you know."

"Well, neither did I, so I guess that makes us even."

"Even? I don't think so."

Spencer tilted his head.

"I owe you, big time, for what you did."

"Just doing my job."

"Oh, please. At least let me buy you a cup of coffee."

Spencer eyed his mug. It was empty.

"Come on. From one working stiff to another."

Spencer smiled. "You forgot, I'm not working. But, sure ... another cup of coffee would be nice."

The two ended up talking for well over an hour, long enough for the sunlight to dim and the afternoon to give way to evening. Spencer told Rowena about his new assignment, which she thought sounded exciting, and Rowena told him all about her job at the hospital and her efforts at working toward a nursing degree, which Spencer thought was both admirable and brave.

Once these tales had been exchanged, and their cups were empty, there was a brief lull in the conversation, and Spencer and Rowena both wondered to themselves if they should allow the other to go on his or her merry way.

It was then that Rowena's eyes finally caught on Spencer's stack of books. "Boy, look at all of these. I guess you writers have to read a lot, too, huh?"

"When we can."

"All I have time for are my textbooks. Sometimes, not even those." Rowena glanced down at the handbag by her side, a thick anatomy text peeking out from the top.

She turned back to Spencer's stack, with its array of colorful titles and cover art. "These look so much more interesting, too. *Human Bondage. Look Homeward, Angel. Poisonwood Bible.* And hey, this one sounds pretty..."

Rowena grabbed a volume from the middle of the stack, like drawing straws or picking a winning lottery ticket. "*Leaves of Grass.* What's this one about?"

Spencer stared at the book, then back at Rowena, struck speechless.

Rowena misinterpreted. "Oh. Have you not read it yet?"

"No, no! I have. *Many* times," Spencer clarified. "It's a book of poetry, not a novel like the others. And I guess it's about ... us. Our country, our lives, our ideals; all the great things around us. Being aware of the possibilities."

"Wow. That sounds pretty great. Like, important, too." She stared at the book, leafed through its pages. "I don't suppose I could borrow it sometime?"

"Take it."

"No. I can't do that."

"Sure you can. I have another copy at home. Take it. I'm serious."

"Okay." Rowena wasn't sure what this meant. Was it her cue to leave? Or was she just over-thinking things again, trying to see some kind of hidden message that wasn't even there? "I guess I should get going. Don't want to be late for work."

"No. We don't want that," Spencer said, although he felt himself wishing that she would.

Rowena got up. "Well ... nice seeing you. And thanks again." She waved the book and stuck it inside her bag. "For everything."

"My pleasure. Who knows, maybe we'll bump into each other again sometime."

"Right. Who knows?"

The two shared a smile. Then, all their salutations complete, Rowena turned to go. But before she could fully disappear around the corner, something made her stop. She turned back. "By the way, you aren't still dating that girl I saw you with at the pumpkin patch, are you? I think her name was Nikki?"

"No." Spencer cleared his throat, a stray bit of heartache still lingering in his voice. "No, I'm not."

"Good," Rowena replied. "That's good. You're better than that."

Satisfied, she turned to leave.

Then, another couple of feet, and she stopped again. "Are you absolutely *sure* there isn't something I could do to repay you?" Rowena tilted her head and batted her eyelashes, a gesture as openly flirtatious as she would allow herself under the circumstances.

It was enough. Spencer leaned forward in his seat, clearly intrigued.

"Well," he said, looking around to make sure that no one else could hear them, "I did have a dream one time about a girl in a nurse's uniform."

Rowena smiled. "Is that right?"

Spencer nodded with an eager schoolboy charm.

"Well, sometimes, you know, if you're lucky, dreams do come true."

And sometimes, Spencer thought, it happens right when you least expect it—in this case, twice in one week.

A headline appeared before his eyes, in large-type letters: HERO REPORTER WINS BIG PROMOTION, WOOS PRETTY NURSE.

And with it, his destiny suddenly seemed, like the headline itself, to be all laid out clearly in front of him now, arrow-straight and silky smooth, like a golden road running all the way to the horizon.

V

TOTAL RECALL

40

TABLE FOR FOUR

When you're alone or unhappy, a day can feel like a century. When you're in love and things are going your way, a year passes in the blink of an eye. It was now February 2006. In the last two years, much had happened, and much had changed. But some things had also stayed pretty much the same.

"Pretty swanky joint you picked out here, old gal. Forty bucks for a steak? I better get the whole damn cow for that price."

"Don't worry, Rockefeller, this one's on me. Not that you need another huge slab of meat, anyway. God forbid you'd order the fish for a change."

"Thought you didn't believe in God."

"Being with you, maybe I should start."

Missy Carver and Todd Tisdale sat in a corner table at a fancy restaurant called, appropriately enough, Moxie, still sparring back and forth just as they had on that night back in early 2004, when Todd was on the brink of losing everything and Missy had come in from out of the rain to help him turn the tide.

Since that time, Todd had followed his Missy's advice down to the letter, and it had all worked out better than he could have ever hoped. Like Missy suggested, Todd had given up his space and closed the shop temporarily, sold off some of his merchandise, and consolidated his debts. With a second mortgage on his house, he was able to re-open just three months later in a new location, right between an event planner and a florist, and just up the block from a jeweler. This new, more synergistic location brought a marked rise in business, and with a lower rent—negotiated by Missy at her bad-cop best— to boot.

Missy also helped Todd when the inevitable occurred and Lana filed for divorce. While she cited irreconcilable differences as the cause for the split, the trial lawyer that Missy helped Todd retain—her former "dream date," Steve Manning— counterclaimed for alienation of affections and fraud. At trial, Steve did a bang-up job of making star witness Drago Petronowicz look like a gigantic home-wrecker and Lana a heartless conniver, while presenting Todd as a saintly victim of circumstance.

Not surprisingly, "Team Tisdale" came out on top, with Steve even securing a reimbursement of expenses from Lana—all of which, it should be noted, actually got paid by the lumbering Drago, who was now engaged to Lana himself and, with his new, fully-guaranteed, 5-year, $35 million dollar NBA contract, could easily afford such outlays.

Another major issue in the case was young Alek. Since Todd hadn't been able to complete his formal adoption of the boy, and the marriage was so short lived, Lana had argued that any requests for visitation should be denied. Steve was able to show that Lana's prolonged absences in the latter stages of the marriage, while pursuing her adulterous relations with Mr. Petronowicz, had left Todd as primary caregiver. Alek himself supported this claim on the stand and, in a final statement that brought closet-softie Todd to tears, further stated that Todd had been the closest thing to a father that he'd ever had.

The end result was that Todd got partial custody of the boy. Alek stayed with him every other weekend, and he was allowed to spend two afternoons a week at the shop, too, helping out or doing homework or just listening to Todd's ever-sage advice.

As for Missy, her good deeds were rewarded in kind. While Todd surely would not have met the prerequisites that she had laid out for Heidi the Yenta Matchmaker back in the day, it was precisely this inappropriateness that, ironically enough, made him such a good match.

Unlike most of the professional men that she had previously sought out, Todd had no problem with Missy's Type-A business persona. He was happy to let her take the lead on that front, and to benefit from her obvious flair for it. In fact, he found her über-careerwoman shtick endlessly amusing, and it provided no shortage of ammo for him when they had their little tiffs—a ribbing that Missy secretly enjoyed, because it forced her to loosen up and not take herself so seriously all the time.

Indeed, this was how Todd had proved most endearing. Although he may not have been very polished or couth, he was a fun guy to have around, and he always kept things in the proper perspective. For him, work was a means to an end, not the end itself, and he slowly got Missy to see things this way as well. Not always, mind you, but often enough that she was able to shed her Super-Realtor shackles every once in a while, for the occasional flyaway weekend, or in the bedroom, where, as Todd noted in his usual ribald manner, "The buck stops here, if you catch my drift."

Todd's exaggerated wink, for the benefit of the other couple at the table, made it clear that he still retained some alpha-dog moments for himself, a claim that Missy notably didn't dispute, though she nevertheless did her best to appear mortified by it.

"Keep it down, cowboy. I've got *clients* here, for crying out loud."

"Oh, you love it and you know it," Todd said, as he grabbed her around the waist and nuzzled her neck.

Missy blushed in a manner that suggested this was true, then self-consciously broke it off to address a nearby table with a little wave and a hand-to-ear gesture that told them she would be calling later with an update.

As she did so, Todd turned to their dining companions. "She loves me. But her parents love me even more. You should see when we go out for dinner with *them*."

Missy turned back with a sigh, resigned. "Who would have ever guessed, right? Todd Tisdale, hometown football hero. You'd think he was Joe Montana or something the way my father carries on. And my mother? Don't even get me started."

"Ah, Mamie. A shameless flirt, that one. Don't know why it didn't pass down to her little Melissa Louise here, but—"

"Watch it, slick. I have a steak knife right here, you know."

"Okay, okay, I'll behave."

Todd laughed, and the other couple joined in, while Missy tried her best not to. It wasn't the first time they'd been out together, so they all knew the routine.

"So, enough about us. Tell us what's going on with you two."

"Yeah, right. After all, you're the reason we're here tonight."

Before they could get in a word, Todd grabbed his glass and raised it. "In fact, while we're at it, I'd like to get the ball rolling and make a little toast."

Missy rolled her eyes. "Here we go. Lock up your liquor cabinets."

Todd ignored her. "To Rowena Pickett, the best damn nurse in town!"

The other man at the table, and Rowena's date, Spencer Brine, seconded it. "Hear, hear. Congratulations, Ro. You deserve it."

The four clinked glasses, Todd downing his with his usual gusto.

Missy then chimed in with a toast of her own. "And to you, too, Spencer, for finally getting the recognition *you* deserve."

Rowena turned to Spencer, beaming, even happier for him than she was for herself. "I'm so proud of you, baby." To the others, she added, "You should see the job offers he's been getting."

Spencer shrugged. "With the material I've had to work with, it was pretty easy. The stories practically wrote themselves."

"Oh, I doubt that," Missy said, quickly dismissing Spencer's attempt at modesty.

"You stuck it to the guy, but good," Todd added approvingly. "And he deserves it, too. The big jerk-off."

"You know, the truth is, Arnold's not such a bad guy, really. He just got in over his head. I think he just assumed he could run roughshod up here the same way that he did down in Hollywood."

"Like I said, he's a jerk-off."

"He's made a lot of mistakes, alright. And he displayed a lot of hubris—"

"A lot of what?"

"Hubris, Todd," Missy clarified pointedly. "It means he was the victim of his own swollen ego. Sound familiar?"

Todd cleared his throat, chastened. "I guess we all screw up sometimes."

"Some in bigger ways than others," Spencer added, in an attempt to soften the blow. "But at least he's willing to own up to it now."

"And that's saying a lot, coming from a hard-core liberal like yourself," Missy noted, before turning back to Todd, in a teasing tone, "Spencer and I have a history, you know."

Todd snorted. "Right. The big date. Tell me this: who *haven't* you dated?"

Missy fired right back. "Says the guy who's been married three times."

"That's right. And if you think there's gonna be a fourth, you're nuts."

As Todd and Missy traded another round of barbed repartee, which for them served as a manner of foreplay, some might begin to wonder how these two couples wound up in the same room, much less at the same table. Though Todd knew Rowena from her brief tenure at the tanning salon, and Missy had served as Spencer's realtor as well as going out on one less-than-magical date with him, their current friendship actually derived from Missy and Rowena.

Back when they were high school classmates, the two women had never run in the same circles—not even in the same hemispheres. But as the old adage goes, time heals all wounds, and when they crossed paths again more than a decade later, they discovered that they had far more in common than either of them would have ever thought possible.

Perhaps the biggest thing was their shared experience taking care of their parents. This topic had arisen when Rowena appeared at Missy's office one day looking for help in selling her mom's house. Rowena had stayed at Connie's for nearly two years, taking care of her while also working at the hospital and attending school. But as her mother's condition had declined, and the demands on her own time had grown, it had simply become too much for her to handle by herself, particularly in such a hard-to-monitor setting. The difficult decision was made to place her in a well-regarded local convalescent facility, The Golden Years Retirement Village, where the staff would be better able to assure that she wouldn't wander off, and take care of her various medical needs.

Fortunately, this transition had proven easier than expected. With her bed and her favorite chair and her TV set brought over from the house for familiarity, Connie had settled right in, rocking in her chair and watching Oprah and humming the same old song as always, which Rowena finally figured out was "Somewhere My Love," by Ray Conniff, the song she and Eddie had played for the first dance at their wedding.

But with Connie now safely and comfortably ensconced, this left Rowena needing to find a new place of her own. At first, there had been some talk about moving in with Spencer, but both of them were wary of repeating their past mistakes. And if that weren't enough, they had also seen how their respective past mistakes had joined forces to create even *bigger* mistakes. Randy and Nikki, their respective exes, had indeed crossed paths in the past, just as Rowena had always suspected, and— as Nikki announced in her break-up note to Spencer—they had also eloped to Reno, only to divorce bitterly six months later, before subsequently discovering that Nikki was pregnant with twins, which resulted in a second quickie marriage that was even shakier than the first one, now with the added pressure of a pair of babies added to the mix.

As a result of all this, Spencer and Rowena had wisely decided to take things a bit slower this time around. Rowena thus turned again to new pal Missy, who quickly found her a brand new, stylish loft-style townhouse just a few blocks from the hospital, which also put her within shouting distance of her nursing school and from Spencer's place, too.

And while the place couldn't have been any more perfect for Rowena's needs, it was worth noting that Missy had a larger-than-usual vested interest in the outcome, as she was not only the listing agent on the deal, but also the developer behind it.

Oh, yes. A mere two years into its existence, Carver Properties was flourishing, and Missy, never one to be satisfied with mere success, had advanced her little fiefdom into the next realm by not only brokering, but also now *creating* properties. "The Lofts in Old Sacramento" was the first of many such developments that she was planning, and it was only the beginning of what she predicted would be a full-scale downtown renaissance, not unlike the one Todd had predicted upon Arnold's ascendance—except this time, it would be a renaissance masterminded by her.

Better still, and on a more personal front, it was a plan that also allowed her to gracefully nudge her mother, Mamie, off her desk and out of her apprentice-realtor position, a job she'd never really had the passion or the aptitude for, and instead install her, along with her father, Cliff, as live-in landlords for the property. It was a role that suited them both far better, and also—even more importantly—finally got them moved out of her house, a far-too-long-in-gestation event that had nearly sent her lunging for her pills again.

It was Rowena who had first noticed Missy's increasingly frazzled state during these busy days of growth and transition. And it was Rowena who had been genuinely concerned enough about it enough, and insightful enough, that Missy had finally come clean about everything, from the pills and the purging to the wild chain of events and circumstances that had surrounded it all. But while Missy had worried that Rowena would think less of her for it, Rowena was merely impressed anew by what a remarkably strong person she was, conquering her addictions all by herself like she had.

With Rowena's support, Missy was able to beat down these reinvigorated urges, suppress the anxieties, and work her way through the crisis without a relapse. Bonding them even further, Rowena promised Missy that she would keep everything they had discussed a secret, as if she was a doctor rather than merely a nurse-trainee. She had harbored secrets of her own, after all, and knew the value of keeping them that way.

As a result, Missy to able to protect her image as some kind of indomitable wonder woman—a "machine," as Rowena's friends used to put it, although Rowena herself now knew better. And that was the way Missy preferred to keep it, especially with

Todd, the prototypical big-man-on-campus she had always so scrupulously avoided, who had nevertheless evolved into a lover of a far more deep and enduring sort than she would have ever expected, much less planned. It was a conceit that allowed her to cope with the inherent vulnerability that any romantic relationship naturally brought with it, much less one as serious as this.

This was, in fact, the last little secret that Missy had kept all to herself. Despite all of her many successes and triumphs, when it came to real romance, Todd had been her first, and her only. He was, for better or worse, the love of her life.

As if reading her mind, Todd suddenly grabbed her and pulled her close. "So now that Rowena's finished with school and you're the big hotshot flavor-of-the-month newsguy, what's next for you two?"

"Spencer, you always used to talk about moving back to New York City. Not that I want you to, of course. I don't." A beat. Missy couldn't help herself, adding, "*But*, if you do, I could get you a great deal on both your places."

Spencer laughed. "I'm sure you could, Carver. I have no doubt. And the truth is," he said, turning to Rowena to get her nod of approval, "we talked about it. And there are some good opportunities for me there. But Rowena's mom is still here—"

"And," Rowena chimed in passionately, "I just got hired on at Mercy full-time. I mean, I walked the picket line with these people, fighting the proposed budget cuts ... and I still can't believe it, but we actually won! We beat Arnold Schwarzenegger! I can't leave now. It wouldn't be right."

"My little political activist," Spencer replied, beaming proudly.

Then, turning to the others, "Besides, where am I going to find better material than I've got right here? Despite everything, Schwarzenegger might actually get elected again, you know."

"God help us."

"God better help him, too," Todd added. "Any more fuckups like this first go-round and he'll be lucky to get out of town alive, believe you me."

Spencer sat back with an amused smile, reveling in Todd's tough talk, even if in truth it was just as hollow as Arnold's campaign promises. "Good old Sacramento."

"Damn straight."

"I have to admit, on top of everything else, the place has kind of grown on me."

"It does that."

"Yes, it does. It most certainly does."

Spencer pulled Rowena close, and Todd followed suit with Missy. Then, they just sat there, in the middle of the boisterous dining room, none of them saying another word, just smiling at each other like crazy people. And for that one bright, shining moment, the four of them felt completely at peace with the world and their own places in it. Free to bask in the love that they had found, the happiness they shared, and the belief that this bounty of goodwill and good fortune would simply linger for them, on and on, forever and ever.

Even though, after everything they had been through, they all should have known better.

CPSIA information can be obtained at www.ICGtesting.com
Printed in the USA
LVOW080906191011

251139LV00001B/91/P